SIC SEMPER TYRANNIS

THE WEREWOLF HUNTRESS

BOOK 1

SAVANNAH LYNN MISNER

Published by Simply Savannah Lynn Press
Design and distribution by Bublish

ISBN: 978-1-647047-54-2 (paperback)
ISBN: 978-1-647047-53-5 (eBook)

www.SavannahLynnMisner.com

This book is dedicated to my family. Thank you for putting up with me and supporting me throughout this five-year-long process. Our hard work is finally paying off! Thanks, Daddy-O for financially backing me and Mom for the many rounds of editing before we finally said THE END. You guys are the best!

CHAPTER 1

AVENGER

When I was fourteen, murderers killed my family in cold blood. *Rogue werewolf* murderers. Why they left me alive, I may never know, and I don't care. What I *do* care about? Revenge.

To the human world, I'm just a nineteen-year-old girl. As for the werewolf world? They know better. To them, I am the Avenger. And no, I don't go after humans and all that shit, only the supernatural world.

Oh, if you're wondering? No, vampires do not exist. Sorry to burst your bubble, you sad Twilight fans. Anyway, on all my victims I carve *AM* for Avenger Mikos. In fact, a deadbeat rogue was about to wear my signature.

Slowing down, fleabag? Good.

My heart thunders in my chest as I race through the dark forest. The werewolf pedophile I'm hunting will be dead in about three seconds, and its body handed over to the nearest pack. Not that I like these packs. I merely hate rapists and gangs more.

"Shift or I'll shoot. And you don't want me to do that because I'll make it slow and painful."

The disgusting excuse for a half-human stops in his tracks and shifts. Acidic bile rises in my throat, looking at him in all his manhood. He saunters toward me, but I stand my ground, not moving an inch for this fleabag.

"So, shoot, Girly. It's not like you can hit me, anyway. I'm not afraid of you."

A menacing chuckle rattles from deep in his throat. He runs his dirt crusted fingers through his wretched mop of hair. I aim straight at his head. He cackles wildly.

Over his laugh, I warn, "Oh, but you should be afraid. Since your kind always evades punishment for your crimes, it is my job to punish you. I can't protect all humans from scum like you, but you can be damn well sure I'll *avenge* them. Perhaps you've heard of me?"

I allow a smile to tug at my lips as his expression changes from amused to confused. When the weight of the word *avenge* strikes him, the look of confusion contorts to shock.

"You don't look like the Avenger. It's a dude, not a weak little schoolgirl."

It's my turn to smile. It isn't uncommon for the werewolves to believe that the Avenger is a male. I mean, this society's version of a *strong female* is a woke pussy hat-wearing, squealing woman who blames everyone else for her problems. So, why wouldn't they expect the Avenger to be a dude? When a truly strong woman is before them, they can't comprehend it.

I shrug one shoulder. "What can I say? I have raw natural talent."

"You don't have the guts to pull the trigger."

My smile remains, but it doesn't reach my eyes. "Next time you'll think twice before gang-raping a twelve-year-old girl."

He stretches his arms wide, palms up in mock innocence, like this is big news to him.

"*That's* what this is about? There were four others. Why are you coming after me?"

I scoff. "Are you kidding me? The Albany State Police force handled the *human* convicts, but you somehow escaped. That ends now."

Before he can respond, my finger pulls the trigger, and one more evil soul departs from this Earth.

Number 954, check.

I abandon the body near a pack border and go on my merry way to where my 2018 Acura NSX waits outside the forest line. I may or may not have stolen it from a gang bust as reimbursement for attempting to run. I mean, they bought it with stolen drug money, then I stole it from them. Two wrongs make a right, in this case.

Closer to my car, the sound of low whimpering reaches my ears. *Griffin.* My Kugsha—wolf dog breed—waits for me, patiently but not quietly.

I never let him out when we're near wolf packs, so he stays locked up in the car, much to his despair. Otherwise, he would attack the wolves. Besides, he's family. So, I protect him with everything I have.

I slide into the front seat, the leather cool and soft under my burning thighs.

"Hey bubby, mommy killed another evil person today. Yeah, who's a good boy?" I baby talk him as I squish his face chubs. He licks my face, inspecting me for wounds. "Let's go home."

We don't really have a home per se, more like apartments or motels, the latter being our latest temporary home. After arriving at the motel, I grab my luggage and trudge inside, Griffin in tow. The routine is always the same. I strip down and take a cold shower, then pull on my boy shorts and sports bra. After that, I clean my weapons and reload the clips.

Tonight, I have one more hit. Might as well watch some TV until then. I land on a teen kids' channel, the mother place of crappy shit shows, filled with fake relationships and stupid problems. These high school dramas that they portray as life-altering are downright stupid.

Here I am, fighting for my life against the supernatural, while these chicks complain about their lame boyfriends talking to other dumb, slutty chicks. The girl likes a boy, but the girl doesn't think the boy likes her. Girl gets makeover like every other girl but still thinks she is an individual with a unique personality. Boy notices girl, and they live happily ever after.

Ugh, shoot me.

Mushy romcom flicks all have near identical plots, and they are all stupid. "Romance is dead, love doesn't exist, and screw love at first sight." Griffin takes my outburst as an invitation to jump onto the bed with me.

"*Griffin.* You jumped on my AK-47. Are you trying to get *shot*? Soviet bullets aren't exactly the easiest to pull out."

His insolent stare says, "What ya' gonna to do about it, bitch?"

I'm not surprised, though; I *am* his owner. Ultimate sass bitch right here, and Griffin is my loyal sidekick. We are Rapunzel and Pascal, Anakin and Ahsoka, and Maverick and Goose. The best duos ever.

I sigh. "Well, we have an exchange going down in twenty-four hours, and mama's got to prepare. Time to pick up shop."

I force myself up and glance around our dismal room. You know that deep gut-wrenching feeling when you lose something close to you? When everything around drifts on by like you don't even exist? Well, it sucks. The only thing left in my life that I care about is Griffin. There is no one in this world that even remembers who I once was.

I can't lie, though. What I have become is nothing I wish to be re-membered for. If my parents saw me now, what would they think of me? Thankfully, they can't see it. "On to Montana."

I snatch my phone and tap the music icon. I scroll through a dozen playlists, till I find my favorite shuffle. My rock-rap begins, and I dial it up full blast.

I load up one bag with the little I own. My emergency clothes consist of jeans, tank tops, and sweatshirts. Yeah, yeah, I get it. I'm not one for variety, but I really don't care. When you are constantly running for your life, airy spring dresses aren't exactly the wardrobe of choice. My parents used to say they had three sons, not two. I never wore dresses or skirts of my own volition. I can honestly say I didn't mind wearing them to church or a nice wedding, but these days I have no use for a fancy dress.

The other duffels hold knives, rations, and, of course, my baby, Diablo. Diablo is my sniper rifle; a Barrett M82. It is my weapon of choice when dealing with the fleabags.

I change into a fresh pair of skinny jeans and a black tank top and finish the ensemble off with some military-grade boots and a bulletproof vest. After a quick check of my weather app, I shrug my black leather jacket on to protect against the cold front coming in overnight. Packing complete—a mere three bags–and I sling the duffle over my shoulder and whistle for Griffin. I clip his harness on and we bid farewell to our one-room dump.

I close the trunk and walk around to the driver's seat. "Griffin, let's go."

Griffin bounds into the front seat and sits shotgun beside me. I start the car, and the engine rumbles to life. Before pulling out of the dump, I hit play on my favorite playlist I call *New Queen*. I skip through some songs before finding the one I wanted. I sing along at the top of my lungs as I pull out onto the open road.

By the end of the song, Griffin and I are jamming out to "The Score" at 3 A.M. It will take another four hours of driving to reach Charleston and another three to prepare and scope out the territory.

I receive all my information from an anonymous source I met on the dark web. Well, I actually have a police radio and travel to wherever they report a prisoner escape from a high-security prison. The escapees are usually werewolves, but sometimes they are merely evil humans. Either way, they all end up dead if they come into my crosshairs.

If they are human, I leave the bodies near a police station or burn them. If they are werewolves, I discard them near the closest pack borders with 'AM' carved into their chests each time. I mean, why be a scary teenage werewolf huntress, if no wolves know about it?

Four playlists and two stops at the greatest restaurant in the world—Taco Bell—later, we arrive in Charleston, Montana. *'Welcome to Montana. Home of Kings.'* It may seem like just a simple slogan, but to the supernatural, it is home to the Werewolf King.

Under my breath, I mutter, "Kill me now, because this is probably the dumbest thing I've done so far." Griffin's left ear twitches in response.

I dread this 'mission', but there is a huge exchange going down and I cannot have those weapons on the street. The aftermath would be catastrophic. For the humans, at least.

I stop at the first motel I see and pull into the parking lot, locking Griffin in the car when I get out. As I approach the check-in desk, the odor of stale cigarettes and cheap alcohol assaults my nostrils. My eyes actually burn at the stench. The receptionist—a weathered woman whose day job was likely at a strip club, and who bore the remains of yesterday's attempted smoky eye along with the smell of STDs and vodka—exhaled smoke out of her nose.

"I would like your cheapest room for one night, please."

Before she answers, she hacks up mystery crap into her elbow. She rasps, "All the rooms are cheap here, honey. $37.95. Room 145."

I hand her cash, and she stuffs it in her bra. She shoves a key ring with a matted rabbit's tail across the counter.

Disgusting.

I mutter a quick, insincere thanks and head back out.

No need to stay more than one night when no one must know who I am. Not that it is a big deal. Everyone who *has* seen my face ends up dead. So far, everyone ignores the teenage girl in dark clothes with a huge wolf dog. It's like I am a ghost. It may seem sad, but it is perfect for me.

Also perfect for me, I have plenty of redneck ingenuity. Who knew it would come in handy? I used to be bullied by people because I was not 'like them.' Thank God for all my middle-class friends, though. We kept each other strong and made sure no one was swept into the modern, city world my generation was falling for.

Those were the days, binge eating fast food in Walmart parking lots and entertaining ourselves with simply a fire pit and old newspapers. I never thought I would say I actually missed the guys who purposely embarrassed me in front of my crush when I had foolishly told them who I liked. Suffice to say of those days, I will never look at "no trespassing" signs and strapless bras the same way again.

The moment I open the door to our room, I notice—without surprise—the air here is stale. It's obvious they've never considered opening a window after what I can only imagine a rowdy group of college frat boys finished a round of beer and more likely than not, a stripper. I scrunch my nose at the thought of breathing secondhand sex air. I finish unloading my bags and clutch Griffin's leash, leading him further into our run-down little room. It comprises of one small twin bed, a bathroom, and a closet. I toss one duffle onto the bed and heave my suitcase onto the dresser.

Little secret: the suitcase is not full of clothes, but a beautiful assortment of my favorite weapons: a Barrett M82, an AK-47, an M4 carbine, an Astra Cub 22 short pocket pistol, and a bunch of other stuff. A glance at the time alerts me I have exactly twelve hours till I need to be at the drop-off location, so a nap is in order.

The nap was wonderful, even with only three kicks to the face from Griffin. He is my best friend, but he can be a pain. He acts like he owns every place we go. When we were hiding out at a little back woods motel, Griffin jumped onto the cot of a bed and triggered one of my rifles to go off because I left a round in the chamber. It was my fault, but I swear he purposely stepped on it.

He has this special glint in his eyes when he does something he is not supposed to. I rise groggily and push Griffin off my bed. He lands on the floor with a thump. He pokes his head up, and if looks could kill, I would be six feet under.

"Try me, little rat."

I glare at Griffin, who scowls in return and lays his head down. Smirking, I climb off the bed and pull a dark green sweatshirt two threads short of being a rag over my head. My dad always taught my siblings and I that if you're going to buy something, squeeze every cent out of it, and even then, it can still be useful in other ways.

I settle on the edge of the mattress and don a bulletproof vest and military-grade combat boots. I head over to the dresser, lifted my Barrett M82, and load all my ammunition into the magazines. Tonight is the night of the drop-off, and I need to be four hours early, minimum. I sling my weapon over my shoulders and shrug on my jacket to hide the barrel. Not that I suppose the people there will notice or stop me. I snag my phone from the nightstand and my duffle, and dash for the door.

"Griffin, come."

Griffin saunters to me and sits. He knows the routine. I slip his harness over his head and connect his leash. Stuffing my emergency escape clothes and supplies into my duffle, along with my Barrett M82 under my coat, we exit the motel room, locking it behind us. Walking through the empty, dingy, gray hallways reminds me of that horror movie with those twin girls standing in the distance. I think they later eat your brains and lay eggs in your stomach, or something. I never actually saw the movie, but that's my best guess. The frosty night air nips at my exposed skin, and I quicken my step toward my car.

My baby looks so out of place. A handsome car in a dump. I duck inside, with Griffin right behind me. We screech out of the empty parking lot blaring some For King and Country.

One thing about me: I live for my music. You will always find me with a boom box or headphones. I remember my mom telling me I would get ear infections or lose my hearing altogether because of all the loud music. It never stopped me, though. Music was how I expressed my feelings without having to say a word. Not that anyone will ever notice if I stopped speaking altogether.

I return my focus to the virtually empty highway and take the pull off onto an older road. Griffin and I approach the drop-off site. It isn't a cool abandoned building or a dirty strip club, but a simple underpass. Not James Bond material at all. Shifting the car into park, I stretch my legs, popping my back.

"Here we are bud, time to get comfy. We're gonna be here a while."

The overpass has plenty of coverage and a nice parking lot a few hundred yards away. The perfect spot for a sniper to hide. *Like me.* I park my car at the far end, out of their sight. My shuffle is annoying me, and it has to change. I press skip once, twice, three times, but nothing captures my interest. Instead, I flip through the radio till I find my favorite channel, 79, better known as Disney Radio. It reminds me of the childlike innocence I don't have anymore. I love me some "Why Don't We". I recline my seat and snuggle into my heated, luxury leather bucket seat and play the long game of doing nothing and waiting.

An hour…

Two hours…

Three hours…

"Ugh, how long does it take to hand over money for some stupid knock-off weapons?"

Griffin, also restless and growing impatient, shifts around beneath my feet. It could be worse, though. I could be crouched in the dirt, on my stomach, in the elements. I'll pass on that. Why shoot people from an uncomfortable location when you may well shoot from your own car? And right *not* on schedule, the vans filled with the men I was about to murder finally show up.

Ah, at last. Time to fire.

The recoil of the first round is hard but firm in my shoulder and my body instantly adjusts to the firepower I am so used to. The echo of the shot underneath the overpass rattles in my chest. Down below, no one comprehends what is happening, but as they drop like flies, panic causes them to turn on each other.

I may have to shoot some humans, as well.

Honestly? A flicker of guilt knots my gut. It does not last, though. The four in the front were easy to take down. They had made themselves completely vulnerable, practically begging to be shot. Safe to guess they weren't expecting anyone to know about their brief exchange, let alone someone doing something about it.

No one ever sees me coming, and never will unless I want them to. The other nine are too busy running around like headless chickens to notice where I am and who I am killing. It is only about a minute until the shouts stop, and silence envelops the night. One straggles back into a van, but alas, they don't have bulletproof glass. With every single criminal dead, Griffin and I can at last take our prize. I duck back into my car, closing the sunroof behind me.

Every assassin knows not to approach the bodies for at least thirty minutes. So, I pop my headphones in, crank up some 90's rock over the radio, and consider what my reward might be. Preferably, a few hundred grand and maybe some Glocks or some Pistols. I fist-pump the air when my favorite oldies song comes on, "Never Say Die", from the best movie ever: *Iron Eagle*. That movie was ahead of its time. A complete classic and totally underrated. More people should watch that series. More than that, I wished I was from that time.

As the last song on my playlist ends, I shift into drive and coast down the hill to the dump.

It's good to be bad.

Or good, depending on what side you are on. I tug my skull mask over my head and jump out, Griffin hot on my tail. He absolutely loves coming with me. I'm not sure if I should be worried about his sanity or not. His fascination with dead bodies might be concerning. I turned out okay. Sort of.

I hold my breath as I approach the motionless forms of crumpled flesh on the ground. I don't like dead bodies, but who does? Pro-tip, avoid looking into their eyes. Even demons like Hitler once had souls. In my experience, humans are naturally corrupt, but it's not as if a five-year-old one day decided he wanted to be a gang rapist and murderer. I pitied them. The children they once were, that is.

With an empty duffel in hand, I move toward the van.

Got to get me some money and weapons of mass destruction. I'll turn them over to the police. Like a good law-abiding citizen would, obviously.

I never took my headphones out, and why would I? If I did, I wouldn't be able to pretend I was in a music video that was topping the billboard charts. My boots pound the dirt as I dubstep, then ballet pirouette to the money, feeling like Star Lord. Dancing is something from my former life I still love, and honestly, I think I was pretty good at. Getting over the leotards and sequins up my butt was another thing. But anyhow, back to what and who I am robbing.

Touching old, hairy, dead mafia men's hands makes my skin crawl. Shooting them fine. Carving 'AM' into their chests, I'm all in. But touching their hands that have done the unspeakable, who knows where, to who knows who? No thank you, I reject the devil.

I nudge the gang bangers icy hands off my money with the tip of my boot and take what is now mine. I stand, glancing around.

"Now, where are the other three briefcases?"

Looks like a few of the humans tried to run. They didn't make it far, obviously. As much as I try to detach myself emotionally from the scene around me, I can acknowledge standing in the middle of a murder scene is a little unnerving.

The bullet-ridden bodies littering the blood-soaked ground are sur-real and *too* real at the same time. Rigor mortis is most likely set in. My skin crawls, and that is my cue that my time is up here. I scan the ground until my trained gaze locates the prize. The last case had slid underneath one van. Not fun to retrieve. I line all the cases in the dirt, locks facing up. Those three briefcase locks are no match for my Remington. I could probably unlock them manually, but I don't have the patience.

Three shots later and the money is mine. I mentally high-five myself. I'm like James Bond up in this joint… except I am a female, and I am real. I stuff the cash into my duffle bag, which doesn't take too long when everything is in rolls of hundreds.

"Math lesson, Griffin. You ready? I'm taking 500,000 dollars in all hundreds. So, how many bills will I be stuffing in my bag? 500,000 divided by one hundred is…" I wait for Griffin, who blinks in boredom back. "Five thousand, done. I am stealing five thousand bills. You're a math genius now. You're welcome."

Half a million dollars and five thousand paper cuts later, I stretch my sore back. Time for the firepower. I slap my thigh a few times to signal Griffin to heel by my side. He bounds over from the other van, tail wagging and tongue lolling. We rummage through the weapons. It's a crappy exchange, to be honest. A bunch of AKs, a few different handguns, and screwed-up modified rifles and sawed-off shotguns. Not much worth keeping. I like my weapons to actually work and be legal. I follow the law mostly. The exchange was not a fair one, let me tell you, and someone would have eventually learned. Once they realized they were getting ripped off, all hell would have broken loose. I simply saved them a shoot-out later. I continue to mess with the shit weapons, making sure I find all the valuable ones.

Griffin's sudden low growl and backing toward me snaps me to the present. Through the vans' rearview mirror, I see ten or twelve men walk out of the tree line with what looks like military-grade M4 Carbines, aimed right at *me*.

"Looks like we've overstayed our welcome here. Griffin."

The packs rarely cared if I entered their territory. Yeah, a few Alphas didn't like me running around killing rogues, but I'm doing them a favor. To them, I'd say get over it. Kiss my ass.

Wait. Don't.

I don't ever intend on touching one of *those* mutts, let alone allowing them to touch me.

They continue to approach yet say nothing. I am the first to talk.

Over my shoulder I say, "This doesn't concern you. Leave me *be*."

I refuse to give them the respect of turning around. I've dealt with fleabags before. When you don't show submission, they go nuts. It is a dominant Alpha wolf thing. A wolf low growls. So, I face him, prepared to shut the mutt up. Griffin stays right on my heels, forever my backup.

The guy, who I assume is an Alpha, says, "You need to come with us."

At this, I raise an eyebrow. He has dominance written all over him, plus the others follow his command.

Several thoughts fly unbidden through my mind. *He's kind of hot. Why am I slightly light-headed? Snap out of it…*

"No can do. Why are you even here? Last I checked, Alpha's don't bother with rogues. Now prance on back to your precious pack and ivory tower. I'll be on my way."

I spin and walk away. The cock of about a dozen M4s halted me mid-stride.

Damn it.

Under my mask, a half-smile tugs the corner of my lips. In my most menacing tone, I say, "That was a mistake. Leave me to my business, and you can resume your pathetic werewolf lives."

"Grab him."

I'm not a 'he', Alpha ass, but you wouldn't know that.

The wolves who *did* find out were all dead, so no harm, no foul.

"I warned you. Griffin, shall we show our friends what happens when wolves mess with a badass?"

Two guys charge me, but I sidestep away, kicking one in the groin and throat punching the other. They fall. No matter how strong a werewolf is, a groin kick and throat punch will always hurt like hell.

Griffin lunges at the Alpha, but something unexpected happens. As soon as he comes within two feet, Griffin turns all happy puppy on him, licking his hand. His tail sweeps a cloud of dust as he wags it.

He only does that for me. Now, I am pissed.

I punch some guy in the face and kick another in the balls. Another comes from behind and gets me in a devil's headlock. My hands shoot straight up to my throat, struggling to pry this guy's biceps off me, to no avail.

"Let go, you raggedy mutt." I buck and kick with all my might. My neck burns as he tightens his hold on me. I dig my nails into his arm, trying like hell to rip his skin.

"Freeze, or we will open fire."

It is fair to say an M4 is something you don't mess with. Plus, the slugs are a bitch to pull out of your body. Still, I am not ready to give up yet. The guy holding me mutters some profanities as my nails scratched at his face. If he doesn't let go soon, I won't be able to breathe.

Another warning. "Drop the bag. Don't do something you'll regret."

Despite the warnings—or maybe because of them—I struggle in vain under four huge werewolves who now hold on to parts of me.

I'm so screwed now, but maybe...

One man keeps leaning back on his heels, meaning I could easily knock him over. I slam my knee into his calf and send him tumbling down. Without giving them a chance to react, I butt my head and swing my fists into whatever flesh they find. Miraculously, I break free from my choke-hold. I run about one yard before they tackled me. *Well, that is leaving a fun-looking bruise.* I need to visit a chiropractor after this.

I struggle to spot Griffin, but one of the goons mashes my face down in the dirt.

"Cade, it's one dude. Hold him steady."

I'm a her, not him, douche bag.

The two speak in low voices to each other. The rough hand squashing my cheek into the dirt made it near impossible to hear them. I'm jerked to standing again as their leader calls out a command to take my hood off. *That* I hear clearly.

No.

Seven to one. This is *so* not a fair fight. Plus, they are werewolves and I'm human. Where the hell was the ref?

I call foul.

The blond one—Cade, assumably—has a tight grip on my neck, and my instinct is to continue attempting to escape, so that's what I keep working to accomplish. He keeps reaching for my head, and I keep not letting him. I duck and thrash around, infuriating him more. His agitation showed in his grunts and growls and his wolf surfaces. Even though this dude is pissed, the Alpha behind him is even *more* pissed.

Alpha butt-turd mutters to himself. "Do I have to do everything myself?"

He reaches for my hood.

No, no, no, I can't divulge who I am.

I jerk violently to evade his hands, but he clamps them so hard on my skull my head might explode. He rips it off with such force my hair flies around, destroying my braid.

"What... the... frick...?"

"The Avenger is... *a girl*?"

"*Mine.*"

The moment he growls that one word, the other four guys holding me let go, instantly backing away. I use the unexpected moment of freedom to send a kick to their leader's face and run for it. I don't need to call Griffin. He is instantly by my side.

"Took ya long enough to show your face, buddy."

For a moment there I thought he switched sides.

I have about a five-second head start and intend to make it count. I fling open the car door and Griffin leaps in. As quickly as it opens, the door slams closed, and my foot smashes the gas pedal. Something—or someone—strikes the trunk, clearly attempting to stop me, but I am long gone.

"That's the closest we've ever been to being caught. Let's not make this a normal thing, huh, Griffin?"

I debate whether I should go back to my motel, but I have too much necessary stuff there. I mean, I lost $500,000 to those fleabags. *Ugh*. That would help me so much and now it's gone.

"Oh well, I guess I'll have to track more rogues with a bounty of cash. We're gonna be skimping a little now."

But that will be harder than it sounds. My gut says I got lucky, but the war is not over yet. I swerve to a stop at the motel and jump out as quick as humanly possible.

"Come on Griffin. We gotta go *now*. Wolves will be on our tails soon if we don't get a move on it."

I have never packed my bags so quickly in all my hunting days. Thankfully, my beautiful 2018 Acura NSX — that I *may* have tricked out a little so it could beat a werewolf—is challenged by no one. Quarter mile race shops in LAX are elite if you wanna do a little something, something to your ride. I re-harness Griffin, hump two of my bags onto my shoulders and tuck one under my free arm and sprint to the car.

"Alright time to bounce. Werewolves will be here in ten, but *we* won't." Minutes later, we are booking it down the back roads to freedom.

"Griffin, how about we drive a few hundred miles and make camp?" He slow blinks and pants at me.

Food, you dumb human.

"Fine, we'll stop for Arby's first, then set up camp."

Darkness still owns the night as I approach the city line. A couple hundred feet more. In the distance, a small light glows. The closer we get, the more it grows. It is only when we are too close to stop I realize what those glowing lights are.

Three enormous trucks, a good dozen wolves, and the asshole of the century block my path to freedom. I speed up.

Your blockade won't stop me.

That is until they pulled out M4 Carbines and aim them at my car. I screech to a stop, thirty feet from the asshole.

"Well shit, Griffin. I can't see how we're getting out of this one." I mutter a quick prayer as I brace myself.

Wow, I really pissed them off.

"Avenger, come out with your hands up."

I rev the engine, as a way of saying 'Hell no.' Griffin growls.

"Well Griffin, if we go down, it might as well be by the royals." Under my breath, I add, "Death by the tyrants sounds fitting for us."

I yank at my armor and pull my hood over my head. Last, but not least, my hand weapon of choice, 9mm with a silver camo wrap and blood-red accents.

"Let's go meet the mutts." Griffin and I exit the car. I look fierce, may I say. Skinny jeans, black tank, heeled boots, skull mask. I'm the pinnacle of a modern badass. I feel like Letty from *Fast and Furious*, car and all.

"You need something, Alpha?" I have evaded plenty of Alphas and I don't intend to stop now.

"Come with me and no one will get hurt."

I roll my eyes. Not likely. Someone will get hurt. I am merely making sure it isn't me.

"Now, why would I do such a thing, *pup*?"

The Alpha strolls toward me. I hold my ground. I will not show I am internally screaming at myself. I make no move toward my 9, but hold his stare.

He says, "I don't want to do this."

"Well, I *do*. So, Alpha, I win, I leave. If you win.... well, that *won't* happen."

I crane-kick him in the face. *Ouch.* Growls erupt from all around.

Oh plug it. You're dead now. Game on.

He growls, wiping his mouth. "Bad move, mate."

I smirk. I brought blood.

Wait. Did he just call me mate? No. Couldn't have. Focus, damn it.

"Call off your army, Alpha. You don't want to get involved in my business. Plus, it's not nice to aim weapons at someone you just met."

Our brief stare-down ends with the Alpha giving the order. "Stand down."

The wolves lower their weapons. That makes me feel *so* much better. Without warning, Griffin snaps at the Alpha's ankle, then barks viciously. But it's like there is an invisible leash holding him back from attacking.

Glad you finally realized whose team you're on.

The Alpha is unfazed. Not a surprise, though. A dog is hardly a threat to a werewolf. Griffin is more here for my mental stability.

"Griffin, don't bite the runts. We don't hunt the less fortunate."

Griffin prowls around, growling at the wolves. When the Alpha isn't looking, I throw a kick to the gut again, but this time he is prepared and steps to the side.

I toss a verbal shot instead. "For the Alpha of Alpha's, you're pretty stupid."

He grips my arm, twisting it behind me and pulling me toward him.

No, thank you.

I pivot and elbow him with my free arm. Griffin jumps onto his back, latching onto the scruff of his neck and collar, and causing him to let go.

Good boy.

I grab *his* arms and sweep his legs out from under him, pinning him in the dirt.

His eyes darken. "You wanna fight? Let's go."

I smirk, my face inches from his.

Real fighting time.

"Bring it, puppy."

He breaks one hand free and tries to shove me off. I lock onto his wrists, forcing them down at his sides, then jam my knees on top of his wrists. He easily rips free and throws me off him. We stand and square off, both panting. I roundhouse kick him again in the gut. He doubles over with a grunt. I tackle him again, straddling his chest, pinning his arms above his head.

Right when I think I have him defeated, he rolls us, placing him on top of me. I fake submit until he relaxes, and I knee him in his jewels and stand, reaching for my boot knife.

He, as swiftly, knocks it out of my hand and grabs me by the throat, pulling me hard against his chest. With a savage grin, he rips the hood off my head once again.

He's been playing with me the whole time.

This fight was won from the beginning. His wolfish smirk widens, showing perfect, white teeth. His breath is hot on my face as he glowers down at me. "On my command, open fire on the dog."

"No. Don't." I flail, but his grip on my throat tightens, making me wince in pain. I thrash and claw at his hand. My nails draw blood.

"Come willingly and maybe I *won't* blow his brains out."

"What the *hell* do you even want?"

"You."

Then… darkness.

CHAPTER 3

ULYSSES

Earlier in the day…

»Someone get me a damn coffee."

I yell at no one in particular. In a pack of twenty-seven thousand, and as King of all Alphas, you would imagine I could have a coffee when requested.

"Well, a please now and then would go a long way."

"Shut it, Axel."

Axel is my annoying-ass wolf. We telecommunicate. He never shuts up and I must sit and listen. My receptionist scurries into my office with a coffee in one hand and memos in the other.

"Sorry, Alpha. Here you go. Beta Coleman is in the lobby, and he requests you immediately."

She hands me the coffee and memos, then collects my 'out' files.

"Yes, send him in."

Coleman enters with a pile of thick yellow folders. "Nine-hundred-fifty-three."

I glance up.

This is what he bothers me with, numbers? I already went through high school.

"What?" I ask in a droll tone.

"Nine-hundred-fifty-three. That's how many rogues the Avenger killed."

"Yeah, and it's getting on my nerves. We can't have a vigilante assassin running around killing wolves, even if they are rogues. Did you find anything useful for catching the bastard?"

He slaps a file down, puffing his chest out in triumph.

"Well, it's your lucky day, boss. The Red Sun pack border patrol just discovered another body, killed by guess who? The Avenger."

He parks himself on my desk and seizes the coffee, gulping it down like a parched whale.

"Ugh, that's the worst coffee I've ever had. Black, plain coffee? Where is the cream, the sugar? Haven't you ever heard of literally anything to add flavor?"

He wipes off his mouth on his shirt. I still can't believe *he* is my Beta.

"Get your ass off my desk. Are you sure about this? Is it *actually* the Avenger? You haven't been right the past three times."

He snorts. "One, I had faulty information. How was I supposed to work with that bullshit? And two, who else kills werewolves and carves 'AM' into their chests and leaves them at pack borders?"

He flings his hands in the air like a pouty kid who got called out for misbehaving. I grimace at him. Beta Coleman has been my best friend since we could pick up a 9mm, but he still sometimes has the maturity level of a six-year-old. Still, there never was a better Beta.

After a moment, he adds, "Okay, fine, so he's gone, and we have a cold trail again."

I pound my fists on the desk. We've been trying to catch this son of a bitch for seven months, and he always escapes. Three different times we had him in our sights, and he got away.

"Not exactly, boss. We were down by the wharf and met a rather interesting character. He had a few outstanding warrants that he didn't want the police to notice. Lucky us. So, when we threatened to tip off the cops, he sang. There is a big exchange going down tonight, and our convict friend thinks the Avenger will be there."

"Alright, this is good. Get me ten of the top warriors, armed with M4 Glocks. What time is the exchange tonight?"

"Seven P.M. That gives us four hours to prepare. What's our course of action, Alpha?"

"We wait for the exchange to go down and check if this guy shows up. We bring him into custody for questioning. No one takes a shot at him unless I say so. Prepare the troops for a debriefing in one hour."

"Yes, Alpha."

Finally, some peace to get some work done. My peace is short-lived though, as a barrel of sunshine charges in.

"Lassie." Corrine, my baby sister, barges into my office and jumps onto my lap.

"Hey CC, what are you doing here and where's mom?"

"I'm right here, Ulysses," announces their mother from the doorway, "and I have a suggestion for your office. How about we put an elevator in here? Chasing this crazy child around all day does a number on my back."

"You're the one who had another kid at forty."

I receive a gentle slap on the head and giggling from Corrine.

I concede, "Okay, I'll consider it, but we have more pressing matters to deal with than elevators in the pack house. I hate to kick you guys out, but you need to go. I have a very important meeting in forty-five minutes."

"Can I come?"

"No CC, this is a special meeting."

They both nod and exit, closing the door behind them.

Cade clears his throat. "Alpha, everyone is in the meeting room."

"Thank you, Cade." We stride into the pack's conference room to join my Gamma, Delta, and ten of the best warriors.

"Alright, we found the location of the Avenger and we are closing in tonight. You all have your weapons and understand the drill. No one will fire at him till I give the command, understood?"

"Yes, Alpha." Thirteen voices respond.

"We are taking three vans. We split in thirty. Dismissed."

Spencer, always inquisitive for battle strategy. pipes up. "Hey Alpha, what should we do when we capture him? What's the aim?"

"Get him off the streets and stop him from killing more. It's our job as the royal pack to protect our citizens, and he's a threat."

"Yes, but he's killing rogues, and the pack sort of loves him. Especially the girls. They talk about him like he's Ryan Reynolds or something."

"You're mad because Emmalyn talks about him and not you. She's not your mate dude, get over it," Coleman says while slapping Spencer's back.

"You found yours; your life is great. I'm twenty-one and still haven't found mine. My life is hell without her."

I raise my eyebrow.

"Sorry, Alpha."

"Move out boys."

Three vans of the world's most powerful werewolves load up. No one speaks, and the air is heavy with silence. At an underpass, we set up shop.

"Alpha, the troops are in place," Spencer says through the mind link.

"Good. Any sign of the exchange?"

"Not yet, Sir."

"Alright. Hold the position and keep watch."

One hour, two hours, three hours…

"We have a car pulling into the lot, sir."

"Keep watch for the Avenger. No one is to shoot him, understood?"

Beside me, Coleman, Cade, Spencer, and ten of our best warriors wait, stationed around the drop-off zone. I squat next to three other guys hiding from the mafia and the Avenger. *Nice.*

"Alpha, two cars are approaching from the east and south."

"Alright boys, listen up. The Avenger should appear any minute, eyes, and ears open."

Out in the distance, a black van opens the rear door and six men climb out. The other black van also stops, and seven men step out with three briefcases. They exchange weapons, briefcases, and such.

Maybe the Avenger isn't showing up after all.

"Alpha, four men in the front of the vans are down, and I smell blood."

"Good, Spencer, keep watch-"

"Ulysses, *five* more men down."

On the ground, the exchange seems to go to hell. Guns are drawn and shouts ring out.

"Alpha, four more down. Everyone is dead. No visual on the Avenger."

"Alright, everyone. Hold position."

We wait there in the tree line for what feels like an eternity, despite being only around thirty minutes.

"Alpha, we have movement."

Around a hundred yards away, a luxury sports car appears.

"You seeing this, Ulysses?"

The door opens and out comes a skinny, all black clad man and a gigantic dog. They move with caution toward the vans. The guy snatches a briefcase from the hands of the dead mafia and turns in a slow circle, presumably to locate the others. Meanwhile, the dog noses around the dead bodies, inspecting each one. Three clean shots later the locks are blown off, and the guy stuffs huge bundles of cash into his duffle. He looks to be counting them in groups as he went.

"Waiting for your orders, Alpha," Coleman says through their mind link.

"Start closing in. Do not let him notice you."

Eleven fighters close in on the Avenger. He doesn't seem to notice us, messing still with the weapons in the rear of one van. The dog prowls around, not caring about the thirteen dead rogue wolves and human bodies littering the ground. He lifts his massive snout into the air, sniffing.

He can't know we're here, right? Wrong.

The skinny guy freezes when the dog lets out a low growl in our direction.

"This doesn't concern you, leave me be," said who we can assume is the Avenger.

"Anyone else think that looks like a girl?"

"Quiet, Cade. Focus. Orders, Alpha?"

"Show ourselves, but proceed with caution."

We leave our hiding places and step into the open night. He's good, but no one can take down an Alpha King, his Beta, Gamma, and ten of his toughest elite warriors. The masked man stops messing with the weapons truck and turns.

How did he hear us?

"You need to come with us." I state, using my Alpha tone.

He laughs and declines the command. The beast of a dog stalks closer, growling.

The Avenger walks away with the dog, the money, and a good selection of guns. The only part of him I saw was his mouth and eyes… with *eyeliner?*

"Alpha, should we close in?"

"Yes. M4's up."

Thirteen werewolf soldiers raise their military-grade, M4 Carbines at the black-clad figure. At the unmistakable sound of guns cocking, the Avenger halts.

"That was a mistake. Leave me to my business."

"Grab him." I jerk my head at the Avenger.

The Avenger makes it clear he and his dog aren't going down without a fight.

Three warriors seize his shoulders, but to no avail. The dog, Griffin, lunges at me. Using my Alpha stare, the so-called vicious dog becomes a well-trained puppy by my side. I stroke his head. The Avenger punches Spencer in the nose and kicks a warrior in the groin. Coleman tightens his grip on his arm and yanks back.

The Avenger struggles in vain against my warriors. "Let go, you mutt."

That shriek sounded feminine. Cade is right.

It takes the threat of open fire for the Avenger to cease struggling. I continue. "Drop the bag. Don't do something you'll regret." He drops the bag.

"Cade, it's one dude. Hold him steady." Seven warriors pin the Avenger down on his knees.

"Alpha, care to test our theory? He must be a girl. Look. Those are clearly boobs and curves."

When he said that, my wolf feels a pang of… *jealousy*?

"Take the damn hood off." The Avenger resists more violently than ever. Axel is getting pissed.

I can take no more of their incompetence. "Do I have to handle everything myself?" I take his head in my Alpha grip and rip off the mask.

"What… the… *frick*…?"

"The Avenger is… *a girl*?"

"*Mine*."

The Avenger sends an unexpected flying kick to my face that drops me, coughing blood into the dirt.

When my fog clears, my gut clenches. Her lower body strength is something else because I actually felt that blow in my rib cage.

My mate is driving away hot. Damn, she got away.

"Coleman, radio back to the pack. The Avenger escaped. Station six wolves at every border road. She is our Luna. We can't let her leave Charleston."

Their eyes widen and several jaws drop.

Well, this day is about to be a whole lot more interesting.

Coleman is the first to regain his composure. "Yes, Alpha. But she is armed. How do you suggest we approach her?"

It is a good point. She may wound my pack and herself.

"Use the tranquilizers. Do not approach her yet. We understand she can easily kill wolves. Proceed with caution." I receive twelve *yes, Alphas.* I rake my hands through my hair. A migraine is coming on.

How the hell did I get a human mate? It isn't unheard of, but it is extremely rare. And the Avenger? The Avenger is a girl and my mate.

I have to keep repeating it to myself to make it sink in. The drive to the pack house is quiet. What must my pack be thinking right now? To be fair, I'm not sure what *I* would think if my Alpha was mated to a werewolf killing machine.

I cannot allow myself to worry about *that* right now. All they need to do is fall in line and let me handle everything, just like always. Being Alpha of Alpha's is stressful, yes. But it's a role I willingly accept. The pack house—though not a castle, but a vast mansion in Montana—and the entire city of Charleston is werewolf town, and it is mine.

The silence of the journey home breaks the moment I step through the estate doors. The smell of teenage werewolf angst and rage wafts from across the law. With only two steps through the doors, I am harassed in my own home.

"Ulysses Carter Ronan. What did you do?"

Ah, my sister. My lovely, lovely sister. The middle child of my parents. I may be the twenty-five-year-old Alpha of Alphas, but my sister bosses me around, nevertheless.

"You are *so* dead. Why the hell would you go after the Avenger? Are you stupid?"

Her screechy voice pierces my sensitive eardrums. Her poor, unlucky future mate. He'd better never make her unhappy. *Ouch.*

"Aubrey, lower the volume on the siren that is your voice."

She rolls her eyes. "Shut up and listen, big bro. Why are you trying to get yourself killed, and how the hell did you get all the stupid genes?"

I blink at her.

"*Speak.*" Her shriek echoes throughout the mansion.

"Okay. First, I'm *not* going to die. I am Alpha of Alpha's, thank you. So, you still owe me respect."

She slaps my arm. "Hey dumbass, I have Alpha blood, too, and you're my brother. I don't need to show you anything. Now, why did you go after the Avenger?"

"You *know* why, Abbs. Now, I must bring our Luna home." Her eyes widen to bowling balls.

"Who is she? *Where* is she??"

"Well, that's the thing." I brace for her reaction. "My mate is the Avenger. It turns out *he* is a *she* and is on the run. She is presently trying to escape town, so I gotta go."

Before she closes her gaping mouth, I spin away from her and bark my orders. "Coleman, assemble everyone in the conference now and triple the warrior count. NOW."

"Yes, Alpha."

I storm to the conference room, not wanting to deal with anyone's shit.

My mate is the Avenger, and she is on the run.

"You're all aware the reconnaissance and receiving mission earlier was a big bust. The Avenger is a girl and your future Luna. She is trying to escape town as we speak, and we have little time."

Giving each a pointed stare, I place my palms on the table as my Warriors Elite listen intently. "We must stop her before she reaches the border. You are all being armed with Tranquilizers and are being given full authority to fire when given the chance. Under no circumstances can she leave. Stop her at all costs but proceed with caution. She is extremely dangerous and kills werewolves without a second thought. Roll out."

We speed out toward the two roads that lead into this city, and blockade both to stop the Avenger. Fifteen others join me at the back road exit. If my intuition is right—and it always is—she will take the less traveled road.

"Alpha, we laid out the metal tire chain and the men are ready. What else should we do?"

"She has a dog with her. If you can, bring the dog, too."

"Incoming car. West exit."

I narrow my gaze on the horizon. "Snipers at the ready, hold your fire."

The car charges toward us, showing no signs of stopping. At the thirty yards mark, she skids to a stop. Smoke rises from the rubber of her tires. I tell her to come out.

She revs the engine in reply. Axel growls at the disrespect.

I try again. "Come quietly and no one will get hurt."

The door opens, and the Avenger climbs out with her dog as if they are about to take a night-time stroll. Her head-to-toe body armor and weapons belie her casual manner.

She looks pretty dangerous.

Being harsh to my mate fills me with guilt, but I *need* my Luna. My *pack* needs her. The world of werewolves needs her, too. And we all need her alive.

I sense Axel striving to surface. The hairs on the back of my neck rise, and I shudder at the sense that Axel is about to rip something to shreds.

The Avenger—*my mate*—rests her hands on her slight hips, cocks her head, and calls me *pup*.

Fiery one, isn't she?

Axel begs to mark our mate, but I will not let him. I do the next best thing. I walk straight up to her. It requires all my might to not take her. Her entire body tenses, perhaps sensing the impending battle that I aim so desperately to avoid. Her hands curl into fists at her sides.

We can't fight our mate. Axel screams in my head.

My voice is low, for only her ears when I say, "I don't want to do this."

Everyone knows Alpha's never beg, but mates are every wolf's weakness. Don't misunderstand, though, having a mate doesn't make you weak. It strengthens your wolf.

"Well, I *do*." She offers a wager… then kicks me in the face again. Axel is beyond pissed.

"Bad move, mate."

If I keep Axel at bay inside me any longer, I am going to rip myself open from the inside. I release the floodgates and the world fades to a fuzzy gray for a second before Axel takes over control.

She aims her weapon at my face. Growls erupt from all around us. My warriors itch to jump into action, but I shoot them down. I am doing this myself.

Well, you pull the tail, you get the wolf. Game on.

Her smirk is downright mischievous as she gives her audacious orders.

She senses the sniper's weapons on her, and yet she is not afraid. She is either crazy or has a death wish. Or both.

"Stand down."

The warriors lower their weapons but remain at the ready, waiting for the second Coleman gives the okay to fire at will to save their Alpha. Out of nowhere, that dog of hers lunges and snaps at my leg. He seems more on edge than Axel, barking hysterically at me, yet not leaving his owner too far behind.

"Griffin, don't bite the runts." There is laughter in her voice.

The dog-wolf stalks around, growling at my warriors. Daring them to intervene in his master's business with me. She remains still, regaining her composure. I cannot yet tell if she will be the most powerful Luna Queen ever… or the most dangerous. Suddenly, a stinging blow slams my jaw. *She kicked me in the face… again.*

"For an Alpha, you're pretty stupid."

I seize her arm, spin her so her back is against my chest, and restrain her with a headlock. The damn feral girl sinks her teeth into my forearm and jabs her elbow into my gut. Somehow, she gets behind me and jumps on my back, knocking me to the ground.

I flip underneath her and allow her to pin my arms between our chests. Her breath is hot and rapid against my throat.

I am the Alpha of Alpha's, allowing myself to be pinned by a human. Bad optics for my pack, but so worth it.

I can't help but grin. "You wanna fight? Let's go."

A growl edges my words. Axel and I exchange control. My irises darken, and my hands curl into claws.

She smirks back. "Bring it, puppy."

In an act of mutual sportsmanship, she releases my wrists, and I let her stand. We square up. Her eyes dart around until they land on her dog. I seize the opportunity and throw the first punch. It's a light one, and she dodges it, catching my arm and yanking it behind my back. I back kick her onto the asphalt.

She groans and heaves herself up. Axel growls at me in my head for being too rough. I shake my head to stop Axel from taking over more than he already has. She crouches and charges into my gut, and we stumble backward.

She uses my imbalance to her advantage and swipes my legs from under me. I fall back hard, adding a new pain to the ache in my gut. Like a rabid spider monkey, she is on top of me again and pinning my wrists. This time, above my head.

I see that gleam in your eyes. Think you have me, huh?

I roll her with ease and pin *her* to the dirt. She bucks me off and jumps up, simultaneously reaching into her boot and unsheathing a sharp knife. My jaw clenches.

I can't hurt her, but I need her to return with me, alive and unharmed.

Her furry beast lets out a sharp bark, and she takes a step closer to him. It's then I realize her one true weakness. To my men, I order, "Grab the dog."

At those words, she freezes. I seize the moment and charge her, knocking the knife out of her hand. I catch my mate by the throat and yank her to my chest, taking her hood off with my free hand.

I tell my sniper to prepare to open fire on her beloved dog. Her eyes fill with wild terror. Guilt stabs at my heart.

"No. Don't." She struggles in my iron grip.

I offer to not kill her dog if she comes without a fight. In response to my generous offer, she tries to maul my face again. Her little claws draw blood. It hurts, but I won't show it. This wild cat sure can scrap.

"Tell me what you want from me."

"You," I whisper. She never sees the needle coming.

Lights out for her. She instantly falls limp.

Wolf's bane. Works every time.

"Well, *that* was fun… our Luna is quite the fighter," Coleman mutters under his breath. I gaze down at the half-angel, half-demon in my arms.

"Spencer, radio back home. Have Dr. Preston at the ready and clear the pack house."

"Yes, Sir."

The wolf-dog growls at me as soon as I walk toward the car, cradling my mate. Man's best friend realizes his master is unresponsive and starts circling me as if I am his next meal.

"Coleman, what do you suggest I do with *that*?" I ask, motioning to the giant, growling dog.

"Well, if you hope to keep your mate happy, I would probably take him with us."

"Bring him. Throw him in the truck."

Coleman attempts to grab the dog's collar but the beast snaps at him, drawing blood. I laugh at his stupidity.

Never grab a dog if they don't know you. Especially when his owner is unconscious because of you.

"Crap. That little jerk bit me."

"We drugged his master. Why would he trust us? Leave him be. If he wants to follow, he will. Let's get back home. Cade, you can drive my mate's car back."

Cade nods and the caravan of wolves drives off in single file. The ride is short and quiet. I sit in the back, my mate curled up in my lap. I gaze down at her. She is knocked out good. Although for how long, I can't guess. I remove the bulletproof vest, but the other gear will have to wait.

When we arrive, I carry my mate to our new room. I vow to bring her to the pack hospital in the morning. She could use a checkup. No telling if she has visited a doctor, considering how many wolves want her dead. I brush a wayward strand of hair off her forehead.

We'll deal with that tomorrow, but first, you require sleep, mate.

I lay her down on my bed and cover her with blankets, not bothering to take off her clothes, aside from her jacket and boots. I stretch out alongside her, burrowing my face into her neck, and fall asleep, inhaling her scent.

I wake to the sound of a soft moaning.

SHIT. She's waking up.

I bolt out of bed to the bathroom.

I must have a tranquilizer somewhere. Ah-ha.

I spy it, right next to the toothpaste and .22 rounds. Pretty normal stuff to have in a bathroom if you ask me. I hurriedly fill up a syringe and inject it into her neck just as her eyes flutter open.

That was too close…

I use the mind link. *"Coleman, get Dr. Preston to the medical wing."*

"Yes, Alpha."

After I mind link Coleman, I gather my stuff to head out. Our pack hospital is significant in size because the humans use it as well. As the King of all Alphas, I must pay for my pack somehow, and it brings in a lot of revenue. We also have a hospital for emergencies, and this definitely qualifies as an emergency. I lift my mate, being careful with her head. I hurry toward the hospital wing where Coleman waits at the entrance.

He rapid fires questions as I approach. "Why is she still asleep? Did you drug her again? When will you wake her?"

Stopping in the entrance, I take a second to compose myself and answer Coleman. "I'd rather have her asleep while she gets her checkup. We don't know what she would do to us. This is safer for all parties involved."

The doctor enters with Spencer and Cade trailing behind.

I offer a terse nod. "Dr. Preston."

She moves with purpose to the exam table and pats it. "Alpha. Please, bring her here." Dr. Preston is a short, petite woman with silver hair. A simple white lab coat covers a light blue shirt and black pants. No frills, all business.

After a brief hesitation, I lay my mate on the hospital bed. The doctor seizes a pair of fabric shears from a tray beside the bed and cuts her shirt down the middle, exposing her bra and bare skin. I seethe as Axel prowls around in my head, begging to be let out.

No one is allowed to look at my mate like that.

The doctor freezes, gulps and says, "S-sir, if it is okay with you, I have to remove her clothes to fully examine her. Perhaps you could wait outside the room. Surely, this girl poses no threat to require such heavy guarding."

I give the doctor a wary smirk. "She's the Avenger we have been hunting."

"Wait, Alpha. *This* is the Avenger who killed hundreds of werewolves? He—I mean *she*—is a-a teenage… *girl*?"

"Yes, but keep this to yourself. She wears a target on her back. Run a full exam, too. I'm pretty sure she hasn't been to a doctor in a long time. She'll need your expertise. There is no telling what diseases she has."

She bobs her head once and continues her assessment of the patient. My phone buzzes in my pocket. Fishing it out, I glance down at the screen, keeping the doctor in my peripheral view.

'Alpha, you are requested in the office,' the text read. I roll my head back, squeezing my eyes shut at the returning migraine.

Now, really? I just found my mate and now I have to leave her for an office meeting?

I march to the door, calling out orders. "Doc, keep her under. If she awakens, she will most likely destroy the place. Spencer, Cade? Guard this door." I give each a pointed stare. "And it's not for her protection, but for everyone in this hospital. If she wakes up, we are screwed. Coleman, you're coming with me."

I leave them scared and concerned. It's best if everyone involved understands just how hard it will be to convince my mate to be Luna of the creatures she kills.

When I at last reach my office, it is to discover my parents at my desk, my mother rummaging through my drawers.

"Mom, Dad, why did you call me here? I'm in the middle of something important."

My mother launches herself from my seat and pulls me into a hug. "Son, we came as soon as we heard. I'm so happy for you."

My father wags a finger at me. "We were getting worried about you, but we are so happy you found your Luna."

"Is it Emmalyn? I always told you she was your mate. She will be a wonderful queen; oh, I am so excited," she squeals. Coleman and I exchange a wary glance.

Boy, are they wrong.

"No, it's not Emmalyn. My mate is… human."

Silence.

"That's impossible… a human mate… you're an Alpha King. That simply won't work." My mother paces, the pitch of her voice getting higher by the second.

"Son, are you sure she is your mate? Perhaps you just thought she was. You need a strong Luna Queen, not a-a *human*."

I snarl, "I know who my mate is. And how dare you undermine her ability to lead?"

Everyone cowers at Axel's Alpha voice. How dare they insinuate I don't recognize my mate? I have waited six years for her, and they believe I wouldn't know her when I saw her?

My mother draws a cautious step toward me. "Okay, we understand she is your mate. Could we hear her name?" She touches my arm and softens her voice further. The one-eighty in her attitude gives me whip lash.

It dawns on me. I never got her name. Not that I had a chance to, really. She was too busy struggling to claw my eyes out and give me a concussion.

My own mate and I don't even know her name. Boy, that's stupid of me.

I swallow the lump in my throat and look away. Not exactly my brightest moment. "I didn't catch her name. She is at our hospital. Which is where I'll be going now."

I turn to leave, hoping to avoid a conversation about that last part.

"Wait. Why is she at the pack hospital?" My mother demands. Oh, so *now* she cares?

Without facing her, I mumble, "I knocked her out."

Thanks to stupid superior werewolf hearing, nothing gets past her. She gasps and marches toward me. Most likely to smack me senseless, rightfully so. I duck to the side as her hand flies up.

"Ulysses Carter Ronan, you *knocked out* your mate? You better start talking right now."

A low growl rumbles in my throat as she tries to whack me. I restrain her gently, holding both her wrists until she submits.

No one tells the King of Alpha's what to do.

But also, no son dares cross his mother. That is a death wish, no matter what rank you are.

"Your mother asked you a question, son."

My father raised me to respect all people. I would like to believe I'm a fair and just Alpha, but I have grown a reputation for being rough and cold-hearted toward rogues. My Beta jokes it is because I haven't met my mate yet and that she will tame that last bit of primal animal in me.

I'll admit, I have a zero-tolerance policy toward rogues, and it shows when looking at our numbers. Our pack prisons hold a plethora of wolves. I'm hoping that now that I've found my mate – one who shares my disdain for rogues – my pack will not only grow stronger but strengthen *all* wolf packs around the world.

My mother's voice brings me back to the present. "*Ulysses.* Answer me."

Coleman and I exchange glances that say, "*this should be interesting.*"

Before she shrieks out another admonition, I raise a hand to stop her. "I knocked her out because she put up a huge fight."

My mother tries to speak again, but once more I cut her off before she utters a word. "And before you ask, she is the Avenger."

Well, she had nothing to say now.

I let my words sink in, then deliver the rest of the news. "It turns out the *guy* who killed hundreds of werewolves is not only a human, but a teenage girl who is my mate."

And to top it all off, she won't stay with the beast she kills for a living.

Before anyone responds, my phone rings. I retrieve it from my back pocket.

"*What?*" I growl.

The voice of the person on the other end trembles. "Umm, I'm sorry for bothering you Alpha… but the Luna's *dog* is here, and your sister found him. She brought the dog into her room and barricaded the door. W-what should we do, Alpha?"

Only my eight-year-old sister would befriend a werewolf assassin's dog and take him into her pink explosion of a bedroom.

I roughly massage the deep crease that has formed in my brow. "Leave her be. It won't harm her but keep me updated."

"Also, sir, the Pack Doctor requests you return immediately. She says it's urgent. It's about the Luna."

I bolt from the room, leaving my parents without a word. I race through the pack house, dodging wolves and elders. At the hospital ward, I brush past Spencer and Cade, who bow in submission and move aside.

"What's wrong, Doc?"

"Oh. Alpha, I hadn't expected you here so soon… umm, well, you should probably prepare yourself…"

My migraine throbs against my skull. I rub my temples and heave a long sigh. Can it ever just be good news? "What did you learn? This was supposed to be a *routine* check-up."

She shifts her weight and averts her gaze. Never withhold information from an Alpha. My lip curls menacingly and I stalk toward her. My eye color has probably changed to gold already—the sure sign I am extremely pissed.

The words come out guttural. "Spit it out."

Axel has *almost* taken full control. If I relinquish complete command, who knows who might make it out alive.

She approaches my mate and removes a clipboard off the side table, flipping through a few pages. "Well, it's not exactly a diagnosis but a theory, really." She hesitates. "I better show you. Besides the basic tattoos, she has some, not *normal* markings."

Dr. Preston leads me to the bedside of my sleeping mate. She raises my mate's hospital gown. I am not prepared for what I see. Her legs are scored with five-inch-long white and brown jagged lines. My brain refuses to comprehend what they are.

Claw marks.

Not wanting to believe it, I ask the doctor to confirm. "What are *those*?" My fury shakes even my voice. If they are what I suspect, someone will pay for those marks.

"Well, I'm not one hundred percent positive, but the distinct patterns likely signify an animal attack. I *suppose* they could be from self-harm, abuse, or perhaps from battle scars." She taps the side of her mouth and concedes, "But the most logical source is werewolf…"

I let out a deep snarl. Whoever hurt her, I will hunt them down and kill them, even if they are family. I can only imagine how she got these scars. Part of me doesn't *want* to. I couldn't live with myself knowing she'd been in harm's way, and I hadn't protected her. Dr. Preston clears her throat, breaking me from my train of thought.

"Alpha, that's not all…"

I nod for her to continue, using all my strength to stop Axel from surfacing.

"Well, s-she has a tattoo burned into her skin. It's on her thigh. The letters JN. I'm not sure what it means. Although I have a few theories. It can be gang-related, an initiation of sorts."

I lose all control right there. My phone cracks in half in my grip. *Someone* or *something* abused my mate, and they had the audacity to mark her precious skin. Axel takes over again, and my transformation begins. My body convulses as my wolf surges through me. My hands fly to my head and grip at my hair in agony.

"Gamma Spencer, Delta Cade, the Alpha is shifting." Doctor Preston shouts yet remains at my mate's side. Spencer and Cade burst in and shove me into the hall before I injure anyone in my shift. Out of my mate's presence, they both yell at me.

"Alpha. Calm down. Getting angry won't help your mate," Spencer pleads.

Cade screams at me, hoping to snap me back into reality. "If you don't calm down, you will hurt *her.* Think about what you are doing. She's tough. She is the Avenger, for crying out loud."

My heart pounds in my head, making everything and everyone hard to hear. I recover control, finally no longer merely a passenger in my body. My eyes return to their normal color and I see clearly again, no longer a gray blur. They back away from my heaving body, and Axel calms down inside my mind where he belongs. I straighten and dust myself off, regaining my composure. An Alpha cannot lose control like that. It doesn't set a good example. I clear my throat and address the Doctor.

"Thank you, Dr. Preston. Do a full exam on her. Cat scans, MRIs, blood tests for anything out of the ordinary. Leave nothing unchecked. Do whatever you have to. I give my full permission."

She nods and resumes her work on my mate. I face my Gamma and Delta. I can't hide the pain in my eyes.

"Stand guard. No one enters this room unless they are medical professionals. Understood?"

They put on brave faces, ready for battle or whatever might occur.

In somber unison, they say, "Yes, Alpha."

I have to let off a little steam, and I know exactly where. I mind link with Coleman, telling him where I'll be. I exit the hospital ward and head back to the main building.

Once through the kitchen door, I storm into the yard. I don't even bother shifting into Axel's wolf. He is already pissed enough and changing into my enormous wolf will not help. I speed off bullet fast and begin my stress-relieving rampage run. Dodging trees and leaping over fallen debris, I maneuver to a place where I can calm Axel and both our nerves. On the outskirts of the forest line is a small treehouse I'd built when I was younger. Coleman and I had spent long weekends perfecting it.

I lean against the base of the tree, staring up into the sky. *What the hell do I do? My mate is human. The Avenger, no less.*

She most likely hates me. And was abused by either herself or her family. She *has* to stay here with me. The real question is, *how was I supposed to do that?* A small giggle from behind me interrupts my thoughts. Before I can react to the little devil, she tackles me around my legs, knocking me down.

"Lassie."

Little sisters are annoying, but you can't help but love them. Even if you don't display it in public. And I had *twice* the trouble.

"CC, what have you done now?" I ask, referring to the dog-wolf behind her. She drops her gaze and fidgets with her shirt.

She rapid fires without taking a breath. "Can I keep him? I found him outside the pack house, and Coleman said he belonged to your mate, but she couldn't take care of him so, could I? PLEEEEASE."

I chuckle and hold a hand up to stop the barrage. "You can keep an eye on him for now, but when my mate wakes up, she will expect him back."

In reply, she attacks my neck with hugs, and thanks me profusely.

I half-heartedly fend her off. "All right, all right, come on, let's get you both home. Mom is probably looking for you."

Corrine climbs onto my back for a piggyback ride home.

"Mommy and daddy were busy, and I'm really bored."

"Well, you can't go exploring alone. You need someone with you. You realize that."

"I had someone with me. Grey followed me."

I assume Grey is the dog. Still, I ask, "Who's Grey?"

Corrine points to my mate's dog, who has taken a strange interest in my baby sister. He seems content to stay around, most likely because his owner is unconscious in the pack hospital.

I ask her, "Where did you find him?"

Corrine perches on my shoulders, playing with my hair. In typical childlike nonchalance, she says, "He was scratching at the back door and Coleman told me to let him be because he was dangerous, but he was really just hungry. I brought him inside and he was really friendly, so we shared my Pop Tart. Coleman said he needed someone to watch him till his owner wakes up because she was sleeping. Does she always take really long naps?"

I sigh. "You can keep him. But don't bring him inside."

She bangs on my head like a bongo. *There's why you never tell an eight-year-old she can't bring her best friend inside.*

"Lassie. He needs to come inside. He can't sleep outside. How is he supposed to play dress-up with me?"

Dare I ever take away a puppy from a possessive child?

I relent. "Okay, fine. Bring him inside. Just don't tell mom."

"Don't tell mom, what?"

Damn.

An angry mama bear greets us at the patio door upon our arrival.

"Corrine Margaret Ronan. Where did you go? And *what* is that?"

She points to 'Grey' behind us. I set Corrine down and she runs to our mother.

"Mommy. Look what Lassie is letting me keep."

She pats her thigh and, to my surprise, Grey trots over to her, tail wagging and all.

"Ulysses. Whose dog is that?"

"She's my mate's dog. He followed the vans here when we knocked her out. Corrine will keep him till she wakes up. My mate said his name was Griffin."

My mom bends over to pet Grey—or Griffin—whatever its name is. He behaves like an innocent, adorable puppy, wagging his tail as she rubs behind his ears. Never would they believe that only yesterday he—along with his owner—had tried to kill me. Yeah, that would be an interesting conversation.

"Lassie even said he can come inside and play with me," Corrine says, jumping up and down.

My mom glares at me, but she cannot legitimately do anything because it is *my* house.

"Why don't we give him a bath? He looks atrocious."

"Yes. Grey and I will go get the bath towels."

Corrine dashes inside with Grey on her heels. I would do anything to keep her happy. It is my job as a brother to protect my little sister, and that's exactly what I intend.

CHAPTER 5

ULYSSES

"So, he belongs to your mate?"

I tilt my head and brace myself for wherever this conversation is heading. My mother—an imperious, restless woman full of exasperated sighs, nitpicking, and inquisitions on all matters—smooths her already perfect hair with an elegant hand.

"I'm so happy you found your mate, Ulysses. But I'm also concerned about you. She's human and *you* are a Royal Alpha. You realize she cannot lead us properly? She doesn't even know a thing about us. And you require a strong heir to rule after you." She cups my face in her palms and compels me to meet her gaze. "She won't be able to give you that. You should consider another she-wolf instead."

Axel judders. My mother releases my face when my jaw clenches, noticing the inner conflict between me and my wolf. Werewolves are possessive of their mates, especially Alphas.

How dare she question me?

Mate bonds are unbreakable unless you reject them. As for my mate, she is strong and independent, and can clearly defend herself. She will be the most exceptional Luna this pack has ever seen.

"Mother. I will not reject her. She will be the next Luna of the Alpha's Dark Sun Pack, and no one will ever stop me or her. You will do well for yourself to never mention rejecting her again."

Her wolf whimpers in submission. I hate to use my Alpha voice on my mother, but Axel is trying to surface for a full-on rampage.

"I'll check on her now."

"Coleman, I need you and Jackie in the office."

"Yes Alpha, we'll be there in five."

I stomp through the house, ignoring the members ducking into corridors and out of my way to avoid me. They know to stay well out of the way of their Alpha King when I am in this state. Once alone with my thoughts, I allow myself to wonder what it might be like when she accepts me. Though I can't imagine it happening soon, I hope she'll see me for who I truly am.

Axel is already attempting to mark her and restraining him becomes more and more a challenge. I have power, but my wolf——when unleashed, is even more powerful. When he wants something, he will get it.

My thoughts drift toward what our pups would look like. Though human mates are rare, they can still have werewolf children, since the wolf gene is dominant. As for having human children? That would be unlikely. Either way, I don't care.

Coleman and Jackie are trying for pups, along with most of the warriors who don't already have them. It is a duty of werewolves to reproduce young to keep the numbers up and breed strong young fighters. It is also a source of pride and joy to bring life into our world.

I make my way to my office, where my Beta and his mate wait.

Without preamble, I announce, "As you both heard, my mate is unconscious in the hospital. Coleman, did you tell Jackie who she is?"

Jackie gasps and jolts in her chair at the word *unconscious*. We practically grew up together, and she is the most loving person I know. Whenever anyone needs help, she is always the first person to offer a helping hand. Her compassion and dutifulness is why she has been performing the tasks of Luna.

She regains her composure. "No Alpha, just that you found her."

"Well Jackie, as Coleman already knows, my mate is the Avenger who we have been tracking for some time now and…"

Jackie jumps out of her chair and waves her arms in the air to interrupt all talking. "Wait. The Avenger is a female? And your *mate*? He's… She's the most dangerous werewolf in practically the world."

"Yes, I know…"

In true Jackie fashion, she exclaims, "That is so *awesome*. I can't believe that our Luna is the vigilante Avenger. I can't believe the Avenger is a *girl*. Is she pretty? Have you marked her yet? Can I meet her now?"

I raise an eyebrow at Coleman to inform him his mate should stop talking. Coleman wraps his arms around Jackie, and she instantly melts. However, her gaze still trained on me, waiting for an answer.

"Jackie, let Ulysses talk now. He has important things to explain."

"Sorry, I was excited that our Luna is the Avenger werewolf warrior."

Coleman and I exchange knowing glances.

"She isn't a werewolf. She's… human."

Her face goes blank, unable to register what I have said. A new torrent of questions begins. I close my eyes, sit down at my desk, and kneed my temples.

"You have a human mate? How is that even possible? I mean, I'm totally happy for you, but—no offense—how can you convince her to stay here and become our Luna? She killed hundreds of werewolves in her lifetime. Plus, she sort of hates our kind. Is that why she is unconscious? Did you have to knock her out to get her here? Is she okay?"

I again look to Coleman to shut his mate down. Jackie is… hyperactive. As are my mother, my sisters, and seemingly every female I know. Maybe it is hereditary for our pack females. Regardless, it gives me a headache. My mate seems to be the opposite. A woman of few words, and when she *did* speak, pure venom poured out. Coleman embraces Jackie once more. Jackie blushes, relaxing into her mate's arms again. Axel whines in anticipation of our mate in my arms. But something tells me that won't be happening for a while.

Jackie bites her lip, picking at Coleman's fingertips, which he often let her do to ease her nerves. "Sorry… I was blabbering, wasn't I?"

Coleman gently bumps her forehead with his. "Yes, baby, you were. Now listen to what Ulysses says."

I really do not enjoy talking about women's undergarments–surprise, I know—so I blurt my next orders. "She has next to nothing with her, so I'll need you to go shopping and buy her more clothes and girl stuff. She has one bag and half of it shouldn't even be wearable. I wouldn't even know where to start. You're a better fit for the job than…"

Jackie laughs her head off. "Wait, so you're telling me you called me here to go bra shopping?"

Axel growls, annoyed that Jackie has disrespected us. But I would not punish her. Jackie is like a sister, and she knows where the limits are. I lift my mate's duffle bag from beside my desk and hand it over to her.

"Yes. Go through this, too. I feel like it would be more appropriate for a girl and not a random guy she doesn't know."

Jackie takes the duffle and carries it over to the couch on the back wall, giving herself plenty of space, and plops down to sort and organize my mate's clothes. Coleman perches behind Jackie and wraps his arms around her waist. While they handle that unwanted task, I sort through paperwork. The companionable silence is interrupted when Jackie gasps.

"Umm, Alpha…"

I glance up to see Jackie holding a .357 Magnum Revolver by the barrel, dangling it pinched between her fingers like you would a mystery zip-lock bag from last year's backpack. Coleman removes the gun from his mate's grasp and checks the safety.

"Why am I not surprised?"

I sigh to myself, walk around my desk to the seating area that is now littered with my mate's things. We rifle through the bag and discover a few other revolvers and a dozen various-sized knives and throwing stars mixed in with several pairs of jeans, a few hoodies, and plenty of camo green shirts and tank tops. I half expect a Gilly suit in here.

"Well, your mate's not one for variety. When she wakes up, we will have a very serious conversation about fashion and the color *green*."

I smirk. Jackie is as girly as God makes them. She loves fashion and shopping at the mall. Coleman has trudged into the pack house many times, saying he will never enter a mall of his free will ever again.

"We should let her wake up first before you traumatize her at the mall with your shopping skills."

Jackie slaps Coleman on the back of his head.

I interrupt their playful bickering. "Coleman, put all those weapons in a safe somewhere."

"Yes, Alpha. Where are you going?"

"To the surveillance room for some investigating."

I leave my office—with Coleman disposing of the many weapons and Jackie designing my mate's new wardrobe with mad glee—and make my way down the long, winding halls.

Not only is the place massive, it is also especially advanced for a werewolf pack. We have a surveillance room, weapons vault, hospital, rogue prison, presidential sized kitchen, media room, gaming room, and a well-equipped gym.

The surveillance room is on the upstairs level of the second pack building. At all times, there are seven to ten men working. They survey the pack borders and keep rogues under control using advanced technology.

I open the heavy metal door and step inside.

"Alpha, what are you doing here? Our next evaluation isn't for another three weeks." A teen boy about seventeen asks, already sweating at the presumption of a surprise inspection.

"No, I need to speak with Chief Eric." I jerk my chin in the Chief's direction.

"Ah, Alpha, what do I owe this pleasure?"

Eric reaches out and shakes my hand with a warm smile. The chief is a burly man—a *silver fox,* as my mother calls him—who smokes cigars and shoots skeet with the grandkids, much to his daughter's and wife's chagrin. He has kind but astute eyes and is always ready with a warm hug for the younger pups. He's a man I find impossible to dislike and easy to trust.

"I need a facial recognition for someone."

I hand him my cell phone with a photo of my mate from a windshield cam from one of the vans and a photo I snapped of her asleep.

It's not creepy, it is thorough.

"I see. Care to share who this young lady is?"

I ponder not disclosing this one piece of information for a second. The pack will find out, eventually.

"She is my mate."

His expression remains neutral as he moves to the computers. Asking no further questions, he does as I ask.

"I'll have an answer in an hour."

I thank him and head to the hospital room. Even from such a distance, I detect her scent. I recognize hints of black teakwood and vanilla underneath traces of cigarettes and motel stench, and I allow myself to wonder what she might smell like after she showers off those offending odors.

I enter the room as Dr. Preston extracts a needle from my mate's shoulder. Axel instantly growls and Dr. Preston drops the needle with a frightened yelp.

I hasten to my mate's side, checking her over for any wounds. My instincts cause me to overreact, and I have to bring them under control. I remind myself the good doctor wouldn't harm her Luna Queen. No one would dare. I swivel back to the doctor, who has hastily gathered her supplies.

The doctor's words are hurried. "You're back already. The tests are conclusive, and I've observed some very interesting results." She averts her gaze to the floor and silence fills the room as she fuddles with her clipboard.

"*Well*, what were they?"

She walks over to the bedside and lifts a medium-sized folder.

"Her outer physical health is okay, despite some major scars and bruises, which is to be expected. Her blood tests came back negative for mostly everything except Hashimoto's disease. Hypothyroidism, when severe, can cause your metabolism to slow down, which can lead to weight gain, fatigue, and other symptoms. She has gone against the grain and maintained great physical condition. With medication, her thyroid will be fine..." She takes a deep breath before continuing. "But she seems to have anovulation. I'm very sorry, Alpha."

My brow creases. "Why are you sorry? What is anovulation?"

Her expression turns mournful, and in a gentle tone says, "Anovulation means lack of ovulation or absent ovulation. Ovulation is the release of an egg from the ovary. This must happen to achieve pregnancy naturally. Medically induced..."

I wave off her doctor's lingo. "English, Doc."

"In layman's terms, she is infertile, unable to produce an heir. She... she *can't* have children."

It feels like someone put a freight train on my lungs and my heart skips a beat at not being able to raise a family with the one person I am meant to be with.

I wonder if she knows.

"How can this happen?"

"Well, it can be genetic, or in rare cases, it may be due to intense cervical damage." She clasps her hands together and looks skyward before continuing. "How do I put this? The brute force alone of an unwanted sexual encounter could tear the vaginal wall, which can cause many problems other than the obvious physical ones."

Understanding dawns. The rage at the implications of what the doctor said makes Axel ready to surface.

"Rape? Is that what you are saying happened to her?"

"I-I mean, it's one theory, but with the claw scars, it makes sense."

I don't let her finish explaining. Axel takes over. I tear out of the ward and bolt into the yard. I let the clothes rip and fall from my body as I shift into my wolf. Had I shifted inside the hospital, no telling what damage we could've done. I let Axel take charge, and our paws dig and rake into the dirt as we race through the forest, sprinting over fallen trees and dodging boulders and brush.

When we slow at last, I don't bother changing back. We end up at the lake, where we lay down on the shoreline. Axel's thoughts mingle with my own, giving me a new migraine.

How did this happen? How is this happening?

My beautiful mate had already had such a hard life. Being the future Luna will only make it harder. How can I convince her to even stay here? My mind skips around to every worst-case scenario of what might have happened to her to leave those nasty marks, burns, and damage.

I can always force her to stay, but my gut tells me her freedom is something she values above all else. My ruminations are disrupted by a sound from the forest line. Someone is there. Axel growls until Spencer appears with a set of clothes. He throws them down onto a rock, and Axel snatches them between his teeth and runs into the thick bush. I shift and pull on the gym shorts and a t-shirt.

"Care to share why you stormed out of the pack house like that? You scared the crap out of the Doc," Spencer calls from the waterline, staring into the distance as I walk up behind him.

"My mate." I snarl. I don't feel like playing show and tell with him. This is not something I want the entire pack to know. He glances over at me and cocks one eyebrow. I break eye contact and look back out onto the lake, ignoring his mental question.

"That bad, huh? Well, at least you still have her, right? She is still alive and here." He bends down, scoops up a smooth rock, and skims it across the water's surface. "She'll be a great Luna. She is a fighter, no matter what Dr. Preston discovered. You'll get through whatever this is."

"Thanks, man."

He claps me on the shoulder. "No problem. Anything for my Alpha. It's getting late, we better get back."

We shift into our wolves for the run back. After returning to the pack house and changing, I go straight to the surveillance room to check in with Chief Bronson. I pray to God above he's uncovered something, *anything*. If I learn a little about her past, it might help her accept me and, more importantly, overcome her demons.

Or completely freak her out looking like a stalker.

As I move through the halls, my mind races. I have to hope this turns out well. This can go south in no time for me and anyone in my mate's way. I slam open the surveillance room door and everyone jumps up.

"Alpha, I'm glad you're here. We couldn't uncover much, but we *did* find a rather interesting news article."

Eric slips a sheet of paper from a folder on his desk and hands me a printout of a news article dated 2014.

> *"Bear attack outside of Winchester, VA.*
> *Late one night in December, the Mikos family of six*
> *went out for a camping trip on the Appalachian Trail and*

were brutally attacked and killed by what the police assume was an unfortunate bear encounter. Several bodies were recovered from the campsite. The body of the oldest daughter, Westries Clary Mikos, was never recovered. Police suspect foul play was involved with her disappearance, but no leads have been fruitful. If you get any information, please contact the Winchester City Police. Picture of Westries below."

When I finish reading the article, I pull the picture of my young mate from under the paper clip to get a better look. It is definitely her—a younger, happier version of her—and she was stunning. Her smile magnified her radiance through the picture. In it, she is hugging the puppy version of Griffin close to her face. Based on the size of the pup, they must have adopted him not long before the camping trip. Griffin was so tiny compared to how huge—almost wolf-sized—he is now. They both have matured into their adult selves.

But more significantly, she is so different from the young woman now laying in one of my hospital beds. The version in the picture had no scars, burns, or tattoos. She appears content, wonder-filled, and without a care in the world.

Chief Bronson opens another folder and spreads out several sheets. "I also pulled out some police reports from the city. The assailant was definitely *not* a bear. In fact, Winchester rarely had bear encounters. It was undeniably a werewolf attack."

The chief raps a blunt finger on the nearest page, sliding it across to me. "The police report also said that there were three different-sized claw marks, meaning three rogues were there that night. It also said none of the family's phones were recovered, just destroyed clothes and tents. They found 9mm and six bullet casings two hundred yards away from where the bodies were discovered. Safe to say something messed up happened there, and someone tried to cover it up."

That's why she kills rogue wolves. They killed her family.

It doesn't take a genius to understand she is avenging her family. The real question is, how did a fourteen-year-old girl escape three rogue wolves? The present-day version of her, I wouldn't be surprised. But I cannot imagine a young girl able to do much damage.

The chief closes the folder and squints at me. "So, when were you planning on telling me your mate was the Avenger?"

I glance away, raking my hand through my hair. I pinch the bridge of my nose as I turn back to him, nodding in confirmation.

He smirks. "Yeah, I figured. The photo you handed me was dated the time and day you and the Warriors Elite went after the Avenger. You didn't bring back a murderous wolf, but an unconscious girl. So, I just put two and two together, which equals your mate is the Avenger."

I sigh. "Yes, she is the Avenger and presently she is unconscious because I had to get her here without her killing anyone. And this is not common knowledge, so I would appreciate it if you kept this on the down-low."

He offers a terse nod. "Well, at least our Luna won't be a pushover. She is a scrapper."

"Agreed. Thank you, Eric."

I take the file from him and return to my poor mate with a different perspective on her. Saying she is a fighter is an understatement. She is a fighter on all levels, physical, mental, and emotional. I step into her hospital room to see Dr. Preston filling a syringe with clear liquid. They had changed her clothes.

I snarl. "Who undressed her?"

It better not have been a man.

The doctor is wary but composed. "Hello again, Alpha. Beta female Jackie said you wanted her in fresh clothes. And this," she gives the syringe a gentle shake, "is Synthroid for her hypothyroidism. It's usually in pill form, but until you decide to wake her, we'll have to inject it into her system every day." She pauses, then asks, "When *do* you intend to wake her, exactly? You can't keep her under forever."

It is a question I haven't determined an answer to yet.

With my eyes on my mate, I ask the doctor, "What do you suggest from a medical perspective?"

"Well, we should take her off Propofol and let her body wake up on her own. She also needs to detoxify from the wolfsbane."

"Can I take her back to her bedroom?"

She must have expected my question, because she hands me a plastic box with seven injections. I accept the box and scoop my mate into my arms, cradling her head against my chest.

"Oh, and Alpha, if she's really as dangerous as we believe, handcuffs wouldn't be a bad idea. At least until you're sure she won't try to *kill* anyone."

The doctor's last words to me echo in my mind as I carry my mate back out and up the stairs to our bedroom. I nudge the door open with the toe of my boot and close it with my heel, trying not to wake anyone up. I lay her on the right side of my king size bed and tuck the blankets up high over her. She looks so peaceful when she is sleeping.

She will definitely not be peaceful when she is awake and trying to kill me.

I chuckle at that, but then I remember what the Doc said.

"… if she's really as dangerous as we believe, handcuffs wouldn't be a bad idea. At least until you're sure she won't try to kill anyone."

It will serve me best to remember she is still the Avenger and will not cease attempting to kill me until she understands the mate bond. I walk to my closet and rummage through my old utility duffle bag, pushing aside tasers, tranquilizers, and chloroform until, *jackpot.* Two pairs of handcuffs.

I remove her hand from under the covers and cuff her right hand to the right head post, aiming to make it as comfortable as possible. I fold her left hand across her belly. Once satisfied with her comfort and secureness, I head off for a shower. As the steaming water washes away my tension, I contemplate my next steps in trying to convince the werewolf assassin to be the mate of one.

Can humans feel the mate bond like werewolves?

I am aware human mates occur, but it is rare. In recent years, I can recall only one. An Alpha of my pack in California had asked if his Beta could accept a human mate. I'd said yes, though I'd also wondered at how many of these human mates actually stayed with their mates.

A hundred other questions fly through my mind as I crawl into bed next to my lovely mate, careful not to squash her. I curl around her and rest my chin on her shoulder, her hair against my forehead and my nose to her neck. I fall asleep breathing in her scent.

CHAPTER 6

ULYSSES

awaken to the screams of my mother at my sister.

"Corrine Ronan, *get back here*. You cannot have that *dog* wearing your sisters' clothes."

"I have to, mom. My clothes are too small."

Thumping of feet fall on the wood floor, and I groan. This is why I need a vacation, preferably with my mate. Or even better, my parents could move out. I bury my head in my pillow next to my mate and wrap my arm around her waist.

Dear God, I wish she was awake so I could hold her, and she would hold me back.

Holding her calmed Axel, despite her lack of response.

If she was awake, she would try to kill me.

"Alpha, Jackie is requesting your presence in your office."

"I am on my way, Coleman."

I slide out of bed and saunter to my closet. I shake out a pair of dark wash jeans and tug a blue button-down shirt off a hanger. I have never been picky when it comes to clothes, but an Alpha King must dress to impress. After I change, I amble into my bathroom and squeeze some toothpaste onto my toothbrush. I brush for two minutes on each rack.

What? Can't a devilishly handsome Alpha have good dental hygiene?

Not that it matters. Werewolves don't get sick or have physical problems, because we heal almost instantly.

I comb my hair and exit the bathroom. I am loath to leave, but duty calls. Even with guards stationed right outside the door, I hesitate to leave her.

I look one last time at my mate sleeping on my bed and go. I stroll along, smiling at the few wolves I come across, calmed by the knowledge I have my mate. Her lingering scent on me, plus knowing that she is in the safest pack house, pacifies Axel as well.

The sound of little feet and paws running around the corner alert me before Corrine and Griffin barrel into me. I catch Corrine by the shoulders and set her back up on her feet.

"Where do you think you two are going? And why is Griffin wearing Aubrey's shirt?"

"Lassie. You must hide us. Mommy is coming, and she wants to take Griffin's new clothes. He *needs* clothes. It is *cold* outside."

I shake my head at my baby sister and crouch to meet her eye to eye.

"CC, he is a *dog*. He doesn't need clothes. He has fur, like our wolves. You wouldn't put a shirt on a werewolf, now, would you?"

"No… but he *isn't* a werewolf and look. He is so happy."

CC points to Griffin, who wags his tail in obvious contentment. No one would believe me if I told them that this dog had tried to kill me not too long ago.

From somewhere in the house, an unmistakable voice bellows. "Corrine. Give me my shirt."

"If you don't want to get caught, I suggest you hide downstairs. Go."

Corrine raises a thumbs up and sprints down the hall. I laugh, shaking my head, and continue toward my office.

I open my doors and instantly regret giving Jackie my credit card. I barely spy Coleman and Jackie over the piles and piles of bags.

Coleman flings his hands up in frustration and mutters, "Sorry, she got carried away at the mall. I-I couldn't stop her. It's like the hulk married a Kardashian and had a fashion crazy hulk, baby."

Jackie glares at him. How can someone so tiny do so much damage?

"When did you have time to do all this? I gave you my credit card yesterday."

Jackie yanks garments out of bags and folds them expertly, not even bothering to glance up at me.

"Well, it's a funny story, really. I had called ahead last night to see if some of the werewolf-owned shops would open early for their future Luna Queen. They were a little upset when I told them that the Luna couldn't come yet but were ecstatic to learn the Luna would wear their clothes."

"Wait, Jackie. You told them I found my mate?"

"Well yeah, it's not like it's a secret, right? I mean, you are announcing it soon. We have been waiting forever to find her and you did. So, anyway…"

I gawk at her. My nostrils flair and I inhale a deep breath, trying to calm myself. I should've known she would spill it. Although, I regrettably never told her otherwise.

"I found a wide variety of clothes. Everything from jumpers to some rather nice dresses I'd like to see Westries wear for me one day. Oh. My absolute favorite thing is this."

Jackie holds up a forest green dress. It has a high-low cut and thin straps. Axel and I yearn to see my mate in it.

"It could be an announcement dress. In no way will it suffice for a coronation gown, though. For that, we will do some serious searching."

Coleman chimes in. "She originally wanted to get the hot pink version, but I convinced her to try another route. Hot pink is way too obnoxious."

Jackie smacks Coleman's chest. She is wearing a hot pink shirt and denim shorts.

"I meant on anyone else. It looks great on you, babe."

"I can't imagine Westries wearing it either. You guys made a good choice."

They both stare at me in shock. What did I say?

"Is that her name? Is she awake? Can I meet her?"

Jackie jumps up and down. Coleman tries to hold her in one place. He catches her belt loop and pulls her into an embrace.

"No, she isn't awake. And before you ask—I had Chief Eric run a facial ID on her. It doesn't look too good…"

"What do you mean, not too good?"

I motion for them to sit. Jackie curls up in Coleman's lap and they wait with expectant eyes. I extract the news article from my back pocket and toss it on the table.

"Well, all the information I have is from a police report in Winchester, VA."

I thrust my chin to the paper. "Read it and you will understand."

Coleman snatches it up, opening it with Jackie peering over his shoulder. They both read in silence. I study them as they scan the document and see pain in their eyes. Wolves receive a physical connection with their Alpha and Luna. They have a desire to protect them, and when the Luna and Alpha are sad, they are sad too. Coleman refolds the paper and Jackie wipes a stray tear from her cheek.

"We also uncovered police and autopsy reports of the family. The reports say the cause of death were bears, but we now know they were rogue werewolves."

"So, that's why?" He mind links with me for the rest of the question. *… she hunts down werewolves?*

I nod.

"This is horrible. No *wonder* she hates us. I would hate me to if… wait. If the rogues killed her whole family, how did she survive? I can't imagine a young human girl fighting off grown male werewolves."

"That is one question we haven't been able to answer. We can only wait till she wakes up."

They both exhale loudly and lean back, taking in the new information about their Luna Queen.

"Do not share this information until further notice. Jackie, thank you for doing this for me. I appreciate it. Now, help me carry all this to the guest room."

They scoop up bags into their arms.

"I have one question, though. How did you get all this in so little time?"

"It is a superpower. Right, babe?"

Coleman scoffs, and I laugh.

"Yes, babe. It is your superpower. A super evil power…" Coleman tries to mumble the last part, but Jackie hears it and throws a fistful of shirts at her mate.

"Hey. I use it for good *and* evil. Just don't piss me off and I won't use it on you."

When we reach the guest room, I walk ahead and open the bedroom door. We toss all the bags on the bed and Coleman and I turn to leave.

"Where are you two going?"

We gape at each other, eyebrows raised, then at Jackie.

"Work?"

"Pack training?"

She purses her lips, shakes her head, and wags her finger in a *come here* motion at us.

"I don't think so. You are helping me."

"With what?" I ask, annoyed that we are still here.

She chucks a pile of jeans at me. "To *organize*. You can't just throw all of this on her bed and expect her to understand what the heck to do with it. You both will sit here and help me. No arguing. This is *your* mate, Ulysses."

We groan and stomp back to the bed. Jackie hands each of us a bag and demonstrates how to *properly* fold shirts and pants for optimum space efficacy.

"So, when you fold any type of pants, you fold in thirds. For shirts, fold into thirds or fourths, and for shorts, stack them. Got it?"

"Does she do this to all your clothes?" I whisper to Coleman.

"She folds my boxers into squares and rolls my socks. She even labeled the drawers with little white stickers."

I snicker at the last part. Jackie is not only bubbly and talkative, but extremely well organized. Just last month, she reorganized my entire office. I am not complaining, but she went a little overboard on the labeled boxes in the closet.

"Don't judge the system because it works. This will be the most organized closet you've ever seen."

"Nope, I am not organizing this."

Coleman hurls a pink and black bag across the room and wipes his hands on his pants like the contents are toxic. Jackie glares at her mate, curling her lips into a scowl, and retrieves the bag. She dumps the contents on the bed. A dozen bras of various shapes and colors are now strewn everywhere. Coleman pokes at one of them with a folded bag as if it might bite his hand if he gets too close. Jackie collects them all and stuffs them in a different bag.

"What are you? Five? You act as if you've never seen a bra before."

Jackie twirls a bra on her finger, devilishly smirking at us. Coleman blushes and mumbles something about five-year-olds under his breath. Jackie informs us we need to carry all the folded clothes to the drawers and put them in the correctly labeled sections. She loads our arms up with folded shirts and shorts.

"Tell me again why we have to do this? We are the Royal Alpha and Beta and we are folding girl clothes. This is beneath us, Jackie."

"Because, Coleman, you are my mate and I said so. What ever happened to chivalry?"

Jackie pivots and snaps up a bag of toiletries and stalks off to the bathroom, huffing all the way.

"Your mate is crazy…" I whisper to Coleman, who bobs his head in agreement and hisses *'ya' think'*. Jackie hears and yells at us again.

"Alright, get out. You're making me lose brain cells. Remove yourselves from my presence, now!"

She chases us with an Old Navy bag and we book it out of there. We end up in the lounge, where I make my way behind the bar and snag two glasses and a bottle of scotch. Coleman perches at the bar while I pour the two drinks. Work can wait a minute.

And I could use some alcohol in my system to numb my senses a little.

I hand my Beta his glass, and he chugs it in two seconds flat. He moves on to the whole scotch bottle and pops the top.

"Chill. Jackie hates it when you get intoxicated."

He slams the glass bottle onto the granite.

"You know as well as I, we can't get drunk. And I need this, no I earned this."

"She's your mate, dude."

He grimaces and peers down at his empty container, then raises an eyebrow at me. I reach under the bar and locate another bottle of liquor, setting it on the bar. Coleman swipes it and before I even pour a glass, he gulps it down, too.

He'll feel this burn tomorrow.

"Okay, what is wrong with you? You are never like *this*."

He bangs another bottle down and rakes his fingers through his hair. No less restless, he springs up and clomps behind the bar himself. I move out and claim a seat at the bar, staring at my Beta expectantly.

"Start talking."

"So, you know Jackie has wanted kids for a year now. Well, she thinks she can't have kids and is in denial now. She has been organizing everything in our room five times over. She organized the bathroom, where the towels are in the drawers and our toothbrushes are hanging in plastic bags on the hooks."

It is heart-wrenching for a werewolf to not be able to have pups. Traditionally, wolves shift when they are thirteen and partner with their mates when they are seventeen. Most mated couples have pups within the first five years of their meeting. When a werewolf meets their mate, marking happens within hours of the pair meeting. Completing the mate bond often takes about a week. Coleman and Jackie met almost three years ago and have been trying for pups for almost four months now.

I say the only thing I can, which is the truth. "I don't know how any of this shit works, but I guess you just have to have faith everything will work out."

He nods and guzzles down the last drop of scotch. Little does he know what similar situations we are both truly in.

CHAPTER 7

AVENGER

Ouch. Okay, let's take in our surroundings.

I am in a silent, immense bedroom, decorated in rustic colors and deer horns. I attempt to sit up, but fail. Someone has handcuffed one of my wrists to a bedpost.

Morons.

Do they think that these will hold me? Because all I have to do is unscrew the top and lift, done.

Within three swift seconds, the shackles are gone, my wrists loose, and my escape in motion. That's when I notice my clothes are gone.

Someone changed my clothes.

I am in shorts and my tank top now. I go straight to a closet across from the bed. Inside are a crap ton of jeans and dress shirts.

This must be the Alpha's room.

I don't suppose he'll mind if I borrow some of his stuff. They are all my size too, which makes me think someone brought these in for me. I slip on skinny jeans and an oversized boyfriend t-shirt. It's not mine, but it's what I would wear normally, so who cares? This bastard drugged me and brought me to his house. I'll take whatever the hell I want.

Where is Griffin?

The thought of Griffin sends a wave of fear and rage through me. I race to the colossal wooden double doors, keeping me in this hellhole.

Damn it. Locked.

Well, I've never been good at obeying rules, or locks, or annoying werewolves.

So, bring it.

I guess they didn't realize I can unlock the door from the inside with the hidden button on the side of the frame. When you are in my line of work, escaping and/or getting into places you shouldn't be in becomes second nature. This so happens to be a pretty common door, and they hadn't changed the lock from the one that comes from the manufacturer. That was his first mistake. Now, how the hell am I to find Griffin, escape, and all the while go unnoticed by hundreds of werewolves?

Geez. This place is like some giant rustic hunting mansion or the King's palace or whatever.

Two sets of footsteps and two voices approach. Time to become scarce. I duck into the closest room I find unlocked. A pink princess room covered in purple wallflowers and a floor littered with plastic dolls assaults my vision. I tiptoe further into the bedroom. The bed has a giant pink canopy covered in a plethora of stuffed animals and fuzzy pillows. I didn't think this many shades of pink existed, it sort of gave me a headache. But to each their own.

Says one voice outside the room, "Sir, we're not sure how much longer she'll be out for. Waking up from medically induced comas happens on their own. You can't force it; her body will decide when she is ready. Dr. Preston expects she'll wake up soon, though."

The other replies, "Cade, thank you for stating the obvious. Bring Dr. Preston up to my room. I want to run a few extra blood tests."

I hear a light sneeze and I jump into a defensive posture. But nothing prepared me for what was behind me. A giant furry beast barreled into my chest, knocking me off balance and onto the carpet.

"*Griffin*. There you are." I hug my best friend tightly around his neck while he licks my face, whining softly.

"You know Grey, too?" A small voice speaks. A girl, probably around seven or eight, sits at a table surrounded by stuffed animals and teacups.

I nudge Griffin aside—keeping a possessive arm around him—and sit up on my knees, eying the girl. "Umm, yeah. My name is Westries. What's yours?"

She awards me the hugest smile and bounces over to us and balances a tiara on Griffin's head. His tail thumps and swishes back and forth, like he is *happy* to be wearing a crown.

Traitor.

"I'm Corrine. My brother said that Grey belongs to his mate, but she is sleeping, so I can take care of him for now."

Mate? Brother? She's a royal.

That's all the information I require.

Time to run.

"Well, *Grey* is my dog. His name is Griffin. I've had him for five years. Where is the back door?"

"He's *your* dog? Well, can I still hang out with him? I've never had a puppy before. My daddy always said no."

Great. Now I feel bad, I'm taking her best friend. Way to go, Westries.

And ironic that the werewolves aren't allowed to have a dog, considering they *are* one.

I inch toward the door. "Yes, you can still visit him, but we got to get home now before people realize I am missing. Could you please help us? It would mean a lot."

I muster my best pitiful puppy face. She smiles at me.

"Okay, I'll help. It'll be like playing spies, right?"

"Sure, yeah. We'll play spies. Can you do that for me?"

She nods vigorously, excited to play a game.

"Go distract your brother, okay? Can you take me to the garage, too?"

The girl catches ahold of my hand to lead me out of her room. She cracks open the door, peaking out both ways before pulling me out into the empty corridor. She tugs me and Griffin toward a flight of stairs and we creep down them single file. We reach a door protected by an alarm and she presses a series of buttons. Seconds later, it swings open and there he is, my 2018 Acura NSX.

"Coleman said they left the keys in the glove compartment." Corrine looks up at me with the saddest face I've ever seen. "Do you have to leave?"

Ugh. Don't make this harder, kid.

"I'm sorry Corry, but Griffin and I must get home. Can you still play spies with us and distract your brother? I am too sad to say goodbye."

"Yeah, I can still play. Mom says quitters never win, so I have to finish the game. Can I say goodbye?"

"Yes, you can say goodbye."

Corrine drops to her little knees before Griffin and attaches herself to his neck.

"I won't ever forget you, Grey. Please don't forget me." From face deep in his fur, I hear her muffled voice say, "You won't let him forget me, right?"

A stab of grief pierces my heart. She reminds me so much of my little sister. I miss her. I squat in front of her.

"Yes, honey, I'll make sure he remembers you."

She untangles herself from the dog and throws her small body at me. After a stunned moment, I hug her back.

"Alright, you know the plan. Griffin and I are going home and you're to distract your brother."

She offers a solemn but dutiful nod.

"And hey, keep up the excellent work, soldier."

She smiles and Griffin and I climb into my car, and I dig around for the keys. Corrine is right. They are in the glove compartment. They also left their garage door opener.

Ha. Thank you, whoever was naïve enough to do that.

"Time to bounce Griff."

I press the door opener and the ornate entry lifts. When the opening is big enough, we peel out. Zero to one-fifty in two seconds.

CHAPTER 8

ULYSSES

end up in the kitchen for a quick break. The sound of footsteps behind me halts my pillaging through the fridge for a soda.

Corrine, in a most proper sounding tone, says, "Hello, brother. How are you today?"

Who is this and what have they done to my sister? Plus, she always calls me Lassie.

I slit my eyes at her. Well, she isn't suspicious *at all.* "What are you hiding?"

"I'm not hiding anything. I was playing spies with Westries and we…"

"Wait. Corrine, did you say *Westries*?"

Her face contorts from weirdly professional to scared and nervous.

"Corrine, I'm not mad at you, but where did she go?"

"She said she had to go home, and I was supposed to distract you. We were playing spies, and I showed her the garage…"

I mind link with my Beta.

"Coleman, Westries escaped and possibly has a car. I need wolves to get a visual on her now."

"Yes, Alpha right away."

I tear out of the kitchen and into the garage as quickly as my legs can carry me. I grab the keys to my 2018 Ferrari 488. The garage door is already open and if I don't race after her, she will be long gone. The smell of fuel and tire burn out still in the air tells me she can't be that far ahead.

Within minutes, I spot her car speeding down the back road ahead. How can I get her to stop without running her off the road? In the distance, wolves run along the tree line, trying to get to their Luna. They will protect her with their lives and understand we need her back at the pack house.

Ahead, a dozen wolves blockade the road and Westries screeches to a stop, barely missing my warriors. I stop my car right behind hers, blocking her in. She leaps out, closing the car door before her dog could join her. Her expression is wild-eyed, and she is wielding a cowboy rifle ready to fire.

She sneers at the closest wolf. "Move. *Now.*"

Where did she even get that?

She presses the barrel of the gun to his head. He watches his Luna without flinching.

She doesn't realize that every single wolf here would die for her in a heartbeat. Even if she's the one ready to murder them all.

Another car rumbled from behind me. Hannah and Jackie jump out of a Ford F150.

"Westries," I call out. "No one here will hurt you."

She whips around and points the barrel straight at me. Scattered growls erupt from the pack. She may be the Luna, but I am the Alpha.

A flicker of confusion makes the barrel lower slightly. "W-who the hell are you talking about?"

The gun barrel jerks up again and Grey growls at me.

"I know who you are, Avenger." I draw the name out. "*Westries... Clary... Mikos.*"

Her face contorts with rage. I hear her heart racing a million miles an hour. Her arms shake. She lowers her chin and glares daggers while stalking in my direction. Her eyes scan the wary crowd around her and then train on me. The rifle barrel now aims right at my heart. Her finger, still off the trigger, twitches.

"How the *hell* do you know me and why won't you let me leave?"

She is an open book of emotions—fury, confusion, and fear—and being surrounded by twenty werewolves helps nothing.

Jackie attempts to calm her. "Westries, please calm down. We won't hurt you."

Westries sweeps her weapon at Jackie. Coleman lets out a warning growl from deep in his chest. His mate bond obliges him to protect her, and he shifts to his wolf form and moves toward Westries, who turns her weapon on him, her finger now on the trigger.

In one stride, I am in front of my mate, disregarding her rifle and pushing her behind me. I warn my Beta through our mind link.

I will kill even you to protect Westries. Back off. Now.

Coleman's wolf glares back, but I know he hears and understands my words. He looks behind me at Westries, who has backed away from both of us but not lowered her weapon.

Fine, Alpha. But you might consider protecting me *from* her.

Jackie pleads from behind Coleman. "Coleman, it's okay. Westries, please return to the pack house with me and talk this out. We have many things to discuss." Her tone becomes conciliatory. "Granted, Ulysses didn't go about this correctly at all, but please give this a chance."

Westries' wary gaze shifts from each of the three before her, landing last on Jackie. "I have nothing to discuss with any of you. I came here for business and that's it. Packs leave me alone and I leave them alone. And who the frick is Ulysses?"

I face her again and answer. "*I* am Ulysses."

Westries approaches and jabs the barrel against my chest. Most men would cower, or at least back away, when an AK-47 is held to their chest, but I'm no mere man.

She sniffs in contempt. "And I don't care. Let me go and I won't blow your heart out of your chest cavity."

Her attitude will be a challenge to tame, but I never back down from a good fight. Her little evil glint is honestly adorable. I smile. That pisses her off more.

Whoops.

I remind her of the facts. "Twenty warriors and an Alpha surround you. You are not going anywhere. You are coming with us. Now please, set the rifle down. There is no way out, Westries."

She scoffs and cocks the lever back. She glowers straight into my eyes. Axel howls happily that she's made eye contact. Her face shows no emotion.

My warriors creep closer as the tension rises. She continues to glare into my soul.

Okay. The hard way it is, mate.

I resign myself to knowing she will never set down that rifle unless it's taken. I applaud her for that. She glances to her side, catching a small movement from the surrounding wolves. I see my opportunity.

In one swift succession, I knock the barrel of the gun downward with my forearm, yank her toward me, and break her grip on the stalk of her rifle. She yelps in indignation, but I allow no time for her to fight back. I rip it out of her grasp and use my heel to push her calf, so she is kneeling. I shove her onto her belly and discard the rifle.

Straddling her back, I hold her arms behind her. Over my shoulder, I say, "Cade, handcuffs."

Cade—now back in human form—rushes over and hands me stainless steel handcuffs. Westries struggles under my iron grip as I closed the cuffs around her wrists.

In between her wrestling and grunting, she shouts at me. "What is your *deal*, flea bag? I didn't do anything to your pack."

Still holding her wrists, I help her up and walk her to a van and hoist her in, closing the door behind us. She, consistent as always, persists in struggling under my grip. I latch her cuffs to one of the prisoner chairs. Perhaps realizing the futility—or conserving her energy—she stops fighting and resorts to death staring into my soul instead. I sit across from her and wait for her to speak.

She seethes at me and through gritted teeth, and says, "You forgot my dog."

After a deep breath, in my most placating voice, I tell her, "I *didn't* leave him. Jackie got him into the Ford and is bringing him home, too. I'm insulted that you would even think such a thing."

She bucks against the seat in outrage. "*That* is not my home."

"It is now, princess."

"Don't call me princess. I am not your damn conquest."

Spencer and Cade hop into the driver's and shotgun seats, and we pull out into the road.

Smirking, I tell her, "I'll call you whatever I like, baby."

She jerks forward and tries in vain to wriggle out of the handcuffs. Most likely to go for my throat. I lean back and relax. We designed those handcuffs to stop a rogue werewolf from escaping. It will hold a teenage girl. She struggles under her restraints a few minutes longer. When she finally gives up, she breaks the silence.

"Are you ever going to tell me why the hell I am here? I'm not a threat to your pack. I am innocent."

Cade blurts from the front seat, "*Innocent*? Really? You have killed hundreds of werewolves in your lifetime."

Westries again shows no emotion as she glances over at the metal-holed wall in between us and Spencer and Cade. If looks could kill, Cade would be paralyzed.

Her voice shakes with contempt and rage. "They are *murderers*, *rapists*, child *molesters*, members of MS-13 gangs… the list goes on. You werewolves claim you're for peace and justice, but that is complete *bullcrap*. Rogue werewolves get away with *literal* murder and never suffer the consequences of their actions."

She aims her glare at me. "And your precious *King* does nothing to stop it. You Alphas protect your packs and don't care about anyone else, but if a rogue wanders in *your* territory, all *hell* breaks loose. Do you ever wonder what happens to the rogues that are in human territory? I can tell you firsthand. You werewolves *revolt* me."

That hits deep, but it is true. Werewolves do only care about their packs and mates.

When you're right, you're right, my Luna.

The rest of the car ride is completely silent but for the continual hum of the engine. The back of the van is closed off except for the rear door, which is covered with stainless steel bars and one window. Westries glowers out the window, not making eye contact with me anymore.

The silence is killing me.

We arrive at the pack after seven agonizing minutes. Cade and Spencer come around to let us out. They open both doors with a loud creaking swoosh and the bright afternoon sun greets us.

I lean over Westries to unlock her handcuffs. When I brush past her, our shoulders met, and sparks shoot through my body. Does she feel it, too? I raise her and push her to the open door. When Cade and Spencer seize each of her arms, I suppress a selfish growl. She is capable of a lot of damage, and we can take no chances.

A moment of irony hits me as I observe the scene before me. Had I been told a month ago that my mate is the Avenger, and it would take the entire Warriors Elite to subdue her, I would never have believed it.

The boys lead Westries up the grand entrance toward the ornately carved wooden double doors leading into my office. I follow directly behind, while the rest flank us.

I could get used to this angle of her.

One of my men springs ahead, opens the door, and leads all ten of us in. I take my place behind my desk, with Coleman to my right. Cade and Spencer sit Westries in the chair opposite me. They hold position on either side of her in case *someone* has any bright ideas.

Hannah and Jackie had followed them and now stand back against the wall, both wearing matching worried expressions. Whether they are worried for their mates or their Luna, I am uncertain. Three-pack warriors guard the exit, blocking all means of escape. Once everyone settles, I open my mouth to speak, but my mate beats me to it.

"What do you want?" Westries tries affecting a bored monotone.

Knowing how easy it is to rile her, I reply, "Well, that's a problematic question, *princess.*"

She hisses through her teeth. "Don't call me princess."

Jackie mind links with me.

Antagonizing her does not help matters.

But she drives me to it, Jackie.

You're the Alpha, *Ulysses.*

After a quick glance at Jackie—who gives a pointed look and head nod from me to Westries—I sigh to myself, feeling a twinge of defeat, and fold my hands on my desk.

"Well, if the name fits…"

Jackie interrupts me. "You're Ulysses' mate and we really need you. You are our future Luna."

CHAPTER 9
ULYSSES

ell, that was one way of setting about this.

I arch an eyebrow at Jackie, and she clamps her hand over her mouth. I return my attention to Westries. Her face is unreadable.

"Sorry…" Jackie whispers under her breath.

My mate's placid expression contorts. With a derisive laugh, she says, "I know werewolves are delusional, but this takes the cake. Hilarious. Real funny. You have my attention." Her laughter ceases and her eyes narrow. "Now, why am I *really* here?"

Coleman stomps over to his mate, growling while pulling her into his arms. He scowls at Westries.

"Aw, poor Beta. Did I insult your mate? Can you not take a blow to your ego?"

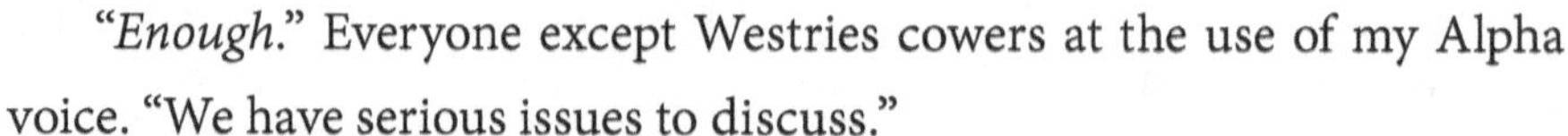

"Enough." Everyone except Westries cowers at the use of my Alpha voice. "We have serious issues to discuss."

Westries says, "Oh, yes, please. The sooner we figure this out, the sooner I can *go away.*"

I tip my head down. "You aren't leaving anytime soon."

She licks her lips and crosses her arms, tipping *her* head down at me.

Her eyes sparkle with an evil glint. "Wanna bet?"

No one ever questions me like she has done. She has denied, sassed, contradicted, and challenged me in two minutes. She moves to stand, but Cade and Spencer shove her back down.

"Cade, take off the cuffs."

Everyone's eyes widen. Westries grins like the Cheshire Cat. She is amused by this whole drama.

"I wouldn't try that if you care about the people in this room, *Alpha.*"

I ignore her and nod to Cade. He hesitates before slipping the key out of his pocket. The moment the cuffs are off, Westries springs to her feet. Everyone flinches. She does not attack anyone, but instead rubs her wrists.

She smirks, obviously enjoying the discomfort she's caused. "Well, that is much better. Now, I can talk to you mutts face to face."

Coleman holds Jackie closer to his chest, narrowing his eyes at Westries. A scattering of grumbles and growls erupt from around the room at her insult.

Over her shoulder she snorts, "Oh, hush, pups."

I quiet them with one raised hand.

She faces me and asks, "Now, who do you want dead? Because, if you wanted *me* dead, you would've done it by now. So, who were you incompetent at killing that I—a *human*, no less—need to handle for you?"

She plops back into the chair, crosses her arms, and props her feet on my desk.

She'll be damn near impossible to tame. But perhaps I don't want to tame such a wild spirit.

"Well, you're right about one thing. I *do* need you, but not to *assassinate* anyone. My name is Ulysses Carter Ronan, and I am the *precious* Alpha King. My pack is the Alpha's Dark Sun, and you have been killing rogues in my territory."

I pause, allowing her a moment to absorb the information. Then I explain what I know will be hardest for her to accept. "You are my mate, our Luna Queen, and you cannot leave Charleston. I *know* you, Westries Clary Mikos. Perhaps better than you know yourself."

Westries studies me, her head cocked. She sweeps her heels off my desk and leans onto my desk seductively, staring straight into my soul. "Wow. Charming speech. But cut the crap, *Alpha*. I don't have time for this shit. *This* is wasting my time."

I lean forward, too, so that our foreheads nearly touch and reciprocate her sardonic tone. "And just where do you need to be? You have an assassination deadline?"

"Yes, actually." She says it like it is the most obvious thing in the world.

"This isn't a joke, Westries. You really are our Luna." Jackie chimes in from Coleman's arms. Coleman buries his chin into his mate's neck while she continues to talk.

"We need you in our pack. Without you, our pack will crumble. A Luna makes a pack stronger, and she helps nourish the young. Plus…"

Westries interrupts. "I *know* what a *Luna* is. Do you really think I could accomplish the things I have without knowing how packs work? I'm also aware packs have survived without one, so you don't *need* me. And if you want a *nurturing* Luna, you better seek someone else."

Westries faces the rest of the people in the office. "And a Luna Queen? *Pfft.* That would be a *disaster,* detrimental actually. Imagine this: The *Avenger* as your *beloved* Luna. Twenty bucks say they'd all reject me. Not that I believe a word that comes out of your mouths." Westries laughs.

I've had enough. This is not a request or a deliberation. "We know all you have done, and it doesn't matter. As my mate and this packs' Luna, you *will* stay here and be as such."

I move from around my desk to loom over her. "Whatever makes you so certain you won't be a good Luna is wrong. This is your home now and you won't be leaving anytime soon, Westries. So, if I were you, I would get used to it."

Without taking my attention off her, I said, "Cade, Spencer. Lead your Luna to her *new* room. One of you must be with her at all times and double the patrols outside. Dismissed."

As my Delta and Gamma lead her out of my office, my mate scowls daggers at me. Everyone else takes their cues to depart as well. Everyone except Coleman.

With no trace of resentment from our standoff earlier, he snorts, "Seriously, your Alpha voice? She is already pissed at you, and you think yelling at her like that will convince her? No offence, bro, but that's stupid."

I glower at my Beta, who simply crosses his arms and leans back.

I throw my hands in the air. "What am I supposed to say? She is being impossible. If I give her a choice, she'll leave me. This pack needs her. I need her. The world *literally* needs her. I don't know what I'm supposed to do."

I slam my fists on my desk. Coleman does not flinch. We have been best friends since we could walk, so he is used to me and my Alpha voice. He might even be immune.

Coleman's tone turns cajoling. "She's killed hundreds of our kind for *whatever* reason. She *hates* us. And now, she's a prisoner in a house belonging to the very group she despises. What did you think she would do? Why would you believe just because you say you're both mates, she'll magically accept us?"

He has a good point. I soften my tone. "I just… what should I say to her? 'Hey, I know werewolves murdered your entire family, and that's why you hunt them down. Oh, and I also know about what happened to you, *and* I saw your scars.' I mean, that's straightforward."

Coleman blinks. Next, he does something only a lifelong friend of the Alpha would dare. He slaps me on the back of the head. Axel's agitation flares.

"What the heck, man?" I rub the stinging spot on my scalp.

"You really are stupid. *Yes*, that's kind of exactly what you should say. Just *talk* to her, get to know her a little before you go all possessive Alpha on her. She is a human, and the Avenger, at that. She will not accept you as normal she-wolves would." He claps his hands on my shoulders. "Go to her, have an actual conversation."

I rub my chin and gaze at the ceiling. Coleman groans and drops himself in a chair across from my desk and I sit back in mine. Cradling his head in his hands, he massages his scalp. I swivel my chair side to side as I study the ceiling texture. Maybe breaking the news to her with eight other wolves was not such a great idea. Also, Jackie blurting it out wasn't exactly how I'd planned to tell her, either. I really do need to get better at this whole mate thing.

I scan through the mental list of offenses. So far, I have knocked her out, kidnapped her, invaded her privacy by doing a full-body exam, ran a background check into her personal life, hand-cuffed her to my bed, and kidnapped her again.

I thump my fist on the desk and rise. "Okay fine, I'll go talk to her."

I better not regret this.

CHAPTER 10

WESTRIES

My luck completely sucks.

I've woken up chained to some mutt's bed, made one cute little friend and escaped, got captured again, and learned I'm the mate of the Alpha King. *If* anything they said was even true. In a million years, I'd never have imagined I have a mate, but God does crazy things.

I can't be a Luna. I murder these werewolves; I could never lead them.

I refuse to show it, but I am completely terrified. Who wouldn't be? Any of those wolves might kill me at any second. I am unarmed and defenseless. Sure, I know self-defense, but these are werewolves with the strength of ten men. It surprises even me how long God has kept me alive working in my field of expertise. Must be for a reason, right?

I really hope I'm right.

The one with the sharp cheek bones—*Cade*—interrupts my ruminations. "I'm sorry I have to do this Luna, but it's Alpha's orders."

The silence resumes as the two dunderheads lead me through the enormous mansion.

We eventually end up before a double door. They each take a door handle—maintaining their vise-like grips on my arms—and swing them open. My jaw drops as my gaze travels across the room. It is the same room I'd awoken in, chained to the bed. I hadn't taken the time to admire it, what with my escape attempt and all.

Okay. It's a gorgeous bedroom.

The words leave my mouth before I can check them. "If this is your version of a prison, I'm never leaving. I'll take this over motels any day."

After my continual throwing of insults at them, the idea I instead have accidentally complimented them sickens me.

Cade and Spencer gape at me like I had grown two heads.

They are so weird, for mutts, at least.

"What?" I snap.

They glance at each other, then at me, and smile like idiots.

Cade stammers, "W-we feel that you'll make a great Luna. We have been waiting for you for a long time."

Adds Spencer, "Yeah, and we believe you'll balance Ulysses out."

I stare blankly at them, wondering if they could really be this dumb. They return my stare, their expressions hopeful and expectant.

Cade mistakenly thinks I didn't hear him. "I said you'll make a great Luna Queen, and…"

"Oh, I heard what you said. I'm just not doing it. I'll be leaving very soon."

"Like hell you are."

The unmistakable voice behind Spencer and Cade belongs to none other than Alpha himself. This man pushes all my damn buttons. He doesn't even have to speak to make me want to formulate a thousand ways to kick him when he's down.

"You will not be leaving this house, little mate." He steps between the men, inches away from me. "Cade, Spencer, you're dismissed."

The men leave, closing the doors quietly behind them.

Must be nice having the privilege of leaving.

I cross my arms and stare him down, daring him to break first. He is so casual, almost smug, and it is pissing me off. I step closer to him, entering a literal wolf's den. He does not move as he stares down at me. My nostrils flare. He seems to notice he is getting under my skin and breaks the stare-off.

"You have a duty to this pack. You can't just walk away."

Is it my imagination, or did he sound almost apologetic? Can't be.

"Says you, as of this morning." I reply. "If you haven't noticed, I'm not too fond of you or your kind."

His ice-blue eyes bore into my soul. A rebellious part of my brain notices how beautifully the blue fades to green around his pupils. For a second, I swear I see a flash of pain in those spectacular eyes, and my gut twists.

I swallow the rising flutter in my throat. "W-whose room is this, anyway?"

My crossed arms are now more defense than defiance. The closeness of our bodies is too much. I step away from him toward the large window doors that lead to a rustic patio overlooking the mountains and greenery.

"This is your half of our suite. You may go anywhere except outside. Don't bother attempting escape. I have guards everywhere."

I grit my teeth, not even bothering to acknowledge a thing he says. In the distance, I see the town and I momentarily wonder how long it would take if I *ran* there. I sense him behind me, probably reading my thoughts about escape through these woods.

"You may be able to hold me prisoner here, but I am *definitely* not sharing a bed with you. Forget it."

I face him, which is a mistake. He steps even closer, our faces only inches apart. "Why are you so difficult?"

"Why are *you* such an asshole?" I retort.

Another wordless stare down ensues. He is a full head and a half taller than me, and if I wasn't so pissed off, I'd probably fear him. Not that I'd show it. This is a test of wills and stubbornness that I win the moment he spins away and storms toward the door.

I splay my hands on my hips and raise my chin.

At the doors, Ulysses faces me, still standing by the window.

"Are you *coming*?"

Does he expect me to heel at his side like a puppy? Ha. As if I'd budge for an ass Alpha with anger issues. I will never give him the satisfaction.

"Are you going to tell me *where*?"

A thunderous roar explodes from him. I'm pretty sure China could hear. He stomps to me. I offer him my most devilish smirk.

You can confine me, but you will never break me or my attitude.

What can I say? I have always been a cocky little asshole, and just because I *apparently* had a mate, I will not be changing.

"We are going to your new room because this one doesn't seem to meet your *standards*."

"Lead the way, fluffy boy." I gesture to the door, as if I am not the one who, moments ago, refused to budge. His fault, by the way. Make someone feel like a caged animal in a corner, and of course, they'll lash out.

"You are walking a very thin line here, Westries. Axel is not one to mess with, and if you continue to play with him like this, I'll have no choice but to take you right here, right now. We wouldn't want *that*, now *would* we?"

I have no desire to die today, but he went *there*. He tiptoed a line and suggested *that*, and I react the only way I know how. I bitch slap him and run out faster than the rats off the Titanic. My heart pumps, and I fight back the lump in my throat forming as the horrifying memories assault me.

When I get far enough away from that monster—who wisely has stayed put—I stop next to a huge brown door. I am officially lost. My heart rate slows, and my breathing steadies as I lean against the wall. I scratch my nails through my hair, groaning over the mess I have gotten myself into.

I have *never* wanted a relationship. I certainly never even believed it was *possible* for a human to have a mate. One thing I am certain: mates do not treat each other like this. These dogs rave about how a mate is your other half and you strive to do right by them. Devil's advocate plays louder than my voice of reason.

It is not completely his fault, though. He doesn't know what happened to me.

Why am I defending him? I want out of here. I'll escape the first chance I get.

It is better to be lost and moving than lost and a sitting duck, so I wander aimlessly around. After two more rights, I stop. I could die in this hallway, alone and lost. There are worse places to die than a log cabin mansion, but my emotions are screwed around at the moment. The only way I'll survive is if I check all the rooms for an exit.

I open one door.

An empty bedroom. Nope.

Behind another door is a dance studio with floor to ceiling mirrors. That other part of my brain chimes in again.

I'll have to come back here sometime when I'm bored. These wolves really cater to any and every need. It honestly annoys me with how wealthy this place is. Like, did you really have to imitate the royal monarch's house? Material things don't equal success or at the very least, comfortability.

I shake my head hard to clear the intrusive thoughts. Two bedrooms later, I walk in on someone. *Whoops.*

"Sorry, wrong room. I-I'm lost…"

I pull the door close, but the girl shouts at me to stop.

"No, wait. Don't go," I open it again, and the girl smiles. "I'm Aubrey, and *you* must be Westries."

"Is it that obvious?" I scratch my neck nervously.

How does everyone already know me? I dislike people knowing who I am.

Aubrey chuckles. "Sort of. I mean, you're the only human in this town, so I took a not-so-wild guess. Well, anyway, this is my room. Have you seen your room yet? Of course, you haven't. If you had, you probably wouldn't be *lost.*"

She tilts her head and plants her hands on her hips. "Why *are* you wandering around here? Did my brother forget to show you around or, more likely, do something stupid again? He *did*, didn't he? I told him not to be an asshole, but he knows no other way of life." She grimaces. "I'm rambling, aren't I? Sorry, I'm excited!"

She sounds exactly like Daya, my sister. Constantly talking, and so innocent. Not a care in the world.

Despite myself, I smile. "Ah, let's see. No, I haven't seen my room yet. I was wandering around because I'm hiding from Ulysses. And yes, to the last question."

"Cool. So, let me bring you to your room." Aubrey clutches my hand and leads me out of her room. "Come on, it's down the hall."

These hallways are huge. I wonder if they're extra-large to accommodate their dog-extra personality.

We pass five doors along the hall—a hall so wide, I can flip a full cartwheel from one wall to another—and come to a dead end. Again, I have to at least acknowledge the fact that these werewolves are loaded.

I guess I can hang around for just a little while.

Damn those intrusive thoughts.

As we walk toward one particular door, something clicks in my brain. I *have* been here before.

"This looks familiar..."

Aubrey faces me.

"Oh, well, that's Ulysses' room, and Corrine's is on the other side of the house, four doors to the right."

I am right back where I freaking started. Great.

I've gone around in a giant freaking circle. I groan. "Of *course*."

Aubrey opens the door, and my mind is blown. It is the most beautiful bedroom I have ever seen.

Well, I guess that doesn't mean much because I have been living in motels, but whatever.

"It's one of the guest rooms. I hope you don't mind."

I blurt, "No, this is awesome compared to where I've been living."

Her brow creases, and she opens her mouth to speak, but snaps it shut again.

She obviously has questions but is too polite to ask them. "It's okay to ask. I really don't mind. I've lived in motels for a while now simply because I move… a lot."

Can I be any less inconspicuous? Move around? Her expression changes and she claps her hands together and bounces up and down as if she's meeting someone famous.

"Oh, my gosh. How could I forget? You're the *Avenger*. That is *totally* awesome. You are so badass."

Well, that isn't the reaction I expected. I honestly figured they would either hate me, be afraid of me, or wish me dead. Not… whatever *this* is.

I shift my weight from one foot to the other and dig my fists in my pockets. "Umm, thanks, I guess. I wasn't really expecting anyone to think it was *awesome*. I thought you werewolves would hate me or I don't know—"

"Why would we hate *you*? You're a superhero around here. Bringing down all those rogues like that? You've taken out more rogues than, like, anyone, EVER. Well, at first you sort of became like one of those stories you tell young kids when they misbehave, but that's when everyone thought you were some rogue vigilante on a killing spree."

She reaches out and grips my shoulders, leaning in like she is telling me a tremendous secret. "No one ever thought that the Avenger would be some teenage human girl. No offense. *And* my brother's mate? Like that's crazy."

Just when I think she's done, she goes on. "Plus, someone started a rumor that you were a hot, buff hunky dude or something and some she-wolves literally fawn over you and…"

She covers her mouth with her hands and giggles.

At this, I have to stop her. I'm no dude, and that's just crazy. "WAIT, re-wind. Wolves *fawn* over me? Like, chick flick sort of Pedro Pascal, fawn?"

She-wolves think I am some hot rogue werewolf and talk about me? I did not expect that.

"Yeah, a rumor started that you were this super-hot male rogue were-wolf. Some pack females talk about you and wish you were their mate. Boy, they'll be shocked when they find out you're a human girl."

Aubrey doubled over, laughing. I laugh a little, too. It *is* pretty funny.

"So, how many people *know* about me? I mean, like, know I'm human and the Avenger?"

"Not to mention the Luna Queen. This is going down in *history*. Oh, I am so excited!"

Her excitement would make you think it's *her* getting all these so-called blessings.

I raise my hands, palms out, to ward off her aggressive enthusiasm. "I haven't agreed to *anything*. I'm still a prisoner here, technically speaking."

"*Please* consider it, Westries. Our pack and the world need you. We can't survive without you." She stares at me intensely, her entire demeanor and excitement doing a one-eighty.

"So, I've been told."

An awkward silence falls over the room.

I cannot be a Luna Queen, I just can't.

I *hate* werewolves. I hunt them down and kill them. I cannot lead them.

Although, these guys don't seem so bad.

Who am I kidding? They kidnapped me, threatened me, and were now keeping me captive. The only mutts I don't want to strangle are Ulysses' two sisters.

How can such an asshole have such sweet, adorable sisters?

Aubrey attempts to ease the awkwardness that has fallen between us. "Well, umm anyway, have you seen any more of the pack house? Or did my stupid brother perp walk you up the stairs like a criminal?"

"Just a prison car and the Alpha's office. Also, I woke up chained to a bedpost this morning, so, whatever room that was."

She winces. "Yeah, sorry about that… Everyone kept saying how dangerous you were, and some people wanted you in the pack prison, but Ulysses didn't want you to wake up there. So, they settled for his bedroom, but you had to have handcuffs on." She gives a pointed look at my hands. "Guess they didn't work, did they?"

Her expression turns wary and she steps back and folds her arms.

"Not in the least." I say, attempting to smile, crack a joke, anything to make her more comfortable around me again.

She takes another cautious step backward. "You won't hurt me though, right? To like escape or anything because I would have to tell Ulysses if…"

Her face has gone pale but for two dots of color on her cheeks.

I soften my voice. "No, you're probably the only one I *don't* want to strangle. We're good."

Gosh, this isn't what I wanted.

She studies my face a moment before smiling widely, then she takes my hand and drags me back down the hallway.

Over her shoulder, she says, "Okay, I'm taking you to my favorite rooms. We'll start with the dance studio, then the media room, the game room, the kitchen, living room, library, gym…"

I stop hard, nearly yanking her off her feet. "Did you say a gym?

I *love* the gym. It's where I release steam, anger, or whatever shit I'm going through.

"Yeah. Does that interest you? I'm guessing you're not a mall shopping sort of girl, huh?"

I shake my head no.

She raises one shoulder in a shrug, then tugs my hand. "Dang! Well, anyway, let's go."

Oh shit, I just dug my grave. May I rest in peace or pieces? Whichever comes first... and I think I know which one it will be.

CHAPTER 11

WESTRIES

Aubrey shows me around the entire pack house. Each room is as beautiful as the last.

As my tour guide walks me through almost all the rooms, I learn from her that not all high-ranking wolves live there, although they may use the activity rooms. Aubrey says the only people who live here are the Alpha along with his parents and siblings, his Beta, Gamma, Delta and their mates, and a few others. After a very long hour and a half, we end the tour in the kitchen.

"And now for my favorite room: the kitchen. I *live* here. So, are you hungry?"

Aubrey combs through the fridge, hauling out random articles of food.

"We have pop tarts, barbeque chips, Oreos, Sprite, and my personal favorite, bacon-covered donut holes."

"Oh, hand me the barbeque chips. Wait, bacon-covered donuts?"

"Yes. I *love* them."

I shrug, resigning myself to the moment. "Okay, grab the sodas, and let's watch a movie."

I shuffle over to the counter and filled my arms with the junk food and follow Aubrey to the media room.

Aubrey side-eyes me and asks, "So, what do you do for fun?"

"That's a hard question. I don't really do fun, *but* I love collecting things."

Aubrey stops and raises an eyebrow. "Could you be any less vague? Give me details, girl."

I hesitate, then sigh. "Fine, but it's not normal. Like rifles, state coins, buttons…"

Aubrey gapes before bursting out laughing.

"That's the most random stuff I've ever heard. Why *buttons*?"

"They are lightweight, and they amuse me."

She lifts both eyebrows at me. "And the rifles?"

"My job."

She accepts this without questions or laughter and instead continues to talk about aimless stuff, which I tune out to admire the house. The pack house is genuinely beautiful, and I have seen many. Most packs have a decent-sized pack house and keep them pretty clean, but they were still dumps.

Regardless of what the pack's livelihood is like, I still drop the bodies of my victims at their borders. I assume the richer and more pomp packs despised me the most. After all, it has to bruise their pride to be unable to catch me. Now I'm wondering if it's that they don't appreciate me leaving them rogue scum to dirty up their precious digs.

Stop caring, damn it.

I tune back into Aubrey's latest story. "And that's how I noticed I was allergic to shellfish. The moral of the story, never go to your cousin's house on April 1st. Especially when they have a deep fascination for pranks and have access to exotic fish."

"Yeah, that's why I don't do relatives. They make your life a hell of a lot more muddled."

"Preach, sister. If I could lock my siblings in the dungeon, I completely would."

Maybe this won't be so bad.

She lets me walk in first. The media room is decorated with beanbag chairs, a giant leather couch, a coffee table, gamer chairs, and a huge flat-screen TV. We spread our goodies across the table and get snug on the beanbag chairs. I lay a blanket over my legs and snatch the potato chips. Aubrey swipes the remote and opens Amazon Prime.

Aubrey asks, "What do you want to watch?"

I answer around a mouthful of chips. "*Psych*. I love that show."

"Okay, *Psych* it is."

We start on season one and binge eat our snacks.

Aubrey laughs her head off as Shawn gives Gus another random nickname while investigating a crime scene he wasn't even supposed to be at. I can't recall the last time I've been this carefree and chill. I don't even remember the last time I had *any* female interaction. It is refreshing. Even if I've never enjoyed all the stuff girls like and talk about, I still appreciate the company of someone other than a smart-ass dog who loves to complicate my life more.

Griffin.

My heart constricts at the thought of my dog, but Aubrey interrupts my thoughts. "So, tell me about yourself."

I wipe the chip crumbs on my blanket and twist toward her. "What do you want to know?"

"Where did you get your tattoo?" She points to my tribal swirl sleeve tattoo. "It is so striking."

"Maine, and thanks. It is not the only one, either."

"Show me." She squeals, bounces closer, pulling a pillow to her face, and smiles like an idiot.

She gazes at me like I am about to share the story of the century. Her eyes glow with anticipation. It is slightly terrifying, to be honest.

"I'll show you later. Keep asking questions."

She stuffs some chips in her mouth, turns her gaze up to the ceiling for a moment, then asks, "What's your favorite color?"

"Red."

"Favorite pass time?"

"Going to the gym or range."

"Favorite animal?"

Ooff, this is hard to explain.

"Don't jump to conclusions, but a wolf…"

"*Really*? I wouldn't have predicted that. No offense."

"Yeah, I *adore* wolves and dogs. I'm not too fond of werewolves." I wait a beat, then add, "You're not that bad, though."

A huge Cheshire Cat grin spreads across her face.

"What about me?"

Aubrey and I both look up. In the doorway are Corrine and Griffin. Griffin charges in and jumps into my lap like he hadn't seen me in years. His tail bangs against the couch as I stroke his head.

Corrine remains motionless, her little lip quivering. She scratches her arm. In a shaky voice, tears about to break through, she asks, "Are you mad at me?"

Ah, she must be talking about letting her brother find out about me.

I wrestle Griffin off my lap and hurry over to her. I kneel to her level. "Aw, honey. It's okay. I'm not angry at you. You didn't do anything wrong."

"But now you can't go home because I messed up the game…"

Corrine whimpers, and a few fat tears roll down her cheeks. Out of sisterly instinct, I wipe them away with my thumb.

"It's okay, honey. It means I'll be staying around longer, and you can still hang out with Griffin."

Her face immediately lights up. "Really?"

"Yes, really. Now, watch a movie with us."

I scoop Corrine onto my hip and walk to the couch. We continue watching *Psych*, but now with both Corrine *and* Aubrey laughing their heads off.

With her little lisp, Corrine asks, "Westly? can Griffin sleep with me again tonight?"

"Yes, I'm sure he would love that."

After two more episodes, Corrine falls asleep in my lap.

Aubrey breaks our silence. "She *really* likes you, so you know."

I catch the underlying warning in her words. "She's a kid. I would never act rough towards her." I am slightly insulted that she would believe I'd be cruel to a child.

Aubrey softens her tone. "She has never connected with someone this quickly. Sure, she's only eight, but she never talks to anyone. Just our family, Coleman, and occasionally Jackie. This is a pretty big deal for her. You should feel honored."

I smile. I have never really been speechless before. I always have a smartass remark, but this warms my heart. A rare occurrence, given my profession. It *is* nice to feel special and warm sometimes.

"W-would you join me and my family for dinner?" Aubrey bites her bottom lip.

I weigh the pros and cons.

Con, I'll have to be in the same room as them. Pro, I never back down from a challenge and never will. The biggest con, Alpha Ass will presumably make me come.

I ask anyway. "Who *exactly* will be there?"

She glances down at her hands and fidgets with the blanket.

"My parents, Coleman, Jackie, Spencer, Cade, Hannah, Corrine, a pack elder or two, a-and Ulysses."

Of course, he would be there. It is his house. Why wouldn't he be there? Yes or no? Do I even have a choice? That answer would be no.

"Fine, I'll go."

This causes Aubrey to sound off a loud squeal as she jumps up and down.

She is adorable, even if she is my enemy's sister.

"Great. Let's go, because dinner is in twenty minutes." She shakes her sleeping sister. "Corry, wake up and put something decent on that is not your pajamas. Don't make me call mother."

Corrine jerks awake and stumble-ran out, Griffin at her heels.

Looks like he has a new favorite person.

He deserves someone who will dress him up as a princess repeatedly and do the special things that little girls do with their dogs.

A sudden panic sets in as I notice my attire. *"Wait.* Twenty minutes? I look like I came from a Goodwill in Venezuela. I don't even know who's clothes I'm wearing, for crying out loud. I found these in the closet from the room I woke up in."

Aubrey waves my concern away. "Don't worry. Ulysses planned for this and had Jackie and I go shopping the other day."

"B-but I just got here yesterday. When did you have time?"

"Well, they knocked you out for, like, a day, so we had a good twenty-four hours. Anyway, let's go. Jackie is waiting for us."

This girl will be the death of me.

She grasps my hand and yanks me through the house. My arm is ripping, but thankfully we end right back up in my room. Aubrey slams the door open, where a girl stands in the middle of the room. Bags, bags, and more bags of clothes surround her.

I'm so dead.

The familiar-faced girl lets out an exasperated huff. "*Finally.* You're here. I thought you'd never show up. I'm sorry, I feel like we started off on the wrong foot. Hi, I'm Jackie, Beta Female. I am so delighted to have a Luna, finally." She stops abruptly and hisses to herself, "Okay, focus," before continuing. "Anyway, we need to get you ready."

I'm going to die in a fashion inferno. Please spare me and kill me now.

Jackie and Aubrey simultaneously grip my arms and throw me onto the bench at the foot of my bed. They dig through a million bags of clothes that they have apparently bought for me. For only knowing me less than 24 hours, they sure have done a lot for me. It sort of made me feel guilty for trying to escape from them.

Holy crap, eighty percent of all this is pink. I hate pink.

Like, being given the choice between being punched and wearing pink, I would rather get punched.

Jackie holds up a skimpy pink and white cocktail dress with a sweetheart neckline. "Okay, I'm thinking we go with this."

"Nuh-uh. *No.* Please don't make me wear that. Oh my gosh, that is… so pink…"

Aubrey cajoles. "Oh, come *on.* It's *so* cute and Ulysses will *die* if he sees you in it."

Both girls giggle like idiots. I cross my arms and scowl at them.

They are crazy.

I groan. "Shoot me, please shoot me."

"So, what *will* you wear?" Aubrey pouts, throwing all the clothes in her arms on the floor.

I pick my way through the mess to the one pile they haven't yet gone through. I discover jeans, sweatpants, blouses, and plain T-shirts. After sifting through the garments, I pick out an outfit.

Jackie screeches when she sees what I've chosen. "You *cannot* wear that."

I sincerely do not think it is that bad. Jeans and a cropped sweatshirt. Something I wear daily.

I look down at the clothes, then at the girls. "It's jeans and a shirt. What's wrong with it?"

Jackie cries, "What's *wrong* with it? You are meeting Ulysses' parents. You have to make a good impression, and *that* is not an option." She wags a disdainful finger at the clothes in my hand.

Jackie and Aubrey continue to argue about which blouse to wear, so I take things into my own hands. I change into jeans and a tank top. I tuck the tank top into my jeans and slip on a brown leather jacket.

I spy my duffle bag in the corner and rummage through it for my dad's dog tags and combat boots.

I interrupt their bickering. "Can we go now?"

Aubrey and Jackie's heads jerk up. Both pairs of eyes scan my change in attire.

Jackie folds her arms, leans back in appraisal, and deadpans, "Well, that's one way of going about this…"

Aubrey takes my hand and again drags me out of a room.

Do they ever do anything calmly here?

"We don't have time for this. Come on."

"Okay, game plan time. Listen carefully. My mother: don't get on her bad side. My father: same, but don't be a pushover either. Elder Danielle is *such* a grandma. Be adorable and you should be fine. Now, Elder Corbin, he is essentially a good ole boy, so be southern with him and you'll be great."

I reply, "Or, I can be my normal self, and let the chips fall where they may."

Aubrey laughs at my *joke*. "Oh, good luck. Props on being daring… or *stupid*."

This should be fun.

We walk into the pack kitchen, and my heart rate quickens.

Why am I so nervous?

I head count. A dozen werewolves fill the room.

That's why.

I tuck myself into the corner, arms at my sides, my damp hands clenched into white-knuckled fists. I glance around, looking for Ulysses.

Why am I even caring where Ulysses is? I hate him.

The smell of Chanel N°5 hits my nostrils, making my nose crinkle. A bleached blonde wolf tramp sidles up to me wearing five-inch heels and a three-inch skirt.

This is the definition of slut.

"So, you must be the human girl that *my* mate is taking *pity* on."

Game on.

I sneer. "And you must be the she-wolf the males call on when they want an *easy* one night stand."

Everyone falls silent.

Whoops.

I refuse to cower and instead hold my ground while the blonde stares death daggers at me. An elderly gentleman approaches us. Power and strength radiate from him.

Old Alpha, if I had to guess.

"You must be Westries. I am Benjamin Ronan, Ulysses' father."

Called it.

He reaches out to shake my hand. Not wanting to be rude, I accept the handshake.

There is a twinkle in his eyes when he teases, "Firm grip you got there for a human."

I banter back. "I'll take that as a *compliment,* sir."

Benjamin lets out a fatherly chuckle. I try my hardest to not be charmed.

"That you will, my darling. That you will. This is my mate, Molly, Ulysses' mother."

I extend my hand to shake hers, but she grimaces at me and recoils.

She obviously does not like me at all.

I wish I could keep my mouth shut, but low and behold, my mouth has a mind of its own. "If you have a problem with me, Miss, please *tell* me. I realize ninety-nine percent of the people in this room don't like me." I gaze around, daring them all, lastly her. "And I'm not a huge fan of you guys, either. But presently, I'm not allowed to leave the house, so I *apologize* that you have to deal with my *awful* presence."

The look on her face is positively priceless, and Benjamin's snort only makes it better. I hear a grandpa-sized laugh. I see the source over in the dining room; a large, cuddly looking man in jeans and a cowboy hat. He rises with painstaking slowness and makes his way toward us, using a cane to steady his gait. He reminds me of a Santa—not the gross mall kind—but the sweet, lovable kind from the movies. I know immediately he is the Elder Corbin.

"You, child, are a breath of fresh air. We can use a spitfire around here. I never imagined it would be a human who taught Emmalyn and Molly some respect."

I preen. "You would be stunned by what us mere *humans* can accomplish when we put our minds to it."

He takes my arm and loops it through his, leading me away from the shocked faces and toward the dining room table. Behind us, Molly and Emmalyn mutter to each other. He sits me in front of him and resumes gnawing on his sunflower seeds.

He points a sunflower shell at me and winks. "Oh, I know what you've put your mind to. You are quite a strong young woman. Mind if I ask why?"

He wants to know why I hunt down his kind and mercilessly murder them, and whether or not they deserve it.

They all deserve what they had coming. But I would never harm the innocent, ever.

I straighten and jut my chin, but glance away when I reply. "Everyone has their reasons for what they do. My reasons, though, might not be justifiable to your kind. I did what was best in my own eyes and that's all anyone can."

A gruff yet smooth voice speaks from behind. "Very profound, little one. Perhaps one day you'll tell *me* why."

I shift in my chair to take in dark jeans, a forest green plaid flannel shirt, and that damn arrogant face framed by mussed chocolate hair.

Ulysses.

Our eyes lock and sparks ignite in my brain.

Why does he make me feel like this?

My stomach fills with butterflies and I'm dizzy. My heart inexplicably howls for me to jump into his arms, but my brain says, '*hell no*'.

"Ahh, Alpha," said my companion, "I was talking to your beautiful mate here. I look forward to seeing what she does as Luna."

Ulysses' gaze flickers to him, then he returns that intense gaze to me and says, "As do I."

Then, he does the most unexpected thing possible. Ulysses *smiles* at me. My traitorous heart pounds so violently, I fear he sees it.

"What are you talking about? This human cannot be Luna. I thought we explained this. *Emmalyn* will become Luna Queen."

Molly yelled like a toddler who was told they couldn't have candy before bed. All eyes and ears follow the show playing out before them. Coleman, Jackie, Cade, Spencer, Hannah, Aubrey, Corrine, Benjamin, Molly, Emmalyn, Elder Daniele, Elder Corbin, and Ulysses all stare from her, to Ulysses, to me.

I swallow hard and stand. "Listen, it's clear I'm not wanted here, and I really don't *want* to be here anyway, so I'll be in my room. It was a pleasure meeting you all. *Most* of you. Elder Corbin, I truly hope we can talk again. Excuse me."

CHAPTER 12

ULYSSES

She slapped me. She *slapped* me and ran.

My words come back to me. *I'll have no choice but to take you right here, right now.*

Why do I suck at this so much? I can't believe I said that. I'd conjured the memory of what she feared the most.

I'm so fucking dumb.

Axel yells at me in my head for being such an asshole. I ignore him and call out to Aubrey through our mind link.

"Aubrey, I screwed up big time. Westries is around in the pack house. Please find her and just be her friend."

"On it, big bro. Please don't mess this up again, Ulysses. There's only so much I can do."

I need to get better at talking to women. More specifically, the woman whose life has been shit and whose own mate is making it more complicated for her. How can she accept me if I keep letting my temper get in the way?

"Aubrey, did you find my mate?"

"You're an idiot. That's all I have to say."

"What are you guys doing now?"

"I am taking your mate on a tour of the pack house because someone was too busy locking her up to do it."

I bite back my instinctive response, which is that I've been busy trying to stop her from running away from me to give her the official tour.

"Okay. I'm sorry. What are you doing after that?"

"We are having a movie day in the media room after I show her the kitchen."

"Fine. Find out what she likes."

"Or you could do it yourself by talking to her."

"Just… figure something out."

"Fine."

I end our link and turn my attention to Axel, who paces around in my head like a caged lion. He is pissed, and I mean a crap ton. We both need to blow off steam.

Time to go for a run.

I check the time. Dinner is in five hours. I cede to him with a warning.

You know how mom feels if we don't show up presentable.

Yeah, yeah, now let's go.

I head out the patio door, removing my clothes. Then, I give Axel control.

The monstrous black wolf with razor-sharp claws and teeth that is my other half throws a mini tantrum because we cannot agree on where to go.

I want to go to the lake.

Axel growls inside my head in annoyance. *We always go to the lake.*

Oh, come on. Let's find some place special for Westries.

Sometimes having another voice in my mind comforts me because someone always has my back. Other times, he won't shut up and has nothing but smartass comments.

Axel concedes. *Our mate needs an extraordinary place.*

My consciousness melts away as I give Axel more control. I become a passenger in my wolf's body as his paws pound into the dirt. We inhale the musky scent of deer and wild animals in the wind. My enhanced senses make everything brighter, vibrant, and more exciting. I spot a single flea on the back of a squirrel, smell a buck five hundred yards out, and hear the rushing of a waterfall.

Go there, to the falls.

The modest waterfall cascades into a turquoise lake and looming pine trees surround it, making it the perfect place to bring my mate… as soon as she stops wanting to run, kill me, or anything else she cooks up in that marvelous brain of hers.

My sister interrupted my peace.

Ulysses. You need to get back home, stat. Mom's wondering where the crap you are. Hurry back.

I'm coming. Don't leave her alone with mom.

On it.

My mind returns to my wolf.

Axel, we gotta get home.

He chuffs and rakes a clawed paw through the packed earth and shakes his massive head.

We cannot let mother be in the same room as Westries.

He turns us away from the falls toward home.

Let's go, then.

Mother has it set in her mind that Emmalyn will be my mate. She believes a human could never run a pack, and though I haven't known Westries long, something told me if someone insults her, she won't back down.

The image of the two strong-willed women in confrontation spurs us faster through the woods in a race against the clock to beat my parents to dinner. The pack house is almost in sight, and I can almost hear the smartass comments and arguing start. I slam through my bedroom door and, with adrenalin-shaking hands, change into something more presentable. At top speed, I tear down the hallways until I reach the kitchen just in time to hear the sweet sound of my mate's ever combative voice.

"… and I'm not a huge fan of you guys either. But presently, I'm forbidden from leaving the house, so I apologize if you have to deal with my ghastly presence."

I hesitate outside the doorway, waiting to see who might respond to my mate. I suspect the comment is directed at my mother, so when a voice other than the formidable Molly Ronan replies, I am caught by surprise.

"You, child, are a breath of fresh air. We could use a spitfire around here. I never thought a human would teach Emmalyn and Molly respect."

Elder Corbin. He has joined us for dinner this evening, after all. He has always been an important figure in my life and if he does not accept my mate, it will make it harder on Westries.

I slip into the room as Elder Corbin leads Westries to the table. Nearly all eyes are on her. Westries' reply is no less than I expect from her.

"It would surprise you what us mere humans can accomplish when we put our minds to it."

Oh, I understand what she's capable of, and I'm impressed.

The Elder asks what makes her so strong. He cannot yet know she does it for revenge, *if* that is even the real reason. I hold my breath, awaiting her answer.

"Everyone has their reasons for what they do. My reasons, though, might not be acceptable to your kind. I did what was best. That's all anyone can do."

Time to make my entrance.

"Very profound, little one. Perhaps one day you'll tell *me* why."

My mate whips around in the chair. The hint of a blush colors her cheeks. All gazes shift to me, but mine is only for her. Everything and everyone in the room disappears for a moment. Elder Corbin breaks the spell. "Ah, Alpha. I was just talking to your delightful mate here. I completely look forward to seeing what she does as Luna."

I force my gaze away from her to acknowledge the Elder. "As do I."

My heightened senses are attuned to my mate's every action and emotion. When her heart rate speeds, I smile at the thought of her being flustered around me. The smile dies on my lips at the sound of my mother's voice.

"What are you talking about? This *human* can't be Luna. I thought we explained this. Emmalyn will become Luna Queen."

Everyone stops what they are doing to watch the showdown. My nostrils flare and I let out a warning growl at the thought of Emmalyn taking Westries' place as Luna Queen. I expect Westries to come up with a slap come back, but she shocks me.

"Listen, it's evident I'm not wanted here, and I really don't want to be here anyway, so I'll be in my room. It was a pleasure meeting you, *most* of you, at least. Elder Corbin, I hope we can talk again. Excuse me."

My mate, with her chin held high and her back straight, stands from her chair and walks out. Axel is more agitated by the second. I am livid at my mother for insulting her future Luna Queen and saying *Emmalyn* is a better fit. Axel's fury, matched with my own, merges our voices.

We bellow. "What was *that*?"

The Alpha voice alone is enough to cause everyone to cower. They sense what is about to happen. Someone has dared mock and undermine an Alpha's mate. Now, hell is about to break loose.

Emmalyn—not reading the room—sidles up to me. "Come on, baby. Forget the human. She was never *really* your mate. *I* am."

She rubs my shoulders, angering Axel even more.

I snarl. "Remove your hands or they won't be attached to *you* any longer."

Emmalyn yanks back her hands as if scalded and stumbles backward.

"Listen, all of you, and listen well. Undermine or insult Westries again, and you *will* be punished. Threaten, or try to harm her, and you will… be… *punished*."

My gaze travels the room and lingers on my mother, then Emmalyn. "I don't care who you are. I will rip your head off if you so much as blink at her the wrong way. Am I understood?"

A chorus of "yes Alpha's" follows me as I storm from the dining room to my bedroom. I remember it is time for Westries' medicine.

Where the hell did I put it? The bathroom.

I snatch the box from the medicine cabinet and trudged toward Westries' room. As soon as I face the door, I freeze.

Do I knock, or do I enter?

I don't know what to do.

Axel decides for me. *Knock, you idiot.*

My fist hovers an inch from the knotted wood. I have never been hesitant about anything *ever*, but now a girl I haven't known for a week has reduced me to a nervous schoolboy.

I set my jaw and force myself to knock. After waiting a moment with still no answer, I knock again.

"Westries, are you in here? I have something for you."

Silence.

"Okay, I'm coming in."

I open the door to discover an empty room. Axel's impatience simmers at the sight of the vacant space. Once further in, the open patio door catches my eye. Panic surges through both Axel and me.

What if she left? What if she's gone forever?

In three strides, I am at the entrance. In my alarm, I failed to notice the huddled form in the patio corner until a slight movement catches my attention.

Westries.

She is gazing up at the stars, her arms hugging her knees to her chest. My mate has changed out of her military esthetic outfit to black shorts and an oversized, ripped camo t-shirt. Uncertain how to approach her, I stare in silence. She makes no acknowledgement of my presence at first. Then…

"What do you want?"

She unfolds herself and walks to me in the doorway. She stops and leans against the frame, waiting for my answer.

Her defeated tone and her nearness break me from my trance. "I-I brought your Synthroid."

I press the medical box filled with the other six syringes against her hand. Her brow knits together as she gazes from the box to my face, not taking it.

"How did you…"

"When I brought you here, I-I did a medical blood test, for precautions."

Fear and shock drain the color from her face. Anger takes its place.

Through a clenched jaw, she hisses, "I swear, if you did *anything* else, I'll skin you alive."

I use my most calm voice and lie. "No, we didn't."

She doesn't need to know about the other tests.

She eyes me for a long moment before saying, "Fine. Who changed my clothes?"

"Jackie did." I again press the box of syringes into her hand. I nod at it and say, "We can send for the pill version tomorrow."

She accepts the box, then crosses her arms and juts her chin up at me. "Anything else?"

My heart wrenches. Her voice has so much contempt in it. I imagine pulling her into my arms, showing her the tenderness she needs. But as quickly as that image makes my heart rejoice, another steals its place. In this scene, my mate shoves me away and professes her hatred for me. I will not set myself up for such rejection.

Forcing my gaze from her face to over her head, I straighten. I cannot bear to gaze into those eyes any longer. "No, that was all."

I storm out of Westries' room to calm Axel.

I leave everybody gawking. Hearing Molly call me a weak human and suggesting I couldn't lead hurts deeper than I should ever have allowed. I *hate* these creatures.

Remember that. I hunt them and I kill them. I loathe them. Don't forget what they did to me, never forget.

Despite getting lost again, I find my room. I tear off my jeans and jacket and rummage through *my* clothes, not the too pink and girly ones they bought for me. I locate my shorts and army shirt—my version of pajamas—and change.

I twist my hair into a messy bun and take in my new prison in one slow spin. There is a bed with a fur comforter, a gorgeous vaulted rustic ceiling with a chandelier, and a fireplace. Best of all, the room has French doors leading to a small deck. I press my head against the glass pane that leads outside.

Nice.

I flip the lock and step out onto the rustic deck.

I give an involuntary gasp at the stunning sight of the snowcapped mountains, sprawling valleys, lush trees, and crystal-clear lakes stretching out before me. Everything seems so perfect, like it came out of one of those fairytale books dads read to their daughters.

There are two chairs set by the railing, but I sit instead on the deck floor, close to the edge. Everything from the *whooing* of an owl to the howls of a werewolf drift on the pure air to my ears. It almost reassures me that everything might just turn out alright for me.

Almost.

As the sun sinks heavily behind the mountains, and the starry night sky reveals itself, I allow myself to acknowledge again how stunning the place is. Although I've been in Montana for about a month, I have been too busy tracking werewolves to notice before now.

Don't think about the human casualties, Westries. The world is better off without them. They were vulgar, vile people, anyway.

I force my thoughts back to the tranquil beauty surrounding me and away from the darkness in my life and work. Leaning forward, peeking through the rails, the sight of werewolves walking around the grounds catches my attention.

From my third-floor vantage, I see the outside of the house is as fascinating as the inside. A giant pool, multiple gardens, and a gazebo nestle into the lush landscape.

Despite the immense beauty, I return my gaze skyward with a heavy sigh, wishing I was home. Wherever home would have been that day.

My reverie ends at the creak of my bedroom door opening. By the sound of the heavy footsteps, it is a male. The steps pause behind me. I don't need to turn around to know who it is.

Ulysses.

I wish he would leave me alone. If I am to be Belle to Ulysses' Beast and held prisoner, I want to be alone with my books.

And movies. And gym. Okay, so, a modern-day Belle.

I let him stand there awkwardly for a few minutes before asking, "What do you want?"

In the patio's doorway, I meet him, my arms crossed. I might not escape soon, but I am not yet prepared to give up or give in either.

Ulysses stares at me, his expression unreadable. After a moment, he says, "I brought you your Synthroid."

He tries to pass me a container that looks to be filled with syringes. How does he even know I need Synthroid? I have told no one and my pill container is still in the secret compartment in my duffle.

"How did you…"

"When I brought you here, I did a medical blood test, for precautions."

What tests? What did he find out? How much does he know? My blood boils at the thought of someone invading my space like that. "I swear, if you did anything else, I'll skin you alive."

"No, we didn't."

Part of me says to believe him, but the world-weary part suspects he is lying and is livid at that naïve little voice for hoping otherwise.

I don't care. He won't ever know the story.

"Fine. Who changed my clothes?"

"Don't worry. It wasn't me, Jackie did. We can send for the pill version tomorrow."

He tries to hand me the syringes again. This time I accept them. His continued intense, unreadable gaze unnerves the hell out of me. It is like he is trying to read my mind or intimidate me.

I stand straighter and cross my arms tighter. "Anything else?"

He flinches.

Aw, did I hurt the poor puppy's feelings? Well, I don't care.

I grip the hem of my shirt to keep from reaching out and touching his arm.

Fine, I care a little.

He averts his gaze over my head and says, "No, that was all."

Just before he stalks away, his eyes turn black. A sure tell his wolf is trying to surface. I grin.

I think I may have pushed his buttons.

I close the patio door behind me and take another glance at the surrounding room. It looks like a fashion tsunami went off in here. So, with nothing better to do, I clean up my room.

Do you hear yourself? My room? Wow, Westries.

I ignore that voice and tackle my first order of business: dividing the clothes into two piles. One pile for keep, and one pile for Jackie and Aubrey to return to the store. They shouldn't have wasted their money on me, anyway. I throw the clothes onto the floor and begin sorting. Right away, everything pink is in the return pile and jeans are in the keep pile.

I can't believe how much they bought me. I have everything from skirts and blouses to sweatshirts and cargo pants. They probably bought a little of everything because they wouldn't know what I would like.

Thoughtful.

When done, my 'keep' pile—jeans, t-shirts, shorts, and a few nice tops—is smaller than my return pile. That pile comprises a ton of dresses, none that I'd ever wear in a million years. For a moment, I wonder what my life would've been like. Maybe I would have spruced up a little with a nice dress and had a night out with friends. Not anymore. I check the time. Almost nine P.M.

I might as well hit the hay now. No reason to stay awake.

I slump onto the bed and curl myself into a ball. This position doesn't last long. I toss and turn until finally resorting to staring at the ceiling for a good while. I squeeze my eyes shut and hum my favorite song.

"You are my sunshine,
my only sunshine.
You make me happy
when skies are gray…"

I sing the song under my breath over and over. My mom sang this children's hymn to us kids when we were infants. It has been pretty therapeutic for me over the years.

"You'll never know, dear,
how much I love you.
Please don't take my sunshine away…"

My body gives up and sleep overtakes me. Nightmares, here I come.

ULYSSES

She is so aggravating.

I am trying to be sensible here. I even gave her the Synthroid she needs. Yet she still acts so hatefully. I need to calm Axel. He is trying to surface to calm Westries. I pace around my room. My mate should be here with me, not in a room one door away.

I should take a shower.

The hot, steaming water streaming down my back calms Axel. When my shower ends, I step out, letting the water drip to the floor. With a towel wrapped around my waist, I head to my closet and grab my long winter pants. Leaping onto my bed, I grab my phone and flip through my texts from Coleman.

Coleman: Did you talk to her?

Ulysses: Yeah, but it didn't go well.

Coleman: What did you do?

Ulysses: I didn't do anything; she is impossible.

Coleman: You both are too stubborn. You want her to submit, and she most likely never will.

Ulysses: Real encouraging…

Coleman: Give her time and show her you're not as awful as she believes you are. I gotta go. Jackie wants me to get off my phone.

I grab the remote to the TV and flip through the options till I land on the Discovery channel. I stare at the TV for a while, watching as the shows change and change, then peek over at the clock. 11:47. I can't fall asleep, and I know the reason. I have a mate and my wolf wants her here in my arms, but she isn't.

As I am about to turn the lights off and try to sleep, I hear a small knock at my door. I open it to the sight of Griffin charging in, whimpering and acting frantic.

Corrine is not far behind him.

"CC, what are you doing here? It's late. You should be asleep."

"Griffin wanted to come in here. He's acting crazy."

Griffin continues to jump on me, whimpering and whining. That's when it hit me.

Westries.

I run to my mate's room, Griffin and CC on my heels. I burst open the door to my mate's room and my heart goes cold with shock. Her body is convulsing.

She is having a seizure.

I rush to her side and pull her against my chest. What should I do?

Do I wake her up, let it pass?

I realize Corrine is still here.

"CC, take Griffin and go back to your room. It's alright, she… she's cold."

Corrine grabs Griffin's collar and drags the whimpering dog away.

When the door closes behind them, I try to comfort her, whispering in her ear. "Westries? Hey it's okay... you're safe... hey *Bellator*, you're okay. You're okay..."

Westries' tremors subside and her eyes flutter open. Her gaze is fixed and her skin is pallid. The episode has exhausted and disoriented her. I continue to hold her to my chest, and she leans into me. The tender moment is fleeting.

"W-where am I?" she mumbles. "What..."

Her head jerks up, first at her surroundings, then up at my face. She scrambles to get out of my embrace and slides off the bed, backing away from me.

"What are you doing in here?"

She cradles her arms to her chest, avoiding eye contact.

Her breathing is ragged, and she tries to take a deep breath to calm herself.

"Corrine and Griffin came in freaking out... I-I felt the mate bond and...."

"Where is Griffin?"

"I sent him with Corrine."

She takes a deep breath and hugs herself tighter.

Damn it. She needs him right now. Maybe he is her therapy dog.

"Oh. Okay, you can leave now."

"Westries, you're my mate, I can't..."

"Please leave..."

"You're not alright..."

"*I'm fine.*"

"*Bellator*, you need..."

"Ulysses, I'm *fine*. Please *leave*."

I don't object again and get off her bed but hesitate to leave. She backs away into a corner as if fearing me. It's that fearful expression that decides for me. Her breathing is still ragged and uneven as I close the door behind me. Axel yells at me to not leave her alone in this state.

She does not want my comfort, Axel.

I stand outside her closed door. With my wolf hearing, I hear her body slump to the ground as she muffles her cries. Her heart beats erratically and I can hear her shaking.

Even someone as strong as she is can break down.

Although she would never let down her guard if she suspected anyone could hear.

I slide down to the floor, my back against her door, listening to her soft sobs until they subside, and her breathing becomes steady. A low hum drifts from her room to my ears.

The humming becomes singing, and I make out the words through her shaky breaths.

> *"—you make me happy when skies are gray*
> *You'll never know dear, how much I love you*
> *Please don't take my sunshine away*
> *The other night dear, as I lay sleeping*
> *I dreamed I held you in my arms*
> *But when I awoke, dear, I was mistaken*
> *And I hung my head and cried*
> *You are my sunshine, my only sunshine*
> *You make me happy when skies are gray*
> *You'll never know dear, how much I love you*
> *Please don't take my sunshine away."*

By the time my lovely mate has finished singing her song, her heartbeat has steadied and her breathing returns to normal. I stand back up and head off to bed, still longing to comfort my mate.

At five A.M., I sit straight up in bed, unable to sleep thanks to my mate, and wander to my office.

Might as well get a jumpstart on paperwork and make this too early awakening worthwhile.

Just because the Alpha King of the world's werewolves has found his mate, doesn't mean the complicated and time-consuming work pauses for him. I have about ten to fifteen packs in each county or state, depending on the size, and from the day I took over as King at twenty, I have been overrun ever since.

"Coleman, Jake, Owen, come to the office."

"Yes, Alpha."

"Yes, Sir."

"Coming."

I need someone guarding Westries. I don't trust her yet. Plus, I appreciate how much damage she can do. Having Warrior Guards safeguarding her will help thwart her escape plan, which I *know* she is considering. I felt her pain the rest of the night, and it made my wolf infuriated and lethal for whoever caused her this agony. This brave, gutsy woman has been through hell and back, and I will not let her go. I will always be here for her. No matter how long she wants to suffocate me, I will protect her.

After a few extremely slow minutes, Coleman, Jake, and Owen walk in.

"Thank you for coming boys."

"Alpha, what can we do for you?"

I fill Jake and Owen in, even though they've likely heard at least rumors by now. "Well, I found my mate and your Luna Queen. Our concern is she is the Avenger and nineteen and…"

Jake interjects. "Wait, Alpha. So, it is all true? The Avenger, the rogue male wolf who has killed hundreds of rogue werewolves, is a girl and our Luna?"

I glare at him, annoyed that he cut off his Alpha. He wisely cringes back a little.

"Sorry, Alpha..."

"Yes, it's all true. She is not allowed, under any circumstances, to leave the pack house. She doesn't want to stay here, but I can't let her leave either. Jake, Owen, you two are officially her guards. And mind you, you're not protecting *her*, but the other wolves *from* her. I have full confidence that she can hold her own against a wolf, but I'm not so sure wolves are ready for her."

Jake and Owen both shift their weight from one foot to the other. They emit the scent and unease, anxious of the little human they are securing. As they should be.

"Some ground rules. She is the Luna Queen and will be treated as such. Under no circumstances are you to spar with her, unless you ask me first and are prepared to be sore. Do not let unmated males near her. She is your top priority. If she needs something, get it for her, unless the pack's safety is at risk. And most importantly, do *not* let my mother near her. Understood?"

"Yes, Alpha."

"Coleman, take them to Westries and apprise her of the situation."

They each nod and leave my office. They are in for a very eye-opening surprise. A few minutes later, a knock at the door interrupts the paperwork I'd just begun.

"Enter."

In walks my teenage sister, a storming rage.

"Yes?"

"What did you do?"

"What do you mean?"

"Corrine said that Westries woke up convulsing and screaming last night. Why?"

Never trust an eight-year-old to keep a secret. Not that there is any point in keeping a secret from Aubrey. You either tell her or she snoops around to find out. It's the other wolves I don't want to know about her issues. Not right now, at least.

"Westries had a medical episode in her sleep. A-a seizure, it seems. Corrine and Griffin woke me, and I went to her. When she came to, she panicked when she saw it was me and forced me out. Be gentle around her, okay?"

"Be gentle? That girl is a freaking legend. What do you mean, seizure?"

"That's all I know right now, Aubrey. Just… don't let her know you know what happened, okay?"

She taps the side of her jaw a moment, then nods and leaves. Word that I found my mate has spread beyond the immediate pack and it is only a matter of time before they discover who she is.

Coleman interrupts my thoughts with his mind link.

"Ulysses, your mate just outed me twenty bucks."

"How?"

"Corrine and Westries ambushed Jake, Owen, and I when we went to find her, and Corrine said she wanted the five bucks I owed her. Westries got a hold of my wallet and said there weren't any fives, only a twenty, and your sister took it and ran. There really was a five in my wallet."

"Can't say I am surprised."

"Yeah, great…"

"I'll pay you back if it means that much to you."

"Sure, thanks…"

I turn off my mind link and attempt my paperwork again. I have a killer headache right now and my wolf is whining because he wants to see his mate.

"Why not? How is our mate supposed to stay willingly if we don't even know her?"

"We have pack duties, Axel."

"We have no pack without a Luna."

He has a point. The only encounters I've had with Westries have been hostile. I want to get acquainted the right way. I mean, the only things I know about her are that she likes Psych and the gym. Perhaps if

I *accidentally* bump into her, it'll be the icebreaker to getting to know my future Luna Queen.

I set my pen down for the one hundredth time and mind link her guards.

"Jake, Owen, update on Westries."

"We are in the gym room. She is training Corrine how to punch."

Why am I not surprised that the Avenger is teaching my eight-year-old sister how to fight? When my mother finds out, she will have a fit. My mom doesn't want Corrine anywhere near the pack training. Aubrey persuaded her, but she rarely goes, much to my mother's pleasure.

"Remember: do not spar with her. And do not let her near any weapons."

"Yes, Alpha."

I finish an email to the middle eastern packs and open the file of upcoming pack events.

Let's see what we got.

We have a pack dinner a week from yesterday, Jackie's birthday in three weeks, and pack training evaluations in a month. So many things to plan for and so little time to convince Westries to come. How am I going to connect with my mate when she hates me? She isn't a normal girl, either. Meaning none of the typical things girls like will be up her alley.

Okay, what does she like, then?

She has a knack for weapons and fighting. She likes her dog. And my sisters, seemingly. Camo and jeans. And her hot rod car.

That can't be it. Can it?

This is going to be a challenge to tackle later. I refocus on my computer, beginning my tiresome work.

Three hours later...

I crack my back as I stretch. Time to check in again.

"Jake, Owen, update."

"The Luna is in the kitchen washing dishes."

"Why?"

"She was baking a cake with Corrine. And the Luna wants ten pounds of ground beef, but she doesn't want us to ask you."

Well, that's a strange request.

"Do we have permission to get her the beef?"

"Yes, you do. In about an hour, I will come to relieve you of your duties."

"Yes, Alpha."

As I finish my latest report on the rogues in Montana, I ponder why she needs ten pounds of ground beef. What will she do with it? Could it be possible she enjoys cooking? There is so much to learn about her yet.

I can't wait to get to know my mate on a romantic relationship level, too. Is the Westries side softer than the hard as nails Avenger side? Considering her childhood was demolished, her entire family dead, that she hunts and kills rogue werewolves, and she has night terrors…

That hard exterior might be an equally hard interior.

Around two o'clock, I head downstairs to find my mate. I walk down the hall and the delicious smell of ground beef wafts through the air. I reach the kitchen and stop right by the entrance.

"Jake, Owen. You may leave Westries."

"Alone Alpha?"

"I am right outside the door. You may go."

I observe Jake and Owen get up from their seats and Westries turn around, acknowledging them. I step in unnoticed by her, and she yells as Jake and Owen leave.

"Does that mean I can escape now?"

"No can do, *Bellator.*"

Westries jumps, then scowls at me. She turns back to her pan while I sit at the bar.

"What?" She doesn't bother looking back.

"I want to talk with you."

"We *are* talking." She replies.

She is so unreceptive to me. I intend to change that. I join her at the stove and snatch the spoon from her hand.

"*Hey*. I need that." She makes a grab for the spoon.

I hold it higher and wag my finger at her. "I'll give it back *if* you promise to listen."

She huffs in agreement and reaches for the spoon. I give the wooden spoon back and she turns back to her pot.

"Westries. You are, whether you like it, my mate and the Luna Queen."

"Says you."

"Yes, says me." I take a deep breath. "I want to get to know you. Believe it or not, I-I care about you, because you are my mate."

Her expression softens, but she recovers and returns to her scowl.

"*Care* about me? You don't even *know* me."

"We can acquaint ourselves right now. Now, what is your favorite color?"

She quirks an eyebrow at me and mixes her grilling meat. "I can tell you're Aubrey's brother."

Instead of asking what that's supposed to mean, I wait. Just as I am about to give up, she answers.

"Forest green, red, and black."

I grin. "Favorite animal?"

She looks at me like she is deciding what to answer. "A dog. No, a... wolf."

It's my turn to raise an eyebrow. "*You* like *wolves*?"

She takes the pan off the stove and pours the beef into a large bowl. She stares me straight in the eye. "I like *wolves,* not *werewolves.* There is a difference."

I peer closer at what my mate is doing. When it comes to cooking, I'm clueless. I can make peanut butter sandwiches and, if I am feeling ambitious, tuna salad.

"What are you doing?"

"I am making empanadas." She sighs her response as if it's the most obvious thing in the world while she mixes the meat and adds seasoning.

I persist. "So, what have you done today?"

"You mean, while your guards have been holding me hostage all day?"

"Yes."

"Your sister and I hung out."

"Yeah, I heard you conned Coleman out of twenty bucks."

She snorts, and her unguarded smile captivates me.

She catches herself and readopts her professional demeanor. "Hand me that onion, will you?"

I grab Westries her onion on the counter behind me, handing it to her. When our fingertips touch, she jerks her hand away as if scalded and breathes a thank you.

She felt it, too. Sparks. I know it.

Instead of obeying my urge to race around the island to hold her, I channel every ounce of self-control and say as nonchalantly as my heart allows, "Why are you even making this?"

"I was bored, and I haven't had the chance to do this in forever because I live in motels."

A teasing smile tugs at the corners of her mouth. "Are you trying to get to know *me*, or my motives for cooking?"

"Right. What is your favorite pastime?"

"Well," she looks skyward for a moment, "I enjoy going to the gym, knife throwing, and I am an expert marksman. Obviously."

I tilt my head at her as she mixes in the chopped onions. "Something I don't know."

"I used to be in a choir." She doesn't raise her head, but I spy the hint of a blush color her cheeks.

"Maybe you can sing for me sometime."

"*Used* to, I don't sing anymore."

I know you sing, Bellator. I heard you last night, and it was beautiful.

She fries up peppers, onions, and corn, then seasons the mixture. As she combines the ingredients, I watch her. She moves on to the dough, pretending to ignore me, and rolls it into little circles and scoops a spoonful of the beef mixture into the center, then folds it into little half-circles and presses the sides with a fork.

I sit mesmerized as she places the pan back on the stove, fills it with boiling oil, and places the half circles into the oil. They sizzle and pop as she stirs them.

Running full speed into the kitchen, Corrine and Griffin shatter the quiet camaraderie between us.

"Wessy, *Wessy.* Look at Griffin."

It is like the universe flips because Westries completely changes from her annoyed and sassy mood to gentle and loving.

"Woah, he looks so handsome."

Griffin has ponytails and braids all over his body. Corrine has a knack for torturing dogs.

"I even added a bow. What are you making?"

"Try one, then I'll tell you."

Westries hands Corrine a plate with two of the beef things. Corrine stuffs one in her mouth and starts jumping up and down.

"This is so much better than *pizza.*"

Westries laughs.

Oh, how I love her laugh.

She ruffles CC's hair. "I'm glad you like it. They are empanadas."

Corrine and Griffin run back out with a dish full of Westries' empanadas.

She cleans up and sets the beef pockets on a platter, darting glances my way.

I realize that I've been staring, so I blurt, "You are great at this."

She smiles at me, and it's all the encouragement I need. She is the magnet to my steel. Before I am even conscious of the idea, I am behind her, burying my head in her neck as she washes the dishes. I take a deep breath, inhaling her scent.

She gasps and her heart rate quickens. She may try to deny the mate bond, but it is still there and working, because although she tenses, she is not yet pulling away.

"Let go of me." The tremor in her voice belies her command.

Close to her ear, I whisper, "Why?"

"B-because this is *wrong*."

Again, I whisper. "Come with me."

She hesitates. "Where?"

"Outside."

She turns her head and looks into my eyes. They shine with excitement.

Plotting an escape, little one?

I take her chin between my thumb and forefinger. "Don't even think about trying to escape. I have guards everywhere. We want our Luna here."

Westries scowls at me and I wink at her, grab her hand, and lead her outside to the gardens.

"Where are you taking me?"

"Somewhere you'll like."

I lead Westries out of the pack house towards the special place I found. "I am going to shift, and you will ride on my back."

She looks at me like I had grown two heads and retreats, shaking her finger at me.

"No *way*. No *how*. I am *not* riding on your back."

"You don't have a choice, *Bellator*."

She clenches her fists and stomps her foot. "You are the most..."

I take off my pants and my shirt.

She stops mid-rant and screeches, "*What* are you doing?

"I have to take them off or they'll rip."

She mutters. "Well, warn me next time…" as she turns around, although it's not fast enough for me not to see yet another blush creep into her cheeks.

Westries continues her muttering and I catch the words 'horny wolves.' I consider letting her know I am not some *horny wolf*. I love my mate.

But you'll learn that in time, Bellator.

CHAPTER 15

WESTRIES

I climb out of bed on shaky legs after a very uneasy night's sleep. I can't believe *he* heard me having a seizure. Usually, Griffin helps me with them, waking me up and calming me. It turns out he went to find Ulysses instead of doing his job.

Yay.

I need to blow off pent-up steam, so I am hunting down the gym Aubrey showed me yesterday. But first, my iPod. I check my duffle to make sure it is still in my hidden compartment.

The wolves didn't do a good job checking this bag. Ha, dummies. If I'd had a bomb in there, they wouldn't be the wiser.

On tiptoes, I creep out of my room, head down the hall with the best genre by far—country, of course—playing in my ears. I expect running into at least a few wolves, but I haven't even seen any yet.

Weird.

When I finally find the gym room, I beeline for the weights. My biceps may not be *huge*, but I have *some* power for what I do. I lift thirty pounds overhead while singing along to "R U Crazy" by Connor Maynard.

Before I know it, an hour and a half passes.

Time to change and de-sweatify myself before I run into anyone.

I make it back to my suite with no encounters from wolves. I clean off in the shower, just to get the stink off me, slip on dark green cargo pants, a black tank top, and boots.

Well, what should I do now?

I guess I'll go find Corrine and Griffin. I stroll along the hall to Corrine's bedroom and knock a few times on her door.

"What's the password?"

Password? I don't know eight-year-old's very well, but I have this one figured out.

"Pop-tarts."

Corrine's jaw dropped.

"How'd you know?"

"You ate the entire box yesterday."

"Oh, I really like Pop Tarts. Mom says they aren't good for me, but she wasn't there."

I can't help but laugh at her. She's so much like me at that age. She seizes my hand and leads me into her room. Griffin is peacefully sitting on her bed in a 'Daddy's Princess' t-shirt.

"Oh, my..."

"Do you like it? He even helped me pick it out."

"It looks like *you* forgot to dress."

Corrine is still in a pink, fluffy nightgown, messy hair and all. She looks at her clothes and runs over to the bedroom door. She disappears into what I assume is a closet. When she comes back out, it's with a crap ton of clothes in her hands.

"I can't decide."

Oh gosh, it's all pink… I'm perplexed here.

"Umm, well, how about these?"

I hand her skinny jeans and a pink camo shirt. She stares at me for a second before snatching the clothes and running into the bathroom. Three seconds later, she comes bounding out again, looking like a mini-me. Despite the pink.

"So, what should we do today? What about playing dolls or having a tea party?"

This girl has eternal energy.

"What do you want to do today?"

"No one is going to be in the pack house today, so we should play forts."

"What are *forts*?"

"It's where we make forts with the couch cushions and chairs, and we have swords and shields, and we run around and attack each other and rescue knights and slay dragons. We even eat macaroni and cheese in our forts."

"Alright, let's go play forts."

Corrine grabs my hand and we barrel out of the room. Corrine charges through the house like a freight train to the living room, me in tow. She pulls cushions, blankets, and decorative pillows off the couches, stacks most of them in my arms, and orders me to bring them to the kitchen. Once there, she proceeds to expertly build a fort with the table as the frame while I watch.

"You have to help, or you can't come inside."

"Oh, right. Let's build."

We continue to build our fort, and I have to say we are doing a damn good job. There is a front and back exit. Corrine informs me the back one is a secret. We cover the top with blankets and add a flag that is actually a kitchen rag. We fill the inside with more blankets and ornamental pillows. Corrine runs into the pantry and returns with a mountain of snacks.

"Get inside now. We have to plan our attack."

"Attack on who?"

"I'll tell you when you get inside. They could be listening."

All three of us crawl inside our fort.

It's pretty spacious in here, I mean I can sit up all the way.

Corrine hides the chips and gummies under the blankets.

"Here's the battle plan. Coleman will be here any minute. We are going to kidnap him."

"*Why* exactly?"

"Because he owes me five dollars, and he needs to pay."

I consider asking why an adult owes an eight-year-old five dollars, but instead say, "Good enough for me. Do I get a weapon?"

Corrine hands me a plastic sword and tells me to hide behind the table and wait for her command. Griffin accompanies me out of the fort to the table. I crouch under a chair and turn to my furry partner.

"I need you still. You know that, right Griff? You left me hanging last night."

He licks my nose and lays his head on my arm. Corrine climbs out and hides behind the kitchen door. She makes all sorts of hand signals, from a butterfly to reindeer ears. I nod, as if I know what she is saying when it's the opposite. I hear footsteps in the distance. These wolves are terrible at being quiet. I can hear them from a mile away.

I see him and two other guys in the door, then hear a warrior cry that sounds like a female tiny version of Tarzan. Corrine shows herself and charges at the three men, who seem like they are used to this. She jumps onto Coleman's back and screams while banging his head with the plastic sword.

"WESSY, GET THE ROPE."

Oh, right, I have a job here. I tumble out of my hiding place, a plastic sword in one hand and a pink sparkly jump rope in the other. Coleman is playing along, albeit warily, when he sees me.

I tell him, "Sorry, *Beta boy*, but the boss says you need to be restrained."

I secure Coleman, who allows it, as the two other male wolves stand there, confused.

"Beta, should we do something?" One guy asks.

"No, just watch her. *This* is normal, believe it or not."

Watch who? Little old me? I've done nothing wrong. Yet.

"Wait, this is her? This is the *Avenger?*"

Hey, I may not look like a cruel, savage, rogue, but I got some kick in me. I resent the cynicism.

"The one and only, fleabag. Don't act so astonished. I am tiny but mighty."

He growls at me.

"Hey watch it. There's a little girl here. Innocent ears."

I point at Corrine.

"Hey, this is a hostage situation. You can't talk to him. Only I can. Now, where's the dough, punk?"

I snort at that last order from Corrine. It sounds like she has been watching *Law and Order* or something. This is my sort of kid.

"What are you talking about?"

"You owe me five bucks. Now show me the moola or die by the hand of my sword."

Corrine holds the plastic sword up to his neck with the bold warrior face of an eight-year-old. Coleman rolls his eyes and motions to his back.

"Fine, my wallet is in my back pocket."

"Westries, please remove his wallet and retrieve my reward."

Damn, kid. Where did this dominance come from?

I reach into Coleman's back pocket, find his wallet, and open it. I feel like Loki right now.

Payback time.

"Well, no fives. But I found a twenty."

I flap the twenty at Corrine.

"I'll take it. That can be interest."

Corrine abducts the money and runs out of the kitchen.

"Come on, Griffin."

Griffin scrambles out after Corrine, leaving me feeling foolish in front of the three wolves I'm now alone with and who are gawking at me.

Coleman makes an exaggerated *ahem* sound.

"What do you want?" I mumble.

"Could you be a pal and untie me, please?"

"I *could*. But that would be doing a wolf a favor, and I don't do those." I say matter-of-factly.

He only clucks his tongue and tilts his head at me.

"Fine." I untie him and hand him his wallet.

He accepts it and opens it. "There *was* a five in here."

"Oops." I shrug.

He growls at me, cramming his wallet back into his pocket.

"Anyway, these are your guards and…"

"I don't need guards. It's *very* clear I can handle myself around over-grown puppy wannabes."

I plant my feet and cross my arms. The two dudes seem to be in their twenties. They stare at me.

Creepy.

"They aren't for your protection. They are…"

"Wait. You're telling me Ulysses wants *these* two to protect you guys *from me*? I can't… I can't."

I laugh my head off, and Coleman glares at me, clearly annoyed.

"You suck at listening, don't you? This is Jake and Owen. They are basically going to be your babysitters."

"Seriously, babysitters? Why not just lock me in my room?"

"Believe me, that was my idea, but your mate didn't want that, so here we are."

"He's not my mate."

"We'll see. I have to head to pack training, so she's all yours, boys."

Coleman walks away and leaves me with the two stone soldiers.

"Do you guys talk or…"

They say nothing as they stare at me with impassive expressions.

Wessy. I need you.

"Well, I'm going to the living room now. Do you…"

Oh, forget it.

I walk away from the zombie-like wolves and into the living room where Corrine has constructed a hasty secondary fort. She and Griffin are inside, their heads poking out. I sigh and crawl into the small opening.

"Now that we have resources, we can buy more weapons."

Corrine waggles the twenty-dollar bill I tricked Coleman into giving her. I may have misjudged this little bundle of energy in all pink. Griffin—still wearing his 'Daddy's Princess' t-shirt—wags his tail.

Confession. Aside from the whole being held against my will *and* apparently the mate to the Alpha King part, I am sort of liking it here. I mean, they *are* still wolves and that's… *meh.* But otherwise, it's not so bad.

Listen to yourself, Westries. You've lost your mind.

"What should we buy? Swords, a bow and arrow, shield? Ooh, what about a catapult?"

"You know, the greatest weapon you have is one you don't even need to buy."

She looks up at me with wide eyes.

"What? Tell me."

"Well, we'll have to go to the gym for that."

"Let's go, then."

We crawl out of our fort to discover Jake and Owen watching me. Do they ever smile or is this their natural appearance?

"Okay, freak one and freak two. *We* are going to the gym room. So, are you guys going to follow, stalk maybe…"

They stand in unison and walk toward us.

That answers that question.

Corrine and I run down the halls, my bodyguards thudding and thumping not far behind with Corrine in the lead. Her laughter, her exuberance… she reminds me so much of my little sister. We enter the gym room and Corrine stands there, confused.

"So, what are we doing here?"

"I'm going to teach you how to punch. So, come stand over here."

I lead Corrine over to a punching bag and demonstrate a basic punch. "Now, your turn."

She scrunches up her face. "But I'm too little. I won't be any good at it."

"Who says you're too little?"

She looks down and shuffles her feet.

"Other kids… and my mom. She doesn't like it when I play with my swords because I'm the princess and it's not ladylike."

"Well, that's plain stupid. You are not too little. You're the perfect size and you'll do great. Why don't you try once?"

I show her a proper punch once more and help her set her feet. She punches the bag once and smiles. She tries again. This time with more power. For an eight-year-old, at least.

"See? That was awesome."

She keeps working on her punches and stance, all the while Jake and Owen stand watch. She's honestly not bad. My dad taught me everything I know when *I* was eight. Plus, I've done a little street fighting, so I picked up another thing or two. My street name was Lady Death. I didn't pick it.

After a while of punching the sandbag, Corrine looks at her fists.

"Why are my knuckles shedding its skin?"

"It's because your hands aren't used to this kind of work. If you keep practicing, your hands will form these."

I show her my callused palms and knuckles. She feels them.

"When will I get them?"

"If you practice hard, you might get smaller versions in, like, a month."

"Then can I spar with you?"

Jake and Owen close in on me.

"Settle down, goon squad."

As if I would spar their eight-year-old werewolf princess.

"That's not a good idea, honey. I only spar with people around my age and *size*."

"Like him?"

Corrine points to Jake behind me, who looks petrified. I smirk.

"Yeah, I guess."

"Spar him."

I could use a refresher with my skills.

My last fight against Ulysses and the other werewolves serves as a reminder my skills need a little brushing up. I mean, I know I am tough, but werewolves are always going to be stronger, period. It would be fun to test my strength on someone who technically cannot harm me, though.

"Please."

I raise a quizzical eyebrow at Jake and smile. "You up for a *human* sparring partner, Jake?"

He blinks at me.

Corrine skips over and grabs his arm, shaking it. "Please… Please… PLEASE."

"Ah, leave him alone. Corry. He won't do it. He is scared that he'll lose to a *girl*."

Jake and Owen exchange glances, their jaws clenching and unclenching. When they look back at me, their eyes are flickering from black to their natural colors. Their wolves are trying to surface.

I think I may have pushed some buttons a little too much. Their wolves need to prove something now. Time to back off, I guess.

I rub my hands together and say, "What *else* can we do today?"

Corrine argues, then notices the posturing of the two werewolves and thinks better of it. "Well, it *is* almost lunchtime."

I give her a wink. "So, how about you show me around the kitchen, and we whip up lunch?"

"Yes."

All four of us enter the huge ass kitchen and I beeline to the fridge and open the doors. It's practically empty.

What the hell?

Werewolves eat five times more than humans, so why is this thing bare?

"Hey statues, why is the fridge empty? Do you guys not eat human food? I thought you were crazy rich, or something. Imagine that. The Alpha King is too broke to buy food."

They remain mute and continue to watch me from the bar.

I throw my head back and groan. They are getting on my nerves. "Could you answer, *please*?"

Jake hesitates, looks at Owen, who shrugs, and speaks. "We usually order takeout. The elders and their mates go out to dinner or eat at their own homes normally. So, we get, like, pizza and stuff."

"This will not do." I say, doing my best Mary Poppins impersonation.

Corrine giggles.

I take another quick assessment of the fridge and freezer. "How about we make frozen berry pie? Since that's all you have."

Corrine runs to the pantry and gets out the flour, baking soda, and other dough-making ingredients.

Over her shoulder, she calls, "Can we make our own dough? I enjoy rolling dough."

"Sure. Bring a chair over so you can reach."

We prepare the dough. Corrine insists we don't use whisks and should use our hands *completely*. I explain to her it isn't sanitary, but she says she will wash her hands extra good, so I agreed. We start by thawing the giant fruity ice block I uncovered in the freezer.

"Hang on. This'll go faster if we cut it apart."

I unsheathe a knife from a knife storage block on the counter and am about to cut the fruit popsicle apart when Owen strides over and plucks the knife from my hand.

"*Hey.* I am using that. If I wanted to hurt someone, I would've done it by now, dumbass." I give him a menacing smile and add, "Plus, I wouldn't kill Corry. I would kill you."

Owen grimaces. "You really like pushing people's buttons?"

"Ah-ha. He speaks."

"Yes, I speak. Now, could you make my job easier and not kill anyone?"

I chuckle. "Where's the fun in that?"

He glares at me and returns to his bar stool, both statues silent once again.

"Fine, no knife. Corry, we have to use a microwave. I trained at the online Nigerian Culinary School. Much better resources than this." I yell at the two douche bags behind me.

Corrine giggles, amused by my dramatics, which gives me warm fuzzies. Sure, I act tough, but I have a weakness for children. After all, I hunt their rapists, killers, and murderers, so it should be obvious I hate people who abuse the innocent, sweet children who are God's gifts to humanity.

Even werewolf children.

We work on our pie while the berries boil on the stove. I roll the dough out onto the counter into a circle and cover it in flour.

Corrine and I lift the fluffy pastry and lay it in the pan. I pour the hot boiled fruit over the dough.

"Alright, open the oven for me."

Corrine runs over to the oven and lowers the steaming door. I slide the glass pan over the metal bars and close the door.

"Can Griffin and I go play while we wait?"

I nod and start cleaning up the flour from the floor that Corrine spilled. I fill the sink with the pots and pans from Corrine wanting a bowl of hot fruit. Two sets of eyes bore into me while I hum a tune. From the corner of my eye, I catch Jake nudge Owen and nod at me. Owen clears his throat but says nothing.

"Whatever it is, just say it."

"Why have you been hanging out with Corrine all day?"

I stare at him, confused.

"I mean, don't you hate us?"

"Ah. You're wondering why I kill hundreds of werewolves, yet I play with an eight-year-old werewolf all afternoon, hmm?"

I dry my hands on a dish towel and contemplate my answer before speaking. "I don't hate *you*. It's your *kind* I hate. Plus, she is a kid, perfectly innocent. I have no resentment for your youth. Mine was taken and I won't do that to her."

They look puzzled but ask no more questions. I finish washing the dishes and set the last pot on a towel. When I turn around to face Jake and Owen, it's to see they haven't taken their eyes off me.

"So, are you going to stare at me for the rest of the day or do I get privacy?"

Owen shakes his head no. I want to do something by myself or at least semi by myself.

Are they going to stand outside the bathroom while I do my business? Geez.

"Can I ask you guys a question?"

Jake and Owen raise their eyebrows.

"So, Ulysses is *supposedly* my *mate,* right? And that makes me Luna Queen, and you have to listen to the Luna, right?"

Owen narrows his gaze at me like I'm conjuring an evil plan.

"I'm not coming up with an escape plan if that's what you're thinking, so chill. Now anyway, if I ask you guys to get me something harmless, would you get it?"

They look at each other.

Owen speaks. "What do you have in mind?"

"Ten pounds of ground beef."

"*Why?*" Jake asks, nervous about what evil doings I might inflict with a dead cow ground to a pulp.

"Because I haven't been able to use a gourmet kitchen in five years and I want to practice. It's *cooking.* You could even watch me the entire time."

"I can ask the Alpha…"

Why does everything revolve around Ulysses? Why can't they get me what I need without talking to him?

"Couldn't you just get me the meat? Besides, what harm could I cause with a dead cow? Salmonella poisoning?"

They both look at each other. Mind linking, I suspect.

"You *could* talk out loud, instead of mind linking."

They startle, then Jake speaks.

"When do you need it?"

Yes. Thank you, Jesus.

"One hour?"

"Fine. I'll send an Omega out to the store and…"

"Ooh, and four peppers, an onion, two cloves of garlic, and four corn cobs."

They look at each other, then back at me.

"Fine."

I offer a slightly sarcastic curtsy. "Thank you."

A few minutes later, the sound of chairs scraping the floor startles me.

They're leaving?

I ask, "Does that mean I can escape now?"

"No can do, *Bellator.*"

The sound of Ulysses' voice startles the crap out of me, which pisses me off. Rather than acknowledge him, I keep cooking. Of course, this doesn't deter *him.* Instead, he starts a barrage of *get to know you* questions, and the next thing I know, I'm agreeing to follow him outside.

CHAPTER 16

WESTRIES

What am I doing?

Riding on a werewolves' back, that's what. Behind me, Ulysses' bones snap and break into their new form. I am terrified to turn around right now. I hate being this close to werewolves without a weapon. It makes me feel weak and wussy. A wet nose nudges my back, and I baby step around. Towering in front of me is an enormous black wolf with silvery white tips. I barely meet his shoulders, and that scares me. He stares at me, then lowers onto his belly. He chuffs and jerks his head over his massive shoulder, motioning for me to get on his back.

"This is stupid…"

Muttering to myself, I climb on Ulysses' back, slipping my fingers into his thick coat and clinging. He glances back at me with those daunting werewolf eyes, then bursts off into the forest. We are going so fast; I can barely open my eyes. The brown and green blur of trees wiz by and a peek over my shoulder shows the pack house isn't even visible anymore.

I allow the tug at my lips to become a smile. This is the closest thing to freedom that I've seen in a while. Ulysses slows to a trot.

I am unprepared for the sight before us when we emerge from the tree line into a grand haven. A majestic waterfall rushes into a shimmering lake. Mountains surround this secret sanctuary… and us. Ahead lies a small beach covered with smooth, tiny pebbles on the shoreline, and trees like skyscrapers stand solemn sentry around the edges of the lake, making a private little utopia.

He crouches low and I climb off, then disappears into the forest line. *Hopefully to put clothes on.*

I trudge to the edge of the shore and sit beside the freezing water. The pure, crisp air fills my lungs in a slow drawn breath and I crane my neck so my face can feel the sun.

I could get used to this… and most likely must.

As tough as I know I am, even I can admit no one can escape the Royal Alpha's wolves. Especially someone whose been marked as the mate of the Alpha King himself. What's the point of being hopeful when hope has died? I must resign myself to being stuck here in this gilded prison.

Fine. But I can't be Ulysses' mate or their Luna. I can't be. I hate them.

The idea of someone *made* for you, to always love you, to protect you? Sounds great, sure. Even I could use that in my life. But love a *wolf*?

Never.

"What are you thinking about, Bellator?"

Ulysses—now in jeans, a flannel shirt, and boots—stares down at me. He looks like a mountain man if I ever saw one.

Avoiding his question, I ask my own. "*Bellator.* Is that Latin or something?"

Ulysses sits next to me.

That's too close, buddy.

I scoot away, which makes him growl. I rarely flinch, but I did this time. However, I recovered well, though.

Ulysses takes a deep breath and we both fix our attention to the water.

"It is Latin. How did you know?"

"When I was in, like, eighth grade, they made us study Latin. I hated it."

I chuckle at the memory. My mom tried as best she could to help me with my declinations, but we both got upset at the rule exceptions. At least we sucked together.

"After that school year, I switched to French, which also sucked, but that is a story for another day."

"So, do you know what it means?"

"What part of 'I sucked' did you not get?"

He rolls his eyes at me. "It means warrior."

Heat rises into my face when he says that. I turn away, busying myself with searching for the perfect stone to skip across the water until the heat subsides.

Stop blushing, you idiot. Be tough, damn it.

Ulysses either doesn't notice or is pretending not to notice.

He continues his interrogation. "Tell me more about yourself, your hobbies, favorite TV shows and movies, and your family."

A surge of anger makes me throw the smooth stone in my hand harder than necessary.

I don't do public sharing, dude. People don't care about me, and I don't care about them. That's how it's been and always will be.

"Do you always ask such cliché questions?"

He forces a quick burst of air through his nose and shakes his head. However, he is grinning as he, too, picks up a rock and skims it deftly across the water's surface.

He tries again. "You said your favorite colors are forest green and red. Why?"

"I like forest green because it's the color of nature, of life. I like red because it's the color of blood that we share."

"Very profound. How old are you?"

"Nineteen. How old are you?"

Raising his eyebrow and flashing that cocky grin of his, he says "I thought I was asking the questions?"

"Well, I don't know you either. So, answer."

"I am twenty-five."

I'm silent for a minute, taking in this news.

He is twenty-five. And we are mates? That is a big age gap if you ask me. Not that anyone cares what I think.

Oblivious to my surprise at our age difference, he resumes.

"Favorite hobbies?"

"I already answered that."

"I know, but you *must* have more hobbies."

He pokes my side and smiles.

Ugh. I love his smile. I can't fall for him.

It won't end well for me *or* him. I can't give him what he wants. I have too much baggage, too many problems. Guys hate girl drama, and that probably goes double for an Alpha King.

"What about you?"

He scratches his cheek and leans back onto his elbows. I look at him stretched out beside me. His eyes are so blue, I could drown in them. My gut twists at the thought of waking up in his arms one day.

"Well, as the Alpha of Alpha's, I do a lot of paperwork and pack stuff. When I *do* get a break, I train with the pack and travel to other packs worldwide for meetings and conferences."

"What sort of training?"

I pull my knees to my chest and lay my cheek on them. I usually am not this comfortable around people, but somehow, I feel safe around Ulysses, and that scares me.

It scares me to feel safe again. How's that for a contradiction?

"We train in wolf form, but we also train in hand-to-hand combat."

"You train with weapons, right? M4 Carbines? I mean, I noticed when… well, you know…" I smirk. That's what started it all.

"Umm yeah, we do. Or at least the Warriors Elite do. What about you and that AK-47? Where did that even come from? I swear we searched the whole car."

He lolls his head back so he can pierce my stupid heart with those eyes of his, waiting for my answer.

"Heh, funny story. I've gotten good at hiding weapons in plain sight." After I keep him hanging first, I fess up. "I hid it under the hood, behind the engine. You guys missed a few things in the duffle, too."

He jolts upright and leans closer.

"*Please* tell me we didn't miss any weapons?"

I laugh. They did an awful job.

"Well," I tick off each missed item. "My Synthroid meds, iPhone, throwing knives, oh, and an Astra Cub 22 short pocket pistol…"

I blink and offer a beatific smile. He drops his head into his hands and moans. But a thought must have jumped into his mind because he lowers his hands and stares at me as if puzzling out a complex mystery plot.

His head tilts and his words come slowly. "And you haven't used them to escape?"

Do I confess what I am mortified to say? That staying here is not that bad, and I have grown to *like* it here. That I like a *few* of the wolves. That I…

Don't you do it, Westries. Tell him only the technical facts… not the mushy feelings ones.

I thrust my chin and direct my answer at the lake instead of his too blue, too intense eyes. "Listen, I don't kill the innocent. Only those who deserve it. So, I hope I haven't made that impression. I may not like all wolves, but I will never go against my morals."

It's not the answer to his question, but I'm hoping he won't notice. He is silent, so I chance a glance at him to see his lips curve into a smile.

"What?" I ask, annoyed that he is staring and smiling at me so charmingly.

"Nothing." He shrugs. "I didn't expect that."

"What did you expect? A *murderous* monster?" I ask, crossing my arms and squinting at him. I mean, it adds to my badassery M.O. if it was what he had expected. But this new, annoying, *caring* part of me hopes that's not it.

He raises his hands, palms out like he's stopping traffic to ward off the suggestion. "No, of course not. As you've learned from my sisters, we consider you a hero in most places." He considers, then clarifies. "Well, at *first,* people feared you, but as soon as they realized you are only after rogues, things changed."

"Aubrey said some people thought *I* must be a rogue." I snort-laugh and add, "Like, a hot guy rogue."

He laughs and folds his arms across his chest. "Yeah, people—females, in particular—did. Honestly, you got on my nerves."

"Why?" I ask, leaning forward.

He pauses for a second, like he doesn't want to answer. "Well, you were a vigilante. I mean, we saw you went after rogues, but we knew nothing else. What is the correlation between you and the rogues, Westries?"

I chew my lip. I am growing more comfortable around him, but not *that* comfortable. But I never back down, nor do I fear him. That will be my downfall. I answer his question.

"They were dangerous wolves who were hurting my people, humans. I had a bone to pick with them, anyway. They were all rapists, drug dealers, or illegal gun traffickers. My world is safer without them in it, so I did something."

"How does someone start something like that, anyway? How do you know about our existence?"

I fix my gaze out at the serene water again. I won't answer his question. He could never convince me to, and he'll think I'm being cryptic.

Let him think that or whatever else. He can call it my stubbornness or my superpower, for all I care.

"How does anyone find out anything? An accident, at the wrong place, at the wrong time." I stand up and brush off my pants. "I don't want to talk about this anymore."

He grabs my forearm before I can stomp toward the tree line.

"Hey. It's alright, you don't have to answer. If you want to leave, we can. Just wait a sec. I'll be right back."

He disappears into the darkening forest line and reemerges as his wolf. I permit myself an unabashed moment to take in his changed form. Most of the wolves I've seen are raggedy and ugly. He is neither. His wolf is huge and powerful. His coat looks as if he had been at the groomers, so shiny and soft.

I try in vain to resist the urge to stroke his soft head, and I don't realize I've failed until my hand is outstretched. His eyes light up, and he meets my fingertips halfway. After a moment, he lowers himself to the ground, giving me easier access to pet his colossal head. Even laying down, his head is level with my chest. I sink on the ground beside him and the second I do, Ulysses' wolf lays his chin in my lap. I am trembling under his weight with the flutter of thousands of butterflies in my belly. He tilts his head up at me.

I give a wobbly grin. "This is *weird*, if you were wondering."

He sniffs and nudges my hand, then lays back in obvious contentment.

I gaze up at the sky. "You realize it is going to be pitch black soon? I don't want to be out this late…"

He chuffs at me, annoyed I want to leave.

"Don't give me that attitude. It is dark and cold, plus don't you have something to do somewhere, anywhere?"

He gives me the wolf version of a sigh and stands, bending enough to let me on. I grip his neck fur and he charges through the forest the moment I give the signal I'm ready.

A short time later, he trots up to the back door and I slip off his back. He walks back to the tree line and comes back out in his clothes.

"We better go through the other door."

"Why? This one is literally two feet away."

He mumbles something I don't quite catch.

I step closer and cup my hand to my ear. "Sorry, no werewolf hearing. What was that?"

"My mother."

Is he blushing? Oh, my God. He's blushing.

I snort. "*Really*? Your mother? *That's* why we can't use this door?"

"Listen, you are not on her good side right now, so let's not make it worse."

A surge of indignation floods my entire body.

What the actual hell? If I'm his mate, then he should have my *back, not hers. Wait a minute. Why do I care?*

I fall back on my crutch: sarcasm. "I'm not scared of a mama wolf who thinks she can intimidate me just because I'm human. But obviously, *you* are."

He mutters something about crazy-ass mate and fiery spirit but I stopped listening. I charge forward and open the door to hear yelling and whimpering.

"*Honestly*. Are you trying to kill us all? She could have poisoned it."

I follow the sound of the screaming into the kitchen with Ulysses hot on my heels. I instantly regret my choice.

Ulysses' mom and dad, Coleman, Jackie, Aubrey, and Corrine are semi-circle around the granite island. They turn to me and Molly stalks towards me.

"*You.*"

"Me." I gather my full, not very high height and meet her glare, mocking her tone.

"How *dare* you? You *human*. You…"

"If your version of an insult is naming my species, you suck at insulting people. Perhaps you should be a biologist instead?"

Aubrey snorts from behind Molly, while Molly grinds her teeth. Miss Prissy whips around and glares at her daughter, then spins back to me and starts waving her finger in my face.

"You have no right teaching my daughter whatever assassin voodoo you commit. And what are *those*? You seriously tried to poison this pack? You are in serious trouble."

Ulysses growls from behind me, wrapping one of his hands around my waist. I don't object because it rattles his mother. And, if I'm being honest with myself, it somehow feels right.

"You are forgetting your place, mother."

I place my hand on Ulysses' chest. We make intense eye contact and I tell him with my eyes to *back off. I got this*. He remains at my back, his hands now resting on my hips. I can't tell if it's possessiveness, protectiveness, or support. Maybe it's all three. Regardless, it somehow gives me the courage to go on.

To his mother, I offer a wide smile that doesn't reach my eyes.

"First, *assassin voodoo*? Really? All I did was boost her confidence. Something that a certain *someone* is not helping her with. And two, I did not poison anyone. I was bored. That's what happens when you are under house arrest in a werewolf pack house with nothing to do. If I wanted you dead, you wouldn't be poisoned. You would have a bullet in your head like everyone else. I am sorry if that is graphic, but it's true."

Benjamin growls from behind Molly, warning me to stop talking.

I continue anyway. "But I don't want anyone dead. And I honestly hope I don't have the reputation that I brutally kill the innocent because I don't. And if anyone asks in the future, someone else explain that to them, because I am tired of explaining this."

I take a deep breath, then one by one meet the eyes of every person in the room. "The wolves I killed were unacceptable wolves who were hurting my people. They were all rapists, drug dealers, or illegal gun traffickers. Yeah, that doesn't always justify taking a life, but my world is safer without them in it. I couldn't stand by knowing what was going on, so I did something about it. And if you have a problem with that, try to keep your species in check. You royals may only see them as pests that only cause trouble, but for me, they are demons from hell."

Griffin trots out from behind Corrine and jumps up, putting his front paws on my shoulders, and licks at my chin. He knows, he always knows when I need him. I lightly push him away and stride out of the kitchen, leaving a dumbstruck silent room. I keep my placid demeanor as I walk up the stairs and down the hall with my furry comrade by my side. Once behind my bedroom door, I strip my clothes off, turn on the steaming water, and climb in the tub. It is only then I am safe enough to allow myself to crumple. Leaning my head against the beige warm wall, I let the memories flood back.

I wasn't always a dark person, but the things I've done and seen can turn even the happiest soul dark. I play devil's advocate in my mind once again.

I kill wolves and sometimes humans…

but I saved more lives than I took.

I can justify what I did.

Sure, but one day, it will come back to bite me.

I suffered too, if anyone cared.

Everyone must face the consequences of their actions, regardless of their intentions.

This, I know. I also know I'm messed up. PTSD, they call it. I don't need to pay a doctor to tell me I have it. I can self-diagnose just fine.

I never let it become an excuse for whatever I screw up at, though. Instead, I use it to better myself and commit myself to overcome my difficulties.

When I finish my internal counseling session, I rinse off the terrible memories, step out of the shower, and wrap a towel around my waist. Griffin sprawls on my bed, rolling around on my pillows. I rummage through my new clothes drawers and grab a sports bra and sweatpants, then jump on my bed with Griffin and scroll through my Spotify. My 80's rock playlist is just right for my mood, and I turn it up full blast. I roll off the bed and drag my duffle bag onto the duvet and empty the contents.

They did a sucky job of clearing this bag. I extract the throwing knives and .22 short pocket pistol and stuff them in the bedside drawer.

Ya never know when they might come in handy.

CHAPTER 17

ULYSSES

We were having a connection, a genuine connection. She was spending time with me. The mate bond is growing, and her walls are crumbling. But all good things must end, and she now wants to go home. I hadn't realized how dark it is getting, so I take Westries back through the woods to the pack house. We arrive at the back door as the crickets start their chirrups and I let Westries off my back.

The moment I return from changing my clothes, I regret having brought Westries to this entrance. Yelling and screaming seeps out into the night air from inside. Three words ring out: *murderer, human,* and *Avenger.*

"We better go through the other door…"

"Why?"

Why is she so combative about everything?

"My mother." After I am forced to repeat myself, a new regret replaces the first.

Her eyes blaze from an internal furnace. "Really? Your mother? That's why we can't use *this* door?"

"Listen, you are not on her good side right now, so let's not make it worse."

That was a mistake to say.

She glares at me, crossing her arms, and giving me that scary eye.

"Try me."

"Seriously, crazy mate, going to get herself killed." I mutter to myself as Westries walks through the threshold.

The screaming becomes clearer, and I can tell instantly who and what it's about.

This should be good.

"Honestly. Are you trying to kill us? She could have poisoned it."

Westries strolls into the kitchen, with me right behind her. It appears the entire gang is here to witness the ensuing battle.

Great.

All heads turn to Westries as my mom storms toward her. The others observe them as if watching a tennis match where, instead of a little yellow ball, they hurl words at one another.

"*You.*"

"Me."

"How *dare* you? You human. You-"

"If your version of an insult is naming my species, you suck at insulting people. Maybe you should be a biologist instead?"

Aubrey snorts from behind my mom. My mother glares at her, then turns back to my mate.

And it's on.

When she goes too far in her attack, I growl and wrap my arm around my mate's waist… and she doesn't object.

"You are forgetting your place, mother."

Westries turns around and places her hand on my chest.

I hope she didn't feel the jump in my heartbeat.

Westries delivers a strong volley in return, but when she mentions putting bullets into rogues, my father growls, warning Westries. He stares at me and I stare back. We may be father and son, but our mates will always come first.

Fortunately, Westries softens her harsh words. She finishes with a final retort.

"You royals may only see them as pests that only cause trouble, but for me, they are demons from hell."

Westries pushes me away, and Griffin bounds over to her. He puts his huge paws on her chest and licks her. I can't help but feel jealous.

She rubs his head and leaves the kitchen. My wolf growls for the second time at people doubting our mate, so I speak.

"Need I remind you what happens to people who dare undermine the future Luna Queen? Father, you would be wise to keep your mate under control."

Axel comes to the surface. I don't wish to hold him under control much longer. So, I don't.

CHAPTER 18

AXEL

I charge out of the kitchen, looking for Westries. I can't believe those wolves. They dare say she might poison her own pack. This is blasphemy. My mate is their future Luna Queen, and they better respect her. I storm through the halls of the pack house in Ulysses' form.

If only I could use my control of Ulysses' body to punish them as they deserve.

Ulysses is yelling at me, warning he'll take control again, because he thinks I'll do something rash. I won't. I want my mate. At her door, I don't bother knocking.

She is laying on her bed, playing on her phone, Griffin drapes across her lap. I swear that dog gets more attention than her own mate.

"Ever hear of knocking?"

I ignore her and take her phone away, throwing it to the floor.

"*Hey.* I was using that."

I disregard her protest and pull her into my arms. Griffin jumps off the bed and runs out the door.

Good boy.

"Ulysses, let *go.* I don't like hugs."

She squirms around in my grip, but I hold her tighter and bury my head in her neck.

"I am not Ulysses."

She stops struggling and tilts her head back at me.

"Y-you're his wolf? But… how? I thought he could only shift into you?" She squints at me.

"And you thought you understood everything about us. Yes, Westries. I am Axel and you are my mate."

"Well, *Axel,* could you please let go? I don't like physical contact." She shoves at Ulysses' chest.

I huff but let her go. She slides over to sit in front of me, her legs crossed like a pretzel. She plays with her hair and alternates between staring at me and looking everywhere but at me.

She is shy. How unexpected. And adorable.

I do my best to soften the gruffness of my voice. "Why don't you like physical contact?"

"I just don't. Why did you take over for Ulysses?"

"His mother disrespected her future Luna Queen, and Ulysses gave me control."

She gapes at me for a second, then leans over to the side table and reaches for something. From the nightstand drawer, she extracts a small pistol and holds it out to me.

It is my turn to gape. "Why are you giving me this?"

"I figured you'd want this since you don't trust me yet."

I squint at her. "You think I don't trust you?"

"Well, Ulysses doesn't. Hell, I wouldn't trust me either, to be honest." She nods at the pistol still in her outstretched hand and waggles it at me.

I push it back toward her. "No, keep it. I won't leave you helpless here."

She hesitates, then smiles and returns the pistol to the drawer. She looks back at me, her smile now sly and her eyes twinkling with mischief. "I am not helpless. Trust me. I could take your warriors any day."

I chuckle. "Oh, really?"

"Yes. In fact, I have already, remember? Didn't it take five wolves to hold me down?"

It *had* taken a lot of wolves to hold her down. Luckily for them, they hadn't gotten too rough with her.

Mate is feisty. I like her, Ulysses.

I see that, Axel. Time's up.

"Ulysses wants control again, so I have to go."

"W-will I get to talk to you again?"

Mate likes us.

"You... want to talk to *me* again?"

"Well, I like you so much..." Impulse overrules my sense. I grab my mate and bring her against my chest for a hug. Realizing what I did, I release her. "Sorry, I forgot."

"No, no, it's fine. I don't mind it occasionally." Shyness creeps back into her voice. "From people I know, that is."

CHAPTER 19

I regain control from Axel to see Westries sitting crisscross in front of me, a curious expression on her face. I scan her from head to toe. "Did he do anything?"

Westries tilts her head. "Can you not see what was happening?"

"Usually, I can." I am loath to admit this, but the words come out, regardless. "He blocked me out."

Westries makes a small *hmph* sound and pulls the fluffy blanket around her more, like a human burrito. Neither of us says anything after that, so I stand to leave.

As I reach the door, she speaks. "Where are you going?" I turn around, unable to hide the surprise from my expression.

"You want me… to stay?"

Her brow furrows. "*Not* the entire night. But to talk for a while?"

I grin. My mate wants to spend time with us. The bond is growing. I return to where she sits at the foot of the bed in her burrito blanket and sit beside her.

Forcing nonchalance, I ask, "What do you want to talk about?" Westries pulls the camo green blanket tighter around her shoulders, turning herself into an even more adorable little burrito. "I don't know. What are you doing tomorrow?"

"I have training with the pack in human form and I need to order caterers for a pack dinner."

"What pack dinner? And doesn't this pack have cooks on staff?"

She has a question for everything.

"Well, this pack has relatively thirty thousand wolves. Although a few hundred are attending."

"Cool. So, the pack training tomorrow, can I come?"

I raise an eyebrow at her.

What game is she playing?

"Why do you want to come?"

She shrugs from deep inside her burrito fortress. "I am bored in the house, and I like training."

"Ah, I don't know…" I rub the back of my neck. How do I feel about my mate sparring with grown werewolves? I mean, I realize she can handle it, but I'm not sure if I want it.

"Come on, please. I can take it. If anything, you should be worried about whoever I spar with."

She flings off the blanket from her shoulders, crosses her arms, and pouts. I roll my eyes and groan, giving in.

"Fine, you can come. Meet me in the kitchen at ten A.M."

My mate springs off the bed like a lithe cat, claps and does a victory dance. It is the first time I glimpse the carefree girl she might have become had life not been so cruel to her.

While one part of my brain makes the observation, the other side makes another. She is wearing only a sports bra and sweatpants.

My gaze travels over her body. From her graceful neck to her toned arms, then on to her taut abdomen and jutting hipbones.

Get a hold of yourself, Ulysses.

I force my gaze back to her arms, one of which is wrapped in a beautiful tribal black system tattoo which starts at her wrist and ends around her clavicle.

My voice is husky. "Where did you get your tattoos?" I reach out to trace one swirl on her arm. She shivers under my touch. I can't help but be proud of the mate bonds' response to my touch.

"Which one?"

"You have more than this one?" I point to her tattoo.

My mate makes a half turn, so that her back is to me. She gathers her hair and sweeps it aside to expose a giant wolf's claw and the words, "I have not yet begun to fight."

I run my fingertip over the famous words by John Paul Jones. "It's beautiful."

She offers her profile, resting her chin on her shoulder, and says, "Thanks. I had it done when I was sixteen."

I raise my eyebrows at her. "Sixteen and they let you?

She lets her long hair swing back in place and faces me again. "No one asks questions there."

I nod, understanding.

There is a new silence between us now. One unlike the many others before. Dare I call it companionable? Whatever it may be, I am unwilling to do anything to ruin it.

Like take her in my arms, and…

"I better go to sleep now." I step away from her, perhaps abruptly. "We have a long day tomorrow."

If my sudden declaration surprises or confuses Westries, she masks it well. She opens her mouth to speak, but then changes her mind and nods. The moment she climbs back into her bed and under her covers, Griffin bounds through the doorway and joins her, curling up next to my mate.

At the door, I call, "Good night, Westries."

Her soft reply echoes sweetly in my head. "Night, Ulysses."

C H A P T E R   2 0

Westries

Griffin woke me twice in the night because of nightmares and panic attacks. I don't know what I would do without him. He has been my absolute hero. This time, Ulysses didn't come in my room, but I know he hovered outside the door.

How could I miss him walking around? He is like Godzilla.

Anyway. I've overslept and must now try to make my way out from under the still sleeping Griffin and climb out of bed.

I swear, this dog is half mutant sloth and half couch potato.

The clock reads 9:23 am. I walk over to my overly organized drawers and retrieve my one gym outfit. A pair of gray leggings, a sports bra, and a black tank top. I yank a brush through my hair and toss it into a high ponytail. Time check: 9:37.

"Griffin. Get your furry butt up. Let's go, boy."

I run through the halls with Griffin loping behind, and beeline for the kitchen. From the fridge, I pull out milk, eggs, ham, and bacon. I can and will make killer omelets for breakfast.

"Hey Griff, is it weird that we haven't run into anyone?"

Griffin sneezes and lays down in a beam of sunshine streaming through the windows. Honestly, I am counting my blessings to have this time alone.

As if summoned by my thoughts, five Warriors Elites lumber into the kitchen. I can tell them apart from the other wolves, thanks to their tattoos.

I sigh, ignore them, and say to Griffin, "What's that saying again? Never put your eggs all in one basket?"

I continue to stir my eggs. Their eyes burn holes in the back of my head.

In a sing-song voice, I say, "If you want some, all you have to do is ask."

I spin around with the hot pan and set it on a trivet. Whistling, I set out a dozen plates, forks, and napkins, serve myself, and hop up onto the countertop to eat. I stab a forkful of steaming deliciousness, but before I can take a bite, I have to snap these knuckleheads out of their trance.

"Are you guys mute, too, or…"

One guy serves himself a plate. The guy to his left slaps his arm.

"What the hell are you doing? She could've poisoned it. You remember who she is, right?"

"Yeah, but I'm hungry and it smells fine. You didn't poison it, did you?"

They look at me and I cackle.

"You wolves and your poison obsession. No. Poison is for cowards." I roll my eyes and pop the heaping serving into my mouth. Around the mouthful, I add, "I'm eating it. See?"

More to myself than to them, I mutter, "And where would I even get poison? I'm under house arrest if you didn't already know."

They nod and sulk at me as they serve themselves. They sit at the table and eat like skittish crows.

After I'm sure they've each had a bite, I say, "Although, I *do* know how to make a stomach bug poison with bleach and paprika."

They drop their forks in a clatter and growl low at me. I'm trying so hard not to burst out laughing.

None other than their Alpha strides into the kitchen just then and sighs. "She didn't poison it. You guys are fine."

I stick my tongue out at him for ruining my fun. "Buzz kill…" I mutter, stuffing more eggs into my mouth.

"You will have plenty of time to have your fun with them in the ring."

"What do you mean, Alpha?" A wolf asks, placing his plate into the sink.

"Today is human form training day. Westries will join us."

Another wolf pipes in.

"We can't fight our Luna."

"Why not?" Ulysses asks.

"We could hurt her. She's human."

"So?"

They turn to me.

I jump from the cabinet, placing my plate in the sink, rinsing it.

"You remember who I am, right? I think I'll manage."

"But what if we hurt her, Alpha?" They look to him for answers, like I am a delicate creature. I am *not* delicate, just marginally bruisable compared to werewolves.

"I'll heal. It's no big deal. Don't go easy on me. Use your full strength. Now could we go? I am bored."

They all nod, and we begin our trek to the warehouse down the road. I run ahead, but I sense someone catching up.

"Hey. I, uh, wanted to introduce myself. I'm Paul." He reaches out and shakes my hand as we walk.

"Westries, but you knew that."

"Yeah. All the Warriors Elite know now."

"How many know, *exactly*?"

He glances skyward, seemingly to count, then gives up. "Well, the whole pack knows Ulysses found his mate, but no one knows who or what you are."

"Good."

We walk in silence until we arrive at the pack warehouse. There are LOTS of wolves around in all forms. Without a gun, or knives, or any defensive weapons except for my biceps—which I'm not ashamed to admit I've nicknamed Smith and Wesson—I am nervous. I was about to walk through the door when someone grabs my arm pulling me aside.

Ulysses.

"Hey." I toss the greeting out.

His gaze is as intense as ever. "I need to talk to you."

"You are." I slow blink, knowing it'll irritate him.

Ulysses rolls his eyes and continues. "Less smart-ass comments, Wes. Now listen, there are a lot of wolves here today and not everyone knows about... *it.*"

"Which *it*? Because there are several *its.*"

"Let's start with the human part for today. The only ones here are Warriors Elite or high-ranking wolves, but it is going to get out eventually, so here's the plan..."

"Wait. Why do we need a plan? Why can't I go inside and spar with them?"

His expression screams a sarcastic, '*Really?*'

"Did you forget that this town comprises of all wolves? You are the only human here. They will know instantly. Luckily, many of the wolves inside already do, so I guess we don't *have* to announce it tonight. So, stay close for now."

I nod, not wanting to argue anymore and follow Ulysses inside the building. I have counted sixty-seven wolves. Not bad. All across the warehouse, there are wolves training in what appears to be the coolest gym ever. Some are pumping iron weights; others are sparring while a few are even using weapons on each other.

Around the perimeter of the vast room are jumping boxes, climbing ropes, punching bags, medicine balls, and a lot of bench presses.

I could live here, it's so awesome.

In fact, I would so love to join in, but Ulysses has me on a short leash.

As if reading my thoughts, Ulysses shoots a warning glance at me before he walks over to Jake and Owen, my prison guards. His back is to me, so I watch him for a moment.

Dummy, his back is to you. Escape.

He is distracted, but one glance around the room is enough to know I wouldn't get far. Still, this might be a great time to find a hiding place where I can scope out an escape route.

I look up and notice the climbing ropes connect to the metal ceiling rafters. Perfect.

If anyone looks over, it'll appear I'm just climbing for exercise.

I climb up one rope and make it to the top. Below, Ulysses is still engrossed in conversation and the pack is too busy training to pay attention to me. At the far end, I spy a maintenance ladder. It ends on the main floor beside a metal door.

Ha, a back door. I'll just go on out and get some fresh air.

So, concentrating on my footing, I balance-beam walk along the metal rafters toward my goal. Once safely at the maintenance ladder, I climb down the rungs and creep over to the door. My back is against the wall, watchful of everyone in the room. I try the handle.

Unlocked. Yes.

When it's open enough to wedge my foot, I toe it open wide enough for me to slip through and pull it closed gently, as if I am diffusing a bomb.

Once shut and no alarms ringing or furious shouting greeting my exit, I close my eyes, lean against the door, and exhale the breath I hadn't realized I'd been holding.

I startle. I am *not* outside, but in a corridor with a staircase leading down.

Well, now what should I do?

Curiosity wins, and I hurry down the two flights of metal stairs. At the bottom, across from me, there is a door that says 'Penitentiary,' and I, of course, try that handle as well.

Unlocked again. This must be my lucky day.

Beyond this door is a long, dimly lit corridor. The walls are beige and mottled with water stains, and the sickly, yellow-tinged lights flicker.

What is this, a haunted house cliché? Should I expect the boogeyman to jump out and get killed?

I wish I brought my pistol, or knives, or *anything*. Yet, I cannot get myself to turn back. At the end of the hallway, there is another door with a huge lock. I pull the metal handle with all my strength and struggle to open the enormous door. I look around and I am in the center of what I think is the pack prison.

Sure, most people run in the opposite direction, but I trust I am safe. It *is* the Royal prison, so it must have durability. Still, I skim the sidewall across the cells, lest any of them reach through the bars to grab me.

My sneakers make but a small *slap, slap* sound on the cement floor, but it's noise enough to alert the imprisoned wolves. Like dominos in reverse, they line up along the bars and jeer at me.

"Ooh, look what we got here. A human."

"You look lost, honey."

"Hey, there is room in here, sweetheart."

I ignore the taunts and continue down the long row. The heckling continues as I round the corners, exploring. The first level leads to a second lower level, separated by five wide stairs.

Quite the assortment of wolves you've got here, Ulysses.

Some look around twenty and others look like fifty, but the one thing they have in common is they all look creepy and gross. I try to tell myself I've seen enough. But then there's that little voice that says there must be *something* more interesting in here than these losers.

Yeah, yeah, I know. Curiosity killed the cat.

"But satisfaction brought it back." My voice bounces against the walls.

It's then that I hear whimpering and stop, listening harder.

I quicken my pace toward the noise and come to a cell with no mates on either side. Inside is a small boy, maybe a year or two younger than Corrine.

"Hey, hey, little man. What are *you* doing in here?"

The boy jolts and scoots deeper into the cell, burying his head in his knees.

I crouch to get eye level. "Hey, it's okay. I won't hurt you. I'm a friend."

He continues to cry.

The harried voices of Ulysses and Coleman follow the unmistakable sound of that metal door banging open.

"WESTRIES. Where the hell are you?"

I don't acknowledge him. Right now, I am more concerned with soothing a little boy in a *prison*. Ulysses' boots clomp and hammer on the metal stairs, like a beast barreling my way. When they reach me, I stand and face them. Ulysses' fury is matched only by my own.

As he draws breath to yell, I snarl through clenched teeth. "Open the cell."

He ignores, or doesn't hear me in his own rage. "*Where have you been?* What the *hell* were you thinking, coming down here, of all places?"

"Open the *door.*" My voice shakes with anger.

He glances from my face to the cell beside me, then his tone turns cajoling. "*Why* in the hell would you come down here, Westries? It's a prison. You could've gotten hurt or worse. And…"

"Ulysses. Open. The. Door."

He looks at me, warily, and I cross my arms. We are at an impasse.

Fine. I'll go around you, mate.

I lock the Warrior Elite who'd trailed behind his master and Beta in my gaze. I recognize him now as the one I'd met earlier. Paul.

Good. I can tell he's eager to please.

"Open the door."

He darts confused, nervous glances between us. "Luna, I-I can't. It is not safe."

They forget I know my position as Luna commands the obedience of all pack members. They must follow any orders coming from their Alpha *and* Luna. So, I cross my arms and stare daggers at the guard.

"Now."

"Y-yes, Luna."

The guard averts his eyes from his masters in submission and unlocks the door, almost dropping the keys. The moment the gate screeches open wide enough, I dash to the little boy hugging his legs. I scoop him up and wait out his brief freak out, all the while murmuring words of comfort.

"Hey, hey it's okay… I won't hurt you."

He stops, looks into my eyes. He must see the promise of safety in them, because his struggles cease, and he wraps his skinny, filthy arms around my neck and buries his face in my hair. The child is shivering from fear and trauma, and it breaks my heart.

I storm out of the disgusting cell to discover Jake and Owen had joined the party and now stand in my way.

"Move," I command.

They both step aside and I walk up the stairs, the little boy still crying and sniffling into my neck. He is no heavier than the weights I lift, but I fear Ulysses will change his mind and give the order to stop me, so I hurry up the staircases, through the gym, and outside in the fresh air in record time.

My voice comes out breathless as I say, "Hey. My name is Westries. What is yours?"

He lifts his head, wincing at the bright light, and whispers, "It's Patrick."

"That's a very handsome name. How old are you, Patrick?"

Patrick holds up one hand and one finger.

Six-years old? Those bastards. How could they?

Despite my renewed fury, I force a cheerful reply. "Wow, you are so grown up."

Patrick sniffs and raises his chin. "My brother says I am very mature for my age."

He grabs a strand of my hair and starts twisting it. His shyness and fear melt away as he openly gapes at me. I smile at his adorableness.

"A-are we friends now?"

"Of course, buddy. I'll be whatever you need me to be."

He smiles and hugs me tightly.

I barely understand him when he says, "You're my bear now."

I pull my head back and raise a questioning eyebrow at him.

"Your what?"

"You are my bear. Your name is Bear, now."

Welp, that does it. I am mush.

My heart melts on the spot. I ruffle his dirty hair and shift him to my other hip. He isn't too heavy for a six-year-old, but the walk and weight need to change.

"I love it. Now, can you tell me *why* on earth you were in the pack prison?"

He messes with my hair again and speaks quieter.

"We came onto the Alpha's land without permission. My brother warned me we could go to jail for it. But…" He shrugged. "Wherever he goes, I go."

I stop in my tracks and look at the child. I can't believe Ulysses put a six-year-old boy in a prison filled with grown men.

Even if he is a rogue, he's just a kid. A terrified little boy.

"Where is your brother?"

"They took them."

"Who's them?"

"The Alpha."

I stop mid-sentence when Coleman approaches. "Where is Westries?"

I give him a strange look. "What do you mean? She is right... behind me..."

I turn around to where my mate was just standing, only to not see her. Her scent is fading, almost vanished. I follow it over to the climbing rope. If she climbed up, she would've walked along the metal beams to the maintenance ladder. Which is right next to the...

Pack prison.

"Coleman, Jake, Owen. Westries went to the prison. She cannot, under any circumstances, be down there. Who knows what the hell she is getting into?"

We race through the door and to the prison.

I should've been watching her. I know how daring she is.

Plus, she is a trouble magnet. Axel is fuming that she blatantly left us. As soon as we pass through the metal door, the rogue wolves yell and jeer. My focus is only on where my mate has gotten off to.

"Westries is in here. I can smell her."

Her scent is everywhere. She must have gone down every row.

"*Westries.* Where the hell are you?"

I track her down the secondary stairs. This is where I find her, kneeling by a cell. She stands and crosses her arms.

Instead of apologizing, she has the audacity to bark an order. "Open the cell."

"Where have you been?" I hit her with a barrage of questions, yelling loud enough for the words to echo. I almost felt bad, but she came down to a prison without thinking of the consequences.

The little minx is unfazed. She repeats her command, as if I'm a servant. This is getting us nowhere. So, I try a gentler approach. This riles her up more than before.

"*Ulysses.* Open. The. Door."

It's then I think to look inside the cell she's hyper-focused on. Toward the back and in the shadows, there is a huddled figure, smaller than the rest of the prison guests. I try to recall who this might be, but I've left the inmate detail on my subordinates while I focus on other matters.

When I fail to move fast enough for her liking, she orders Paul instead. "Open the door."

"Luna, I-I can't it is not safe."

She stares death at him and crosses her arms. I swear even I almost cowered at the power in her voice. Not that I'd ever admit it.

Fine, brave one. You want in, I'll allow it.

When I offer no argument, Paul jumps forward and opens the door. Westries walks straight in. I am ready, should this rogue decide to attack, though.

In the back corner of the cell is a little rogue boy. I'm mortified to realize I have only a vague recollection of my men saying they'd caught some trespassers recently.

Had I been so preoccupied to not hear it was a child they'd captured?

Westries' fury is palpable when she shoots hate filled daggers my way. She picks up the small boy, and he freaks out. She only holds him tighter, whispering soothing words to him.

The little boy clings to her like a spider monkey. She brushes past me and when Jake and Owen stand in her way, she orders them to move. I mind link with them.

Do as she says.

They listen to their Luna and let her pass with the sniffling boy. As soon as she is out of earshot, I speak.

"Jake, Owen. Follow her."

They nod and walk out of the prison.

"Coleman, who was that kid?"

"He was the rogue who trespassed with his brother a few weeks back."

Damn. I am in so much trouble with Westries.

I nod, scratching my neck. The optics on this are bad. I am not so hardened that my heart didn't clench at the sight of that small, ragged child locked alone in this wretched cell.

Surely, my mate cannot believe otherwise.

"And where is his brother now?"

"The questioning ward, Alpha."

"Send him extra rations."

I make my way back toward the pack house. I am in no hurry to get there, and I slow Coleman's pace with my own.

Coleman curses under his breath and exclaims, "How did she even know about that place?"

"Like hell if I know. All I do know is that she is pissed."

"Yeah, angry mates are no fun. Believe me. When I said Jackie's parents were overbearing, I nearly died from the screaming."

"Great…"

We walk the rest of the way in silence and part ways when the pack house comes into view. I search the immediate rooms for my mate. The last place I try is her bedroom, where I hear the shower running.

I knock hesitantly. I don't *think* she will yell at me. She might smartass me to death, but she cannot be mad at me for something I knew nothing about.

"Bellator? You in there?"

"Go away."

I slowly open the door to see Westries standing before her bed, folding a pile of jeans and shirts.

"Listen, I'm sorry about all that."

She crosses her arms.

Yep. Definitely pissed.

Axel growls in my head at her questioning of my dominance.

She cranes her head forward. "For?"

Isn't it obvious?

I sigh in resignation. "I didn't know he was in there. Well, I knew, but I am pretty sure I did not know how old he was."

She rolls her eyes and scoffs at me.

"Ulysses. He is *six* years old. How the *hell* did he even get put in there?"

"He and his brother trespassed on our land, and we arrested them."

She stomps closer to me with a renewed fury blazing in her eyes. "So, because some *kids* trespassed on your precious land, you put a *six-year-old* in a prison meant for full-grown werewolf adults? He hasn't even turned yet. That is really fucked up."

Axel is becoming unruly. A loud growl erupts from my chest. Westries doesn't even flinch and instead shoves me away with one palm.

"Don't you growl at me. I've been around werewolves for a long time, and your growls don't scare me. You're going to have to try a lot harder than that."

I grasp both her shoulders and pull her to me, getting straight in her face. "I am your mate and your King. You will respect me. NEVER raise your voice at me."

Westries wrenches free and steps back from my hold.

"I have a *President*, not a king. We *humans* got rid of those tyrants a long time ago. And as far as I am concerned," she inhales, then yells, "I have no mate."

That is the last straw.

It is my last coherent thought. In a flash, I have enveloped her in a rough embrace. Axel and I sink our canines into the tender flesh between our mate's throat and shoulder. She gasps for breath, tearing at my shirt. Axel sinks his teeth deeper into her neck. Her hands fall away limp, and she collapses into my arms.

As I stare down at her in shock, the bathroom door opens and out walks a little boy with wet hair and baggy clothes.

His already pallid face blanches and his eyes go wide when he sees Westries gasping for breath. He charges at me and unleashes a flurry of punches on the back of my legs.

He wails. "What did you do to my Bear?"

He abandons his assault and squirms around me to get to Westries. The boy tugs her shirt hem and begs her to wake up.

I feel for her pulse. She is not dead, but she is passed out. I lower myself down to my knees, taking Westries with me and supporting her head with my arm. All the while, the small boy cries pitifully.

I mind link with my most trusted few. "Coleman, Jackie, Cade, Hannah, Spencer. I need you in Westries' room, fast. It's an emergency."

"Yes, Alpha."

Within ten seconds, the five of them barrel into Westries' room. The little boy backs up in fear and squats next to the bedside table.

"What the hell happened in here?"

"What does it look like?" I ask in annoyance.

I am on the ground with my mate's head in my lap and Spencer hurries to my side and checks for a pulse.

To Hannah and Jackie, I nod in the boy's direction and they busy themselves with coaxing him out of the corner.

Coleman, in a low voice, asks, "Did you mark her?"

I meet his gaze, then look away. Ashamed. "Yes, Axel and I lost control and marked her. Why did she pass out?"

"Why do you think, genius? She is *human*. You are an Alpha King. Read between the lines."

Aubrey, no doubt eavesdropping outside the door, storms in, verbal guns blazing.

"You need to learn how to control your temper because after this, I'll be shocked if she decides to even stay here with you."

She folds her arms and shakes her head in disgust. Axel growls at the thought of our mate leaving us and my eyes flash gold.

"Mate is not leaving us."

"Then control your damn temper."

Just as I open my mouth to warn her of her place, Westries shoots up, gasping for air. Everyone lets out a breath I don't think we knew we were holding. She is dazed and her wild eyes search every face in the room as she stands. Her wobbly legs give out and I catch her.

She notices it's me and shoves me away and stumble-walks backward toward her bed. When she leaves my arms, I am instantly colder. The small boy in the corner crawls out and runs to Westries, jumping in her arms. She falls back onto the bed and pulls the boy closer.

"Don't leave me again bear, everyone always leaves…"

It is like the child's need for her restores her strength. She straightens her back and hugs him. "Never, baby."

She stands, still holding the child, and almost falls over. Instinct has me at her side in an instant to steady her. Again, she shoves me off with her free arm. She walks toward the door, but Spencer and Cade block her.

"If I wasn't holding Patrick right now, you wouldn't have your *balls*."

They both gulp and move over to the side.

"You are not going anywhere." At Jackie's wordless admonishment, I soften my words. "You need to be checked out."

"Oh no, I don't. At least not by you."

Jackie tries. "You passed out. You need a doctor."

She scoffs and hands Patrick to Aubrey, who tries to calm down the whimpering boy. Westries charges toward me and stops, only to wave a finger in my face. She sways a little, as if drunk.

"Listen, wolfy king. I have survived perfectly fine in the supernatural world *without* you. So, I don't need you now. Werewolves have done enough, thank you. And this," she points to the black and gray imprint mark forming on her neck, "Is only proving my point."

She returns to Aubrey, who hands her back Patrick, and storms out of her room with Aubrey on her heels.

Before leaving, Aubrey—perhaps emboldened by her Luna —speaks. "For the King of werewolves, you are pretty stupid, you know." She slams the door behind her for added effect.

Jackie asks, "Should we follow them, Alpha?"

I run my hands through my hair. A migraine is starting and I rub my temples.

"Yes, Jackie and Hannah, go with them. Try to… I don't know, smooth this over? Convince her not to hate me, I guess?"

They nod and leave to find wherever my mate has gone off to. I pace the room while the boys watch. No one speaks. When it's clear I'm not talking, Cade ventures the question on all their minds.

"Did you… force mark her?"

"Yes. I force marked her."

Coleman mutters from underneath his breath. "Well, this will not go well…"

I explode. "You don't think I *know* that? My mate hates our kind. Hunts and kills them, for fuck's sake. She won't give me a chance. Not now, anyway. That wall I'd been chipping away at is now ten times higher."

They exchange glances, but Spencer is the one to engage. "Well, have you even talked about what it means to be Luna Queen? And I mean actually *talked* about it where she completely understands? Also, the time at the office does not count."

I think about it for a moment. We've talked *around* things. But I've yet to give her the details. Now that she is marked, there is no more time for ambiguity. Westries must know her role in this life.

My silence is answer enough for Spencer. "Exactly. And with this new kid, it is only going to be more complicated."

I grunt in agreement.

"She *is* oddly protective of that kid. And why the hell did you two move when she told you to? I directly ordered you not to."

Spencer and Cade shuffle uncomfortably.

"She used an Alpha voice. Our wolves forced us to. Is that even possible?"

Coleman scoffs and crosses his arms.

"We are way past *possible*."

"No kidding…"

I rub my hands over my face as my migraine grows.

"Well, what are we going to do now?"

"Let's start by finding our mates."

All four of us nod and walk out of the bedroom and follow the scent of food cooking in the kitchen. As we approach, the faint sound of giggles reaches my ears. We enter to discover Aubrey and Westries frying up what looks like bananas, while Hannah and Jackie slice apples. Giggling turns to guffaws at the table, where Corrine is laughing at Patrick, who is covered in white powder.

"Well, then. What do we have here?"

Hannah grins at Cade and walks over to him, kissing his cheek.

"The kids were hungry, so Westries is teaching us how to make plantains and fried fritters."

Westries, as if nothing unusual had just occurred upstairs, smiles while taking a wet rag to Patrick's face, wiping off whatever he was covered with.

"Yeah, and those two tried to open the powdered sugar and failed." Aubrey laughs, pointing at the little kids.

A cell phone buzzes. Westries pulls out her iPhone and casually looks at the caller ID.

Who could be calling my mate?

Coleman raises an eyebrow. "Where did you…"

She waves a dismissive hand at him. "You guys suck at searching bags. Excuse me for a second." Westries walks into the living room, answering the phone.

I force nonchalance. "So, what else is happening?" I asked, leaning up against the cabinets.

"We were just cooking, Alpha. Your mate is really nice and, umm, less violent than I expected." Hannah says, within the arms of her mate.

I nod and look back towards my mate, pacing back and forth. *Don't say anything. Just let her be.*

"So, what are we going to do with b-o-y?" Jackie asks from her bar stool where she is still cutting apples.

"I can spell, you know. I am six, not five."

Everyone chuckles at the two children now playing with an iPad on the kitchen floor as if they've known each other forever.

I open the pack link so we can talk freely.

"Well, he should never have been in the prisons, to begin with, and that is on me."

"That's on us. One of us should have known." Coleman emphasizes reassuringly.

"I think he is adorable, and Corrine seems to enjoy having him around."

"How did she find out?"

Aubrey answers. *"She just ran down here and started talking to him. They seem to just have clicked."*

We all glance at each other knowingly.

"You don't think…"

"Could they…"

"I guess we won't know for a few years.

I don't know how I feel about the possibility of my little sister having a mate with Patrick yet.

"Aw, they are so cute," Aubrey says, jumping up and down a little.

They are still kids, and they might not even be mates. They are just sitting on the floor together playing Minecraft while petting Griffin, who has happily made his way into the kitchen.

"Hey."

We break the mind link to see Westries trying to get our attention.

"I have to go into town."

I raise an eyebrow. "Why?"

"I am meeting someone. And before you ask, no, you can't know who it is."

I don't bother telling her I will find out who it is, because it will piss her off more. Plus, I'm completely thrown by her overall attitude. Twenty minutes ago, I thought she might never speak to me again. Now, she's acting… normal.

Normal for her, at least.

I risk invoking her anger with another question. "Can I know *why* you need to go?"

"Meeting an old friend." She stares at me with a blank face. However, a tiny speck of mischief twinkles in her eyes.

Jackie, caught between us like a tennis umpire, bursts out with, "Oh, I have an idea. How about we *all* go, and it can be a fun outing for everyone? Plus, Patrick needs some clothes."

Aubrey agrees with Jackie's idea, and they enthusiastically plan where we are all going to go.

I sigh and glance at my watch. It's a little past 1:00.

"So, what *are* you doing? If this is an escape plan, you will fail," Coleman says, crossing his arms at his Luna.

Westries looks up from her phone and scoffs.

"That is on a need-to-know basis, and you don't need to know. Also, if I wanted to escape, I would've done it a long time ago. Underestimating me will be your downfall."

I can't help but smile in pride at my mate.

She is a fighter. I don't doubt it for a second. I glance at her neck and see a large black and gray wolf surrounded by tribal swirls that match her arm. My wolf wags his tail in delight at the sight of our mark on Westries.

"Can we at least know where and when?"

She huffs, but answers. "Today at four P.M. in the shopping mall."

Jackie squeals in delight. "That works perfectly. We can leave in, like, thirty minutes and go straight to the mall. Stop at the food court for a snack and then shop. At, like, four you can go meet the mystery person, and then we'll go home." The excitement in her voice is almost scary. "Alright. Everyone, meet back here in, like, twenty minutes and we will leave."

So much for never going to the mall again.

Everyone nods and heads back to whatever they were doing. Spencer and Coleman walk out, whispering to each other.

"She is going to kill me with shopping."

"I heard THAT."

"Run…" Jackie chases the boys out with a spatula.

Aubrey and Westries continue to fry up the bananas while I watch the entire surreal scene.

They scoop the browned bananas out of the pan and place them on a plate covered in paper towels. Hannah sprinkles powdered sugar on them. The apples sizzle as Westries dips each one in cinnamon before they cool completely. Corrine and Patrick stand and climb on the chairs for a better look. They hold out their bowls and Aubrey gives them both some of each fried fruit.

"Corrine, when you are done, why don't you show Patrick all your toys?"

Both kids nod and run out of the room, mouths full of fruit. The girls are cleaning up when my mate glances at me, then speaks.

"I will do it. You guys go get ready."

"You sure?"

Westries nods and Hannah and Aubrey leave. She washes the dishes and loads them into the dishwasher, keeping her back to me. The tension in the air is thicker than the grease in her frying pan.

If you won't talk first, I will.

"Where did you learn all this?"

"My Abuela." She jerks her chin at the plate on the counter. "You can have one. I promise I didn't poison it."

I take one apple and pop it into my mouth. My mouth waters in delight. "Wow, this is great."

"Thanks." she says, still not making eye contact with me.

"Don't hate me." I hesitate, then add. "Please."

She turns around and looks into my eyes. Like she is trying to decipher my every thought. She bites her lip and rubs her teeth together, still not breaking contact. "It would have been nice to have had a choice, you know."

She drops her dishtowel on the counter and walks towards the door, but I block her.

"If I could rewind time, and do it over… do it *right*, I would. But I can't. Our people cannot keep waiting for their Luna. Their lives depend on you. Whether you want this or not, you need to understand your importance." I force her to meet my gaze. "They won't survive without you. Please understand that I didn't choose this for you."

A bitter laugh escapes through her lips. "That's how it *always* is, isn't it? Everything is going great until evil is thrust upon you and everything you love is taken away." Her bottom lip quivers. "A-and you never have a single say in the matter. Because death doesn't discriminate between the sinners and the saints, it just takes and takes and takes."

Her voice breaks, and she pushes past me. I let her. I don't think she was referring to being here. *One day, Bellator, you will tell me.*

CHAPTER 22

WESTRIES

I leave my bedroom—Patrick on my hip—for the kitchen.

"Let's get a snack, shall we?"

Patrick's vigorous nod is reply enough.

To keep myself from falling over or thinking too much about what had just occurred, I engage the wary boy in a debate over what we should eat. We agree on making plantains and fried apples. Meanwhile, I argue with myself in my mind.

I hate him.

No, I don't.

I must escape.

I like it here.

I don't belong to him, or anyone.

He has marked me.

I'll get out of this somehow.

I'm staying.

But I hate him.

No, I lo…

I force my brain to shut off. Minutes later, Hannah, Aubrey, and Jackie join us in the kitchen. It's the start of a steady trickle of company, which I suspect is not at all coincidental. Corrine bounds into the kitchen next and hangs out with Patrick like they are old friends. It is honestly the sweetest thing I have seen in a while. The boys saunter in a few minutes later and make small talk.

Ulysses' eyes are on me, but I ignore him. A conversation about what we were doing drifts over and around me as I wipe powdered sugar off Patrick as Corrine laughs her goofy head off. The scene is that of a perfect, happy, *normal* family, and I find it both comforting and alarming. A vibration in my back pocket halts my thoughts. I check the caller ID on my phone screen.

There are only a few select people who have this number.

Coleman asks, "Where did you get…"

I cut him off. "You guys suck at searching bags. Excuse me for a second."

I leave the room to answer the phone.

My tone is cool. "Well, speak of the devil and she will appear."

"You know you love me," says the familiar voice on the other side of the receiver.

I scoff. "Do I really? I'm not sure."

"Yes, you do. Now I have more intelligence for you. But first tell me, how did your mission go?"

I hesitate, then force confidence into my voice. "Exactly like I wanted."

"You sure? Because I heard you got captured, I was growing worried."

I laugh. "The Royals, they became interested in what I was doing…"

"But you're safe now, right?"

"Define safe."

There is a long pause, and for a second, I suspect Ruby has hung up on me.

"Stop talking in riddles and answer the damn question, Wes."

"Gosh, sorry. They captured me. Happy?"

Ruby's voice explodes through the phone. "How are you not dead? You should be dead right now. Wait. How are you answering my call right now?"

"Chill, Ruby. So, um, it turns out the Alpha is my supposed mate."

There is another uncomfortable, slow silence, and I wait for her senses to snap back together.

"But the only pack there is…"

"Yes." I confirm her train of thought.

"Holy *fuck*. Are you serious right now?"

I pull the phone away because her shouting is like a megaphone in my ear.

"Do I ever joke? No. Now, when can we meet for the file?"

"Today at the mall at four P.M., Starbucks. Will you be able to make it?"

"When have I ever failed?"

"Well, you *did* get captured…"

"I can escape anytime I want, but there are some people I actually like here…"

Again, a blistering silence.

"That's… startling. You hate all of them, except me. I am *special*." She says in a proud tone.

I roll my eyes. "Yes, but you won't be for much longer if this information isn't gold."

"Oh, it always is, babe. See you at four."

We hang up, and I walk back into the kitchen. Everyone is staring at each other.

They must be using a mind link.

I shout. "Hey."

They turn their stares at me.

"I need to go into town."

Ulysses raises his eyebrow. "Why?"

"I need to meet someone. And before you ask, no, you can't know who it is."

He nods but his expression says, *I will figure it out.*

Coleman speaks. "Can I at least know *why* you need to go?"

I keep my gaze locked on Ulysses, expressionless. "Meeting an old friend."

Ulysses and I haven't broken eye contact. I narrow my eyes at him, and he smirks.

Jackie pipes up. "Oh, I have an idea. How about we *all* go, and it can be a fun outing for everyone? Plus, we need to get some clothes for Patrick."

I text Ruby with the updated plan as Jackie and Aubrey talk about what stores and places we will go to. This is not ideal, but Patrick needs clothes other than my shorts and a baggy shirt.

"So, what *are* you doing? If this is an escape plan, you *will* fail," Coleman says, crossing his arms.

I glance up from texting Ruby and scoff. "That is on a need-to-know basis, and *you* don't need to know. Also, if I wanted to escape, I would've done it a long time ago. Underestimating me will be your downfall."

I hit send on my text to Ruby, who is like a sister to me. Her bright red hair and faux innocent brown eyes give her a Disney princess appearance—like Merida from Brave mixed with a touch of Maria Hill from Marvel—but it's thoroughly deceiving. Ruby is a force to be reckoned with.

She is a rogue with no pack, but she hates bad rogues as much as I do. Which is why she helps me destroy them, giving me information and tips. Last I heard from her, she was living in Wisconsin. But that was four months ago, so Ruby could be anywhere now.

"Can we at least know where and when?"

I sigh. "Today at four P.M. in the shopping mall."

Jackie squeals with delight, laying out her whole plan in one breath. The excitement in her voice is unbearable. I feel almost bad for Coleman.

Ulysses takes charge. "Alright, then. Everyone, meet back here in twenty minutes and we will leave."

Everyone nods and I turn back to finishing up the plantains and apples. The boys leave and Jackie chases them out. Hannah, Aubrey, and I finish the food in silence, while Ulysses stares at me. I continue to ignore him. Corrine and Patrick hold up bowls and we serve them. They scarf it down in seconds.

"Corrine, if you are done, why don't you show Patrick all your toys?" Aubrey says. They both nod and run out of the kitchen with Griffin.

That dog is seriously living the dream here.

The girls clean, but I stop them.

"I will do it. You guys go get ready."

"You sure?"

As they leave, I turn away and wash the dishes, loading them into the dishwasher. Ignoring Ulysses, who has remained.

"Where did you learn all this?"

"My Abuela. You can have one. I promise I didn't poison it."

I point over to the two plates of food and Ulysses accepts, taking a bite of one. He moans in delight.

"Wow, this is good."

"Thanks."

"I don't want you to hate me, you know."

I face him, finally making eye contact with him.

What doesn't he comprehend here? Isn't it obvious?

I see he's genuinely clueless, so I say, "I just wish I had a choice."

I walk toward the door, but Ulysses stops me, catching my arm. As soon as his hand touches my skin, butterflies fill my stomach.

It must be the mark.

I was afraid of this. The mark is making it so much harder to reject the mate bond… and it's also making my emotions out of whack.

"I wish you did, too. But too many people's lives count on you. They won't survive without you, whether or not you want this. Please understand that I didn't choose this for you."

He really doesn't get it, does he?

"That's how it always is, isn't it? Everything is going great until evil is thrust upon you and everything you love is taken away. And you never have a single say in the matter. Because death doesn't discriminate between the sinners and the saints, it just takes and takes and takes."

I push past him and walk out of the kitchen to return to my room. As soon as I leave him, my heart aches to go back. I ignore the feeling and trudge up the stairs. When I reach my room, I close the door and pull off my gym clothes and change into my streetwear. It is cold, so I also grabbed my leather jacket.

From my bedside drawer, I grab my pistol and load the ammunition, then tuck the weapon in my pants holster on my back and cover it with my jacket. I grab a pair of socks and my combat boots, throw my hair up into a high ponytail, and check the clock.

I have ten minutes, so I hunt for Patrick and Corrine. Four doors down, I hear laughter. In the middle of the room are the two little troublemakers.

"What are you two doing in here?"

"Bear. Come here and look at this."

Patrick skips over to me and grabs my hand, leading me to Corrine's iPad. They are watching the old vines and completely enjoying it.

"Oh my, you found the *vines*. We're all doomed."

They giggle as I grab the iPad, showing them the infamous MAGCON boys. Knowing we have time to kill, I lay down on my stomach with them and watch some vines. Ten minutes later, Jackie is screaming at us to hurry.

"Let's go, you two, before Jackie has a cow."

They jump up and run downstairs, chasing each other. I smile. They remind me of my siblings. Ulysses, Coleman, Jackie, Cade, Spencer, Hannah, and Aubrey are already back in the kitchen, waiting.

"You are late."

"Um, sorry?"

Jackie drags me to the car, everyone else following behind.

She loops her arm through mine and squeezes. "You know this is going to cut into our shopping time."

I squeeze back and pat her hand. "A true pity."

"Don't smart-mouth me, young lady." She punches in the garage code and the doors open.

"Boys in that car, girls in this one. That means you too, Corrine."

"No, Patrick and I wanted to sit together."

"Nope. Now, get in."

Corrine pouts but gets into one of the Sequoias. I glance over to Cade pleadingly and he gets the signal.

"Come on, little man, we can have quality man time."

Patrick shyly looks over at me and I nod reassuringly. We all get into our designated cars and pull away. The car ride is quite a spectacle. The girls sing the entire way, and I *do not*. They sing everything from Frozen to Spice Girls, with about nine out of ten songs very, *very* out of key.

There are a few songs I *would've* sung to, but I am not that comfortable with them… yet. Thanks to impeccable timing, we arrive at the mall as the song "Call Me Maybe" comes on and we exit the vehicle.

Man, I despise that song.

The boys pull up behind us and climb out. Corrine and Patrick are like magnets, because the moment we are out, they are together again.

"Alright, we will divide into four squads. Team Red, Green, Blue, and Magenta."

"Magenta?"

"Yes, Aubrey, *magenta*. We will also be…"

Coleman steps behind his mate, pulling her into his arms. "Or we could just go inside first, baby."

"Yeah, that works too…"

Despite myself, I smile at their adorableness. We move like a pack—Ulysses at the front, me to his right, and the rest flanking us like bowling pins—toward the doors.

"I didn't know you could smile." Ulysses smirks down at me.

The damn butterflies are flapping their wings in my stomach again.

"I *do* smile. Just give me a reason to."

"Oh, I will."

I narrow my eyes at him as we walk through the automatic doors. Audible gasps follow our entrance into the mall.

People, or *wolves,* bow their heads in deference as we pass them. It's all to do with Ulysses, of course. But I'm hyper-aware and uncomfortable with the curious eyes turning my way.

Ulysses, sensing my discomfort, whispers, "They are staring at you because of your scent."

"My… scent?"

Ulysses runs a finger along my throat. "You are human and have an Alpha mark. They now know who my mate is."

Of course. How could I forget?

I rub my neck but then yank my hand back because of the burning sensation.

"Does it hurt?"

I try to harden my heart against the sweet concern in his voice. "Take a wild guess."

"You should've told me. I could've taken you to the pack doctor."

I sniff and raise my chin. "I'll live."

He nods and Jackie grabs my arm, whirling me in her direction like we're square dancing.

Great. Let's just add whiplash to my list of aches and pains.

"Come *on*. We need to focus. Patrick needs clothes and you are helping."

Ulysses says, "We will be out here."

The boys sit on the benches outside the store.

I wish I could do that.

We walk into a store and Jackie and Hannah go straight to the racks of little boy pants.

Patrick, Corrine, and I stand at the entrance like three lost little lambs.

Patrick's voice is wobbly. "My mom used to do all the shopping for me."

Crap. I guess I have to be the adult here, don't I?

I ruffle his hair, smile down at Corrine, and take their little hands in mine. "Same, kid. I am clueless too. We can learn together."

The two kids nod and together, we go through all the graphic t-shirts. This is the only section I would ever shop in. Marvel shirts are life and jeans are a 'go-to' leg wear. Between us all, we find ten pairs he likes.

Corrine does most of the talking, telling us all about her fashion expertise.

I interrupt. "What about this?" I hold up a long sleeve shirt with Captain America and Bucky on it.

Corrine grabs it and pairs it with dark-washed jeans.

"See? They match. The colors can never clash when designing ensembles."

"Whatever would we do without you?"

Corrine giggles, and I search for Hannah, Jackie, and Aubrey and spot them at the changing rooms with piles of clothes waving us over.

Oh, good Lord, I pray for this boy.

"Come on, we better go try some of this stuff on."

How could they find so many outfits? We have only been here for twenty minutes. How did they do all this?

"Do I have to try all that on?" Patrick asks, backing away.

I would be scared too.

"How about this? We try on just a few to see what size you are, then you can just pick through the rest for what you like." I intervene, trying to cool the dangerous situation.

"Good thinking, Westries."

I hand Patrick his superhero outfit, and he walks into the dressing room. A few seconds later, he walks out again.

"I like it and I think it fits."

"Aww, he is so cute."

"Come here, Patrick."

He walks toward me, and I pull off the tags. Jackie's eyes go wide.

"Chill, Jackie. I am going to pay for them. He just needs clothes other than my gym shorts to walk around in."

"Oh, good because I thought… well, we have money, so yeah. Alright, ladies, let's show him what we found."

The three girls hold up outfit after outfit after outfit. Most of the clothes seemed like Boy Band or Justin Bieber clothes that both Patrick and I promptly rejected. In the end, we keep all the stuff Corrine and Patrick pick out and a few outfits the girls found. We move to the cashier, and I pull out my credit card.

Right before I give it to the lady, someone from behind me grabs it and replaces it with theirs.

Ulysses.

His voice tickles my ear. "This is on me."

"You don't have to do this, Ulysses. *I* can pay for it."

"But it's my job to take care of my mate."

He then did the unexpected and kissed my head… and I *let* him.

What is happening to me?

I'm in a daze as the lady hands us the four bags and we leave the store, but I still have enough sense to check my watch. 2:17. I have one hour and forty-three minutes. At the door, we meet up with Cade, Coleman, and Spencer, and resume our mall walk.

Internally, I marvel at the surrealness of the scene.

I'm just walking, talking, and shopping in the stores with a pack of werewolves. Nothing to see here, folks. Totally normal for me.

We only pause for Jackie and Aubrey to run into every other store, where they almost always walk back out with bags of all sizes.

At one such stop, Ulysses asks, "Do you hate shopping, too?"

"Is it that obvious?" I smirk.

He grins back. "Yes, and now imagine your sister having the pin number on your account."

I snort at that. I can imagine Aubrey maxing a credit card out easily. Ulysses blinks at me with shock.

"What?"

"You *laughed*."

"I do have emotions, you know."

A slow smile spreads all the way up to his eyes and my heart stutters at the way he's gazing at me. Since I don't know what to do, I break the unexpectedly intimate moment by blurting the first thing that comes to mind.

"Who's hungry?"

We all sit down at the food court and Hannah and Aubrey come back with cinnamon twists for Corrine and Patrick. The rest talk about what's for dinner, pack training, and other stuff, while I listen, stuffing twists in my mouth.

Hannah announces, "Alright, I have one more stop, and it is *imperative* that we make this stop."

The boys and I shift nervously. We all want the same thing, to finish up here and go home.

Home? Am I referring to it as home?

"Where exactly, Hannah?" Cade asks.

"Well, I called in a special favor and the owner of the bridal shop has closed today just for us."

The life drains from my face and the air in my lungs fades. Hannah takes one glance at me and clarifies.

"Not for a *wedding* dress but for a coronation dress."

I let out a breath I didn't know I was holding.

"Boys, you take the bags to the car and meet us there later."

"Wait, but…"

Jackie and Hannah grab me, pulling me to my doom. The boy's laughter follows us. They will regret this, I swear. The three girls drag me through the mall till we reach a huge corner store.

I gulp as they drag me inside the "princess' dress outbreak." The older woman greets us at the door.

"Hello, Miss Lane."

"Beta Female Jackie, Delta Female Hannah, it truly is an honor. And who is this? Is she who I *think* she is?"

I stand there awkwardly as the old lady approaches.

"I have heard the rumors, but I never expected her to be this lovely."

Heat spreads across my cheeks as she takes my hand.

"I truly believe you will be a grand asset to this kingdom and to us humans."

I raise a questioning eyebrow at her.

"I am a human too, my dear. My mate was a Warrior Elite in the previous King's reign. I can only imagine your surprise when you found out you were the mate of the Alpha King. It scared the dickens out of me when it happened. Just imagine a young fashion designer in her studio working, when a *very* handsome man bursts through the door and swooped me up in his arms."

She laughs for a second, gazing into the distance.

"I threw a good number of bobbins and fabric squares at him before I gave him a chance to talk. But anyway, enough about me. Let us find you a coronation dress fit for a Queen. Girls, I will let you browse. Grab any dress you like. You, my dear, are coming with me."

The girls disappear, and Miss Lane takes me to the back, where the fitting rooms are. She sits me down on a plush chair and sits across from me.

"Tea?"

I nod and she pores us two cups of tea. By the smell it's chamomile. She hands me one cup and takes a seat.

"So, how did you take it?"

I bite my lip and take a sip of tea, waiting for her answer.

"Well, let's just say I tried to escape multiple times." She laughs to herself, most likely reminiscing in a memory.

"I know that feeling."

"So, you have accepted him as your mate, then?"

"I don't really know yet…"

"Well, he must really want you to stay. You have a very large mark. The larger the mark, the more passion that was used. And you are here, aren't you?"

I shrug and sip my tea. A few moments later, the girls came in with at least a few dozen dresses. Everything from short cocktail dresses to the big fluffy demon dresses, which reminded me of Charlotte's dress from Princess and The Frog.

"Holy…"

"Well, girls, you certainly grabbed a large assortment here. Before we start, we need to figure out what color palette works with the Luna's skin tone."

Miss Lane grabs a huge binder and holds it up to my face. She flips through a few pages before showing the one she picked to the girls, who all nod in agreement.

"So Westries, what sort of dress are you thinking of right now?"

I throw my hands wide, palms up. I would wear pants if it were up to me, but no one asked me that.

"Come on Wes. You always know what you want. Why is now any different?"

Aubrey yells at me while holding up her top pick.

"Okay, fine. Only if I *had* to pick. I don't want to look like a princess. I want to look like a formerly evil queen who reluctantly redeemed herself for the side of good."

Miss Lane says, "I think I can make that work."

Jackie and Hannah giggle and Aubrey grumbles to herself. I just sort of sat there awkwardly. Then they organize the dresses on three different racks.

"Oh, could she please still try this one on?"

Jackie holds up a bubble gum pink dress with ruffles and sequins. I grimace. It is so atrocious.

"Jackie, you try to put me in *that,* and I will cut you."

"PLEASEEEEEEE. Just try it."

I shake my head no, warding off the blinding sparkles. I am not looking to be a pageant queen.

"You might *actually* like it."

"No, no, and *no.*"

"Aubrey, tell her."

At that moment, the rest of the gang saunters in. Coleman and Cade go directly to their mates. Coleman wraps his arms around Jackie and Cade does the same with Hannah.

"Babe, tell Westries that she should at *least* try the dress."

"What dress?"

She points to the dress on the rack, and he feigns a retching sound. She elbows his stomach and pouts into his arms.

"Um, it is *very*... pink."

"That would be code for *no*..." Spencer mutters under his breath. A few people snicker, including me.

"And it doesn't match the Luna's palette, so it's out, anyway."

I sit mute as the girls bicker. Ulysses, seeing my discomfort, sits beside me.

"This is *your* fault." I hiss at him, slapping his arm. He chuckles a deep husky laugh and crosses his arms, leaning back into our chair.

"No, it was Jackie, Hannah, and Aubrey's doing. I didn't even know about it till you did."

"Yeah, well, you left me with crazy thing one, two, *and* three. I thought mates were supposed to protect each other, but you threw me to the wolves. *Literally.*"

I slouch and drop my chin in my palms, pouting.

My death will be by tulle and satin. I just know it.

"Aww, I'm sorry, Bellator. I'll do better, I promise."

He wraps his arm around my shoulders. The move is so natural, so *right*, that I let him.

More than let him, welcome him.

"Alright, we will start with the fall color palette, then move to skin tones."

"Still your fault." I whisper to Ulysses, while Jackie grabs my arm, drags me away again.

He calls out, "You *should* try on the pink one."

I whip around, staring daggers at Ulysses, who leans back in the chair, an amused, smug smile on his lips and mischief in his eyes. Miss Lane pulls me into a dressing room and helps me into the first dress.

Why I am complying with this torture, I don't know. This is worse than being stabbed.

She zips up the back and I walk out to the twenty beady eyes staring at me. No one speaks or moves.

I fold my arms in front of me. "I feel stupid…"

Aubrey snorts and Hannah speaks. "It's very pretty on you."

I am wearing a beautiful silver mermaid gown with one sleeve. The dress *is* stunning, but it isn't me.

As if there is a dress out there that is *me.*

"The color doesn't work with your eyes."

We all turn to Corrine, who is like the 'Mr. Thinker' statue, trying to contemplate the meaning of the universe.

"Let's try something with more color, like a fiery red or burgundy." Corrine says waving her hands around dramatically.

"I like that," Miss Lane says, leading me back to the dressing room.

God have mercy on my soul.

Miss Lane helps me into gown number two. This gown is a dark crimson, A-line ball gown. It is not absurdly poofy, but it's close. I walk out again and this time, the boys comment on it.

"You're like a radish with a head." Patrick says, tilting his head from side to side.

Cade and Spencer try to stifle a laugh, and so do I. Corrine slaps his arm.

"Patrick, you cannot say that to a girl. The only right answer is *you're beautiful*. Right, Jackie?"

Jackie and Corrine high-five each other proudly. I can't help but smile. This is pretty entertaining, to be honest. It's like the Kardashians, but fewer tantrums.

"Oh, sorry. You're like a beautiful radish, Bear."

He smiles to himself, proud of his good save. Miss Lane takes me away again. The next dress is a flesh tone with sequins. I walk out again, waiting for the comments.

"I like it. It's like mom's coronation dress, minus shoulder pads."

That Corrine thinks this dress is like Molly's makes me want to gag. I don't want my dress to be like hers.

"For that exact reason, I am saying no," Spencer says from the floor. I mentally mutter a ditto. We go to the back again and about a dozen dresses and a million comments later, I walk out again.

"It's not your color. If you count that as a color…"

"I think the shape is flattering…"

Everyone is talking or arguing, or both. I am bored out of my mind and start meandering around the shop in this navy-blue high low. The further away from the bunch I get, the less of a headache I have. I search through the racks of dozens of exquisite, colorful gowns. One, in particular, catches my eye.

"Do you like that one?"

I jump around to be met by Miss Lane and her warm smile.

"Oh, sorry. I didn't mean to wander away. I just…"

"You are bored. I understand that. You would probably rather be someplace else, right?"

I nod shyly, hoping I didn't offend.

"They are a tough bunch, aren't they? Let's try this one. Something tells me it will drop jaws."

She grabs the gown from the rack, and we return yet again to the changing room, the gang still talking and arguing.

I slip on the forest green ball gown with a floral off-the-shoulder design. I gaze in the changing room mirror and barely recognize myself. If it weren't for my very distinct tattoos, I would believe it was a perfect Instagram picture.

"Just as I thought, *stunning.*"

She undoes my ponytail and lets my mess of hair fall to my shoulders. It feels like a moment from *Say Yes to the Dress* when Randy dolls up a bride.

"Let's show them. Yes?"

She opens the curtains, and gasps erupt throughout the room. I can feel my face warm as everyone stares at me.

I force a laugh. "Is it *that* bad?"

Silence. Then…

"It's gorgeous."

"Who picked this one?"

"It is perfect."

"What about you, Alpha? You haven't said anything this entire time."

Ulysses gapes at me, his hand covering his chin. Then gets up. He strides over to me and traces my jaw with his thumb. I feel like fireworks are going off in my head. He stares into my eyes and everything and everyone fades away.

His voice is husky. "Stunning."

I gulp. "Yeah, it's a beautiful dress."

"I wasn't talking about the dress."

My heart skips a beat and my face flames.

"Aww…" Aubrey says, breaking the silence from behind us.

"Perfect. Now we only have one more dress to find."

Ulysses' hand drops and he moves aside, and when he does, it feels like the sun has moved behind the clouds. But then—as if sensing my feelings—he positions me in front of him, and his warmth radiates through my back. This all plays out in plain sight, for all to see.

Step away from him, damn it. No, stay.

Despite the emotional riot in my brain, I force myself to act as if this is all totally normal. "Another? Jackie, I can't do this for another hour."

"Well, too bad, because you need two dresses. One for the ceremony and one for the reception."

I allow myself to lean back into the arms holding me. Ulysses buries his face into my mark, and I melt into him. I never would have thought this possible, yet it feels so right.

"Was there another you maybe liked?"

I shrug. Everything is sort of fuzzy. Change dresses, receive comments, change dresses, then receive comments, repeat. Jackie and Hannah go through the gowns, trying to find a less *formal* one for the reception. Although I am one hundred percent sure that it will be very formal. Patrick stands up and walks toward me. I lean down to his level, my dress spreading out in every direction.

"I think you look like a princess, Bear."

"Thank you, Patrick."

He traces my arm tattoo at the top and ends up at my hand. "I like this. They make you look like a warrior princess."

Miss Lane gasps, snaps her fingers, then runs to the back. I raise an eyebrow. Seconds later, she comes running back with a black dress covered in lace swirl patterns.

"This one is perfect. I just finished it. I hadn't put it on display yet because I wanted it to go to someone special. *You* are the perfect woman to wear it."

I stand up and walk back toward the dressing room and slip on the gown. It is a tight-fit black silk dress with a long slit and black lace swirls. It has one sleeve and a cape across the other arm, with a low-cut back. The dress reveals all my tattoos in the best way possible, and there are no sequins. It is gorgeous. I walk out for the one-hundredth time and Corrine jumps up this time.

"You're like the Evil Queen from *Once Upon a Time*."

"Is that a good thing?" I laugh, darting glances around the room.

I mean, it sort of is my dream goal.

"YES." Aubrey and Corrine shout.

"Miss Lane, these dresses are unquestionably beautiful, but I can't afford them."

"That is why I am paying for them."

"No, Ulysses, you have bought *enough* for me."

"Too bad." He smirks.

"Neither of you are paying because they are on the house. It would be an honor to have the Luna Queen wearing any of my designs, *two* nevertheless. That's more than I could ever ask for."

I dip my head down, humbled by her generosity. "Thank you."

She pulls me in for a hug and whispers in my ear. "No, thank you for everything… Avenger."

I pull away and stare at her in shock. She winks and packages the dresses back into their appropriate bags.

Jackie says, "Westries? It's 4:07."

"Shit."

I run back to the changing room and put my jeans on again. I walk out and hand Miss Lane the dress, thanking her again. As I dash out, Ulysses stops me.

"I will meet you by the fountains in half an hour."

I counter. "Two hours."

"Forty-five minutes."

"Fine, I'll be there."

Ulysses pulls me into his chest and buries his head in my neck, inhaling my scent. I freeze, not knowing what to do. I gently push him away and he then reluctantly releases me.

"Okay, go." A kaleidoscope of emotions passes across his eyes, and I suddenly see him, *truly* see him.

He is as confused and overwhelmed as I am.

I smile at him, trying to convey a silent reassurance, and rush off toward the food court.

One thing Ruby hates is tardiness, and I know I am going to hear an earful from her for this. I reach Starbucks and walk inside. I am not a fan of fancy frou-frou coffee, so I skip the line for a booth and act like I'm doing something important. Within two minutes, someone from behind me jabs my shoulder.

"*Star Trek* is better than *Star Wars*."

"It is not."

I whip around to be met by a smiling face and two coffees. I stand up to hug her.

"Hey there, Killer."

"Right back at you, Dork."

We sit down across from each other, and she slides the familiar logo cup to my side. "Black."

"Thanks." I raise the hot cup and take a large gulp.

"You are late, by the way."

"By ten minutes. And I was busy being held *captive*."

"Doing what?"

"Trying on dresses." I mutter under my breath. She laughs and sips her iced coffee.

"Liar. You hate dresses. What were you *really* doing?"

"It's true. You and I know I hate dresses, but supposedly, I need one, *two* actually for the coronation ceremony."

Her eyes go wide. "So, you are going through with it? You accepted him?"

"No! I just sort of went with it while we were at the mall. Jackie pulled a fast one on me, okay?"

"Really? Because your mark says *otherwise*." She smirks, then sips her coffee with a taunting glint in her eyes.

"It was an *accident*. I was yelling at him and his wolf, and Axel acted possessive blah, blah, blah. He tried to eat my neck. And what about you, Miss 'I am a rogue and don't need a mate? Miss *I'm gonna act like a crazy cat lady on the road*? I am going to *laugh my ass off* the day you get stuck with someone like Ulysses. Then you can suffer along with me. Oh, and trust me, I will never let you forget it."

She just scowls at me and sips her coffee.

"You will *never* laugh because I don't have a mate."

"Look at *me*. Werewolf huntress of all things and now mated to the Alpha King. The impossible can happen and you better be ready."

She sticks her tongue out at me, and I laugh.

"How is Griffin, by the way?"

"Lazy as ever and living the dream. He made friends with Ulysses' kid sister and has been playing dress up and having tea parties for the past week."

She nods.

"So, about that information…"

"Oh yeah, that. I don't have any…"

"*Ruby.*"

"Sorry. I never said I did, technically…"

I narrow my eyes at her, and she throws her hands up in the air in defense.

"*Fine.* I know one thing. There are feral rogue wolves rumored to be lurking around here. That's all I know."

"Feral?"

"Yep," she says, swirling her straw in the now half-empty cup.

"Your *favorite* kind. How do you plan to get out of the pack house to, you know?"

"I'll figure that out later. Right now, I am enjoying not having guards with me 24/7."

"Like them?" She points to the two boys who are not being very incognito outside the glass window. Cade and Coleman, I should've known.

I slap my hands on the table. "Alright, let's go."

I grab Ruby's hand and lead her to the back employee's exit.

I grumble the entire way. "I can't believe Ulysses sent them here."

"Well, you did let him mark you."

"I did not *let* him."

We sneak out the service door to the maintenance hallway. Right before we walk back out to the public area, Spencer steps out of nowhere.

"Spencer, what are you doing here? Leave me alone. Ulysses *knows* where I am."

"Well, that was before…"

He stops cold and stares behind me. His expression is of adoration and triumph. Like he had just won the lottery. I turn around to see what he is gawking at, but all I see is Ruby, who is petrified. Then it clicks. Spencer and Ruby are *mates*.

Ruby tries to make a break for it but fails. Spencer grabs her and lifts her up.

Ruby's fists beat his back. "Set me *down,* you big oaf."

"*Spencer,*" I admonish. "Set Ruby down. You cannot just start *man-handling* my friend."

"Ruby…? *Wait.* This is who you were meeting?"

"Yes, now set me down, you pig."

Spencer lets Ruby slip back down to the ground and she flies behind me.

"What is the emergency, Spencer?"

Ulysses rushes around the corner to me and starts checking me over for injuries. He lifts my arm and tilts my chin from side to side.

I bat him off. "I am fine, stop."

He stops checking me and wraps his arms around me.

"I came back here because I thought the Luna was trying to escape and…"

"Were you?" Ulysses asks firmly, his eyes going gold for a moment.

"No, I was just trying to go five seconds without Coleman, Cade, Jake, or Owen watching me."

"Who is this?" Ulysses asks, nodding toward Ruby.

"This, if you people would give me five seconds to explain, is my friend Ruby. Who also appears to be *your* new Gamma Female."

Ulysses' gaze questions Spencer, who only nods. "And the problem is…?"

Ruby's voice is defiant. "The problem, *Alpha*, is I don't *want* a mate."

I snicker. "Welcome to my life."

Both Spencer and Ulysses growl, sneering at us. Then Coleman speaks up from behind Spencer.

"Can I suggest that we all go back to the pack house to figure this out? Out of the public eye."

"Fine. But I am staying with Wes."

Ruby crosses her arms and glares at Spencer, who growls at his mate for not wanting to be near him.

"Deal. Let's go Ruby. I'll introduce you to everyone else."

I slip out of Ulysses' grasp and seize Ruby's hand, sprinting toward the group.

"Why did *we* get stuck with the complicated and bipolar mates?"

"I heard that." I yell back to Ulysses, who follows with Spencer, who is grumbling to himself.

"You jinxed me." Ruby's whisper yells at me.

"Well, now I will have someone to complain to all the time."

We walk toward the group, who are giving me weird looks.

I better start explaining.

"Guys, this is Ruby. She was the person I was meeting today, and she is Spencer's mate, blah blah, blah, clear?"

Ruby slaps my arm. Jackie, in true Jackie form, rushes up to hug her.

"Oh, my goodness. We *finally* have all our Royals here. I am so excited."

Ruby backs away. "I am not staying."

"That's what she said." Cade whispers to Hannah, jerking his chin in my direction.

I elbow Cade in the gut. He grunts over in pain and stumbles closer to his mate.

"I never asked for this. I don't want to be Gamma Female, or whatever."

Spencer growls low and is about to interfere when Coleman places his hand on his chest, holding him back. "I suggest we leave now."

The ride back is anything but calm. The girls and boys are separated again, and Ruby sits next to me. Five seconds into the car ride, everyone wants to know how we know each other, where did she come from, and why we were meeting. Ruby answered a few questions and then sank into my side, avoiding everyone.

She never *did* like attention. When we finally arrive back at the pack house, I send Patrick, Corrine, and Aubrey to organize Patrick's new clothes, while the rest of us go straight to the office to figure this shit out. Ulysses, Coleman, Jackie, Spencer, Ruby, Cade, Hannah, and I all space ourselves out in Ulysses' office.

"Okay, Westries. Explain."

"I don't know to what you're referring."

Ulysses low growls and I roll my eyes…

"How many times are you going to growl at her before you realize it won't work?" Ruby says, laughing.

"That's what I said." I lament.

"Holy shit. She's another version of that." Cade mutters, pointing from Ruby to me.

"It's an honor to be compared to the Sass Queen. I thank you."

Ruby mock bows.

"And I am not a '*that*' Cade. I am a she."

Ulysses gives me a pointed stare. "Okay, okay, enough. Westries, explain who this is." He clears his throat and adds, "Please," and I oblige.

"Fine. Everyone, this is Ruby Taylor of the rogue Taylors, here to present to me information on rogue whereabouts."

I added a British accent and a curtsy while Ruby royally waves.

We are platonic soulmates when we are together. She is who I would call if I needed advice or someone to help me bury a dead body.

Ulysses is not amused. "Keep talking and lose the accent and sarcasm."

"That's seriously all that happened. Until your goons showed up and we made a break for it."

"Wait, so are you a hunter too?" Hannah asks from the comfort of her mate's lap.

Ruby laughs. "God, no. No one is that stupid. Well, no one except this one here." She smirks at me. "I am more of the man in the chair character. I snoop around other people's business, find out some crap, and give it to that witch there."

"So, you are a rogue?" Spencer asks, conflicted.

"Yep. Born and raised. Well, technically, I was an orphan, and I ran away when I shifted."

Everyone is somber. You couldn't cut the tension with a diamond blade, it's so thick.

"Please, don't all cry at once. Seriously, don't. I am perfectly fine with what happened. No pack, no rules, no one to hold you down."

"Until now," I mutter.

Ruby glares at me. "I haven't said I am staying. I never wanted a mate, remember?"

"Oh yes, you are." Spencer comes from behind Ruby and pulls her into his chest tightly. Ruby struggles for a second, then gives up, blowing the hair out of her face.

Her defiant voice is muffled by Spencer's shirt. "I never agreed to this. I could still reject you." Still, she's not trying to escape his hold.

"Neither did I, Ruby. You think *I* agreed to all this? I am stuck and I am bringing you down with me."

"Bitch."

"Ho."

"Butthead."

"You love me." I answer.

"I question that right now…" Ruby mutters, trying to pry Spencer's arms off her that are stuck like a vise.

"Yes, you are stuck with me, mate." Ulysses whispers, pulling me into his lap and kissing my mark.

"Wes, help." Ruby pleads.

Poor Ruby. It wasn't long ago I felt completely overwhelmed by all this, too. Time to cut her a break.

I flick the tip of Ulysses' nose, which makes him growl. "Down fluffy."

I stand, grab a pillow, and whack Spencer on the head repeatedly. The moment of shock gives Ruby time to escape. We both stand and run toward the door, leaving Spencer and the pillow.

"I'm showing Ruby around!" I yell as we both bolt down the hall. As soon as we reach a far enough distance away, we slow down.

"So, where are we going?"

"I have some people I would actually like you to meet."

A few doors later, we arrive at Corrine's room. I open the door to find it empty.

"Corrine, Patrick?" I shout into the hallway. This is like a strange game of marco-polo.

"Six doors down!" Aubrey calls back. We walk to a guest room I'd never entered before to find a teenage boy's room.

"Oh, hey guys. This used to be Ulysses' room till he moved to the master bedroom. I figured Patrick would like it now that he is staying."

Patrick runs up to me and takes my hand.

"Bear. Did you see? This room has a TV."

"I see that buddy."

He peeks behind me and sees Ruby. "Bear, who's that?"

"Corrine, Aubrey, Patrick, this is my old friend Ruby. She is going to be staying here with us for a while."

Ruby waves and Corrine strolls over.

"Do you know how to fold pants properly?"

"Um, yes?"

"Good, you can help me."

Corrine drags Ruby over to the pile of clothes on the floor. Patrick and I join in, too, and help fold the clothes. After an hour of cleaning up and reorganizing, our stomachs growl.

Patrick declares, "I'm hungry."

"Me too."

"Wessy, do we have any more Empanadas and fried apples?"

"I don't know. Let's go see."

The six of us, including Griffin, walk downstairs in search of food. I open the fridge and grab the leftovers. Aubrey mans the microwave while Corrine and Patrick sit at the bar stools. I make five plates of snacks and serve the hungry group.

"Uh, Wes? Might want to make that seven plates," Ruby says, pointing behind me. Jake and Owen stand at attention.

"Oh, Ruby, meet statue guard one and statue guard two. Guys this is…"

"Gamma Female Ruby. We have already been informed."

"Are they always…"

"Acting like creepy know-it-alls? Yes. Don't let them fool you though, they aren't as mean as they appear. Can you guys talk like normal people for five seconds and maybe eat? I am sure you can watch me and enjoy breathing at the same time."

They both stared stone-faced, not moving from the entrance.

"Don't make me order you."

They flinch and hesitantly sit down. Aubrey and the two twin turbos run off somewhere, so it is just the four of us and Griffin at my feet. I throw Griffin an empanada and he swallows it whole.

"You have the power to order them?" Ruby asks while biting into her food.

"Yeah, who knew, right? Perk of the job, I guess."

"Then tell them to let us go."

"I am sure Ulysses would override that command if I asked. Right, boys?"

"Do you have ketchup?" Owen asks, stuffing another treat into his mouth.

I roll my eyes and hand him the bottle. He mutters a thank you over all the food stuffed in his mouth.

Ruby forces her attention away from the spectacle of Owen's poor etiquette and says, "So, what happens next? Anything interesting?"

I am about to answer when Ulysses and Spencer come in.

"Depends on how you define interesting." Ulysses says, walking toward me.

I attempt to sidle away to escape his grasp, but Griffin gets underfoot, making me trip right into his enormous arms, a face full of t-shirt.

You smell amazing.

Instead, I say, "You corrupted my dog, jerk."

Ulysses' laughter vibrates in his chest against my cheek.

I could stay like this forever. Wait. No, bad Westries. Bad, bad, Westries.

I glance over at Ruby to see her in the same predicament I am in. *Damn.*

"Okay, okay. Get off me."

I push Ulysses off and take a step back. Ulysses' eyes flicker gold, but he stops himself.

He points a finger at me. "You are coming with me."

"Do I get a say?"

"No." Ulysses pulls me toward the door, but I stop him.

"Wait, what about Ruby?"

"Don't worry, Spencer is taking her on a date, so she will be fine."

"By force…" I mutter under my breath as Ulysses continues to pull my hand.

"What was that?"

"Nothing."

This day has been crazy. We found Patrick in the prison. I forcefully marked my mate, and my Gamma found *his* mate in my assassin mate's best friend. This could not have gone more wrong. Well, at least this day couldn't get any *more* complicated. After Westries and Ruby run out of the office, most everyone is confused and conflicted, especially Spencer and me.

Of course, we have to get complicated mates.

I can't fathom what the pack house is going to be like with the two of them now. Or what the pack is going to think when we have the coronation ceremony.

I honestly couldn't care less, though. She is their Luna, and they need to respect that. Whether my mother will is a different question.

While everyone else makes small talk, I order Owen and Jake to find Westries and Ruby. No telling what damage they are causing now that they were together. The others take their cues to excuse themselves from the office, leaving Spencer and me to commiserate.

"What are we going to do?" He groans, rubbing his hands over his face.

"You tell me, because I am out of ideas."

We sit in silence for a minute before Spencer speaks again.

"What about this? We find them, separate them before they can cause any more damage, and I don't know after…"

"Take them on a date?"

"Yeah, I think that might work…"

Why is this so difficult? Why is talking to my mate so complicated?

An Alpha King and his Gamma can't figure out how to take their mates on dates. It's frankly quite sad. We're like two teenage boys who can't talk to girls. Pathetic.

As the Alpha, I have to take charge. "Well, I guess we'd better hunt them down and get this over with."

We trace their scents to Corrine's room, then my old room, and came up empty. So, we follow them into the kitchen. There stood Westries, Ruby, Owen, and Jake. The girls were laughing, and the boys were sitting at the bar eating leftover empanadas.

"You boys are dismissed. Thank you."

I tell the boys over the mind link. They nod and walk out of the kitchen as they stuff the last bits of food into their mouths.

"So, what happens next? Anything interesting?" Ruby asks, stuffing a whole Empanada in her mouth. Spencer's smile probably grew five sizes.

"Depends on how you define interesting." I say, making our entrance. I walk over to my mate. Griffin doesn't growl but moves so I can embrace my mate. She stiffens up and groans when I hold her.

I think I have a new assistant in crime. Good boy, Griffin.

"You corrupted my dog, jerk." She mutters and struggles to get out of my grip and fails.

She pushes herself off me and I let go. I can feel Axel trying to surface, but I suppress him.

"You are coming with me."

"Do I get a say?"

"No." I pull Westries toward the door, but she comes to a grinding halt.

"Wait, what about Ruby?"

I glance over at Ruby and Spencer, and she is also being dragged grudgingly toward the game room.

"Don't worry, Spencer is taking her on a date, so she will be fine."

"By force…"

"What was that?"

"*Nothing.*"

She quickly says in a sing-song voice and follows me to the back door. We walk to the garage while Westries grumbles to herself about being left in the dark.

"Where are we going? I swear if we are going to the mall again, I will stab you."

"We aren't going to the mall, and what could you possibly stab me with? You are unarmed."

"That's what *you* think."

"I am going to let that slide because I am trying to get you to trust me. So, get in."

I open the garage door and gesture to the black Ford F150 parked inside. She crosses her arms and raises an eyebrow at me.

"Tell me where we are going, then maybe I will get into the creepy guy's car."

"Do you have to be so stubborn?"

"Do *you* have to be so *secretive*?"

I give her a pointed glare and she throws her hands up in defense.

"*Fine.* I'll get in the damn car."

I can't help but smirk. She slides into the co-pilot seat, and I start the ignition. I pull out of the six-car garage and start down the dirt road.

"If you're going to kill me and leave me on the side of the road, can I have at least one request?"

I roll my eyes but glance toward her, giving her a look of 'sure go ahead.'

"Everything I own will go to Griffin. Scratch that, Griffin is the primary beneficiary, but Patrick will reserve 54.84% when he is eighteen. Yeah, that sounds about right. Oh, and Corrine can have my boxing gloves. And I want all my organs donated to science. Except for my middle finger, you can give that to the King."

"Really?"

Her expression says something like, 'no, duh.' "Yes, and I would like it on paper. I would appreciate it if you arranged something."

I banter back. "Okay. Should I have my personal lawyer come by tomorrow to sign the papers?"

"I'll be dead by then, but I am sure you can accomplish this one simple task, right?"

I laugh and shake my head, returning my attention back to the road.

I feel her gaze on me. "Is there something else you want to ask of me?"

"Yes, actually. I…"

I tense, sensing a change in her tone. But as we leave the pack borders, her attention shifts.

"Ah, hey, Mr. Werewolf King, we just passed the Charleston sign. Where are we going?"

"You'll see."

"I hate surprises." She pouts, even crossing her arms, and turns away from me.

"Fine, grumpy. You can man the radio."

She rebounds with head-spinning speed. "Don't have to tell me twice."

She grabs her phone and plugs in the aux cord, shuffles through a few songs before landing on one.

"It's called "Wolves" by Sam Tinnesz. You'll like it."

She hums along to the song but doesn't sing. The lyrics *are* pretty great, I'll admit. We ride in companionable silence, the music filling the space between us. A few songs go by and I notice a common theme between them. They are all about wolves, warriors, and being the new King.

Interesting.

She taps her foot along or plays the drums on the middle console.

I clear my throat. "Nice playlist."

"Thanks." She pauses halfway through her air guitar solo to answer.

Three songs later, we arrive in the quaint nearby town, which consists of mostly good ole boy type humans and a few elders who chose to live further away from the pack. We pull into a parking lot of a big metal building, and her eyes light up.

"You're kidding?"

"Nope, thought you could use some *practice.*"

She wags a finger in my face.

"I do *not* need practice. This is raw talent, thank you very much. Anyway, I didn't bring any of my guns."

I raise my eyebrows at her and open the car door. At the truck bed, I drop the hatch to reveal four large cases.

Westries practically jumps for joy at the sight. She opens one case and lightly touches the contents. She gently lifts the black Barrett M82 out of the case and she pulls the magazine.

"Diablo. I can't believe you kept him."

"Well, I wasn't going to throw them out. These are delicate pieces of machinery."

"You're telling me. Half of these saved my life on more than one occasion."

The very thought of her life in danger causes Axel to stir and I must suppress the urge to growl. She opens another case and gasps.

"Oh, my… Is this an M4 Carbine?"

I pick up the weapon and show Westries, whose jaw is practically on the ground.

"Yep. Standard issue for the Warrior's Elite. This one is mine. You like?"

"Yeah, sweet. Now let's go inside so I can kick your pretty butt."

I bite back an R-rated comment about *her* posterior and instead say, "You wish."

We each take two cases and walk through the metal doors leading to the gun range. At the front desk I sign us in, using the Warriors membership card. From my bag, I extract two headphones and two pairs of glasses. I hand Westries hers and take the other two for myself.

Inside the range there is a long hall and about fifteen stations. Seven of the stations are occupied with people firing an interesting assortment of handguns and rifles.

We take the booth close to the end, far away from the other shooters for good reason. Westries unloads the Barrett while I set up the six targets. Once she finishes loading her ammo, she prepares to fire.

"You ready?"

She nods once.

I give her a thumbs up and Westries lets loose on the targets. She empties the entire magazine in about seven seconds flat.

"How's that?" She asks, reloading her magazine.

"Pretty good for a *girl*." I smirk.

Her mouth curves into an 'o' shape. "Okay, pretty boy. Show me how it's done then."

"That's twice you've called me pretty in one hour. I think you've got a crush on me."

She blushes and shoves her Barrett—barrel facing straight up—at me. "Shut up and shoot."

"With pleasure, Bellator."

I accept it and position myself. I empty the barrel in about five seconds. I smirk triumphantly and hand her back her weapon.

"How was that?"

She sets the Barrett back into the case and grabs her binoculars.

"I would say pretty good, but you missed the ten."

She hands me the binoculars and I peer through them down range. I see her pink target with holes all in the ten and my blue target with holes all in the center, except one. I hand her back the binoculars.

"Really, just because one was in the nine, you are going to deny my talent?"

"That one bullet could be life or death. Precision is key, Mr. Werewolf King."

"Oh, really?"

"Yep," she says, crossing her arms and popping the 'p'. I give in and grab another case. I pull out my Ruger handgun.

"Best two out of three?"

She bobs her head and grabs her own handgun. A Remington. We both stand at our own sections, and I nod to her, giving her the okay. Shots ring out for about twenty seconds till I am out. Westries doesn't stop though and continues to fire down the line, interchanging her magazines accordingly. I gape unabashedly at her as she destroys the target. A few people around us stop to watch. She is truly amazing at what she does.

"You have your hands full with that one, don't you?"

I turn around to see an elderly gentleman in a Vietnam hat.

"Yes, I do. I am honestly scared to get on her bad side."

He chuckles a little and scratches his nose with his thumb.

"I can imagine. She definitely knows what she is doing. You hold on to that one. There aren't many like her left."

"Oh, I intend to."

"Good. But I warn you, if she is anything like my wife, you'd better think of building a range in your yard if you have property."

"That's a good idea. This is her favorite hobby, among *other* things."

She would love that.

"Like?"

"Don't even get me started on that. Let's just say I have a very large gun safe."

He chuckles again, glancing at my mate.

"I'm Jeremy, by the way."

"Ulysses."

The firing stops and I turn back around. Westries sets the Remington down and takes off her headphones. When she sees me and the old man, she steps toward us, smiling.

"Young lady, you have some natural talent there."

"*Oh*, thank you. I'm Westries."

She reaches out and shakes the old man's hand.

"Jeremy. Your boyfriend was just telling me about you."

"All good things, I hope."

Westries nervously glances at me, laughing.

"Oh yes, dear. He is very lucky to have you."

"Aww, thank you and thank you for your service, sir."

"Oh, no need to thank me. I would do it all again and it was the best decision I ever made. It's how I met the love of my life, and I couldn't be happier."

"That's so sweet. What's her name?"

"Annie. After the Paris Peace Accords, they sent me to a physical therapy hospital in Boston and she was my therapist. I, being young, wanted to smoke, and she did not like that. So, she told me if I could reach the cigarettes, I could smoke them. By the time I could reach them, I didn't want to smoke. I just wanted the girl, and the rest is history."

"Oh my, that's beautiful."

"Well, thank you. Now, I must be going. It was a pleasure meeting you both, and I wish you the best."

We shake hands and he disappears back into the lobby.

"You didn't deny it."

Her brow furrows, and she tilts her head.

"That I was your boyfriend."

Her eyes go wide, and she tries to hide her reddening cheeks by turning around and walking in the other direction.

"Aww, is that a blush?"

I wrap my arms around her from behind before she can escape. She wiggles around and I let her go.

"I don't know to what you are referring." She says in a proper tone as she packs up her handgun in its case. I laugh, packing up my own. We collect all our cases and check out at the front desk. It's only after we reload the trunk and climb into the cab that I realize I'm famished. It is almost dark, and I am sure dinner is long finished at the pack house. Pizza, or whatever they ordered tonight, no doubt.

"You want to get some dinner while we are in town?"

"You had me at dinner."

"So where…"

"Taco Bell!" she yells quickly, looking at me with enormous eyes, and I chuckle.

"Taco Bell it is."

The Taco Bell is just down the street, and we pull into the parking lot. Westries jumps out of the car and drags me inside.

Note to self: food is the way to her heart.

There was no one here, so we have the whole place to ourselves.

"What do you want?"

Without hesitating, she responds. "Six hard tacos and three bags of churros… Oh, and a root beer."

I blink at her, eyebrows raised, for a second. She is the most confounding person I have ever met.

"Okay, then. We'll have twelve tacos, six churros, and two drinks, please."

The cashier looks up at me through false eyes, in a failed attempt to seduce me. Axel and I both repulsed at the thought.

"Anything else I can help a *man* like you with?" She licks her lips and plays with the tips of her hair, leaning more onto the register, that is thankfully dividing us.

"I'm pretty sure he doesn't want Gonorrhea, but just in case he does, we know where to find you."

Now standing slightly in front of me, Westries smiles at the cashier, like she didn't just hit on her mate.

"I don't think I was talking to you sis." The woman now just seems pissed off, and I am mildly attracted by the show down happening right before me from my Bellator.

"You are now Chica, so be a dear and swipe my man's card, do your job and we'll be gone before you know it. 'K?" Westries smugly holds her hand out for my card while the other woman mutters an incoherent response and tries to hand me back my credit card. Westries swipes it first, tucking it away.

"Well thank you. Now if you could get our food, that would be just brilliant!"

Begrudgingly, the cashier turns behind her to collect our food. A few seconds later, she tosses down a tray filled with tacos, not bothering to make eye contact.

Westries grabs the tray and takes it to a table.

I guess I am on drink patrol.

I fill up the two large cups with root beer and Pepsi. I debate in my head whether or not to bring up the little scenario that just occurred. Especially the part where she said, "My man." I decide to take it as a win and let her be. I'm not even entirely sure she even *realizes* what she said. We sit down at the table and simultaneously reach in to grab a taco.

"Ah, ha, since you were the first one to touch a taco, you say grace." Westries gives me a sharp look and folds her hands.

Here goes nothing.

"Uh, dear God, thank you for today and this food… and Westries being here with me…"

"Amen."

"Right, amen."

Westries smiles and hands me a taco. We both start eating our food. *One* of us, a lot faster than the other.

"I never imagined you to be a Taco Bell fan."

Her mouth full of food, she replies, "Are you kidding? I practically lived here. Fun fact, motel food sucks, so you have to improvise, eat out, or starve."

"I'll keep that in mind."

"What about you? King of all Werewolves and you're sitting in a roadside Taco Bell at eight at night."

"Yeah, but I am with my mate."

She glances away and stuffs a churro in her mouth.

She is so freaking adorable, with a face full of food.

Axel is salivating at the sight. We are both relieved she isn't afraid to eat in front of us. Clearly not bothered by the fact she eats like a starved beast.

"*What*?"

"Huh?" Westries' voice snaps me out of my trance.

"You are staring. Never seen a girl eat her weight in tacos?"

"I think it's beautiful."

She rolls her eyes and collects our trash.

"That's sickeningly cliché. Come on, Fluffy. Let's go home."

We walk out and head toward the car. An awkward silence takes over and I try to find something light-hearted to say when Westries speaks.

"I want Patrick's brother out of the prison."

She turns to watch me driving, giving me a look somewhere between pleading and despair.

"Ah, so that's what you were going to ask earlier, hm? Well, I can make that happen."

"Tomorrow. And I want to be there when it happens."

Coleman has always told me mates are demanding and complicated, but I figured that was a 'Jackie' sort of thing… until now.

"Why is this so important to you?"

"They're family and family is everything. You never know what you have until you don't have it anymore. They're just kids."

I nod and return my attention to the road. The rest of the ride is silent except for the radio playing lightly.

I pull into the garage and shut the door behind me. Before Westries can jump out of the car, I touch her wrist. She faces me.

"Thank you for coming with me today."

She smiles a genuine grin.

I love her smile.

"You're welcome. A-and thank *you*. Good night, Ulysses."

"Good night, Bellator."

And with that, she's gone.

CHAPTER 25

Westries

He took me to a gun range.

I was so happy, I could almost kiss him. but I didn't. I haven't had that much fun in a good while. Then, to top it off with tacos for dinner? What a night. Even though neither of us called it a date, that's what it was. I don't mind, though, because I got free food. He could convince me to do almost anything with food… not that he needs to know it.

I leave Ulysses in the garage and sail upstairs, already imagining my sweet, marvelous, steaming shower. I open my bedroom door to discover Ruby sprawled on my comforter, going through my duffle bags.

"What exactly do you think you are doing?"

Ruby doesn't even turn around and throws some of my clothes onto the bed.

"Spencer just brought me back and I need PJs."

I walk over to her, grabbing my shorts back from her. She skirts around me and forages through a drawer. I grab her and spin her around, brushing the hair away from her neck. I gasp. There on her neck is her mate mark, barely hidden by her shirt collar.

"Rubes? Did he force mark you? Because if he did, I swear I will castrate him and…"

"Wes. He didn't force me. I *let* him."

I stare at her for a second. She let him? She met him only today!

"What do you…"

"I fell for him, Wes. I can't deny that mate bond. It's too great, he's a Gamma, and the pull is too compelling to ignore. I-I think I finally found a home and someone to care for me."

"What happened to 'I don't need a mate?' Wait, what am I? Chopped liver?"

She shuffles from foot to foot, ignoring my eye contact.

"That was before I knew my mate wouldn't reject me. Someone actually wants me, wants to be with *me*. Please understand, Wes."

"Wait, Rubes, no, *no*. I'm not mad," I say, embracing her in a tight hug.

"I am so excited you have a mate. And as much as it *pains* me to say this, he is a great guy and he will treat you like a princess, literally. Now that we're together again, we can kick the boy's asses and hang out every single day. I could not ask for a better surprise. Now go, lover boy is waiting. Borrow all the clothes you need. You can keep the *sleep*wear, though."

She shoves my arm playfully and kisses my head.

"You are the best. Love you, Wes."

"Love you too, ya' butthead."

She scampers out of my room and closes the door behind her. I walk over to my bathroom and turn the shower on. Between the toilet and bathtub lies Griffin, curled up in the corner.

"Dude, you find the most miserable position to sleep in."

His tail thumps on the tile and he offers a lazy yawn in response.

I peel off my clothes and step into the steaming water. The liquid cascades down my back and washes off the day.

If I could stay here forever, I would, but there are other people in this house, and I'm not rude. I finish up in the shower and turn the water off. The second I step out onto the rug to dry off, Griffin tries to lick my wet legs and I shove him off. Annoyed, he goes to the waterspout to drink the dripping water. There's a chill in the air tonight, so I decide on sweatpants and a tank top. In bed at last, I curl up under the comforter and open my phone to scroll mindlessly through my Pinterest, as I let myself do a mental review of the day.

Today has been an excessively long day with way too many unanticipated events. Maybe tomorrow I can catch a breather. I found a new best friend, went unexpectedly coronation dress shopping, found Ruby, and went on a *supposed* date. Today has been eventful, indeed. A tiny knock at the door interrupts my thoughts.

"It's open." I called out, not glancing up.

The door creaks open and in walks Patrick, dragging a blanket behind him. He trudges into the room, his face cast downward and his voice is meek.

"Can I stay in here tonight?"

"Come here." I say, holding open my arms.

I remember all too well what it's like to be alone. Patrick comes running and jumps on my bed, burrowing his face in my lap.

"Bad dreams?"

He nods, digging in even more.

"Me too, kid."

I cover him with the bedspread and close my eyes. He flips around and curls up to my chest. I freeze for a second, not sure what to do. He sighs in contentment, and I throw my arm over him. My sister used to sleep in my room for the longest time until she decided her room wasn't haunted anymore. I loved having her with me. When she left, I hugged my pillows in solitude.

"Bear, do you know where my brother is?"

"Yes, and I am going to bring him here tomorrow. You'll have your big brother back soon, buddy."

"But you still won't leave me, right?"

"Never." And with that, I fell asleep. A few hours later, I shot up, gasping awake. Patrick was still sleeping peacefully while I was recovering from a mild panic attack. They rarely happen, but when they do, I have Griffin to comfort me.

I turn over to face the clock. 4:23 A.M.

Might as well start the day.

I dress quietly and brush through my lion's mane of hair and pull it into a high ponytail. Before I leave the room, I check on Patrick and tuck the comforter around his sleeping form.

The vast halls of the pack house are empty and peaceful, so I shuffle through my many playlists for one that matches the mood. I wander around till I find the media room. Once there, I enshroud myself in a burrito fortress using four pillows and six blankets to watch one of my favorites: the old *Clone Wars*.

I am about to yell at the TV when Jackie walks in.

"Why are you up at this hour?" Jackie asks while walking into the room.

She is in cupcake pants and a pink, long sleeve pajama shirt. She sits on the single-seater couch and covers her legs with a blanket.

"Couldn't sleep. You?"

"Same? Care to share?"

I shake my head no.

No one will know. I've buried those memories deep inside me and they will *not* be resurfacing… except in my nightmares. Jackie lays her chin on her hands and fidgets.

"Do *you* need to share?"

She obviously has something on her mind. She thinks about it for a second and bites her lip before answering.

"I don't want to be a bother. It's nothing."

"Jackie, it isn't nothing. I am a good listener, and I promise what you say won't leave this room."

She bows her head, then faces me.

"Well, you know Coleman and I are mates and, well, it's just… we are trying, and it's just not working."

I know immediately what she's referring to.

They want kids.

It makes sense now. They are trying to have children and she might be infertile. I can relate to their pain.

"Well, how long have you guys been trying?"

"A while now. He wants kids and I don't think I can give him any…"

A lone tear rolls down her cheek and she wipes it away.

"Just give it time, maybe? I don't really know enough about *that*. I am probably no help, sorry."

"No, it's fine. I really needed to tell someone."

The room is quiet for a few minutes, then I talk.

"Have you gone for a medical opinion about it?"

"No…"

"Maybe you should? At least then you can have a for sure answer."

She nods and we stare at the screen. I am sorry for her. Genuinely. The irony doesn't escape me. I came here hating everything to do with werewolves, yet slowly but surely, they have melted my stone-cold heart.

How did you people… no, you werewolves make your way into my heart?

From Corrine and Aubrey to Coleman, Cade, and Spencer, who make me want to strangle them yet protect them at the same time. Jackie, Hannah, and now Ruby help me deal with my anxiety, whether they know it. Patrick and Griffin just make me want to roll them up in little burritos and take them with me wherever I go. Even Jake and Owen. I care. What's more, I feel—for once in my life—hope.

Then, last but not least of all, *Ulysses*. How do I describe how I feel about him when I cannot understand it? I *want* to hate him, I honestly do, for keeping me here, but I can't. Maybe it's the mate bond, maybe it is my new mark. Either way, when I am around him, my heart and mind are in utter chaos. I don't know what I will do in this predicament, but I know for once in a very long time, the decision will be from my conflicted heart.

Ulysses is a werewolf. A werewolf I am attracted to in every feasible way.

How long can I deny that every fiber of my being begs for me to run into his arms and tell him everything, so maybe he can make it go away?

He can't. And because I care about him, I must protect him... from me.

I want his love. But he deserves someone who is not shattered in every conceivable way. Someone who can give him what he wants, and what this pack and the world need.

Sure, he wants me now, but as soon as he finds out the truth, he will reject me.

If a wolf, once rejected, dies of a broken heart, what might happen to me, a mere human?

I will most definitely die.

My strong and independent act is just that: an act. I am no more than a house of cards painted to look like cement. It is something I've always known, deep down, but I had hoped God had a failsafe for me.

It turns out I am weak. For as much as I know I should leave here and let them move on, I cannot compel myself to do it. So, I'll just convince myself of another lie. Okay, half-truth.

I don't want to leave the pack house with everyone remembering me as the brooding human who couldn't smile or change.

"Do you want to do something today?"

Jackie lifts her chin up from her hands as the movie ends.

"What did you have in mind?"

"I don't know. Maybe you, Hannah, Ruby, and I could come up with something together."

Her expression is dubious. "I don't think Ruby likes us…"

I grin. Then it fades. That *must* mean she thinks *I* like her. Does she also think I have accepted this situation? Is that good or bad?

Ask her, dummy.

Instead, I say, "Oh, she has accepted her role. She came back last night with a fresh mate bond mark and was with Spencer all night. She's a love-sick puppy right now."

Jackie's eyes go wide, and her smile lights her entire face.

"Really? Oh, that's wonderful." Then, as if having read my mind, she asks, "Does that mean *you* accepted, too?"

I squirm in my chair. "Baby steps."

She nods, still smiling ear to ear.

"So, what do you want to do?"

I think about it for a second, then answer. "What about a movie and snack binging day? Nothing better than *doing* nothing and being lazy on a rainy day, right?"

She smiles and jumps off the couch. "I think we will get along just fine. Come on, let's see who else is up and about."

Together, we roam through the house, searching for everyone else. As always, we end up in the kitchen, where I almost gag at the sight before us.

Spencer is practically sucking Ruby's face off.

"Can you please not do that where we eat? I might gouge my eyes out."

Ruby buries her face into Spencer's neck while he scowls at me, wrapping his arms tighter around his mate.

"Nice mark, Rubes."

Ruby lifts her head and winks at me. "I love you, Wes."

She bats her eyelashes a little and pouts.

"Yeah, yeah, I love you too, ya' jerk. Now Spencer, go away because I want my best friend back."

Spencer growls and grips Ruby's waist tighter. She yips in surprise and melts into his arms.

Revolting.

"Don't make me beat your ass. You can survive a few hours without her, now scram."

Spencer whispers something to Ruby that makes her blush, then reluctantly leaves the kitchen. Jackie rummages through the fridge and pantry.

"I'm thinking we start with the *Star Wars* prequels, then *Frozen*, and we'll end with *Transformers*, the new one. Just to mix it up a little."

"There is no logical reason to pick those movies together. And what if someone hasn't seen all the other *Transformers* movies?"

"And what's going on exactly?" Ruby asks as Jackie lays out all the food on the island.

"Well, *we* are having a girls' day, so be a dear and grab the root beer."

Ruby gives me a questioning look. I shrug and pile food into my arms. We shuffle to the media room, listening to Jackie talk about Michael Bay and Harrison Ford movies.

"Still want to stay here?" I jokingly whisper. Ruby elbows me.

"I can hear you guys, you know. Anyway, Hannah is going to meet up with us soon with pizza, but we can start the prequels now."

We spread the snacks out on the coffee table and get comfy on the couch.

Jackie squeals. "Hayden Christensen time."

Twenty minutes later, Hannah arrives. "Seriously, Jackie? The *Phantom Menace*? You pick that every movie night." Hannah says, walking into the room with two pizza boxes.

"Oh, gimme, gimme."

Hannah plops the boxes down and Jackie and I both grab a slice.

"*Yes.* Meat. Oh, how I love you." I say as I kiss my slice.

"What else would you expect? Werewolves love their meat. Now, where are we in the movie?"

"I'm glad you asked."

Jackie goes into deep detail about the plot line so far.

Gosh, this girl loves these actors and their sex appeal.

Can't say I do, but I am honestly scared of what she would do to me if I said that. I'm pretty sure she's only watching this for a certain Jedi Master and not the plot.

"Why do I even ask?" Hannah mutters while grabbing a soda. I stifle a laugh and chug down a root beer.

We watch the movie in relative silence except for when Ruby or Hannah make the occasional comment and Jackie throws something at them.

My stomach growls, which is weird because we have been pigging out all morning. I head to the bathroom.

"Where are you going? This is inexcusable to miss. It's the best part." Jackie whisper yells.

"Chill, I just need to pee."

She nods and turns back to the movie. I walk a little faster toward the toilet and before I know it, I am puking my guts out into the bowl. I rarely ever throw up, unless I am really, and I mean *really*, sick.

What the hell is going on?

My stomach feels like acid and my head is throbbing.

I flush the toilet and wipe my mouth. After I wash my hands and swish water around my mouth, I return to the girls. The movie is just ending as I enter, and I thank God for that. The second one is better, anyway.

"Next movie." Jackie screams as she changes the DVDs and jumps back on the couch between Ruby and Hannah. The movie is so stupid, I almost barf again. Ruby is enjoying it and is reciting lines with Jackie. Of course, they would pick the most mind numbing Disney musical ever created.

I can't focus, my mind is on my stomach. It hasn't settled, so I drink a sprite to calm it down. To top everything off, now my neck and head itch.

I swear if Patrick gave me lice, I am going to beat that little kid.

I'll give him a running start, though. It then occurs to me that Aubrey isn't down here with us. She should be here, too. If I had to endure this, she did too.

"Does Aubrey want to come down for *Frozen*?"

"I'll mind link her."

"Tell her to find Corrine and Patrick, too."

"No," she whines. "No, little kids."

"Please. Just for a bit?"

She groans but does it, anyway. Twenty minutes into *Frozen*, Aubrey comes downstairs with two little devils on her heels.

"Wessy!"

Jackie, Ruby, and Aubrey all hiss a loud '*Shh.*' Patrick and Corrine curl up next to me and mutter a sorry.

"Hey, it's alright. Just whisper for now. I want to ask you something, Patrick."

He slow blinks at me, waiting.

"Does your head itch right now?"

He tilted his head to the side, confused, then scratched it. "No, should it?"

I shake my head no and smile at him. We all continue to watch the movie for a while before Hannah leans over to me.

"Ulysses wants to talk to you. He's in the kitchen."

I nod and stand up. The moment I am on my feet, I doubled over in pain. Hannah stabilizes me, holding my shoulders, and helps me upright.

"Woah, you alright, there?"

"Yeah, just some period cramps, I think. No biggie."

She frowns, eyeing me, and sits back down. I don't have periods anymore. She studies me with suspicion... like she knows. I make my way to the kitchen. Ulysses is sitting at the bar eating a sandwich.

"Where were you this morning? I couldn't find you."

I smirk, walking around him and sit on the cabinet. I grab his sandwich and start eating it. I never got to finish my pizza. "You should've just asked Jackie. We are having a girls' day movie marathon. She picked the *most* obscure trio of movies ever."

"I was going to eat that, you know. And I am very sorry I stole you away from such an important event." He says in a mock tone.

I take another bite of his food, pulled pork on a hot dog bun. *Why am I not surprised?*

"No, *please* steal me away. I mean, it was my idea technically, but I did *not* say to watch *Frozen* and *Transformers* as a follow up."

He laughs and takes his sandwich back.

"*Hey*. I'm eating that."

"There is more in the fridge, you thief."

I grunt and then grudgingly make myself some more food.

Because Ulysses can't share. He is like a literal child!

"You know, you smell different."

I turn around to face Ulysses, completely confused.

"I *smell* different? Really?"

"Wait no, not like that. I meant your scent. It changed."

"Care to elaborate, wolf boy? I don't exactly have your doggy super sniffer."

A low growl rumbles from deep within his chest at me.

I think I may be poking the bear.

I smirk and take a huge bite from my newly made sandwich.

"The scent that distinguishes you as my mate is like black teakwood and vanilla. Now it has a metallic scent to it. Are you on your..."

"Ew, stop and *no*. Rude..."

"Sorry. I was just telling you what it smells like."

With a full mouth of food, I talk. "So, is this what you called me in here for? To tell me about my *bloody* smell?"

"No, that isn't it. You said you wanted to be there when we released Patrick's brother."

"Are you serious? When can we leave?"

"Right now."

"*Yes.*"

I run out of the kitchen, then the realization hits me. I don't know where we are going. I walk back to the kitchen where Ulysses is smirking with his arms crossed.

"Where are we going, exactly?"

He smiles and grabs his car keys. I follow him toward the garage. We climb into his truck and pull away.

I'm about to ask again when he announces, "Back to the prison."

"Couldn't we have walked then?"

"We could've, but I wanted to drive around for a while."

Wait, he tricked me. We aren't going to the pack prison.

"You *said* we were going to the prison. You tricked me, you liar."

I turn away and pout. He can trick me maybe, but he can't stop me from being grumpy. Ulysses chuckles and reaches for my hand, but I slap it away like a five-year-old throwing a tantrum. This only makes him laugh harder and makes me even more mad.

"Butthead..."

"I'm a butthead? Never thought the Alpha of Alpha's would be called a butthead by his mate."

He glances over at me with his own pouting lip, *mocking* me. I stick my tongue out at him.

"Where are we going this time? Or am I not allowed to know *again*?"

"Well, I'm not going to kill you, if that's what you're *still thinking.*"

I glance out the window and I see the trees speeding by.

"Well, I wasn't going to *say it but...*"

He peers over at me with a sad expression, then turns back to the road.

"Do you *really* still think that? No one will ever hurt you here."

"Well, what am I supposed to think? Because I still believe a lot of people are going to have a big problem with me being Luna."

He perks up. "Does that mean you accepted the role?"

"Well, umm, I'm not sure yet. Ruby seems to want to stay and I just…"

To his great credit, he swallows back his obvious disappointment to reassure me. "Hey, it's okay."

"Can we please just change the subject?"

He slows the car to a stop. "We're here."

We are at a shallow, wide river surrounded by trees and mountains. There is a family of deer drinking nearby and birds flying overhead. I spin around, gazing at the beautiful sky that now shows no signs of this morning's thunderstorms. The rain has ended, and the sun now shines overhead. There is not a cloud in sight. How cool would it be as a kid to have your own personal riverfront playground in your own backyard?

"Spill. Why are we here?"

He sheepishly smiles and takes my hand. "Can't a guy just enjoy a beautiful fall day with his mate?"

I raise an eyebrow at him. I am always suspicious of everyone.

No, no, they can't.

"By the way, I was in the middle of a very important movie marathon! And don't you have, like, an entire kingdom to run or something?"

"Yes, but my mate always comes first."

He caresses my jaw with his thumb and then turns away, walking toward the water. Could he be any more confounding?

The answer is yes, he can.

"What are you doing?" I ask, slightly annoyed as Ulysses takes his shoes off.

"It's shallow enough to walk in. Now, come here."

Ulysses reaches a hand out and I shake my head no stubbornly.

"No way. It's cold and I don't *want* to."

"Too bad."

He stalks toward me and I slowly back up, knowing full well he was going to chase me.

"No, don't you dare. If I get wet, you will *pay*."

"I'll take my chances, Bellator."

I turn to run away and don't even make it three feet before Ulysses throws me over his shoulder.

"Ulysses, I am going to *kill* you."

"You know, I kind of like this angle."

"SET ME *DOWN*."

"As you wish, my Queen."

Ulysses drops me into the six inches of water, and I can feel a shiver coming on. I cross my arms and stare daggers at my annoying mate. Now I'm grumpy and I have wet socks!

"Aww, is my little mate pouting?"

I narrow my eyes at Ulysses. He does *not* need to know that I am finding him almost irresistible right now. But then he scoops me into his arms like I weigh no more than air, and instead of wrestling away from his grasp, I wrap my legs around his waist. However, I am still crossing my arms and pouting.

I will not put my arms around him. So there.

His breath teases my ear. "Are you mad, baby?"

"My feet are wet, and you tricked me into coming here." I shiver against him. "How are your feet *not* cold right now?"

"Werewolf genes, babe. I am naturally warm-blooded. I can be your personal radiator."

I drop my forehead against his warm neck and slip my arms through his, around his broad back. Heat emanates from him. He smells fantastic, like the cedar wood and man musk. I have no smartass comment, nor even a coherent thought other than I was content.

He nuzzles my hair with his stubbled cheek and holds me tighter. Just as I allow myself to give in to this intimate moment between us, the strange ache in the pit of my stomach returns, and my abdomen heats. Like the stomach acid from inside me was boiling. I lift my head back up to search Ulysses' eyes.

"Ulysses, do you have any water?"

"Water surrounds us, babe."

I groan and thump my head against his chest. "Set me down, Ulysses. I need water from a bottle, *please*."

His teasing smile fades and he strides out of the water with ease, despite carrying me. With a tenderness I'd not known him possible of, he sets me on a boulder by the bank of the river.

I clutch my stomach. Ulysses runs to the car and rushes back with a plastic bottle. I snatch the water from his hand, gulping it down.

Ulysses' concern is plain to see in his eyes as he rubs my back and pushes the hair out of my face. I want to reassure him, tell him I am fine, and it will pass, but I'm afraid it would be a lie. Something *is* wrong with me. Very wrong.

What is happening to me?

CHAPTER 26

ULYSSES

"Do you want to tell me what that was about?"

I caress Westries' back and hair as she pants, clutching the plastic bottle.

Is she on her period? Did she lie? Aubrey told me periods are the end of the world, but it can't be this bad?

Jackie, Hannah, and Aubrey have complained about cramps many times. They all say it feels like being repeatedly kicked in the gut by a kangaroo with ninja stars. Although I think that's excessive.

"I am fine, just cramps, I think."

"Well, let's get Patrick's brother and get you back home."

I help her back into the truck. She leans up against the window and closes her eyes. I turn on the radio softly, not wanting to wake her up. I drive in silence as my mate sleeps for the ten-minute car ride. Axel, unfortunately, is not silent in my head.

What's wrong with her?

Cramps. She must be on her period.

She can't be.

Why not?

You are an idiot. She can't have pups, so she is not going to have a period. But maybe cramps don't apply?

How could I have forgotten? She can't have children, so her body won't need extra blood. So, where is this pain coming from? Possibilities run through my head as we pull up to the pack prison. I nudge Westries awake. She slaps my hand away.

"Go away, five more minutes."

I chuckle despite my concern.

"We're here. Wake up. Don't you want to be here for Patrick's brother?"

"I'm awake." She bolts up.

Her face is pale but for two dots of color high on her cheeks and her eyes have a glassy shine to them, but I know her well enough now to realize she won't stop until she's accomplished her goal. She is out of the truck before I can open the door for her.

I catch up to her and we walk through the gym toward the entrance of the prison.

Westries clutches my sleeve. "Wait. Where will he stay? Can he stay in the pack house?"

"Of course he can, but there is only one other room left, and it's next to Coleman and Jackie. Granted, now that you're here, they can go back to their house. You know this is highly unorthodox for us."

She rolls her eyes as we walk through the metal-locked door. "Why? The kid is not even legal. How much of a threat could he possibly be?"

"We rarely let prisoners go."

"Ulysses, he is a kid, not a prisoner. He shouldn't have been there to begin with! Listen, if anything happens, I will be responsible."

"You will, hm? Well, I…"

"Oh, and can Patrick and David join the pack?"

Snuck that one in quick.

"Yes, I can do the mind link right now for Patrick and his brother when you meet him."

She wraps her arms around my arm and squeezes, a wordless thank you in her eyes. Then Westries surprises me again by slipping her hand into mine for the rest of the walk. Cade and Spencer stand at attention at the end of the hall.

"Cade, got the keys?"

"Yep, got 'em."

We walk tandem down the halls of the special interrogation cells until we reach the last one.

"Well, he's in there. We will be just outside."

Cade slides the key over the fob and unlocks the door, sliding the door open. Inside the room, a teenage boy huddles in one corner on the cement floor, his head turned away from us.

Westries takes a deep breath and walks in. Axel begs to go in and protect our mate, but I restrain him.

He is just a kid and three of the greatest werewolves are outside.

She kneels to his level. "Hey, David."

At the sound of her voice, he turns. "W-who are *you*?"

"I'm Westries and I am going to get you out of here."

"How do you know my name? Wait. Y-you're human?"

She laughs a little. "Last I checked, yeah, I am human."

"How are you *here*, then?"

"That is a long story for a different day. All you need to know is you're safe now."

"My brother! Do you know where he is?"

"Patrick is safe, too. He even has some new friends to keep him company."

She stands and offers David her hand. His eyes dart to the three men watching from the other side of the bars. When his eyes meet mine, I nod for him to take her hand. Together, they exit the cell.

"This is Spencer, Cade and Ulysses."

David cowers behind Westries when he recognizes who we are. "Y-you're the Alpha King."

"Yes, and *she* is your Luna. You will show respect."

Westries rolls her eyes and turns around to face David, whose eyes are about to pop.

"You're the Alpha King's mate?"

"Yes, but that shouldn't matter. It's just a title, and that's not important right now. Do you want to join Ulysses' pack? Your brother can, too. You can even live in the pack house."

He glances from me to Westries, then back to me.

"You want *me* to join your pack?"

"It was the Lunas idea, and what she says goes," Spencer says from behind me. David's jaw drops.

"He's right, I'm the boss. So, is that a yes?"

David nods timidly, while Westries smiles blissfully.

I lack her enthusiasm but move forward regardless. "Alright, what is your last name?"

"Jettieson, sir."

"I, Alpha of the Alpha's Dark Sun Pack, accept you, David Jettieson, into my pack. Welcome."

Cade and Spencer pat David's back as we walk out again. Westries takes her spot beside me and links her arm through mine as if it is the most natural thing to do. Cade and Spencer talk in low voices to David in front of us. Her hand slips from my forearm and she stops.

"Bellator?"

Her lips part and she sways. Her eyelids flutter.

She is going to faint.

I catch her around her waist just as her knees buckle. Her head lolls briefly, but she is conscious and already struggling to right herself.

"Hey, what was that? You good?" I ask as she stands on her own again.

She forces a laugh. "I think it's just a bad combination of no sleep and junk food. I'm fine, honest. Maybe it's just altitude sickness."

I nod, not believing a word she is saying. Cade and Spencer give questioning looks, to which I shake my head. They understand, as always. The five of us climb into the truck, where Cade and Spencer ask David more questions and fill him in on the rules here. Meanwhile, I watch my mate as she rubs her temples, softly groaning.

At the pack house and we all climb out. "You'll be living in the pack house, as per the Luna's request. You will join pack training and we will evaluate you soon."

David bobs his head in obedience at everything Cade says. We walk into the kitchen where most of the girls are eating a late lunch. Westries heads straight to the sink and fills up a glass of water, winded.

This is not from junk food and insomnia. She is definitely not okay.

"This is David Jettieson. He joined the pack today." Spencer says to the girls.

The newest addition to the pack causes a flurry of questions and excitement from the girls. I stand back and watch everyone. By the sink are Westries and Ruby. Hannah, Jackie, and Spencer surround David at the island, while Cade raids the refrigerator. Aubrey enters.

My ears perk when Ruby says, "Wes, are you alright? You don't look so good," Ruby asks, rubbing my mates back.

"N-no, everything h-hurts…"

My mate needs me.

I take a step toward them.

"Hey guys, I heard Patrick's brother was here." Aubrey says. I glance from my sister to the teen to realize David is staring at Aubrey, love-struck.

He is Aubrey's mate. No.

Axel tries to surface to defend his sister. I hold him back as our combined growl rumbles through my chest.

She is still too young to realize the mate bond. I must stop them.

Ruby screams Westries' name just as I stalk toward David, who is now hiding behind Cade.

"*Ulysses!*"

Aubrey yells, and I snap out of it. Jackie, Hannah, Ruby, and Aubrey are huddled around Westries. I rush to my mate's side. I kneel beside her as her body shudders.

"What is happening?"

"I d-don't know. She said everything hurt, then she collapsed and started shaking."

"We need to get her to my room."

I pick up Westries in my arms and speed toward my room.

"Cade, take care of David. Spencer, get the Doc."

I lay Westries down on my bed. She continues to shake, and I am helpless and clueless to what I should be doing.

"U-Ulysses, I a-am cold."

I grab her a blanket and throw it around her.

"W-what's happening t-to me?"

"I-I don't know yet, but the Doc is coming, okay?"

She pulls the blanket tightly around her. The Doc charges into the room.

"What happened, Alpha? What are her symptoms?" she asks as she examines Westries' body, taking a pulse.

She runs a battery of quick assessments, asking questions all the while as to what she'd eaten, drank and done leading up to now. The shaking has become intermittent tremors.

"She said she was hurting all over, then collapsed, shaking. Earlier, she was really thirsty, and she couldn't walk straight because she was dizzy."

Margaret continues to examine Westries.

She asks, "Have you completed the mate bond, Alpha?"

"*Why?*"

"She is human Alpha. You marked her, and her body is rejecting it," the doctor explains in a low tone.

Axel is surfacing, and I may let him have control.

"Are you saying she is rejecting me?" I yell. My temper battles with my guilt.

"No, Alpha, but human mates are very rare. I don't think we have ever had a human for a Luna *Queen*. My suspicion is her body is having trouble adapting to the power you injected into her when you marked her." She pauses, clasping her hands. "I have a theory. If you complete the mate bond, these reactions just might go away. But there is no way to guarantee that."

"I will not be doing that to her." I growl out.

No way, no how.

"I feared as much. There is nothing I can do, then. Human medicine won't work on werewolf problems. All I can suggest is that you stay as close as possible to her for the time being. The closer to her you are, the less pain she will have. I will inform the others not to bother you. I am sorry, Alpha." She bows and leaves.

I close the door behind her.

"I am so sorry that I did this to you, Bellator. I can make it better, though. I promise." I take off my shirt.

Westries, now more alert, freaks out. "What are you doing?"

She scoots away from me toward the headboard, her arms barely holding her up.

This makes Axel growl, which only made Westries scoot further away.

Her voice shakes. "I will not have *sex* with you."

"What?! No, I am shifting. I would never do that to you."

She hesitantly nods and turns away so I can change. I finish undressing and shift into my enormous black Alpha wolf. I release control to Axel as he climbs onto the bed, barely fitting without squashing our mate.

"What are you doing you big oaf?"

Axel curls around our mate, with one huge paw around Westries, who appears as if she's being smothered alive. He licks her face gently.

She grins, despite herself. "You can't use me as a dog bed. I am in pain here."

Axel whimpers and so do I.

She tries to scoot away, and Axel lays a paw in front of her, blocking the exit.

"Y-you are being a j-jerk…"

Axel lays his head behind Westries, nudging her face with his snout.

"I-is this Ulysses or A-axel?"

Axel chuffs once and licks her face, nudging her neck with his nose.

"Axel, then."

Axel thumps his tail, happily curling around Westries, nudging her mark. Westries cries out in pain and Axel stiffens, careful not to move so he won't cause her pain.

"T-that really burns. D-don't touch t-the mark, p-please?"

Axel is careful as he curls back around Westries, mindful not to touch anywhere near her neck.

Westries shifts under Axel's huge paw.

"You're not going to g-get off me, are you?"

Axel closes his eyes, completely ignoring her question, giving his mate her answer.

"But why do y-you feel the need to b-be right on t-top of me?"

Axel snorts, blowing Westries' hair around her face. She tries to move her hand from under the massive beast but gives up. Axel purrs in a gleeful bliss and I resume control again. Now in charge of my wolf form, I snuggle closer to Westries. She mutters something about fat wolves and too many bucks for dinner.

Her eyelids shutter closed, and she drifts off to sleep. Hopefully tonight she won't have any nightmares. She really needs it. The minutes turn into hours as I watch over my sleeping mate.

Out the tall arched windows of my master suit, creatures of the night wander around for their next meal. I glance down at my mate, snoring lightly under my huge paws. She is the most beautiful creature I have ever seen. Thick waves of long, auburn-brown hair cascade around her face and across her pillow, perfectly framing her features.

I have memorized every one of those features.

Her eyes.

When I first saw her eyes, I thought she wore contacts. They were so unique. When I first met her at the gun drop off, they were bright blue, practically piercing my own eyes. The day she tried to escape, they were a mix of green and ocean blue. By dinner that night, they were dark blue. I don't understand how they change, but they do.

I wish she were awake right now, so I could gaze into them. She would probably slap me, though.

I can't wait for the coronation to see her in the two dresses she picked out yesterday. If Jackie had it her way, Westries would probably have four or five dresses… a complete contradiction to my mate's usual style. Not that I am complaining. In fact, it makes Axel and I feel a lot better knowing she can handle herself in tough situations.

The night wears on and my mind wanders all over the place and eventually sleep beckons. I long to sleep beside my mate in human form, so I raise my paw off her, carefully moving off the king-sized bed. I trot over to the closet and grab a pair of boxers and flannel pants. I slip on the clothes and return to my mate.

Westries has curled her slight form into a tiny ball. I surround her with my body, wrapping my arm around her slight waist. She shifts closer to me, and Axel wags his tail happily in my head. Sleep then overtakes my body as it did my mates.

The bright morning mountain light shines through the open window as my mate stirs beneath me. Axel begs me not to move, so my mate will stay with us longer, but we jinx it. Westries shuffles and suddenly jerks awake. She realizes where she is and tries to pry my arm off her.

"W-what happened last night? Did we…"

"No, nothing happened. Your mark was acting up, so the Doc suggested we spend some time together physically, so the bond heals."

She tucks her hair behind her ear and scooting out from under my arm. Axel softly growls.

She shuffles off the bed, trying to remove herself. "Okay. Well, can I leave now?"

"Why do you do that?"

She stops, barely acknowledging me as she hugs herself.

"Our mate bond is growing. We are getting closer… but then you build another wall around yourself. Why won't you let me in? All I want is for you to be happy and accept me."

I try to take Westries' hands in mine. She allows it, but her hands lay limp in mine.

"I-I just don't… I can't, um, do… *that*."

"Do *what* Westries? Please tell me. You don't understand what I am going through, not being able to help you. You don't think I didn't notice you waking up in the middle of the night screaming? Because I did and Axel is ripping at the inside of my mind, trying to figure out how I can help you."

"I r-really don't need h-help, Ulysses. I can…"

I lean closer to Westries, who slowly backs up. Her breathing and heart rate speed up and her eyes fill with something I can't decipher.

She wants to open up. I can feel it.

I hold her gaze. "Where did those lines on your legs come from, Westries? They are clearly from an animal. You and I can both guess what animal they are from. And the letters on your leg. Someone burned them into your skin. You can tell me everything and anything.”

Because I already know.

Silent tears roll down my beautiful mate's face, and the cause of those tears makes me see red. I force the rage down and focus on her.

“Talk to me, please. Tell me how I can make it better. Tell me how I can help with the pain, to make it go away. I'm your mate. Just say the word and anything or anyone could be yours.”

I take her small face in my hands, slip my fingertips through her hair, and caress her scalp.

She presses her cheek against my palm. “I-I can't…”

She is so close. Take this agony from her.

I pull her forehead to mine. “You don't need to hide from me, from anything anymore, Bellator. I already know. The reason you hunt rogues, what happened to your family… I *know*. But I also know you can't heal if you won't talk about it.”

“Ulysses, you don't *understand…*”

“Then explain it to me. Tell me so I can help you. You are the only person in my life that matters anymore.”

Westries takes a deep bitter breath and then shoves my hand off.

“You don't think I know that? I know how mates work, but that doesn't matter, because no one in this pack or in the world will accept me. I am shattered beyond repair.”

“That doesn't matter. I don't care. We all have our problems.”

“Problems? I have more than just *problems*. I have demons by the thousands. And even if I didn't, the kingdom will never accept me. See what I do for a living. I can't even count how many people want me *dead* right now.”

I snarl at the thought. “Then I'll destroy their rank and take over their pack.” If anyone dared to harm Westries, I'd kill them.

She tries another argument. "I can't rule over werewolves. How could that even work? What do I know about ruling a kingdom and who would even want me?"

"I want you." I grip her shoulders and pull her closer. She shrugs my hands off and backs away.

"No, Ulysses. I can't give you what you need."

"What, what are you talking about?"

Westries wraps her arms tighter around her waist.

She scoffs. "I know you're not stupid. I knew you would've figured it out by now, since you know everything about me, apparently."

"I-I don't understand…"

"Exactly. You wouldn't be able to."

My mate viciously wipes a single tear from her cheek. I reach out to her, but she wards off my touch.

"Try me, Bellator."

Something in her changes. The cornered wild animal look in her eyes goes out, and her coiled body goes limp.

In a voice I've never heard from her—one that is flat, emotionless— she says, "Ulysses. I was raped."

All the air in my lungs leaves me in a whoosh, like I have been gut kicked. I knew, of course, I knew. But hearing the words from her lips, seeing how much *saying* those words took out of her…

Westries claps her hands over her mouth and a sob escapes through them. Crying was not something I thought I would ever see my strong mate do, but even the strong stumble. Her legs quake and I rush to catch her as she falls to the floor. I hold her to my chest as her floodgates open and the tears flow.

I don't know how long we sat there on the carpet, my back rested against the bed, and her cradled in my arms, but as her heart slowed, I picked her up and set her on the bed. She pulled her knees to her chest and buried her face. I push the tear damp strands of hair off her cheek and tuck them behind her ear. Her eyes are red puffy, and her lashes wet.

She has endured enough.

"You don't have to say anything more." I tell her.

"You want to know, I can tell. Just ask me and I'll answer, I promise."

She sits up straighter and wipes her eyes with her sleeve. I sit crisscross in front of my mate, inching closer by request of Axel.

"How did it happen? You don't have to answer that…"

Westries places her hand over my mouth to shut me up.

"Could you just breathe? I swear, you're more nervous than me."

I mime zipping my lips closed.

She pats my cheek and offers a weak smile before staring off into a faraway space in her memories. "My family went camping. We had just bought a camper and Griffin…" She grinned. "He was just a puppy, so we had a lot of excitement and craziness happening all at once."

Westries smooths the fabric of her shirt sleeve, lost in the recollection.

"We were going to be there all weekend. Friday was great. We went hiking and played in a small river and even roasted marshmallows over a fire my brothers built. They were both so proud. Anyway, Saturday came. All day I had this strange feeling we were being watched. I shrugged it off, convinced myself it was probably just a deer or something. I knew if any wild animal came into camp, my dad would protect us."

She bowed her head. "He trained my siblings and I in firearms, so I had full confidence I was safe. Boy, was I wrong. That night, my siblings and I wanted to sleep in a tent outside. So, nighttime came, and we piled into this tiny, two-person tent and my parents went back to the RV."

My mate took a deep, unsteady breath and looks up into my eyes for the first time during this entire conversation. I don't think I have ever seen such despair in someone's eyes before now.

"That night, while everyone was asleep, I woke because I heard voices. Three of them, and they were *not* my parents. The rest happened so fast. It was all a blur. I heard screaming and claws on metal. I unzipped the tent and saw three huge black wolves clawing at the RV. One wolf got the door open and went inside. They dragged my parents out. The darkness in the tree line hid our small tent, so I thought we might be safe. I was wrong. I watched those raggedy wolves turn back into men. Gangly, vile looking men whose faces I'll never forget. Two of them grabbed hold of my parents."

She paused for a moment and rubbed her head with her palms.

"My siblings had woken up, too, by then. I clamped my hands over their mouths, warning them not to make a sound. We saw the largest guy talking to my mom when she spat in his face. Then another guy slammed his knee into her stomach. My dad acted so fast. He took his pistol from his pants and shot the man in the stomach. The other two tried to restrain my dad and failed. There's hope, I remember thinking. Then. I watched him fall to the ground, his neck at an unnatural angle. My little sister screamed and ran toward my dad. I couldn't stop her in time. The guy with tattoos caught her by the neck and clawed her with his hand."

Westries shuddered but continued. "She was so tiny… I-I knew she was dead. The other goon came toward us while the main guy held my sobbing mom down. I didn't know what to do, just that I had to do *something*. So, I grabbed my bear spray and, as he was about to grab my brothers, I sprayed him. He screamed, and I yelled at my brothers to run. They both ran out of the tent for their life."

A single tear rolls down my mate's face as she bows her head. She then continues, her voice shaking.

"I tried to tackle the wolf man while he was blind, and I caught a glimpse of my brothers running off into the trees. I clawed and kicked the man, but he threw me to the ground a few feet away.

It knocked the wind out of me, but I looked for a rock or anything to throw or strike him with. That's when I saw my mother with her neck slashed. The next thing I knew, one guy sat on my stomach and pinned down my arms. I could feel my ribs being crushed; I could barely breathe.

My ears were ringing, and I could see their lips moving, but I didn't hear anything. The guy on top of me said something to the tattoo guy, and he ran off. He then tied up my hands and legs and gagged me with a cloth."

A river of tears runs down her face and she closes her eyes, rocking.

"I c-couldn't move, and I was sure a had a concussion. My v-vision was blurry, and I could barely see a-and my parents and sister's bodies were laying right next to m-me."

She clutches herself tightly, folding over grief. I cannot let her suffer alone in this agony. As gently as if she were a bomb, I pull her against my chest, and she lets me. After a few minutes, Westries lifts her head from my chest. She takes my hand in between both of hers and absently traces my knuckles. I can tell she is ready to finish the story.

She says, "They were dead. The third guy came back and grabbed my neck, pulling me up to my feet. He told me my brothers were dead. I broke down right there and lost the rest of my strength. He let go, and I crumpled to the ground. They were talking, but I ignored them. I should have... but I-I... he started... he started taking my clothes off."

Axel growls loudly, but instead of cowering away or slapping me, Westries snuggled deeper into my embrace.

"I-I tried to fight back. I really did, but t-they were so strong. I fought, and I tried to kick them, but they had the strength of ten men, and I was just too *tired*."

Her hands tighten almost painfully around mine, but I don't mind. She goes on. "I was only fourteen. I was no match for three grown werewolves. They violated me, Ulysses, and there was nothing I could do to stop it."

She cries unabashedly now. They aren't loud sobs, but silent tears.

I speak against her soft hair. "Westries, you have said enough. You don't have to finish."

She nods but continues her story. "They took turns holding me down the entire night. At some point, I think my body shut down and I couldn't physically move anymore. It hurt so badly; I passed out. I woke up later with no one bothering anymore to hold me down. They knew I was in-capacitated. T-they stopped in the morning, and I remember only being able to smell metallic blood. It was still dark out, but the light from the destroyed camper provided enough light to see the m-mauled bodies of my parents. I tried to c-cry, to move, to do anything to get help, but I couldn't."

"The blond guy came over to where they left me. He was carrying a lantern. He said something about being done with 'it'. The last thing I remember seeing before I blacked out again was him lifting the lantern overhead. I-I don't know what they did a-after that. I thought I was dead. I woke up to a bright light and something scratching my face. I remember I started coughing and couldn't get a breath in. I realized the bottom half of my body was buried. Griffin was digging me out. I don't know where he went or how he survived, but he did."

Her body tensed with the memory. "I used whatever strength I had and started digging my legs out. My body hurt so much. I-I have never felt like that before. My shirt was hanging on by threads and it was covered in blood, *my* blood. I made it back to our car that we had parked off the trail and drove home. I got home, and I p-patched what little I could up."

She covers her mouth with her hand and sobs wrack her body. "I was a coward. I ran away. I left. I didn't know what to do or who to call, so I ran. Who would even *believe* my story? I packed a bag, grabbed Griffin, and I got on a bus. I have been running ever since. I am so sorry, Ulysses."

She was in shock. Alone, traumatized, and in shock.

She cries. "You see? I-I am broken. Please just reject me, please. Spare yourself from me. I promise I won't be mad or hold a grudge. It will be better that way. Please."

I can't breathe anymore. Axel can't breathe anymore.

What can I say to something like this? To someone who has no idea how strong they are? Someone who has shown such courage, such spirit despite all obstacles? Someone who never fails to impress me with an Alpha personality and wry humor?

How am I supposed to combat this much pain and emotion?

I pour every ounce of my emotions into my words. "I will never reject you, ever. I don't care that you feel you are broken because you're not. Not to me. You are perfect for me."

She pleads. "I can't rule. I can't be a queen. I can't be your mate. I can't even give you the one thing you actually need. I can't have kids. I can't give you an heir. I am useless. I can't…"

I cut her awful talking short in the only way I know how. I cup her face in my hands and press my lips to hers. I wait for her to slap me off or push me away, but she doesn't.

She draws her head back to search my eyes. Whatever she sees, there is enough for her to let herself go at last. My mate leans in to brush her lips over mine. Axel howls in delight.

She climbs from my lap to face me, our knees touching. She runs her fingertips along my temples and tangles them in my hair while mine pulled her closer from her waist. I trace my finger along her jaw and push myself closer to her. Eventually, I realize we need to breathe, and I pull back, resting my forehead on hers.

Move slowly with her. She is healing.

"Never talk about yourself like that ever again. Okay?" I mean it as a command, not a request.

She nods and places her head against my chest, leaning into me. She asks in a hushed voice, "So, you're not rejecting me?"

"No. Stop asking that, Bellator. It never even crossed my mind."

She nods again, and I pull her back into my lap. I lay us down on the bed, holding my mate close. We lay in silence for a while. Westries draws circles on my chest, and I twist her long brunette hair in between my fingers. Thoughts wander and drift through my head about what we are going to do next. Is she accepting the mate bond? Will we have a coronation for her to become Luna? Will she and I have a future together? I think of her family as well. The in-laws and sibling in-laws I'll never meet.

"What were their names?"

"My sister's name was Daya. She was five years old. I had twin brothers, Ian and Colton. They were six. I miss them every day."

"I can't even imagine what this has been like for you."

She stops drawing on my chest and bites her thumb.

"I have PTSD. That's why I love the gym and the range so much. It's the only place I don't feel weak or powerless."

I prop my head up and pull her to look at me.

"You are not weak. Just the opposite. You realize everyone thought you were a rogue werewolf, right? Did Aubrey tell you the stories?"

She laughs a little, rubbing her eyes with her sleeve.

"Yeah. Did girls really fawn over me?"

"Yep, it totally pissed off Spencer because he had a crush on Emmalyn. She was obsessed with him… well, you."

"She was obsessed with *me*? Really?"

My mate's lips curl into a tiny grin. She notices me staring.

"What?"

"I love your smile."

This makes her blush, which must be a foreign concept because she buries her face in her pillow.

I wrap my arm around her waist and pull her into my chest. She obliges and curls closer.

"Thank you for everything."

"Care to elaborate, my Luna?"

She smirks at me with a raised eyebrow at the nickname.

"I mean, for being here right now, just talking to me. I have never told anyone before. I mean, Ruby knows a little, but not in detail. Also, for accepting what I have become and who I am. This is the first time in a long time where I've felt… *wanted*."

She stares across at me and then I realize what she just implied.

"Does that mean you will stay here and be my mate?"

She bites her lip, pausing for a second then answering.

"Yeah, I think I will."

I don't even let her continue before I tackle her with a hug, kissing her on the lips.

"Thank you. I promise you will not regret it. You just made my life."

"The saying is: Made my *day*."

"No, it has made my *life*."

She grins at me and places her palm on the side of my face. "Just… could we take things slower than normal mates?"

I realize what I am doing and get off her, sitting in front of her now.

"Of course. Can I still hug you, though? Because…"

"Yes, you can still hug me." She laughs. "Just no random hugs from people, please. I do have one question though. What happens when people find out who I am?"

That's definitely a good question. Some people will have a very hard time coping with what their Luna Queen did for a living.

"We'll tell them before it can become a scandal. We can start with this pack slowly and can officially announce it at the coronation. If that's what you want?"

"Are you asking for a date or my permission?" She raises a sassy eyebrow at me.

There's that fiery side again.

"Can I ask for both?"

"You have my permission, and you pick the date, or let Jackie. She seems to have it planned already, anyway. She is scary. Going dress shopping was terrifying."

"Yeah, she really is sometimes. I'll have to talk to her today."

"Can we go get food now? We have been in here all morning. It's almost eleven and I am starving. You've seen me when I'm mad, but you do not want to see me when I'm 'hangry'."

I laugh at her as she crosses her arms and gives what I assume is her 'hangry' face.

"Sure, get dressed and I will meet you downstairs."

She nods and heads toward the door. Before she leaves, she turns to me. "Oh, and Ulysses, could you keep this to yourself, please? The whole family thing?"

"Always."

This is going to be interesting.

CHAPTER 27

Westries

I either just signed my death wish or just created a new dawn for myself. Either way, I hope it is for the better. I cannot deny that I have *feelings* for Ulysses. Whether it is the mate bond or my human hormones, I can full-heartedly say I have fallen for the Werewolf King.

In fact, I've fallen for all of it: the pack house and the land, the girls in all their weirdness, and even the guys. It feels good to have people who care for me. But it feels even better to care about them.

Inside my closet, I grab some shorts and an oversized ripped camo shirt. Dressing down as per usual. I throw my hair in a soft headband and lace up my tennis shoes. One last peek in the mirror before I head out. My shorts cover my burn letter mark, but not the claw marks.

I am not embarrassed by them, but they aren't exactly a lovely sight either. My scars show what I have gone through, how much I have survived. It's probably a dumb decision to wear shorts in the fall, but...

"The cold never bothered me, anyway."

I probably sang that off key, but *Frozen* is probably one of my favorite Disney movies ever, and I never pass up an opportunity to belt out a song or a line.

My stomach reminds me of what I am supposed to be doing as I walk out down the stairs. The smell of bacon is in the air, as is the sound of laughter. I walk into the kitchen and see the entire gang staring at me. I feel like I have two heads.

This is so awkward.

"Are we having a staring contest or...?"

"Wes." Ruby yells, tackling my neck with a hug and then punching my arm. "I thought you were dead. Don't *scare* me like that."

"I'm sorry. Next time my body unwillingly shuts down, I'll just reboot my system and we'll be good to go." I reply.

She shoots a stank eye at me and returns to her mate. Everyone resumes their conversations or cooking, and I join Corrine and Patrick.

"So, what are you two up to?"

"Bear!" Patrick jumps on me, hugging my waist.

"Don't tell me *you* thought I was dead, too?"

"No, I knew you would live, but I wanted you to meet my brother."

I didn't bother telling him we'd already met.

He pulls me over to the enormous kitchen table where David and Coleman are eating and talking.

"David. This is Bear."

David smiles, playing along, as well.

"Luna," He acknowledges, bowing his head somewhat.

"Please, just call me Westries. I am not Luna, yet."

"Yet?" Coleman asks, smirking.

"*Yet.*" I confirm, trying to hide a tiny smile.

He grins, stands up, and walks over to Jackie. He whispers something in her ear. I swear the room shakes from her mad elephant charge toward me.

"OH MY GOSH. You're staying? For real? Does that mean I can start planning the coronation? Please say yes, because I have like a dozen *Pinterest* boards dedicated to this."

"Jackie, *hush.* Not everyone knows yet, and I already told Ulysses you could do it. I figured you would do it either way, so might as well give you full control."

The squeal she emits is ear piercing, and I slam my hands over my ears to protect myself. As she finally stops torturing us, a pair of arms wrap around my waist and a head buries in my neck.

Ulysses.

"I am guessing you told her then."

"Actually, Coleman did. I said the word *yet.*"

Jackie yells as she leaves the room with Aubrey and Corrine hot on her tail. "I am going to need at least five or six personal assistants, and I am taking over the craft room. Aubrey, we have planning to do. Let's get a move on."

I can already tell this is going to be very *extravagant* and not my style at all.

"This is your fault." I whisper to Ulysses, who smirks against my shoulder.

"It was *your* idea to let her take full control. I just didn't argue."

"Well, since you're not in a mood to argue, you'll agree to letting me take her for a bit? Because I *really* need Westries today." Ruby says from across the kitchen.

"Why?" Ulysses grumbles, squeezing my waist tighter.

"She was my best friend first, you are second." Ruby grabs my arm and pulls me away. I shoot Ulysses a pity glance and struggle to keep up with my crazy friend. She tugs me along, ignoring my groaning and whining. She opens her bedroom door and pushes me inside, locking it behind her.

"Really? Locking the door? Who's going to come in? Jackie, Aubrey, Griffin?"

She flaps her hand at me. "Never mind the door. You need to pay attention. I have it on very good authority that the feral wolves will be close to the border tonight. Think you might pay them a visit?"

Her eyes sparkle with mischief and excitement at the prospect. The spark is contagious.

I tap my chin. "Maybe? Do you think you might distract a certain werewolf King?"

"*Pff,* I could do that in my sleep, but can't you just ask if you could leave? I mean, I heard you accepted your position."

I kick my feet up onto the couch across from the bed, crossing my arms.

"Eh, better to ask forgiveness than permission, right? And maybe I accepted, maybe I didn't. You never know."

"Cut the crap, Wes. I *know* you did. You were glowing and all cozy with Mister King of the werewolves. You can tell me."

She sits next to me, nudging my shoulder.

"Fine. I accepted him. I broke down and told him everything and he still wants me, Rubes. I can't help it, it's this stupid mate bond."

She looks at me like 'seriously, you for real right now?'

"It is not *just* the mate bond, you nitwit. You found your soul mate and you feel the connection. You two are made for each other. Stop selling yourself short."

I stop to think about it for a second. Am I really still selling myself short? I don't think so. I accepted the bond and being Luna Queen, but do I *love* him? Love is a strong word, and I haven't known him for long. I have fallen in *something* for him, but love?

Yes.

"Whatever, but can we get back on topic, please? I need my gear, Griffin, and at least two hours, got it?"

She jumps up, mock salutes me, and runs out the door. So much for my casual attire. I leave her room and head back to my own. This should be interesting. Guards all around the house, Ulysses will never let me leave for a mission, and I do not know where any of my weapons are.

Time to do some snooping. And I know just where to start.

I tiptoe my way to Ulysses' office, planning how I am going to conquer this next challenge. I creep toward the door, listening to see if anyone is inside. Silence. I inch the door open and step inside.

There must be a safe in here somewhere.

I wander around his desk, examining everything in sight, then sit in the expensive office chair, staring at his computer. I tap the mouse a few times, but of course, he has a password. So, I move on to a few drawers to find papers and other office junk.

I rummage around until I find a small safe. On the box, there is a keyhole and a thumb pad. I don't have the tools to open it, so I put it back where I found it. I stride over to the closet and open the double doors. Inside are about half a dozen coats and fancy suit jackets. I push them all aside to find an even larger safe with a keypad.

Now, if I was an Alpha king, what would my password be? How about one, two, three, four? Nope.

What about a four to six-letter word? I sit crisscross in front of the safe with my head in my hands.

Dogs… nope.

Wolf… uh-uh.

Alpha… king… how about Ulysses? Nope.

My gut is telling me something, but I don't want to listen. I slowly type in the eight-letter word I am dreading presently:

"Westries." The safe clicks open.

We'll think about this later.

I open the safe doors and peer inside. We have folders, a small shoe box, and my Barrett M82. Jackpot. I check for ammunition, and I find about thirty rounds. I lock the safe back up and take my leave. I have maybe two or three hours before someone notices I am gone. Time to do what I do best, go hunting. One sharp dog whistle later, Griffin comes charging in, knowing exactly what is about to go down.

"You're late. We don't have all day. Let's go."

In the garage, I open the driver's side door, letting Griffin jump in the co-pilot seat. I can only imagine the amount of trouble I will be in if I am caught. Not too much though, because I am Luna of Luna's.

I still can't believe I am actually doing it, but whatever.

I open the garage door and put the pedal to the metal. Knowing Ulysses, he has wolves everywhere, but I hope that they will let the car through.

I don't exactly know where I am heading, but I do know this; when you are searching for a feral rogue, all you really need is a pretty target. Thankfully, I am a good actor, so playing a damsel in distress shouldn't be too hard, if needed. Revolting, but not hard. I drive deeper into the mountainside hoping that Ulysses' scouts won't find me or will at least not bother me. I reach a camping site and slow down to park the car along the trail. Griffin jumps out with me.

I pop the trunk open and take my pistol first, loading it to max capacity. I slide the cool metal into my thigh holster and start on my Barrett, loading the magazines and slinging the strap over my back, still covering most of the barrel with my coat. Next, I take out six smooth throwing knives and slide them into their grips on my forearm. I feel a slight chill as I remove my coat to do so. Winter is coming and I can smell the snow in the air.

I need to find a high vantage point if I am going to attain the element of surprise. Griffin runs ahead along the trail, eager to hunt. I swear that dog loves the chase more than I do. He has helped me track down more than a dozen feral wolves who realized they were now the hunted. Who better to sniff out a wolf than their own kind? I don't know what I would do without him.

In the distance, a large rock formation is visible, perfect for a rifleman's crow nest for hunting wolves from. Climbing is another thing I excel at. With each bolder I climb, I can feel myself growing stronger, tougher, and more like myself again. Griffin, too, has rediscovered his inner Billy goat, and scales the boulders with equal ease. As we reach the top, I can see a good distance away. Not too far up, but just enough so that I can spy on them, but they can't spot me.

I set up shop, getting as comfy as I can, then wait for anything to show itself. I scope out a tree, a rabbit and tried to figure out what my firing range is. I have about two hundred and fifty yards in each direction, with the blind spots being trees and bushes. To the left of me, there is a slight clearing, about the size of an average house.

Now for the hardest part about hunting, waiting. Ninety-nine percent of hunting and tracking is patience. Taking the kill shot is only one small fraction of the arduous task. Griffin mindlessly chews on some sticks at my feet as I peer through the scope on my rifle.

If I were a rogue werewolf, this is exactly where I would be. Vegetation, water, cover, plenty of places to attack and hide from. Forty minutes pass, and I have gone through half a bag of butterscotch. Number one tip when hunting, find a good candy that you can suck on. It will at least give you something to do. Another tip, take the wrapper off beforehand and put them all in a plastic bag, so you won't make too much noise.

The entire bag later and I begin to see things like most hunters do. Chewbacca, a giant spider chasing a hairless mole-rat, and an ostrich trying to peel a banana. I will have you know this is perfectly normal. It happens to everyone, even the best.

My thoughts are cut off at the sound of a loud, feral growl. Then more growling and howling. I take the safety off my weapon and scope around, searching for the source. Out in the field are the first two wolves. One is chasing the other, trying to go after his neck. It is clear who is the rogue and who is the pack warrior. I wait for them to separate and then take my shot.

The feral falls. Dead.

Ulysses' pack warrior frantically peers around for what just happened and where the other invisible attacker came from. He would never guess, or maybe he would. At least a dozen wolves fill the field, with the rogue to pack wolf ratio at five to seven.

Well, now four to six.

They all stand about, probably using their mind link or whatever. The feral wolves growl and one of them lunges at the large brown wolf.

He never even had the chance. He was dead faster than you can say, 'Peter Piper.' The rogue wolves are getting antsy and are about to run when an earth-shaking growl erupts. Springing from the brush is Ulysses in wolf form. I would recognize him anywhere. Griffin sits up intensely next to me, watching this whole saga go down. I can't help but giggle a little at him. He rests his head on a rock, looking down on the werewolves, most likely judging them.

The wolves down below seem to have a growl off because the rogues, or what's left of them, lunge for the pack warriors. I have a clear shot of one, and I take it. I have a feeling Ulysses knows what is going on because he gazes around and then up. He spots me, but I ignore him. Two rogues remain. Rogue One has his neck snapped by a rather large wolf and Rogue Two is about to attack an unsuspecting pack wolf until I shoot him.

The small field is littered with dirty feral rogues. I stand and gather up all the casings from my rifle and all my stuff, cram it into my duffle, walking back to the car. I hear a rustle in the bushes behind me, but I ignore it and load the trunk.

"Westries."

Ooh, someone is in trouble. Oh wait, that would be me.

I turn around, arms crossed, to find seven men in basketball shorts. Two of which are Ulysses and Cade. Ulysses storms up to me, anger and worry etched on his face.

"Yes? Can I *help* you?" I smile sweetly.

"Don't give me that. Why did you leave the pack house? We have been looking for you everywhere. What if you got hurt?"

I scoff. "You're welcome, by the way. Or did you forget I just saved your pack warriors' butts till you arrived? Blondie over there would've had his head ripped off if it weren't for me."

"Oh, I know. Cade mind linked me, saying that bullets were raining from the sky, and it didn't take a genius to figure out who it was." Ulysses is still seething, and his jaw muscles clench and unclench.

I angle my head around him and call out to the nervous guy. "Hey blondie, you might want to pay more attention when you are in the middle of battle. You new, or something?"

"Um, yes Luna, I just graduated from high school, and I will try harder next time."

I walk away, but Ulysses stops me.

He hisses in my ear, so the others don't hear. "We are not done here. You can't just leave like that. What would've happened if you had gotten hurt? Or worse? How could you be so stupid? They could've killed you."

"Ulysses, this is what I do. I may have accepted the mate bond and what comes with being Luna, but you can't just expect me to drop the only thing that has given my life any purpose up until this point. Take me with all the messed-up problems I am, or take nothing, because this is who I really am. The teenage hunter who has a lot of baggage and can hold a grudge like there is no tomorrow. You said you accepted me. Well, this is part of me."

Ulysses stares at me for a second, breathing heavily. He rubs his temples.

From the migraine that is me, I'm sure.

"Cade, take Griffin and the car back, please. The rest of you can return to your patrols."

I give up arguing with Ulysses and groan. I point over to Cade.

"Cade, if there is a single scratch on her, I will neuter you."

"Yeah, yeah, I'll take great care of your car."

I watch as Cade gets into my ride, pushing Griffin over, who growls at him. That sure is going to be a fun ride home.

Home? Oh, forget it, it is my home.

Ulysses and I are now alone on top of the giant rock mountain. He is pacing back and forth as I watch and wait him out. It's only when I realize I'm freezing, do I give in and speak first.

"You do realize it's like thirty degrees out here."

Ulysses glances at me from his pacing yet says nothing.

"Okay, mister moody, how about you tell me what we are doing?"

Nothing.

Fine. I can be stubborn, too.

I sit on the ground, arms crossed, still watching the bipolar werewolf king pacing in front of me. One, three, and then five minutes pass, and I am cold and bored. I lay back on the ground, cross one leg over the other, and prop my head under my arms. I stare up at the sky, counting clouds and birds. Twenty-seven clouds and fourteen birds, not counting one very suspicious vulture, who probably thinks I am dead.

A pair of very muscular arms pull me up and I am pressed against Ulysses' chest. I sit in between Ulysses' legs as he breathes in my scent.

I guess I pissed off Axel big time, and he just needs time to gain control again.

It keeps slipping my mind that I am literally living with killer wolves who could bite my head off. Honestly, I don't care.

In a controlled, calm voice, Ulysses says, "Could you just not do that?"

I play coy. "Be more specific."

"Run off without telling me. I almost tore off my own Beta's head because Axel couldn't find you. It wasn't until Ruby told us what you were doing that I regained control."

"Traitor…" I mutter under my breath as I am spun around so I am facing Ulysses.

"You don't mean that. She was just worried about you, and she was forced to say something because I threatened her mate. Don't blame her. They just want what's best for their Luna and…"

"Ulysses, that is just it. I don't know *how* to be a Luna. I never intended to fall in love, let alone have a mate, let alone an *Alpha* mate, *LET ALONE* the WEREWOLF KING. I am not a proper lady, nor capable of running the entire werewolf world. And what happens when people find out who and what I am? They will reject me and, in turn, you. I can't imagine the thought that I had caused that. And…"

His warm lips pressed against mine catches me off guard. As soon as they were there, they left.

"Is that the only way to stop your rambling?"

I glare at him, crossing my arms, trying to seem mad. I fail.

Ulysses chuckles, pulling me back into his chest.

"Aww, don't pout, Bellator."

"I hate you." I say it with as much confidence as I can. He doesn't believe me.

"No, you fell in love with me. You said so yourself."

I did? Did I really say I loved him?

I bury my face in his shirt to hide the blush that is surely on my face. He holds me tighter. A cold, heavy breeze sweeps through the rocks, and I shiver.

"Hey, wolfman, you werewolves may have endless heat but us humans get cold."

Ulysses jumps up, lifting me with him.

"Oh yeah, I forgot. I'll be right back."

He jumps behind a rock, and I can hear his bones snapping into their new position. Seconds later, a giant black wolf comes trotting out. He towers two or three heads above. In his mouth, he is gripping his shorts. He leans down next to a rock, motioning for me to climb on.

"This is still weird." I mumble as I climb onto his back.

Once I stop squirming around, he takes off running. We will get back to the pack house in under a quarter of the time it took to get here. This is honestly way better than cars and driving. The wind in your face, the feeling of being free out in the forest with trees and nature. I love it.

CHAPTER 28

Ulysses

Now that she has accepted the mate bond, we can plan her coronation… and figure out how to tell the entire werewolf community that their Luna Queen is the Avenger and a human. I don't expect it will be easy, but it is feasible that they will…

Something is off. I don't smell her. That can only mean one thing.

She left. Without a single clue about where she was going or why. Griffin is also gone, and my office had been broken into. Plus her car isn't in the garage. For a solid thirty minutes of ransacking the pack house, I believe maybe she left because she is rejecting us. It isn't until Ruby admits where she is that I regain control.

Westries is going to be the death of me.

No one has ever stood up to me and backtalked me the way she has. It is irritating… and also refreshing.

Now that I know she hasn't run away, my mind turns to the questions in the back of my thoughts.

When will we complete the mate bond? Can humans even go into heat?

We already know having pups is out of the question, but maybe we could explore other options. I haven't had a need to study the werewolf bylaws for such a concern, but adopting an heir may not be accepted or allowed. Axel pipes up in my head.

Screw the bylaws. We will do whatever it takes to make our mate happy. End of story.

Try telling mother that.

That's sounds like a you problem, not a wolf problem.

My problems are your problems.

I am so preoccupied by my thoughts; I barely register we've arrived to the field Ruby sent us. Westries is no doubt hiding in some vantage point, itching to practice her sniper skills. As if knowing my thoughts, a rogue falls to the ground and the sound of the shot follows.

My Elites and I jump into action, and with Westries' help, the rogues are eliminated. I waste no time in finding her, reprimanding her, and promptly forgiving her. She shivers.

I need to shift and get her home.

Once secure on Axel's back, we charge off through the woods. We arrive back at the pack house and before I can lower myself to the ground, Westries jumps off and strides toward the back door. I shift and pull on my basketball shorts, trying to catch up with my stubborn mate.

"Slow down. What's the rush?"

"Hurry, fur butt. Keep up or eat my dust."

Westries reaches for the door handle, and upon opening the door, a whirlwind of arguing spills out. Westries stops flat in her tracks and looks back at me, giving me a knowing glance. We both step inside the door to the kitchen. Our Beta, Gamma, and Delta are standing there arguing with each other, among my siblings, my parents, some elders, and the Jettieson boys. They fail to notice us.

I am about to intervene when a piercing sound rings through the kitchen and dining room. Everyone covers their ears and shuts up. When the sound ends, everyone looks around for the source. I know exactly where and who is responsible. Westries twirled a key ring around her finger as she speaks.

"Much better. Now someone wanna tell me what is going on?"

"*We* don't have to tell you anything. You're human, and you aren't even a part of the pack." Emmalyn sneers, standing next to my mother.

"Think again, honey." Westries smirks and crosses her arms. Almost all the females already know what happened. It is just the elders, pack, and the old Alpha who didn't. Then elder Corbin laughs and hobbles over to us, cane and all.

"This is terrific news. I cannot wait to see what you do as Luna, my dear."

Elder Corbin embraces Westries, who gives into the hug willingly. Emmalyn and my mother are still standing next to the island, dumbfounded.

"What are you saying, Ulysses?"

"Mother, she accepted me as her mate and will be the Luna Queen."

"But we have laws. Laws that I will not tolerate being ignored."

My mother tries to sound dominant and demanding in the situation but fails.

"Actually, there are no bylaws against having a human Luna Queen. No one ever thought it possible, so no laws were created."

"Elder Daniel, you can't possibly be endorsing this?"

"Yes, in fact, I am. We could use a spitfire like her around here."

"I second that. Wes is incredible when it comes to running operations like businesses. She would kill it" Ruby says from the arms of her mate. Emmalyn walks closer to Ruby, her heels clicking against the hardwood floor.

"She would, wouldn't she?"

Ruby's eyes go wide for a second, then return to confidence. I quickly sneak a glance at Westries to read her emotions. Her face is stern, almost like stone, staring at Emmalyn, daring her to speak.

"So, *if* you became Luna Queen, would your devoted subjects get to know about you, or would that be a secret? Don't they deserve to know *what* their precious Queen has done?"

She gazes around the room for someone to answer the question.

"Does anyone remember what she's done? She is a genocidal maniac!?"

Emmalyn is cut off by Westries.

"Enough. I am the Avenger, this is old news people. I am not explaining myself again to someone of such low intellect who clearly didn't get it the first time. Isn't this common news by now for everyone here?"

The room fills with snickering and whispers. Yes, many of them already knew, but I don't think the full severity of the situation has officially worn in yet. Westries sighs.

"Good. No one is surprised. Now, here's your one opportunity for questions from the peanut gallery."

Emmalyn shifts uncomfortably.

Westries' gaze travels around to each person. "If anyone has *anything* they would like to say on the matter, do it now. Condemn me if you must. But understand this: I won't apologize." Her gaze rests on Emmalyn, then my mother. "What I do may be wrong in the eyes of some, but I have saved more lives than I took."

When her gaze finds Elder Corbin, her tone changes, pleading for understanding. "There were little girls sold into slavery and families destroyed because of drugs and gang rape and I just couldn't sit around and do nothing."

Westries' pain and sadness courses through the mate bond into my heart. I reach out to hold my mate in my arms. She lets out a ragged breath. I kiss the top of her head and she leans into me.

The whispers have stopped. Everyone stands with their own mates out of comfort. Ruby pulls herself out of Spencer's grip to console Westries.

"Wes, *I* know you and what you've done. I helped, for crying out loud. Why would we ever condemn you?" Ruby grabs Westries hand, squeezing it lightly.

"Thank you, Ruby. But it is reasonable that no one would want me to be Luna after what I've done. Even I would question a ruler who has done even a fraction that I have."

Jackie comes forward and takes Westries hand, smiling kindly at her. "Why *wouldn't* we? You fight for the weak, you care for random werewolf pups you meet, and you just want to protect the people you care about. What would we condemn?"

"They're right, you know. You will be a great Luna. I mean, at least you could mate Ulysses." Cade laughs, glancing at me. He nods knowingly at me. "You are completely badass, and we would be lucky just to even have you in our pack. We literally have been spending all our time keeping you here and you think we're going to send you away now!?"

"Besides, who likes a boring, proper Luna, anyway?" Hannah says, walking toward her mate.

Everyone has kind things to say to Westries. My parents, however, stand watching us next to the pack elders and Emmalyn.

"And you still want me to be Luna Queen?"

Jackie and Ruby are still holding my mate's hands as she stands in my arms.

"Yes, we do," says Ruby. "If I have to stay, then so do you."

Jackie elbows Westries. "Plus, I already planned your coronation. Oh. And Aubrey and I designed the invitations, too."

Westries laughs. The formerly tense atmosphere in the room is now filled with love and adoration. From the corner of my eye, I spot Emmalyn and my parents slipping out the side door. It's then I notice Elder Corbin watching them as well, a troubled expression on his face.

When he sees me, he adopts a cheerful smile and mouths, "Never mind them." I return my attention to Westries, who is gazing up at me expectantly.

"So…"

I squeeze her and announce, "So, it's settled, then. You are going to become our Luna Queen. We will announce it to the pack tonight, and if Aubrey and Jackie are done with the invitations, we can send them tomorrow."

Westries' face glows as Jackie, Hannah, Ruby, and Aubrey embrace her. Jackie then talks an ear off to Westries about the Coronation and how it will go down. All the girls then drag my mate out of the kitchen, probably toward the art room.

"Congrats, man." Coleman pats my back warmly. "So, she is officially staying?"

I nod at Spencer's question. I am bursting with joy at the realization my mate wants me as her forever partner. My cheeks hurt from smiling like an idiot.

"So, we finally have all the Royals together. I honestly never thought I would see the day." Cade chuckles.

Neither did I. Not even when I found her.

Spencer chimes in. "Tell me about it. Now that everyone is here, the pack should run smoother."

I nod in agreement. Spencer is right. Since we have everyone together now, with each assuming their proper positions, things will be a lot easier.

"What about you, Ulysses? You've been quiet this whole time."

"Just taking it all in. Things are about to become very busy around here."

Cade says, "Knowing Jackie, she already found everything we need."

Now it all just needs to come into play.

"Our mates will be tied up with caterers, decorators, and God knows what else. We're hardly going to see them," I lament.

"She left five minutes ago. You're whipped." Coleman laughs, slapping my shoulder.

"Well, considering I've waited years to find her, I think I can just be a little possessive. I am going to find them."

The other guys agree to find their mates as well. Before I depart, Elder Corbin calls me aside. I'd forgotten he was still here in the chaos.

"Forgive me, Alpha, but I must speak with you."

"Of course, Elder Corbin. What is it?"

"The Luna… she is not weak; we all know that. But I still fear for safety. She *is* just human among some of the most powerful creatures known. I humbly recommend that until the coronation, you keep a close eye on her. We have waited this long for her. I fear if we lose her, the nations will fall."

"Thank you, Elder Corbin. I promise you I will sooner give up my life than let any harm come to the queen. She will be protected at all costs."

He tips his hat and excuses himself.

Now, to find my mate.

I head off to the art room, knowing that is where Jackie would have taken her. As I approach the room, I can hear four voices explaining the ceremony and two other voices arguing. I push open the double doors to see the mess that the art room has become.

Fabric is everywhere, cardstock is thrown onto the floor, and in the middle of it all are three trifold boards and Westries sitting in a chair watching.

"So, the ceremony will be in the Wilson Grand Hall, where you will wear the forest green gown. This is where you receive the crown, be accepted, marry Ulysses, and some other stuff."

Jackie uses a long ruler to tap the second trifold board. "The reception will be just outside in the gardens and courtyard. Between the two events, you will change into your black lace gown. You will mingle with Ulysses and get to know your subjects. Think Met Gala but actually interesting. Listen up, because this is where it gets tricky. When we fly there, we will need…"

"Wait. Jackie. Did you say fly?"

"Yes, I did, now…"

"It isn't going to be here?"

"No, it's going to be in Romania."

"Romania!"

"Yes, Westries. Were you paying attention at all?"

Westries mutters a no and sinks further into the chair. Spencer and Cade slump on the couch, watching while Ruby, Aubrey, and Hannah run through catering brochures. Jackie is trying to explain her trifold boards while Coleman hides off to the side, not wanting to interfere with a ranting Jackie. Westries sees me in the doorway, and we exchange weary glances.

"Slow down, Jackie. You should start with the basics. I completely trust that you can handle everything else."

Jackie grunts and flips through her clipboard. "Well, what should I tell you then?"

Time for me to jump in. "What if you let *me* explain it?"

Jackie collapses next to Coleman on the loveseat. "Fine, but when you can't decide what dessert would be best for the reception and how to book a florist, don't come crying to me."

I nod to her and explain. "The ceremony will take place in Romania because, as history has it, the first werewolf was born there. Depending on when Jackie planned this whole thing, we will fly there a week early to prepare."

Westries picks at the edge of the cushion while biting her lip. "I thought this would be with, like, just your pack and family, not the *whole* werewolf community…"

I push a stray strand of hair behind her ear. "Sorry, but this is the event of the century. A *lot* of people will want to meet you. Jackie, when did you plan this thing exactly?"

Jackie flips through a few pages and slams her finger down on one of them. She nervously mutters something.

"The thing is, I *sort* of messed up the one and the two, so it's in eight days…"

I massage my temples. "Eight days. That means we leave tomorrow."

"Yes, we would leave tomorrow, but it doesn't have to be early. We have a private jet. It will all work out."

"Don't forget the announcement tonight, Wes."

Westries glares at Ruby. "Thanks, Rubes. And no Jackie. I am not wearing a dress."

Jackie groans and throws her binder down again. Coleman wraps his arms around his mate, calming her.

Westries springs up. "Wait, so let me get this straight. *Today* you are going to announce me to the pack, right?"

"Yes."

"Then *tomorrow* we are leaving for Romania for the coronation thing, right?"

"Yes."

"And at that coronation thing, I'll have to talk to people?"

"Most likely, many people have been expecting you and are waiting patiently."

She throws her head back in the chair and stares at the ceiling for a minute. Then she sits up, a new question on her lips.

"Can Patrick and David come? I would want them to be there, please." She begs.

"Yes, of course, they can come. Corrine, Aubrey, and my parents will be there too, but most likely, they will come later."

Or not at all.

Right then, Corrine, Patrick, and David barrel into the art room with Nerf guns firing at each other. Fabric and paper fly everywhere. Not that it makes much of a difference. The room is already a disaster.

Aubrey screams at them to quit it and David throws her a Nerf gun, which she uses on Corrine.

Westries laughs her head off at the chaos surrounding us. It is quite the spectacle. The four kiddos turn on the rest of us and fire away.

Jackie screams and runs, but Coleman uses her as a shield. She howls up a storm at him. Spencer and Ruby throw pillows at the bunch, using whatever they could find as weapons. Hannah and Cade hide behind the art table, shushing each other to stop laughing. Corrine runs out of bullets and screams for the 'calvary'. Griffin charges in wearing a Nerf gun vest covered in Nerf cartridges. Corrine and Patrick yank them off and reload, firing on us even more.

"Freeze, Wolfie boy." I heard my mate say.

I turn to her, and she is smirking and pointing a Nerf handgun right at me.

"Don't you dare. You wouldn't turn against your own mate."

"Think again." She fires once and a single foam bullet bounced off my forehead. Westries doubles over, laughing.

"Oh, it's on."

She stops laughing and curls into a defensive ball around her weapon, but I tackle her and wrestle the gun out of her hand. When I finally get it, she chortles.

"You couldn't hit the broad side of a barn."

I raise an eyebrow and shoot her in the stomach rapidly. She giggles and falls to the ground.

"Is someone ticklish?"

She stops laughing. "No, no, I am not."

I tickle her, causing her to squeal. I pulled her into my lap and continue torturing her.

"Surrender."

"N-never."

I wriggle my fingers at the tender curve of her neck, and she squirmed around even more. "Surrender."

"F-fine! I surrender."

"Victory." Corrine screams at the top of her lungs. The trio start high fiving each other.

Westries stares at me, shocked. "You were in on this?"

"Don't blame me. It was Corrine's idea." I point to Corrine, who preens.

"Corrine, how could you? I'm hurt." Westries yells, rolling around on the ground.

Corrine bounds over and jumps on her stomach, followed by Griffin, quite literally dog piling her. "Aren't you proud? I planned a war."

Westries lifts her head, smiling. "Yes, very proud. But since you started this war, you have to help clean it up."

Corrine sighs and helps Jackie and the other girls clean up. I reach a hand down toward Westries, who grabs it, and I pulled her up.

"I'm mad at you…"

"Are you?"

She tries to let go of my hand. Instead, I pull her closer, burying my face in her neck.

"Let go. We have to clean up in here." She whines, struggling to get out of my grip.

"Guys it's 2:34. The barbeque is in two and a half hours." Jackie yells at everyone. Westries and I pick up the pillows and put the chairs back.

"So, what should I pack for Romanian weather?"

"Well, it's pretty cold, so jeans, long sleeves, jackets, you should have everything you need."

We all pick up the room, or what Jackie lets us pick up. Apparently, it is an *organized* mess. I don't see it. When we finish, Aubrey announces we should all go pack for the trip. David and Patrick look at each other, confused.

"You guys need to pack, too." Westries tells them. "You guys are coming to Romania with us."

"Really?" Patrick asked excitedly.

"Are you sure Luna?"

"David, I asked you to stop calling me that and yes, you both are coming. It would mean a lot to me, plus Aubrey will be there."

David blushes, and I suppress a growl.

"Hey Patrick, why don't you go lay out your clothes? I'll come help you soon."

Patrick skips out, leaving David, my mate, and I in the art room.

"Aubrey's your mate, isn't she?" Westries asks gently. David nods.

Axel growls and Wes elbows me.

"I swear I mean no harm, Alpha, and I…"

"Ulysses will not be a problem. He understands you won't hurt her, and you just want what is best for her, right?"

David's head bobbles.

"He also will be accepting the mate bond, right?"

I cool down Axel, trying not to growl again. Westries slaps my chest with the back of her hand, forcing me to agree.

Damn, I really am whipped.

"Yes, I only ask that you go slow with her and if you break her heart, I'll pummel you." I shake his hand and resist the urge to crush the fine bones under his skin. He bows his head and backs out of the room.

"Was that so hard?" Westries asks.

"No," I mumble.

"But if he hurts her, I will snap his neck."

"Fine, now let's go."

Westries grabs the collar of my shirt, dragging me to our bedroom. *Ours.* My mate and I.

I drag Ulysses through the halls till we reach our bedroom.

"When did you get a jet?" I ask, throwing a pile of jeans and sweatshirts onto the bed.

"King of all werewolves, babe. I own a lot of things you don't know about," Ulysses says, winking at me while he places two suitcases onto the bed.

"So, mister *rich* guy, how many of us are leaving tomorrow?"

Ulysses lays two dress shirts down into the case and then gazes up at the ceiling, counting on his fingers.

"You and me, Coleman, Jackie, Spencer, Ruby, Cade, Hannah, David, Aubrey, Patrick, Corrine, Jake, Owen, Paul, and a few other personal guards."

Wait. We can't forget about my best friend.

"Can Griffin come too? *Please.*"

He looks at me like 'really the dog too'? I give my best puppy eyes possible.

"Fine, he can come. Now get packing. We have a lot to do before we leave tomorrow."

We throw clothes into our suitcases at record speed. Ulysses packs nicer dress clothes while I pack jeans, T-shirts, and sweatshirts. It's cold there, right?

Should I make a good first impression? Nah.

"Done." I holler as I sit on my suitcase, trying to close it. Ulysses helps me zip it closed and sets it to the side.

"You sure you have everything you need?"

"Yep. I am going to help Patrick now," I yell as I run down the halls toward the boys' room. When I walk in, I see David, Aubrey, and Jackie trying to help Patrick pack his suitcase. It appears a tornado has gone through the room.

"Ah, Westries, I'm handing this impossible little devil off to you. I'll be in my room." Jackie says, exhausted, leaving me with the three.

"I am going to help David find some of Ulysses' old clothes. Good luck with him." Aubrey and David leave the room in a hurry. Patrick is running around the room throwing everything from clothes to pillows to a box of cereal into the center of the room.

"Patrick, what exactly are you doing?"

"I'm packing, Bear. Do you want to help me?"

I nod and get on my knees, trying to find his suitcase under the mess.

"I want you to give me seven pairs of pants you like."

Patrick wanders around the room, grabbing various pants, and returns to me with a big wad. He hands me the pile and I fold them, putting them into the case. I do the same thing with his shirts, socks, underwear, and everything else. Before I know it, we have a fully packed suitcase filled with little boys' clothes.

"All done. Now go play before the barbeque."

I set Patrick's suitcase in the corner of his room. I check my phone, 4:36 P.M.

Shoot, the barbeque is in twenty-four minutes.

Jackie is going to kill me. I rush to the kitchen, where everyone is waiting.

"What took you so long?"

"I was helping Patrick. Where's the fire? Geesh."

We're just going outside, aren't we?

"Alright everyone, load up. We have a barbeque to go to."

Okay, so I guess the announcement isn't happening here.

I follow the crowd to the garage, not quite knowing what was going on.

"Where are we going?" I whispered to Aubrey next to me.

"The community center. Most of the town will be there. The local restaurants are providing food and there will be live bands, too."

I gulp. This is all happening faster than I expected, but then again, what the hell do I know about any of this? I am about to jump into the car behind Aubrey when Ulysses grasps my wrist and tugs me with him to the truck.

"You are coming with me, mate."

I roll my eyes and climb into the shotgun.

"Thanks for telling me the announcement is at the community center."

Ulysses pulls out of the garage, leading the caravan of cars to the pack barbeque.

"I thought that was obvious. Where did you think it was going to be?"

"I don't know, here on the patio, maybe… and how many people are coming today? Like, is this going to be a few dozen high-ranking people, or just like anyone?"

"Well, most people have full-time jobs, so it won't be *everyone*. Anyone could come though, it's just whoever shows up. Most people will probably just come for a little while and then leave. It won't be terrible, I promise."

I groan. I am *not* a social person. Small crowds and small get-togethers? *That* I could get into. Large ones? Hard pass. Although, I guess I better get used to it, because I'm sure being a Queen involves a lot of people-ing.

Queen? Really?

Will that ever sink in? I am a killer, ruthless. Now suddenly, I have people to care about, and they care for me back. A family, a pack, a nation.

I am staring out the window when Ulysses turns on country radio. My feet tap along to the beat of the latest country love songs. I love all sorts of music, but country is by far the best. The trees speed by as the songs change. The mountains disappear and the town emerges in the distance.

Part of me wishes I could jump out of this car and run back to the pack house, but there are a dozen people willing to throw me back in the car and force me along. I figure it is best to stay put. Before I know it, I am humming along to yet another country love song. We drive into town and people wave at our caravan of cars. I slide deeper into my chair, heat rushing to my face and my stomach filling with butterflies.

Ulysses reaches over to me and takes my hand, squeezing it reassuringly. We arrive at the community center. It is a large white building surrounded by a park, playground, and picnic tables. There are people everywhere talking, playing, and serving food. I don't know what I was expecting, but it isn't this.

This seems like a friendly chill get-together, not an up-tight party with stuck-up snobs. I open my door and jump out, a cold breeze hitting my face. Ulysses walks up behind me and clasps my hand, looking out at all the people with me.

"You ready?"

"No."

"Perfect."

Perfect? Ha.

Ulysses grins at me and leads me to the picnic tables. I am freaking out here. People notice the large group of us walking toward them and they bow their heads with respect, then return to their conversations. I get a few shocked eyes and whispers. They probably realize I am human or see that I am packing. Boy, are they in for an even bigger surprise.

"Come on, there is someone I want you to meet."

Ulysses drags me through the crowd, and we wind up inside the community center, where all the older people seem to hang out. We stop when an old man and woman approach us. By his warm greeting, it's obvious Ulysses knows them well. I wait politely for the introduction and hope my discomfort doesn't show.

"Westries, this is my grandmother and grandfather. They were Alpha and Luna before my parents."

"Oh, my goodness, she really is human. Well, I say it is about time. We could use a change around here. Oh my, where are my manners? My name is Amia, but you can just call me Me'ma."

I reach my hand out to shake hers, but she wraps me in a death grip hug. The old man guffaws.

"Let go of the poor girl, dear, before you traumatize her."

Amia let me go, still smiling.

"Hello, dear, I am Michael, it is a pleasure to meet you. I hear you accepted becoming Luna Queen."

"Umm, yes, I did."

"Well, that's great. I cannot wait to see what your grandkids will look like."

Both I and Ulysses freeze. I force myself to breathe, inwardly feeling my gut twist and the unmistakable feeling of bile rising in my throat.

Ulysses is quick to cover the pause. "Me'ma please, you just met my mate, and this is the first thing you ask her? We are taking things slow."

Ulysses gazes at me with a tenderness that makes my heart stutter. He takes my hand and firmly squeezes it reassuringly. I wordlessly thank him.

"Oh, I'm sorry, honey. Excuse my forwardness. Ulysses, do you mind if I steal her for a while? I have some people who are just dying to meet her."

Ulysses quirks his eyebrows at me. I wipe my damp hands on my jeans and nod.

"Just don't overwhelm her with all your amazing *social* skills."

Apparently, Amia doesn't know an insult when she hears one, so she loops her arm through mine and leads me away before I can utter a single word of protest.

Amia presents me to three other ladies, whose names I forget the moment she tells them. They were old 'pup' friends of hers and they act overly excited to meet me. Every single person I meet has a billion and one questions, some of which I don't particularly want to answer.

Honestly, werewolves have worse filters than I do.

This goes on for what seems like forever but is only twenty-five agonizing minutes. I swear when I find Ulysses, I will kill him for letting me go with his crazy grandma. I mean, yeah, I agreed to go, but he should warn me. We eventually end up outside under a gazebo.

"And this is my oldest gal, Sue."

I reach my hand out to shake hers, but she squashes me in a bone-crushing hug.

I don't think I will ever get used to this.

"Oh, my goodness. So, it's true. You really are as beautiful as they say."

Heat creeps up my neck and floods my cheeks. I'll never get used to compliments, either.

"She really *is* human. Not that it's *bad.* I just thought the younger wolves were making a ruckus with rumors."

"A ruckus?"

"Oh yes, something like this will be *world* changing. Human mates are a rarity. You could count them all on your fingers and toes. So, you can understand why a human Luna *Queen* is beyond revolutionary."

"So, in your opinion, how many people will, like, *hate* me?"

She rapidly blinks for a second, then answers. "Well, there will always be people who don't like the Luna. But in the end, we will have your back. No matter what."

"Well, that's a relief, I guess."

The ladies launch into a winding conversation while I drift over to the side. My gaze wanders around to all the people talking, eating, and socializing. I back away slowly in search of someone I know, or at least someone my actual age. I stroll aimlessly around for what felt like forever till I end up back outside.

The clean, brisk air hits me straight in the face as I push the heavy doors open. Over in the grass is a giant playground surrounded by a three-foot high fence. There are kids running around playing tag, swinging on an old tire swing, and in the center of it all, a grand oak playscape with dark green accents. Feeling like a total creeper, I sat at the picnic tables and watch the wonder that was the gift from God. The playground, sandboxes, swing sets and jungle gym were all the ultimate child's dream.

One child catches my attention. She seems to be about twelve and has no intention of enjoying this shindig at all. Since awkward and weird is my strong suit, I'm compelled to talk to her. I plop down right next to her against the fence.

"I'm guessing you were forced to be here too?"

She offers that classic 'Who the hell are you?' teenage look. I reached my hand out, and she hesitantly took it.

"I'm Westries."

"Audrey. Wait, aren't you…"

"Yeah, but never mind that. So, what's up, I guess?"

Nice. *That wasn't awkward at all. I don't know how to talk to tweens anymore, actually I never did, but that is beside the point.*

"The sky?"

She is a little smart ass, isn't she?

"Why are you talking to me? No one talks to me."

"Well, why not? Oh, your necklace is beautiful." I say, pointing to an emerald stone around her neck.

"Thanks. It was my mother's. She passed away when I was little. I live with my dad and older brother now."

"I'm sorry about your mother."

"No need to be sorry. She was a firefighter; she died a hero. My brother and dad work at the same fire station now and when I grow up, I'm going to be just like them." She says with a huge smile, crossing her arms over her chest.

"Well, I think that's a great way to honor her."

"Me too." She grins at me and twirls her necklace around in between her fingers.

"So, this is where you ran off to." Audrey and I glance up to see Ulysses leaning over and looking down on us.

"Alpha." Audrey scrambled up and bowed her head.

"No need for that. I see you met the Luna."

"Westries," I correct, giving Ulysses a warning scowl, who hopefully got the point.

"Yes, I did, Alpha."

Ulysses walks around the fence and drapes his arm around my shoulders.

"Excuse me, Luna. It was a pleasure to meet you."

"You, too, Audrey. I hope we can talk again."

She gives a lopsided curtsy.

"How do you do that?" Ulysses faces me and tilts his head to the side.

"What?"

"Make everyone love you the way I do, and they aren't even your mate."

I snort and stroll back to the picnic tables with Ulysses on my heels. "I have no idea what you're talking about. If you mean I can speak properly, then yes, I can make friends, despite the odds *stacked* against me."

Ulysses takes my arm and stops me. "Hey, what do you mean by the odds stacked against you?"

"Well, I didn't exactly put myself in the best circumstances to make friends, considering what I do. Pretending it won't matter, or that they won't see me as being evil, is bonkers." I shrug. "I'm just being realistic here."

"Well, I disagree completely, but if it helps you sleep at night, sure, you are diabolically evil."

He's trying to lighten the moment. I'll play along.

"You got it, and Griffin is second in command in my army of darkness."

Ulysses smiles down at me and splays his hands on my hips and plants a gentle kiss on my lips.

"Come on. We're about to announce you."

"Where are we going?"

"The main hall."

We stroll hand in hand toward the large building where the old ladies with a million questions are. I slow my steps. No one is outside anymore, and I am hoping they all went home and forgot about the announcement.

But no.

He opens the doors to reveal a few hundred people here to watch me in all my embarrassment.

The hall is a vast open room with tall ceilings and giant stained-glass windows. Tables with food and refreshments line the walls and chairs are spread out everywhere. Coleman and Jackie, Spencer and Ruby, and Cade and Hannah are all on the stage. Ulysses weaves us through the crowd, whose heads turn as we pass them by. My feelings of awkwardness earlier are nothing compared to now. It's like they are staring into my soul and judging every part.

Ulysses helps me onto the stage and a hush falls over the room in anticipation of their Alpha's speech. I fidget next to Ruby, who is doing a crap job of holding back laughter at my expense.

"Never thought you'd be here, huh?"

"Shut up." I whisper back.

"Don't act sassy with me, Wes. I'm in the spotlight, too. Trust me, I am in just as must pain as you."

"Not too much pain, I hope." Spencer whispers from behind us. He grabs Ruby's hand and kisses it gently.

"Well, I guess not that much…"

"Is that a blush I see?" I ask, pinching Ruby's cheeks.

She rolls her eyes and bats my hands away. "Wes, the pack is watching us, stop…" She groans and nods her head toward the crowd.

I focus back on Ulysses, who apparently has been talking.

Oops.

"And now I am proud to present your new Gamma Female Ruby."

Spencer and Ruby step forward, and the crowd claps. Later, I won't remember what either of them has said because I've sort of spaced out. Next thing I know, Ruby is nudging me forward. I freeze, trying to analyze the situation.

Ulysses is holding his hand out to me. I am supposed to do something. *Take his hand, dummy.*

I lurch forward and let him draw me to his side under the bright stage lights.

"Now, I would like to introduce my mate, your Luna, and Future Luna Queen, Westries."

It is as if someone announced they are all getting a million dollars every day for life, because the room bursts with cheers and clapping. I drop my chin and smile, and Ulysses squeezes my hand reassuringly.

"I spaced out. What did you tell them, exactly?" I try to yell above the noise. Although I'm pretty sure Ulysses would have heard me even if I whispered.

"Just that I had found you and that you are going to do great things."

"Are we going to tell them…"

"Right now, actually. Alright, alright, settle down now. Most of you may already know or may have heard rumors about what the Luna did for a living, and I am going to clear everything up, once and for all. For the past few months, we have been trying to apprehend the rogue werewolf vigilante called the Avenger, who has been killing rogues and leaving them at pack borders. And I am proud to announce we just recently succeeded."

I elbow Ulysses in the gut playfully, and he chuckles.

"Or rather, she found us."

There are a few murmurs at the *she* part. Ulysses' eyes are filled with adoration and complete contentment as he gazes down at me. I try to absorb his confidence.

He looks back out at the crowd. "I think it might just be best to come straight out with it. *Westries* is the Avenger, and before anyone jumps to conclusions, I would like Westries to briefly explain why."

Some mutters and grumbles ripple through the hall, but the majority quietly wait for me to explain. It is almost impossible to not notice the gaping jaws of several teenage girls in the crowd. What a shock to learn the *guy* they were fawning over is a woman. Ulysses nudges me forward. I move in front of the mic and cleared my throat.

"It's true. I am the Avenger. I don't really know what I am supposed to say, but I can promise you I only did what I had to, to protect my people. Rogues get away with more than they should, and I couldn't stand by and let them. To be honest, I was never really fond of werewolves either, but I found a *family* who changed my mind. I know nothing about being a Luna, let alone a Luna Queen, but I am going to try my best and that I can promise."

I step back to the group, and the gang surrounds me in a show of solidarity.

This is definitely where I want to spend the rest of my life.

We file down the stage stairs and kids of all ages bombard me.

"Are you really the Avenger?"

"How'd you do that since you're human?"

"Why did you not like werewolves?"

"When did you start hunting rogues?"

"Whoa, okay. One question at a time." I laugh and sit down on the edge of the stage. A dozen kids sat around me, hanging off every word I say.

"How about you?" I point to a boy who appears around Patrick's age.

"Umm, well, are you *really* the Avenger?"

"Yes."

I point to a girl who was probably sixteen, who asks, "How'd you do it? Since you're human and all."

"Well, don't underestimate someone because you assume you know their strength. Anyone can accomplish anything if they are determined enough."

"My cousin said you killed innocent people. Is that true?"

Gosh, harsh much.

Sometimes it's like everyone is against me when they don't even know all the facts. Though, if I'd only heard rumors, I would probably fear me, too.

"Well, it depends on how you see things. I did what I had to, to protect my people. Sometimes bad people get away with things and someone must stop them. So, I did. It's a very long story really, probably a little too old for most of you, but I can promise you this; I never hurt any innocent people, only the bad ones."

"So, you're like a superhero?"

Superhero?

I chuckle at her question. "No, not a superhero. Does anyone have any other questions?"

"Yeah, how'd ya' *really* do it?"

I glance up to see three smug teenage boys staring down at the group of children and me. They are waiting for me to screw up.

I stand up and lean against the stage, sizing the three boys up.

"Do *what* exactly?"

"We don't think you actually are the Avenger, and all of this is a ploy to make some human seem tough. What do you even know about killing werewolves?"

Challenge accepted. I whip out my Beretta M9 from behind my jacket and emptied the fifteen rounds into my hand, showing them to the small crowd that had formed.

"The Beretta M9, semi-automatic pistol, holds fifteen rounds used by the United States Armed Forces since 1985." I load the rounds back inside the magazine. "Commonly used in close and long-range self-defense, the M9 has seen action over several wars across the globe. It's your go-to for handguns if you are looking. Now if you're looking for a good sniper rifle, the Barrett M82 is the ultimate choice of weapon. For all the kids listening, or anyone who isn't properly trained, these are not toys, and if you ever see one lying around you: Stop. Don't touch. Leave the area. Tell an adult."

I did the hand motions along with the saying my parents had taught me when I was little. A few of the kids giggle.

"The Barrett M82, also known as the M107 by the U.S. military, is a recoil-operated, semi-automatic sniper system designed by Barrett Firearms Manufacturing company. It is an anti-material rifle which means it is used against military equipment, instead of anti-personal, which means used against combatants, aka bad guys. So yeah, I know a little something."

The three boys' smug expressions are replaced with chagrin and maybe a smidge of grudging admiration. Proved them wrong. The small crowd around me has expanded to include adult werewolves.

"Questions?"

A bunch of hands shoot up. I point to an older girl.

"When you started shooting, what did you start on?"

"BB guns. They are the only way to start your self-defense training, but first, you need to go to ground school."

"What sort of ground school?"

"You *never* pick up any sort of weapon without proper training first. Like, can anyone tell me what color most safeties are?"

One boy spoke. "Red, Luna?"

"Yeah, what's your name, kid?"

"Houston."

"What do you want to do when you grow up?"

"Join the Warriors Elite."

"You're on the right path, then. How old are you?"

"Seventeen."

"Then you can join in a year."

Everyone bows their heads when Ulysses joins me. He pulls me to his side and kisses my head. "You can start a gun safety class when we get back from Romania for anyone who wants to learn more or wants a head start in the Warriors Elite."

I turn sharply to face him. "Are you serious?"

He laughs at my sudden change from seriousness to giddy. "Would that make you happy?"

"YES. I would love that."

The crowd is thinning, and people are waving their goodbyes. There are probably a few dozen left inside, and no one is outside mingling anymore. The sky has darkened, and the party is ending.

I weave through the empty chairs to the snack table. Everything is gone except a platter of veggies.

That figures.

I scoop up the entire plastic dish and sit at an empty table with the plate in my lap.

Don't mind me, a full-grown woman sitting crisscross apple sauce, eating an entire platter of reject veggies.

"I am guessing you're hungry?"

"I haven't had dinner yet. You know what? I can't remember the last time I ate." I whine through a mouth full of snap peas and sour cream.

Ulysses sits across from me and takes the platter away.

"Hey, I was eating that."

"I need to talk to you, and I can't do that if you are going full rabbit on me."

"I'm not a rabbit… what'd you want to talk about?"

Ulysses sets the plastic plate down on the table and sticks a carrot in his mouth. "Do you know what time we are leaving tomorrow?"

I shake my head no.

I don't even know what time it is now.

"The plane takes off at 7:30 and the airport is twenty minutes away from the pack house. And do you know what time it is right *now*?"

Again, I shake my head no. Must he be so cryptic?

"It's 12:38. Past your bedtime."

"I don't have a bedtime. I'm a full-grown woman, damn it."

And it is then that my stupid body betrays me, and I yawn. Ulysses raises an eyebrow, smirking.

He just loves being right, doesn't he?

"*Fine*. Did everyone else already leave?"

"Yeah, they did."

"Then why didn't you come to get me?"

"You just seemed so happy eating the *entire* platter of veggies. I didn't want to interrupt you."

I slap his shoulder setting the tray down and stomp toward the exit doors. The next thing I know, I'm upside down over Ulysses' shoulder, with his forearm holding my ankles, so I don't kick.

"Set me down Ulysses. I am armed and very dangerous."

Ulysses' laughter bellows through the empty hall and his saunter becomes a sprint. I beat my fists on his back, then give up, cross my arms and pout.

This is stupid.

I am being kidnapped again by this lug head. We at last come to a halt and Ulysses sets me safely back on the ground. I glare at the giant.

He laughs even more and opens the passenger door for me.

"My lady."

"Cut the act, fur ball."

I climb into the car, and Ulysses closes the door. He jumps in the driver's seat and starts the engine while I rummage through the various car compartments, searching for my next victim. I reach across Ulysses to search the door for snacks.

"What are you doing?" Ulysses asks, pushing my hands back into my seat, probably so I don't cause a wreck.

"I'm hungry."

"Are you always hungry?" Ulysses laughs.

"Yes."

He rolls his eyes at me and focuses back on the road.

"Behind my seat in the pocket is a pack of thin mints. You can have them… if you share."

My stomach growls when he says thin mints. I snatch the box behind the seat and rip it open, then stuff two in my mouth. In between cookies, I turn on the radio and fold my legs underneath me.

"I said *share*."

I take a cookie and shove it in Ulysses' mouth. "You better not eat the entire box, missy." Half falls out, but he catches it and pops it back into his mouth.

"No promises." I mumble through the cookie crumbs falling out of my mouth. Nonetheless, I keep the promise and alternate one cookie for me, then one to Ulysses until the box is empty.

"So, how early do I have to get up tomorrow if we have to leave by seven?"

"Depends. Are you a morning person?"

I shrug. I get up when I have a good reason, like going to the gym or if I'm on a mission. There's no other reason, really.

"Let's just go for 6:30, alright?"

"Fine."

We drive in companionable silence while music softly plays in the background. He is right, though. I am tired. I make myself a nice pillow out of a sweatshirt and my arms and lay down on the middle console. I'm not sure what happened after that, but the next thing I know, I'm floating on a cloud. The cloud is warm, soft, and… *breathing*? I crack open my right eye to see cloud-man carrying me.

"Mr. Cloud, where are we going?"

"To your room. You fell asleep in the car."

"Okay, but hurry, I want to go back to…"

Whatever.

I sink deep into the warm, muscular cloud. It's like my personal heating pad and blanket in one. The far-off conscious part of my brain hears the creak of a door opening and registers being laid down on a soft bed. The door clicks shut, and that self-aware part of my brain realizes I'm still fully dressed.

Still somewhere between slumber and wakefulness, I sit up, wander into the closet, and peel off my old clothes. I tug on some sweatpants and a tank top. Then, after I almost slam into a wall, I accept it is best if I went to bed.

I collapse into the soft duvet, but I'm not warm like before.

Where is my warm cloud? I want my cloud back.

Again, I get up. This time in search of that cloud. I find clouds' room and make myself comfy in the warm sheets. They smell and feel fresh from the dryer. A door opens, and a burst of steam warms the air. The lights flick on, and I hiss at the piercing brightness.

"*No*, turn it off…"

I whine, burrowing my face in the blanket. The bed dips and the cloud man nudges my shoulder.

"What are you doing here, Bellator?"

I groan. The sleeping side of my brain is fighting to win the battle against the wakeful side.

"You're supposed to be in your room. Why are you in here?"

"I like it in here. It smells like Ulysses."

Mr. Cloud laughs and lays down next to me, covering both of us with a warm blanket. I curl straight up to the heating pad. He wraps an arm around and… *purrs*?

"You sound like a cat…" I murmur.

"Axel is happy, Bellator." He whispers.

"Why?" I whisper back.

"His mate is here."

Blame the cozy warmth, or the sense of security in his arms, or just my two A.M. sleep-stupidity, but from far off I hear myself ask, "Who is his mate?"

"You."

Blissful, dreamless sleep at last overcomes me.

"WHEEP WHOO, WHEEP WHOO, WHEEP WH…"

The alarm clock reads six A.M. On a scale of one to *I will take a hammer to that thing*, I am hammer-y. The bed dips and someone shakes my shoulders.

"Westries, time to wake up. We have to leave soon."

I sit up and rub my eyes. Ulysses kneels in front of me, smiling. He is way too chipper for six A.M.…

"Why are you so cheerful? It's too early to be this happy."

"I just am, Bellator. I set out some clothes for you and we're going to eat on the plane. See you downstairs, *Bella*."

Ulysses kisses my forehead and leaves. I drop back down on the bed onto my clothes. I begrudgingly grab them and stumble to the bathroom. I assess his selection of clothes for me and deem them perfect.

Gosh, he knows me so well.

I twist my hair into a high ponytail and splash water on my face. The mirror tells me I look awful, but I don't have time to care.

I wander into the kitchen where everyone is waiting, appearing tired as I feel. Along the far end are a million suitcases, and five or six giant black dress bags.

"Well, look who decided to wake up."

"Leave me alone Ruby, unless you have a coffee peace offering."

She grins and hands me a steaming mug of black energy. I mutter thanks.

"Alright everyone, the vans are here, so let's make our way outside," Coleman announces.

I have been down here for barely five minutes, and we are already leaving. I chug down the entire mug of coffee and snag my cell phone, following the crowd.

Shit. I forgot about Griffin.

I turn around and jog back to the kitchen.

"Hey, no getting cold feet on me now."

Ulysses has Griffin already with a leash and harness on.

"I was just going to find him." I say, pointing to my furry beast, taking the leash from Ulysses. He kisses my cheek, and that now familiar rush of heat floods my face. Darn hormones.

"Come on, everyone's in the vans."

I follow Ulysses outside in the still predawn darkness, where the taillights of four vans glow. Ulysses leads me to the first one and opens the door for me. Corrine, Aubrey, Patrick, and David are asleep in the back row, and Griffin makes himself snug in the middle row. The van pulls away, and I struggle to not fall asleep again.

Beside me, Ulysses is looking more and more like a pillow. I lay down on his lap and he covers me with his jacket. I drift back asleep to thoughts of what Romania will be like, how I had agreed to any of this, and how will any of this work. But Ulysses is smoothing my hair from my brow in slow, gentle sweeps and my thoughts are replaced by blackness.

"Westries, we're here."

I climb out of the van after him and stretch out my back. Griffin tumbles out of the van, knocking me into Ulysses. He steadies me and grabs Griffin's leash. All four vans are parked on the tarmac where a sleek-looking jet waits. In pairs and singles, we make our way onboard as people load up all our suitcases.

"Griffin isn't going down below, right?"

"No, he can stay with us in the main cabin."

Halfway up the stairs, my stomach fills up with butterflies at the sight of the giant, white jet looming in front of us.

Ugh...

"Ulysses, I've never flown before."

He raises both eyebrows. "Really? I would've thought you had since you go everywhere."

"I drive, not fly. Plus, why would I want to be twenty thousand feet in the air, possibly falling to my death at any second? Yeah, that sounds just *peachy.*"

I swore I never would, but here I am, about to fly.

"Hey, it's alright. I know the pilot, and it's completely safe. There's no need to worry."

Ulysses caresses my hand with his thumb. I try to smile. The plane roars to life and Ulysses leads us. I cling to Ulysses' hand as the engines grow louder. The inside cabin décor is light beige with brown trim. There are two couches, multiple personal chairs, tables, and a dog kennel in the corner, where Griffin instantly makes himself comfortable. Everyone is buckling in, but I freeze, not knowing what to do.

"Go sit down. I'm going to talk to the pilot."

I nod and go to the back of the plane. I sit next to David, who is drinking a soda, on a couch and gaze around to see what everyone else is doing. Patrick and Corrine are sitting together playing on an iPad, while Jackie and Aubrey are gawking at multiple binders. Coleman, Spencer, and Cade are in the front talking. Hannah and Ruby are sleeping in their mate's laps. Meanwhile, I am the only one clenching their chair, freaking out.

"Nervous?"

I turn to David, who is wearing a sympathetic expression.

"Just a little. I don't like planes."

"Me neither." He smiles as he drinks more of his soda.

"Have you told Aubrey she's your mate yet?"

He blushes. I nudge him and he picks at the soda tab.

"Come on, tell me." I beg.

"No. I haven't. Do you think I should? I don't want the Alpha to kill me." He awkwardly laughs to himself.

"Don't worry about him and if he tries, I'll stop him. When can you guys find out? I never really understood that part."

"Well, it's around seventeen, and Aubrey has a while left."

I glance over to Aubrey, who is staring at David. I catch her eye, and she blushes as fiercely as he had.

"What if you just asked her out?"

"She would know I imprinted on her. What if she doesn't like me and the only way for anything to happen is with the imprint?" David panics.

"Stop selling yourself short, David. I am sure she could fall in love with you, even *without* the imprint bond. And when she finally feels the pull, it will only make it even stronger."

He is silent for a moment. "Is that what happened to you?"

Is it? Did I fall in love on my own? Or maybe the mate bond? Why do I keep second guessing myself?

"I don't know, maybe. Probably. I feel *something*, but I've always been bad at deciphering what my feelings mean. I really, *really* like him, but I don't know if I'm capable of *loving*."

"Sure, you are. If not, you wouldn't have rescued Patrick or helped me out, or even stayed at all. I don't know you that well, but I can already tell you have a kind heart. Plus, I've seen the way you two look at each other. I'm no expert, but my parents looked the same way, and to me, that's a pretty good example."

I glance over to where Ulysses is chatting with the guys. He must sense my attention because his head turns and when our eyes meet, a slow smile spreads across his face. When he winks at me, I flush and smile back.

"For whatever it's worth, I think you'll make a great Luna and Luna Queen."

"Thanks, David."

Ulysses walks over and drops onto the couch next to me. "You doing good?"

I nod, but I suppose the rapid leg bounce I'm doing says otherwise.

I am going to die on this plane. I just know it.

"Umm, when are we going to take off exactly? I would like to know when my death spiral is going to start."

Ulysses laughs. "We already took off."

We did? When? I didn't notice. I guess that's good.

My impending doom will be later than I expected. I clench the seat just a little more. We are flying and we are going over an ocean. Nausea rises into my throat and my belly feels hollow.

"Do you have any food?"

Ulysses hands me a fruit cup and a fork. I thank him and take tiny nibbles of watermelon. If I eat too fast, I'll get sick all over this plane.

"You need to eat more than that, Bella." Ulysses says, rubbing my shoulder. I mutter under my breath but finish the fruit cup. Throughout the cabin, people are sleeping, talking, or on their cell phones. I put the fruit cup on the coffee table and go through my playlist on my phone, then put my headphones on and hit play. Thank God I packed my bags yesterday because I completely forgot about it. I dig into my bag and find chargers, my laptop, gun case, and snacks. In other words, all life's necessities.

I glance over at Ulysses to see he is still watching me, so I take an ear bud out and place it in his right ear. Whether it's the food in my stomach, the music, or Ulysses' presence, I relax. A softer track is in order, so I change the song and curl into his side. He rests an arm around me, and I fall asleep again.

Westries' unease is obvious when we load onto the plane. I hadn't considered asking if she'd ever flown before, and now I could kick myself.

Once she settles in, she'll be fine. Hopefully.

Everyone else takes their seats and is talking or going back to sleep. I tell Westries to go sit while I have a word with the captain.

"Captain Darnel?"

"Alpha, I was hoping you'd stop by. How are you?" He rises and shakes my hand.

"Very well. I just want to check on the flight."

"We should arrive around ten A.M. tomorrow morning and all services are available. The lavatory and showers are working."

"Thank you."

He bows in response, and I head back to my seat when Spencer, Cade, and Coleman stop me.

"Never thought you'd be here, huh?"

I lean against the cabin wall, shaking my head at Cades' question. "Nope, not in a million years."

I glance over to Westries, who is sitting on a couch in the way back. Two of the guys are sitting on the couch with Hannah and Ruby asleep on them and Coleman sits across from them with Jackie and Aubrey, going over coronation details. Looks like he got roped into helping.

"Well, we have about a sixteen-hour flight, so get comfortable."

"How are these two already asleep?"

I sit down next to Cade and buckle in as the plane moves. I peek over at Westries, who still seems nervous.

"We all better get some breakfast, too. You're going to need it if you want to stay awake."

"Don't forget the eight-hour time difference."

We talk pack business, how the elders are going to handle the two weeks we'll be gone, the Romanian Alpha and Luna, and the ceremony. I hear my name, and I glance over at Westries, who is talking to David. I am trying not to listen, but that's near impossible when you have super hearing. They are talking about me, and David is reassuring her about something. When our gazes meet, a blush rises in her otherwise pale cheeks.

She needs something to eat, or else she's going to pass out.

I sit down next to Westries on the couch and offer her the fruit cup. She takes it gratefully, but barely eats. Turns out she had no idea we've already taken off. The news seems to calm her, and soon she is snuggled against me. She shares her earbud with me, and we listen to her music until she's asleep.

Enjoy the peace now, Bella. Life is about to get very hectic.

Westries is quietly snoring on my lap, and the rest of the gang has followed suit. It is an endless night and there isn't much to do on the plane, despite its luxurious accommodations.

I am close to falling asleep myself when someone taps my cheek. I open my eyes to discover Patrick staring at me.

"Hey little man, what's up?"

"I had a nightmare. Bear lets me sleep with her when I have nightmares."

I motion for him to join us, and he lays down in front of Westries, who is using my lap as a pillow. Westries wraps her arm around his waist, pulling him closer. I take my sweatshirt and cover their shoulders and untangle the headphones from Westries' hair.

Hmm, what else do you listen to?

I put the earbuds in and hit play on her second most recent playlist.

I don't recognize the songs, but the theme is slow romance. Their melodies are soft, and the lyrics are not what I would have imagined Westries liking. I scroll through her playlists until I find one called *Alpha's Warrior.*

Intriguing.

The first song is "Thunder Struck" by AC/DC. The rest of them are 80's and 90's rock or decent 21st century music. It comes as no surprise she would listen to this stuff. There is everything: Guns N' Roses, AC/DC, Queen, Led Zeppelin, King Kobra, Sam Tinnesz, and Allen Walker.

Now, this playlist, I like.

Coleman comes over and sits in a chair across from the couch, waking me from a sleep I hadn't intended to fall into. Westries' phone is essentially dead. Jackie and Aubrey are *still* going through binder after binder after binder with coronation details. They have endless energy.

"How are you doing, Ulysses?"

"With the flight or…"

"No, you just seem to have your hands full there."

He laughs, motioning at Patrick and Westries sleeping in my lap.

"He had a nightmare, and he apparently sleeps with Westries when he does."

"She is good at it, being Luna. Whether she realizes it or not."

"She is going to be a great one." I whisper, quietly caressing Westries' hair. She stirs and sits up, leaning into my side again with Patrick on her lap.

"I'm asleep, not deaf, but I'll take the compliment." She mutters, still half asleep with her eyes closed.

Coleman chuckles, and I can't help but grin. Westries yawns and blinks slowly.

"What's up guys?"

"Well, you've been asleep for the past four hours, so it's almost lunch."

She hugs Patrick as if he is a teddy bear. She yawns and straightens, pulling him into her lap.

"What is for lunch, anyhow? Since we are a trillion feet in the air, trusting clouds to not let us *die*."

"Salad, fruit cups, and junk food for the little kids."

"Who made that dumb rule? Here, hold my person."

Westries hands me Patrick, and Coleman covers a guffaw with clearing his throat.

Seems like someone is over their fear of flying.

She rummages through the mini-fridge and pantry and fills the crook of her arm with a box of Pop Tarts, fruit cups, and a Jell-O pudding cup. She plops down on the couch and elbows Patrick.

"Hey bud, are you hungry? I have your favorite."

She shakes a Pop Tart in front of Patrick's face, and he shoots up. Westries laughs and hands him two bags. He takes them and runs to Corrine, who is just waking up.

They both giggle and play with the iPad again while shoveling cold Pop Tarts into their little mouths. Westries dumps her junk food haul into my lap and clamps a Pop Tart between her teeth. She snags a Jell-O cup and brings it to a sleeping Ruby and throws it at her stomach.

"Hey wake up."

Ruby jolts and clutches her gut. "*Ow.* I'm going to… wait. Is this cherry?"

"Yep."

Westries pops the 'p' and hands her a spoon, then wanders back over to Coleman and me and sits beside me.

She collects all the snacks in my lap and organizes them in between us. I raise an eyebrow at her, wondering what she is doing.

"I'll take this Jell-O cup and you can have this one."

She takes a red cup and tosses me a green cup. She opens another bag of Pop Tarts and gives me half of one.

"What? I don't get the entire thing?" I ask, waving the dismal offering in front of her.

She narrows her eyes at me and takes a bite of her full-size treat. I slant my eyes, accepting her challenge of a stare-down. I lean in and she continues to chew her pop tart.

"What are you guys doing?" Coleman asks, half concerned, half amused.

"*Shh.*" Westries hisses, flapping her left hand at Coleman, not breaking eye contact. "I need to focus. *Ruby.* I need reinforcements."

From the corner of my eye, I see Ruby jump up and quick walks over to us. She kneels by Westries and feeds her from a bag of chips like this is totally normal. Both maintain earnest faces. Spencer joins my side and gives Coleman a look as he jabs a thumb in our direction.

"Do I want to know what is happening right here?"

Ruby answers. "It's obviously a staring contest, babe, and Westries needs me in her corner."

"To feed her potato chips?"

"*Yes.*" Westries and Ruby shout. Spencer puts his hands up in surrender and sits next to Coleman.

"You're going to blink," says Westries, smirking.

"Oh, yeah? And what makes you so sure of that?"

No sooner do those words come out of my mouth than she blows air into my face, and I blink.

Ruby and Westries high-five each other and open a bigger bag of spicy chips.

They nestle crisscross on the couch next to me and eat the rest of their chips. I shake my head at the duo and return my attention to the guys.

"Where's Cade?"

"Sleeping. And Jackie and Aubrey haven't stopped going over coronation details."

Westries groans next to me and mutters something about 'Crazy, controlling OCD girls with fashion as their evil superpower.' I chuckle at her as the two continue to giggle and stuff more junk food in their mouths.

The girl has an iron gut. It's impressive if I say so myself.

That's undeniably one of my favorite qualities about her. She doesn't care what anyone thinks of her, specifically about eating food.

"I swear those girls never sleep."

"They don't need to. It's a *gift*. Jackie told me" Coleman says, holding up finger quotes.

"I heard that, you lug," Jackie yells from across the plane. The boys stifle a few laughs. From the corner of my eye, I notice Westries taking off her sweatshirt, revealing her black tank top and tattoos. I stare at my mate. She is stunning and not in that beauty pageant, make-up, and glamour way, but a tough, all-American girl, *you got spunk* way.

"There are eyes on Westries, and they aren't ours."

My gaze shifts to the boys who are also watching my mate. I repress a low growl, but realize they are actually looking at her arm, so I glare them down till they turned aside. I curse myself for laying out a tank top with her sweatshirt.

"Hey, Westries, where did you get your tattoos? You've never talked about it."

"No one asked."

"I asked." Aubrey yells from the other cabin.

David and Aubrey are sitting too close and resume what appears to be a deep conversation. Jackie and others made their way into our cabin, so now everyone is sitting with their mates. Westries, done binge-eating, leans into my side and I wrap an arm around her.

"Which one do you want to know about?"

"You have more than that one?" Hannah asks, shocked. The only normal tattoo that is visible on her body is her sleeve of tribal swirls on her right arm that ends up connecting to her mate mark on her neck.

"Yeah." Westries laughed a little, making Axel purr just a little.

"Where?" Jackie asks, leaning in.

Ruby snorts and Westries kicks her shin, making Spencer growl.

"It's on my lower back, I would show you, but I think Axel wouldn't let me." With that, I pull her closer to my chest, making her laugh. Damn right.

"Well, you could at least tell us, right?"

"Sure. I have a wolf's claw on my back with…"

"A *wolf*?" Cade laughs.

"Yes, a *wolf*, Cade. And underneath that, the words '*I have not yet begun to fight.*' I thought it was fitting."

She smirks and crosses her arms, leaning into my shirt. I kiss her head.

"Wait. Aren't you, like, fifteen or something? Don't you need, like, parental permission or something for tattoos?"

"First of all, I'm *nineteen*. I'm legal, thank you. And second, you'd be surprised how much stuff kids can do without parental permission." She pivots to face me. "And how did *you* not know that? I know you did background checks on me, Ulysses."

"Yeah, we did, not gonna lie."

Axel pipes up again in my head.

You did. I had nothing to do with you intruding into our mate's personal life before she wanted to tell us.

Oh, shut it. We had every right to know.

"I'm curious. Why did you accept us, anyway?" Hannah blurts. Jackie slaps her arm. Hannah shrugs and looks back at Wes.

"What is this, 21 questions only for Westries?"

"Yes."

"I don't know." She gazes down at her hands. "It was nice to have a place where I felt wanted and stuff…" Westries mumbles and curls deeper into my side.

Hannah smiles from ear to ear, understanding. This ends "The Q & A", and everyone drifts off to other time passing activities. Westries snatches my phone from the console, leans back against me, and I twirl a strand of her hair in-between my fingers while she plays video games on my cell phone.

Several hours later…

Everyone is still asleep on their random couches and chairs when the wheels of the plane touch down and the skid of rubber on the pavement alerts me of our arrival. I'm sprawled across the cushions with Westries lying on my chest, burrowing her face into my neck. Westries jolts in my lap and groans as she lays back down.

"You good there, Bella?"

Wes clamps her hand over my mouth and groans again.

"Shh. No speaking, headache and hungry, not a good combination."

She removes her hand, and I chuckle. Not a big conversationalist upon waking, duly noted.

As we taxi to the terminal, others are waking, stretching, and yawning. The mountain ranges are already in view out the window.

Westries pushes off me and wakes Patrick and Corrine. I watch the trio as she nudges them tenderly. Corrine has always been good at waking up early, so she is up and booming in a flash. Westries asks her to help wake Patrick.

"Corrine, help me out here. Hey buddy, you gotta wake up. We're here."

Corrine whacks him on the head with a pillow. Poor boy. He groans and sits up. Corrine smirks and hands him an apology Pop Tart. With the littles settled, Westries weaves her way to Ruby and wakes her.

"The car should be at the gate already, Ulysses."

I nod at Cade, who is on his phone, texting. I rub my face and stare out the window again to see we're parked, and the stairs have lined up to the plane door. I feel a weight on my knee and peer down to see Griffin wagging his tail with his head on my lap. Not that long ago he was trying to kill me, and now we're chums. I scratch behind his ears, and he closes his eyes, leaning in.

"Ladies and gentlemen, we have arrived in Bucharest. The local time is 9:26, so we are thirty-four minutes early. I hope you enjoy your stay in the Old Royal State and that you fly with us again."

The intercom clicks off and everyone gathers their belongings. The girls surround Westries, explaining where we are going. I hook Griffin's harness. As I step out onto the top of the stairs, the cool brisk air hits my face. Two black limousines wait out front with staff already loading up our suitcases.

Griffin pulls hard on his leash, trying to get Westries, who is standing in the center of a group of people. I join them when I hear the conversation. Jackie is explaining why the royal pack is in Montana now instead of Romania and how the ceremony will go.

Two days, not that far away. But it still feels like an eternity to wait.

"Oh, and you'll get to see where the old Alpha King and Queen used to live. Oh, oh, oh, and tomorrow you have your crown fitting."

"It is so much fun to see the crown jewels. My mom took my sister and I every summer to visit."

"Wait, no one said I had to wear a crown. I may have agreed to a dress, but I never said I would wear a *crown*."

"You are *royalty*, Wes. That's obviously a given." Ruby says, hip bumping her. Westries slaps her hard on the shoulder, which only makes Ruby laugh harder.

"Ulysses, tell her it's going to be amazing," Jackie squeals, throwing her hands up in the air.

"Yes, all the dresses, jewels, manners lessons, teas, and high heels. Not to mention the etiquette protocols. Oh, and did I mention the castle is a gun-free zone?"

Westries eyes widen, and she plants her fists on her hips. "I *swear* Ulysses, if you aren't joking right now, I will get back on that plane and leave."

"Kidding, Bellator."

I pull her arm into a hug, and she groans and pushes me away.

"You better be."

We climb into the waiting van, off to the next leg of our adventure.

CHAPTER 31

WESTRIES

ell, this has been quite an adventure so far.

Here I am, in a limousine, driving to a royal castle with David, Aubrey, Corrine, Patrick, and Ulysses. I am staring out the window when Ulysses squeezes my hand and asks if I'm nervous.

Am I nervous? Do I seem nervous?

Because I feel fine. I mean, it's not like I'm going to be a queen or anything. Oh, wait. That's *exactly* what is happening. I am becoming Luna Queen to an entire species. A species I despised not so long ago.

That's in the past.

If they can see past all I've done, I can disregard something they personally never did to me.

Aubrey and David sit across from Ulysses and me, talking. Rather, Aubrey is doing all the talking, and he is nodding enthusiastically. They are pretty cute together.

I can't wait for her to find out. It is going to be adorable.

My attention shifts to the scenery outside the limousine windows. Romania is beautiful. It is like we've stepped into a fairytale book… but with cars and cell phones.

We drive for what seems like forever, and I am thinking we'll be in this car for as long as the plane ride. I hate being a passenger in moving vehicles for long periods of time. There is nothing to do and I get motion sickness. Just as I'm about to complain to Ulysses, the top of a castle steeple catches my eye.

That must be where we are going, right?

More of what I can only describe as a colossal castle comes into view between the mountains. Flags matching the ones on the cars wave in the breeze seem to confirm my suspicions.

It has to be the place this death trap on wheels is taking me.

The appearance of the full expanse of the old stone building—nestled between two giant clusters of trees—takes my breath away. A vast courtyard sprawls out front. The walls are varying shades of beige stone with maroon accents and dark green steeple points. It isn't a giant gaudy castle like I half expected, but it is still huge and intimidating.

"What do you think?"

"It's beautiful."

It certainly is. I can't lie. The car stops and Ulysses pops open the door before the chauffeur can round the vehicle, and Griffin is the first one out. I climb out to see an unfamiliar woman petting Griffin's belly. He is thoroughly enjoying it. She is baby talking to him and I'm not sure she has even noticed us standing here.

A smiling, bearded man steps forward. "Ulysses. It's good to see you again."

"Stefan. How long has it been? Two, three years?"

"Must be." Stefan laughs.

The two shake hands and embrace each other. I stand behind Ulysses, still watching the lady who is thoroughly enchanted by Griffin. My guess is that these two are the Alpha and Luna of this pack.

"And who is this young lady? Is this who I think it is?"

Stefan can't be much older than Ulysses, though his beard gives him a sophisticated air. Ulysses takes my hand and tugs me closer to the trio.

"This is Westries, my mate."

His eyes widen comically as he reaches out to shake my hand.

The woman gives Griffin's belly a last pat and stands. "Well, it's about darn time. I'm Daria. I've known Ulysses since we were kids, and you are way overdue. It's a pleasure to meet you and I hope you don't mind."

"Don't mind what?" I ask, glancing from one to the others.

Stefan answers. "That your mate here is going to be highly overprotective and territorial of you since you're human. I am assuming he already put a protection guard in place for you?"

Ulysses narrows his eyes at Stefan, and Stefan just smirks.

I snort.

Everyone assumes that just because I'm human, I need protection from them. Boy, are they in for a surprise.

Ulysses rubs his temples, groaning. Still, a smile peeks out from behind his knuckles.

It's Stefan and Daria's turn to exchange uncertain looks. "Are we missing something?"

"I'm not the one that needs protection. I can handle myself just fine with werewolves, and *he* knows it."

Stefan's eyes go from Ulysses to me. A smirk tugs at one side of his mouth.

"Color me intrigued. Do tell why, Luna."

Ulysses reaches for my waist as if to say, *you don't need to say anything.* Or maybe he is saying, *PLEASE don't say anything.*

"I'm the Avenger."

His jaw drops, and Daria gasps. "WHAT?"

Her high-pitched voice reminds me of Jackie, or a girl who was just told she had Taylor Swift tickets.

I cringe and rub my ear with my shoulder.

Then she says the last thing I expected. "You are freaking amazing!"

This woman must be in her early twenties and here she is, fan girling… over me!

"Ulysses, is she for real?"

He nods, sighs, and looks at me.

Stefan holds his chin and studies me with new appreciation. "Woah…"

I purse my lips. Not the best way to start a conversation, but it will come out, ultimately.

"You know Ulysses has been tracking you down for months, right?"

"Apparently, he is not good at it," I say, smirking.

Ulysses hooks an arm around my waist and pulls me against him.

"Well, you're here, aren't you? I think I did a pretty good job."

"He threatened to kill my dog. I honestly didn't have a *choice*." I say, half laughing.

Daria gasps again. "Alpha. Her *dog*, this innocent little angel? You threatened him?" She ruffles Griffin's face again.

"How else was I supposed to get her here? It wasn't like she was going to come willingly." He gazes down at me. "Were you?"

"Not in the least bit, no." I shake my head, laughing.

"Well, I have many questions. Can we take this conversation inside? Everyone else is already there."

I glance around to see he is right. Everyone has gone in, and the cars have left the courtyard.

Daria says, "You can take Ulysses, but Westries is coming with me. The girls are meeting up with us in the lounge."

"Well…"

Before I could get a second word out, Daria is dragging me away from Ulysses and Stefan. I swear, if these people don't stop dragging me around by my arm, it is going to rip off.

"Where are we going, exactly?"

"I need to show you around. I haven't had new guests in forever."

We walk through the front door, or should I say the giant gate, and *holy freaking cow.* It is like walking into medieval times, yet truly beautiful. Heavy tapestries and paintings adorn the walls and flower filled vases and carved statues of various sizes rest on pillars and tables. Ornate rugs and antique furniture cover the smooth stone floors. She turns left, and we enter what she calls a parlor. Jackie, Ruby, and Hannah are already there on the couches, talking.

"Daria, it's so good to see you again. It's been too long."

Hannah jumps up and hugs Daria.

"I know. You should've come to visit more often. Well, you're here now and with *the Avenger.* Did it never cross your mind to text me?"

"Sorry, it's still new to us."

I sit next to Ruby and throw my legs up on her lap.

"Where's the rest of the gang?"

"The boys or kids?"

"Kids."

"Media room and the guys went outside."

"So, care to share?"

Ruby nudges me and I turn around to face the three sets of eyes staring at me.

"Hmm?"

Daria asks, "How'd you find out Ulysses is your mate?"

"He kidnapped me."

Ruby snorts, and I shoulder bump her.

"Wait, you were serious about that?" Daria asks, leaning in closer.

"As a heart attack."

"I thought you were joking. That doesn't sound like Ulysses at all."

"Yeah, then he cuffed me into a prison car and dragged me back to the pack house to lock me in his room. Although I escaped his room and wandered around for a while."

Daria's eyes widen and Hannah and Jackie exchange woeful glances.

"Okay, *that's* not normal at all, but whatever. Oh, I noticed Aubrey and Corrine with two boys. Who are they? I got the distinct impression the older one is Aubrey's mate?"

"The boys are new pack members. They are super sweet." Jackie exclaims.

"But are they…"

"David is Aubrey's mate, but she doesn't know yet."

The conversation continues, and I answer the latest version of the same questions I've been asked a million times now. Despite being hungry and exhausted, I answer politely and patiently. Thankfully, Daria has snacks for us, but sleep will have to wait. Not for Ruby, though. She has fallen dead asleep, so I am using her arms as cup holders.

Ulysses promised I wouldn't be doing this. Liar.

"Westries?"

"WHAT?" I jump and Ruby shoots up. Thankfully, I am holding my drink, and not her.

"We're going to the closet. Come on."

Ruby and I stand and stretch. I follow Jackie, Hannah, and Daria to the closet.

"Question. Why are we going to a closet?"

"It's where we store all the coronation dresses, since they are all so big. Including yours."

Good thing someone remembered to pack the dresses because I sure didn't.

I still don't get why we have to go see them, though. "What are we going to do? Stare at them?"

"No, Westries. You will try them on, and we'll check for last minute alteration needs. We really need to help you with your irrational fear."

"No! Haven't you all tortured me enough?"

I stop in front of the door that Hannah, Ruby, and Daria have disappeared through.

"Westries Clary Ronan. You will come in here and try on your dress and you will do it with a cheerful attitude."

I do the most logical thing I can think of. I run. Not with dignity or grace, but with screaming, hysteria, snickering… and Jackie chasing me.

"GET BACK HERE."

I dodge random people in the halls yelling apologies as I go, not knowing where I am going at all. Forget pride. I am running for my freaking life. If Jackie gets her claws into me, there is no telling the damage she will do. A voice I recognize reaches my ears and I make a split-second decision to follow it. I run into a wall, but the wall catches me. *Ulysses…* and the other guys.

"GET BACK HERE."

I jump out of Ulysses' arms and hide behind him.

"What are you…"

"There you are, Westries. You can't get out of this. You need to try on your dress and practice walking in it. The coronation is literally tomorrow. You are acting like a child! Tell her Ulysses."

"Technically, I am one and wait! It's *tomorrow*? Yesterday I had a week!"

Jackie rolls her eyes and nods.

"You sort of need to, Bella."

"No. I don't want to." I wail. "I did not agree to this."

I did, but that's irrelevant.

"Come on, Bellator." He drags me along with the help of the guys and a very snarky Jackie.

"I thought you were supposed to be my protector… you're being a traitor."

He chuckles and continues to drag me until we reach the dreaded dress room.

"There you guys are. Where did you go?" Daria asks, confused.

"*Someone* thought she could make a break for it."

"And the guys are here. Why?"

"Because we wanted to see ya'll too." Cade drawls, kissing Hannah's cheek.

"Okay, boys. Go sit down. Girls, all the dresses are in that side room there, and your shoes are on that table. So, have at it."

All the girls head toward the changing room, but what catches *my* eye is the open door I can escape out of. I back up slowly, hoping no one notices. It works, too, till I slam into my werewolf wall. I take a slow turn and meet raised eyebrows and crossed arms.

"Where are *you* going?"

"Restroom?"

"Uh-huh, let's go." Ulysses man-handles me to the changing room. Apparently, I weigh nothing to him because this is just too easy for dumb dumb here.

"Jackie, I found you a runaway."

"Thanks. Just shove her in and guard the door, please."

I give Ulysses the death eye, and he grins in response and shoves me through the door, closing it behind him. The room is smaller, and hooks cover the walls, holding beautiful gowns in clear plastic bags. The four other crack heads are already opening their gowns and zipping each other up. Jackie is in a flowy light blush halter dress, covered with champagne-colored flowers along the top and neck. It is gorgeous.

Ruby is like Merida from Brave. She is wearing a sleeveless teal dress, accented by silver jewels, and her wild red hair flows free. Hannah has on a red long-sleeved dress with large petal flowers trailing up the sleeves and chest. Daria is being zipped up by Ruby, and her dress is a skin toned, off-the-shoulder mermaid gown, which perfectly complements her curves.

Jackie grips my arm and yanks me to the far end where my devil green monstrosity hung. "You can't escape me that easily."

Dread fills every ounce of my being and oozes out of my pores. My dress is huge. Everyone else has reasonably sized dresses they can move in, and here *I* am in a freaking ball gown the size of Texas.

"Let's go, missy, put on the dress."

I snarl a multitude of curse comments under my breath as Jackie straps me into the death trap with zippers and suck in a breath as Jackie zips me into my fabric prison.

"There you go. Now come on. We need to see what this is like with your shoes on."

"*No.*" I whine, knowing I sound pathetic, but not caring. "I don't want to wear shoes."

"You *will* walk out there, and you will put your shoes on. Now come missy."

Jackie walks away, and I face the full body mirror.

The dress is like something a royal monarch would wear and I feel weird in it. I don't want to, but I must join the others outside, so I trudge out the door. Everyone is putting their shoes on, admiring themselves in the mirror, or adjusting straps and other nonsense.

"Hey, Wes, Jackie told me to give these to you."

Ruby hands me a pair of dark green low heels. Thank God they are not four inchers, I would kill my ankles for sure. I lean against the wall and try my best to get my shoes on under all the fluff. I can't.

"Does Cinderella need some help?"

Ulysses looms over me, smirking like an idiot.

"No." Trying and failing again, I sigh in resignation. "Yes."

He takes the shoes from me and slips them onto my feet. I try regaining my balance with the thirty pounds of fluff and heels, but I trip on a petticoat. I fall straight into Ulysses' chest. Thankfully, he catches me.

"You aren't going to do that tomorrow, are you?"

I slap him on the shoulder and then use it to steady myself. Once I stand on my own, I give him a smug smile.

Westries one, shoes zero.

My self-satisfaction is short-lived. I gaze around the room to see everyone is having fun bouncing around in their dresses and here I am, just trying not to fall on my face.

"Why do I have to wear this?"

"Because as much as I wish we could wear comfy clothes the entire time, we are the King and Queen."

"That's no fun. Okay. It fits. Can I take it off now?"

He nods and I wobble-walk to the changing room. I close the door behind me, and I kick off my shoes. But when I try to get the dress off, I realize it is a two-person job.

Well, look at me. The once badass Avenger, now an idiot, jumping around a closet trying to undo a giant dress.

A friendly voice calls out from behind me. "Need any help?"

I bob my head gratefully to Ruby, who undoes the zipper in a second. I grasshopper out of the circle of green fabric and yank my clothes on. I then help Ruby unzip hers. Everyone else comes in to change as well, so I slip out.

"Well, we could take her now?" Cade says, talking to Ulysses, Coleman, and Spencer.

"Take who?" I ask.

Curiosity killed the cat, but I'm not a cat.

They all turn to me, and Ulysses scratches his head. "The royal jewels are here, and we need to try them on, but..."

"What's the problem, then?"

"You're alright with that?"

I look around, confused.

Either I am as oblivious as a bat, or this is just complicated to everyone.

"Why would I not be?"

"Well, you did throw a whole tantrum because you had to try on your own dress."

I shrug. A crown just sits on your head, a dress a whole complicated ordeal. They all exchange dubious expressions, and then the double doors open. Owen, Jake, and Paul enter. Jake holds a giant metal box with a sophisticated lock on it.

"What are *you* guys doing here? I didn't know anyone else was coming."

"Well, we're still your personal protection detail and Paul here came with the crowns."

"Seriously, you're still babysitting me? I'm good now. Promise."

Jake and Owen wear expressions of 'I don't believe you one bit.'

The other girls come out of the changing room and Hannah hugs Paul.

Am I missing something here?

"Hey little sis."

"You have a sister? He's your brother?"

They both stare at me like I asked the most obvious question in the world.

"Yeah, you didn't know?"

"No. No one told me."

Hannah laughs, and Paul opens the special case. Inside are two of the most beautiful crowns I have ever seen. One is a tiara in gold covered in small diamonds. The other is a crown for a male, also in gold, with sharp points on the top. They are both stunning.

"Sit," Daria barks at me.

I obey, dropping onto the couch and staring, awestruck.

"We have had them in the vault for almost five years. The Luna crown has been stored for much longer since Ulysses just found you now."

"Wait. I have to wear that?"

She arches an eyebrow at me. "Yes. Do you not like it? If you don't, we can always add on…"

"No! I love it. It's just… I-I don't want it to fall off my head and break. Especially something as priceless as this."

"Don't worry, we can bobby pin it in, so it won't go anywhere. It's nothing to worry about."

She delicately lifts the jeweled metal and places it on my head. It feels weird and cold. She hands me a mirror, and I gaze into it. Butterflies explode in my stomach. It makes everything so much more real, and I don't know if I like it. I bite my lip and tuck a strand of hair behind my ear. I notice out of the corner of my eye people excusing themselves. I swallow hard and take the crown off my head, placing it on the coffee table. Reality settling in my gut.

"It fits, so I'm just going to just go take a break for a while."

I stand and wave off Ulysses, whose concerned expression only makes it worse. He encircles my wrist in his warm hand.

"Are you alright, Bella?"

"Yeah," my voice cracks. "It's just a lot to take in. Can I have a minute, please?"

He lets go and nods.

I walk out the door, and when I am out of view, I run. My heart was beating fast as I reached the patio door. Instinctively, or maybe accidentally, I find my way to the castle courtyard. I run under the pillars towards who knows where. A high-pitched scream stops me.

It isn't human. It sounds like a horse. I used to ride every other day, once upon a time, but that was a lifetime ago. I move in the direction of the noise, which is coming from a cluster of trees past the courtyard. I step onto the lush green grass and walk toward the copse. It isn't exactly a forest, but trees and mountain ranges surround the castle in a protective ring.

More nickering, snorts and the crunch of branches and sod draws me further in. Tethered to a large oak tree, a giant dapple gray horse rears and yanks on his lead rope. He is tangled in a fallen tree and is distraught.

I feel ya' dude, maybe not in the same way, but the feelings of turmoil are mutual.

I approach him as slowly as I can, but when he sees me, he loses his mind even more. If looks could kill, I would be six under. Beads of sweat drip off his face as he rears and strains against his lead rope, but to no avail. I'm surprised he hasn't snapped his halter yet.

"Hey there buddy, I know you are super pissed right now, but do me a favor and stop ripping your head around like an idiot? I feel you though, being trapped someplace you don't want. I understand."

I am a few yards away from the massive beast, who is still sassing me with his grunts and tail.

I know what you're implying, horse. Don't think you can get away with it.

"You and I are alike in many ways."

He chuffs at me and slaps his tail left and right.

"Give me a second to explain, you big oaf. I mean, you and I are in the same predicament. We both feel trapped and if you let me help you, one of us won't be anymore."

He stops pawing around and breathes heavily, staring at me. I hold my hand up to him and he sniffs it. I use the distraction to grab his lead rope before he can do any more damage. The moment I latch on to the rope, he freaks out again.

"Hey, chill. I'm not going to hurt you. Now, quit it."

He somewhat stops freaking out, and I stroke his head in between his ears. He shoves his head into my hand for more scratches and that's when I know I haven't lost my touch. I unwrap his lead rope, still tangled in the log, and he nudges me with his head.

I rise and take in his form. His dapple-gray coat and black mane are striking.

If Ulysses was a horse, I think this is how he would look. Weird, but somehow true.

I walk him around a little to help calm him. We head toward the open part of the field, where I sit crisscross in the middle of the field. I hold the end of the lead rope while the gray-white beast grazes.

"You know, I feel bad for referring to you as a beast and an oaf. I think I should name you. What about, Blackjack?"

He doesn't bother glancing up from his grazing.

"Fine, Mr. Grumpy. How about Caspian? Steele? Okay try Justice?"

At *Justice*, he lifts his head and whinnies in my face. I don't think he is responding to me, but I'll take it, anyway.

Justice, it is.

"How about we find out where you came from then?"

I spring back up and rub his head right between the eyes. We stroll back toward the castle courtyard. The sun is high in the sky, but it isn't hot at all. In fact, it is the perfect combination between a fall day and summer's sun. Justice's shoes click onto the stone path as we enter through the archways into the courtyard.

I am, like, ninety-nine percent sure that this show-stopping creature has an owner, but that one percent isn't too sure. I mean, the way he acted when he saw a human was interesting, but who am I to judge the way someone trains their horses?

"Oh, my goodness, where did you find him?"

Daria jumps from out of nowhere as I pass a pillar.

"Um, he was tangled in a tree out back that way." I point behind me.

"He probably just escaped again. We have a stable around the tree line, and this one is always escaping. He opens the gates and when we changed those, he just jumped the fence. He is a troublemaker, no doubt."

She reaches out to pet Justice, but he lifts his head out of her reach and pinned his ears at her. Daria sighed and crossed her arms.

"I've never been good with horses. He seems to have taken a liking to you, though."

Justice tries to chew on my shirt, and I nudge him off.

"Is there any chance I could ride today? I swear I've ridden more than just a pony ride once a summer, and all I would need is for you to point me in the direction of the tack shed."

"Of course. It's just past this trail. Should I call Ulysses for you?"

I bite my lip. I sort of want to be by myself for a while.

"Could you maybe give me like thirty minutes first? I just want to clear my mind for a while without him."

She warmly smiles at me and turns to leave. I click at Justice, and we follow the worn grass path toward the stable. I tether him to a low-hanging tree branch and enter the large barn. I suspect I am going to find only English saddles, but I still have a glimmer of hope. I saunter down the rows of large, pampered stalls, and in each is a stuck-up royal horse.

No wonder Justice is always escaping.

Who would want to hang out with a bunch of prissy ponies all day? I open several doors till I find the tack shed.

As I feared, only Dressage saddles line the wall. But then, on the bottom row, I spy an old leather Western saddle. I grab a pad, headstall, reins, girth, and some boots and head back to Justice. Of course, he is just grazing grass with not a care in the world. Except as soon as he hears the jangling of the riding equipment, his ears perk. He paws the ground the moment I start with the pad.

"Oh stop, it's wool and leather. It can't be *that* bad."

I finish with the saddle and grab the bridle, heading to the front of Justice. He nips at me and I swat his nose.

"Listen, you either let me ride with you, or you can go back to that cramped stall with the other royal prissy horses. Take your pick?"

With that, he lets me slide the bit into his mouth. I leave his rope lead on the branch and walk away to attempt to saddle this black bear.

Thank goodness I wore my combat boots today. I slide my left foot into the stirrup and swing my right foot over. Justice shifts his weight on each hoof as I adjust myself.

So far, so good.

I squeeze him in the side a little, and we start off in a walk. After a short while, Justice gets antsy, and I can tell he is trying to go faster.

"Alright then, let's go." I skip every warning and lesson I've ever learned and go straight to galloping.

There is a split second where everything goes in slow motion, and I feel like I am flying. Then everything goes back up to full speed. We are making a giant loop around the castle. We dodge and weave around the trees and the sidewalks, then we leave the grass for the long concrete driveway. Justices' hoofs slam into the black ground as we approach the stairs of the front door. I don't even slow us down as we charge up to the front gate.

CHAPTER 32

When Westries leaves, every fiber of my being tells me to stop her, but something else in me says to let her go, and it isn't Axel.

"What stupid part of you let her go? Because it wasn't me."

"Oh, shut it. Tell me how stopping her is going to help? It's overwhelming enough."

Daria locks the crowns away and everyone leaves the room. I stay there for what feels like forever as Westries runs down the halls.

To get away from us.

To get her bearings.

Eventually, I lose the sound.

I knew this would overwhelm her.

On top of everything that has happened in the past few weeks, this only adds to the stress, whether we'd admit it or not.

Tomorrow isn't going to be much better.

Cade comes to check on me. Except he says nothing and just stares.

"Are you going to stare at me or actually say something?"

"What can I say that won't end up with you killing me?" He laughs.

"I wouldn't *kill* you, just probably be really pissed off. Why *are* you here, anyway?"

"Daria wants me to tell you Westries is fine, and she's made a new friend, too."

My jaw clenches. "Friend? What sort of *friend* are we talking about here?"

"You'll have to see for yourself. Hannah is watching from the front window. It's pretty cool if you ask me."

He gestures for me to follow him. On our way to the front door, Jackie spots us and joins the procession.

"She's heading toward the front gate. She is really flying on that thing."

"What are you talking about?"

Jackie looks from me to Cade. "He doesn't know?"

"Nope."

Two guards open the front door to a giant stone landing. Clanging in the distance reaches my ears, but for the life of me, I cannot figure out what it is. Hannah, Daria, and Stefan approach us when a glistening, black tidal wave jumps out of nowhere to the top of the stairs meeting us. The horse screams bloody murder, bobbing his head while pawing the ground.

It would be a lie to say I'm not at all startled by this unexpected appearance. But to see the horse's rider when all four hoofs meet the ground is more like shock.

Westries.

She guides the sweaty horse in front of us. By her expression, she is as shocked to see us.

"What are you doing on *that*?" I ask.

I prefer knowing what is going on at all times. That Westries is on a horse the size of Axel without my prior knowledge is concerning.

Extremely concerning.

The giant horse shifts his feet and huffs at us, clearly not having any of this.

"Riding?" Her tone is snarky, her expression faux innocence.

"Can you get down then, please?"

She smirks at me and tightens her grip on the reins. "Why? Does this make you nervous?"

Axel growls at her defiance. Westries clicks her heels and the giant black horse walks around us.

"He might not be, but *I* am. Don't hurt yourself up there, Westries."

"Why? You think I might *fall*?"

"*Yes.*" Jackie screeches.

"So, if I do this…"

The giant horse rears up on his back legs and Jackie screams.

"*Westries!*" Jackie admonishes, stamping her foot.

Wes laughs and stops the beast.

"He did it! Not me! Good boy, Justice. You scared the crazy wolf lady."

She swings her leg over the horse and lands beside him, looking like a midget compared to the enormous horse.

"This is Justice. Justice, meet the gang."

Cade reaches out to pet the horse and Justice pins his ears and nips at him. The black devil swishes his tail and flares his nostrils at us.

"*Ow.* Don't tell me this is going to be another one of your pets that hate us?"

Cade cradles his almost lost hand to his chest while Westries strokes Justices' mane.

"I was going to tell you, but I wanted to see what would happen. I don't think he likes dogs…" Westries snorts to herself.

"Well, that's just unsettling and ironic." Hannah mutters.

"Where exactly did you find a *horse*, Bella?"

She shrugs and wraps her arms around Justice's head.

Stefan crosses his arms and says, "He's our barn demon. He never stays in his stall, always tries to run off, won't hold still for a second. I'm just shocked you could get a saddle on him. One time he tried to eat the ponytail off our trainer. He is a complete problem child. Uh, *horse*, I mean."

"Now that's even more perfect." Hannah mutters again, making Cade laugh.

"But he's so sweet. He couldn't possibly have a mean bone in his body. Right, bubby?"

Justice nudges Westries gently. Axel is peeved this horse is getting more attention than us.

"You can have him. No one here can get even within ten feet of him well except for his groom who feeds him that is. But I think there are ulterior motives on that one."

Westries eyes light up and she whips her head to me. I feel like a parent whose kid just asked them if they could have a pony, literally.

"Please, Ulysses? I promise to walk him and feed him every day. *Please*?"

She hugs Justices' head tighter and bats her best puppy dog eyes.

"Can't really say no to that, Ulysses." Stefan says chuckling.

I scowl at him for putting me in this situation.

"Tell you what. If he lets me touch him, you can keep him."

This horse has been trying to eat our hands. He won't let me touch him.

Westries nods enthusiastically. I reach my hand out halfway. Justice doesn't even flinch as he stares at me, daring me to come closer.

"Go all the way now, Ulysses."

Daria laughs. My plan of letting him bite me fails. I reach out and stroke the beast. Westries smirks at me in satisfaction.

"Fine, we can keep him."

"Thank you."

Westries jumps up and down, then latches herself around my neck in a maniacal hug. I wrap my arms around her waist, holding her close, inhaling her scent. She whispers thank you, and I tighten my hold. She then kissed my cheek, and Axel purrs.

"Okay. *Okay.* Let go of each other. No PDA on the front steps. We gotta get ready for tomorrow, so you two need to 'okay' the venue."

"Can I go put Justice away first?"

"No, Westries. You're coming with me. Daria called someone to take him." Jackie states.

A few moments later an older gentleman steps forward and reaches for the reins, which Westries reluctantly hands over. We all follow Stefan and Daria to the throne and ballroom. Westries trails the rest of the group. I take her hand and squeeze it. She half smiles at me and shuffles behind me.

"Are you nervous, Bellator?"

"*No.*" Her answer is too quick, too shrill, to be the truth. "What makes you say that?"

"You're shuffling your feet, not making eye contact, *and* you never act nervous."

"Whatever…"

Two pack warriors open the giant double doors to the throne and ball room. It isn't quite like I remembered. In fact, it seems even larger now. Westries' jaw is on the ground. The doors open to a long, broad corridor with satin curtain covered windows that nearly reach the vaulted ceiling. Massive chandeliers are every twenty feet, and everything is gold crested.

For a second, I forget why my first order as Alpha King was to move the royal pack to Montana. Then I remember that the economic growth, tariffs, and laws are better in America. So, we became American citizens and moved West.

Leaving all this behind.

"Woah…"

"And we'll have everything in gold and burgundies. You, tell me what the status is on the caterers."

Jackie orders people around while Daria finishes the table settings. On the farthest end of the grand room is a set of five stairs leading to two thrones and the locked royal jewels box. On that raised stage is where Westries will be crowned.

"Ulysses, I need to know if you approve of this. It's very important that this coronation is *perfect*."

"Jackie, whatever you do will be great. Maybe you should ask Wes."

Westries wanders around with Ruby observing everything with child-like wonder. At Westries' feet, Griffin follows happily. Westries laughs at something Ruby says, and my heart melts. The entire room is abuzz. People bustle everywhere. Some are setting up tables and chairs, others are folding napkins, arranging flowers, and setting the royal China and antique silverware on the freshly spread tablecloths.

"Can you believe that it's finally here?" Colemans' voice snaps me out of my trance.

"No, I can't honestly. Who would ever have thought we'd be here?"

"No kidding, and Jackie is having a ball with it. No pun intended. I don't think she's ever had this much fun planning something."

"I can tell." I laugh.

"LASSIE."

"Run, Lucius."

The thunder of little feet and the shrieks of innocent staff and pack members explode around us. Three kids are running about with plastic swords and shields. They mad dash directly at us before Jackie and Aubrey intervene.

"Oh, no you don't, Corrine. You, Patrick, and Lucius *cannot* come in here. Jackie and I will not have you breaking something and ruining the decorations."

"Please, sissy? We promise to walk and not touch anything."

Aubrey and Jackie groan and get back to work. Corrine—immediately reneging on her promise—charges at me and jumps in my arms.

"You know Aubrey hates it when you run around her projects."

"I know, but I want Westries to meet Lucius."

"Who's Lucius?"

Westries, Ruby, and Griffin appear behind me and Corrine squirms out of my arms. Patrick, David, Lucius, and Corrine go straight to Westries. I can't really imagine why David, a grown teenage boy, would want to hang around little kids, but Corrine can be very convincing.

"Bear, this is Lucius. He's my age." Patrick says happily, bouncing up and down.

"Well, hello. I'm Westries."

Westries leans down and shakes Lucius' hand. Lucius is almost eight and is the son of Daria and Stefan. They met young and had Lucius almost right away.

"I know. Patrick and Corrine told me all about you. My mom told me stories about you. She said you were a badass bitch, but you can't tell her I told you. She says it's a potty word."

Westries snorts and pinky promises Lucius, before he runs off again with Corrine and Patrick.

"You didn't tell me Daria and Stefan had a kid." Westries crosses her arms.

"Didn't think it was important. Besides, Corrine and Patrick wanted to. You can't be mad at me because I listened to my little sister."

I use her puppy dog eyes trick, adding a head tilt. She rolls her eyes but drops her arms.

"Fine. But I need to know all the things from now on, and I want to hear them from you. I *am* second to the king, after all."

I encircle her waist and she smirks up at me.

"Oh, really? And the king, doesn't he have any say?"

"I don't know. I think I have him pretty much wrapped around my finger."

I raise an eyebrow.

"But don't tell him because I think I have a crush on him, and that's very unprofessional."

She gazes up at me and grins. I smile back and pull her to me. She slips her arms around my waist and buries her head in my chest, sighing.

Against her ear, I tell her, "I promise I won't say anything."

She murmurs an incoherent response and burrows deeper. We sway to no music aside from the synchronized beating of our hearts. I am peripherally aware of everyone leaving the room as they complete their tasks.

The fancy matching armrest chairs surround the dozens of tables, the crystals on the chandeliers sparkle, and the lights are dimmed. The two thrones are freshly dry cleaned and the royal jewels rest on the table between them. Someone has opened the curtains of the thirty-foot-tall stained-glass windows to reveal the beginning of the sunset.

CHAPTER 33

WESTRIES

I'm unsure how long Ulysses and I danced in the throne room as if it's the most natural, normal thing in the world for us to do. I don't remember at what point we stopped and joined the others for dinner, but I *do* know it was pizza.

The jet lag has hit me hard. Presently, I'm lying face down on the couch in my room. Two warm bodies are using me as a cushion. By the snoring of one and the bony knees and elbows of the other, I can tell it is Griffin and Corrine.

The room I am staying in is a quaint royal castle room. Which means it's like a hotel suite on steroids.

Someone lifts a body off me, and magically I can breathe again. Griffin kicks me.

I guess it's time to change into pajamas.

I roll off the couch and land on my back. I grunt and crawl over to my suitcase. My method is either smart or lazy, perhaps both. I shrug on my sweats and t-shirt, then crawl across the floor toward the bed. My head meets the bedpost, and I roll over onto my back to see the tall bed that I must now scale.

I grip the comforter and pull, but instead of raising myself, I've succeeded only in covering myself. I half cry, half grumble and use my legs to kick off the heavy cover, but I fail again.

The floor is my home now. This is where I shall sleep.

At least it's a royal floor and not some apartment floor. It could be worse. A pair of arms wrap around me, lifting me up.

Not today, Satan.

I throw wild, weak punches at the damn thing where the sun doesn't shine. It throws me on the bed, and I reach for my knife from under my pillow and jump on the devil, aiming the knife at its neck.

"Not today, Satan. You shall not have my soul!"

The Devil shoves me down again, snatches my weapon, and pins me down.

"Damn it, woman. I'm not the Devil. Stop trying to kill me."

Whoops… well, how was I supposed to know? Don't grab me when I'm acting like a lunatic.

He collapses on top of me and buries his head next to mine.

"Sorry, I thought you were trying to drag me into the underworld."

He props his head in hand and blinks at me. "What?"

"You heard me."

He drops his head onto my shoulder, shakes it for a moment, then looks at me again. "Why do you have a giant knife under your pillow?"

"Really? After everything, *that's* what surprises you?"

He groans and buries his head into the extra dense fluffy comforter. I smirk and twirl his silky hair in between my fingers.

"No, but in the future, could you warn me, please? I don't want to jump on the couch and become a shish kabob."

"Well…"

"Are you serious?"

"You take me to a foreign country, surround me with werewolves I don't know, and think I would come unarmed? *Pfft*, as if. I'm still not one hundred percent sure your own mother won't kill me, for goodness' sake." I sit up, bumping his head off my shoulder. "I think Emmalyn and her are conspiring to have me disappear *mysteriously*. Also, do you know how awkward it is when people realize I'm a human and they make it very evident on their *face*?"

Before he can respond, another thought hits me. "And another thing, when we bring Justice back home, can I build, like, a small shed or something? He doesn't need anything fancy, just a roof over his head."

Ulysses opens his mouth, but I cover it and continue. "That reminds me, when we get back home, I want to do something. Like volunteer at an animal shelter or, oh… even better, *own* an animal shelter. That would be utterly amazing, and Griffin could even be my assistant manager." I flop back against the pillow and gaze up at the ceiling. "Ugh, that's like a secret dream of mine, right next to astronaut, CEO, and becoming a professional mermaid, but that last one's a little farfetched. Don't you think?"

I gaze back down at Ulysses, who is watching me, smiling.

"What?"

"You talk a lot. I'm tired just listening to you. We are going to sleep now, so shush."

Ulysses props himself on his elbow and turned the nightstand light off, then pulls the tangle of covers over us. I flip over and face plant into my pillow. My mom always told me not to sleep facing down because, the way I sleep, I might suffocate myself. I can't help it, though. It is way more comfortable than my back or side.

I lift my head just enough to ask, "What time…"

"You can sleep in as late as you want. Jackie wants you to meet her and the others in the spa at noon."

"Spa? I don't want to…"

Ulysses pulls me against him and hugs me tight.

"You'll be fine, Bellator. She had the works planned, but I told her to skip waxing."

"Oh gosh, I'll love you eternally for that."

"You better. You know how much scolding I had to endure from Jackie for you?

I laugh and roll around, facing him again.

"Well, then thank you, my hero."

Ulysses scrunches up his face and shakes his head.

"That doesn't sound right. I think we should change that to 'Partners in Crime for Life.'"

I tap my chin and pretend to ponder the title, even though I madly love it. "I agree. That one is much better."

He tucks me in closer and kisses my forehead. I yawn in his face, and he kisses my nose.

"And tomorrow, you will officially be my Luna Queen."

I mash my face in his shirt.

"Don't remind me, I still don't like the concept of all this fancy royal clothes business."

He chuckles and pulls me even closer, if that is even possible.

"Sleep, now… *please*."

"Okay, Bellator, you can sleep. I'll still be here when you wake up."

"Like a creepy stalker…" I mutter under my breath.

The second it seems like I am actually getting rest, the morning rays of sunshine assault my face. I groan and roll over, feeling around for my heating pad, aka werewolf's mate. I can't find it and I'm getting cold. So, I do what's only natural and completely normal. I make sounds that could be confused for whale calls and groan as loud as possible.

If this hunk of Alpha King wants to be my mate, I am going to be clingy and desperate for attention.

I flop over, face up, and starfish my arms out. "*Ulysses.* I need you."

The bathroom door screeches open and out walks Ulysses in his sweatpants.

"What, baby? You *groaned*?"

He mocks me and saunters over. I pout and hug the big fluffy pillow underneath me.

"You lied."

He sits on the edge of the bed and brushes off a strand of my hair.

"You said you'd be here when I woke up and you weren't, so that…"

I didn't even finish scolding Ulysses because he tackles me, smothering me underneath all his weight.

"I can't breathe, you lug. You are squishing me with all your fat."

He laughs and nuzzles his head into my neck.

"All my *fat*? Really, babe? This is all muscle, thank you very much."

"Yeah, well, muscle is heavier than fat, so you are still breaking my spleen. Get off before I stab you with this ornamental pillow."

"I think you are the most aggressive person I've ever met." He rolls off me but holds me tight.

"I resent that. I am an *assertive* person."

"That's what you're calling it, huh?"

I throw a half-hearted punch to his stomach. He *oofs* and grabs my hands before I can hit him again. We poke and tease for a few minutes more, and when I call a truce, he sits up against the headboard.

He is staring out of the stained-glass window, watching the sun rise higher in the sky. I lean against him because I am still freezing. He drapes an arm around my shoulders and brings me closer. When Ulysses kisses my head, I close my eyes in blissful contentment.

We stay like this for a while, neither speaking until Ulysses murmurs, "I want to spend the rest of my life with you."

I suppose he thought I'd fallen asleep, because when I answered, "Me too," he startled.

"Really?"

He adjusts himself so he is in front of me, and I am backed against the headboard. I smile and quirk my eyebrows.

"Yeah. I think I fell for you…"

I pick at the comforter and avert my gaze from his piercing one.

Why is this so uncomfortable? I mean, I've said it, right? That I am in love with a werewolf? I thought I did at some point.

Maybe not coming right out and saying 'I love you' but I've said those words in *other* words, I think. He is silent, so I peek up at Ulysses. I wish I hadn't because the expression he is giving me melts my heart. It's the sort of look that says 'You mean more than the world to me. You mean the universe and beyond.' I bite my lip under the weight of his intense gaze.

"Say it, Bellator."

"W-what?"

"*Tell* me."

I bite my lip hard enough to taste blood. Why is this so difficult? At least for me it is. Eight letters, that's all it is. What's so bad about that?

"I love you." I whisper.

Two toned arms wrap around me and practically squeeze out all the air in my lungs. When I catch my breath again, it's only to be smothered in a barrage of kisses and sweet murmurs from the man I once tried to kill.

And I'm loving every second of this. Wouldn't have guessed it possible, but here we are.

"I have been wanting to hear you say that since we met."

"You mean kidnapped?"

"Kidnapped, met… they're the same thing. I can't wait to spend every second from now on with my beautiful mate."

"Minus bathroom time."

"Fine, minus bathroom time, but every other second you are now glued to my hip."

He kisses my nose and hugs me even tighter. I am being squashed in his embrace, but it is a comforting sort of being squashed.

I pull back and warn him. "You better have pickles and BBQ chips at the ready, then."

He grins. "With donuts covered in bacon?"

"You really *are* made for me."

It is my turn to do the hugging. I probably didn't come close to his squishing ability, though. Ulysses sits up abruptly, pulling me upright with him. He then leans over to the nightstand and takes a burlap bag out of the drawer and sets it in his lap.

"This is something I never thought I would have the privilege of doing, Westries. We haven't known each other long, but it feels like a lifetime. I knew from the moment I saw you, strange as the situation was, it was the start of the best part of my life."

He unties the strings of the bag. "It's been a wild ride and I can't wait to see what we do together next. Whether it's changing the status quo, or showing up my own highly trained warriors, I want to do it all with you."

Ulysses reaches into the burlap sack and extracts a black box. He opens it slowly and says, "I don't really know how to do this, but Westries Clary Mikos, will you be my Luna Queen… and wife?"

Inside the box is a simple gold band with a gray, muted stone in the center, surrounded by diamonds. It is simple, rustic, and perfect. I blink at it for a second and a single, unexpected tear rolls down my cheek. I can't find any words because my throat has closed, so I simply nod.

Ulysses' face lights up and he slides the ring onto my finger. My cheeks are wet with tears, and I wrap my arms around Ulysses' neck.

I, Westries the badass Avenger, am crying, damn it, and I don't even care.

Ulysses' voice shakes when he says, "You realize that was *the* most difficult thing I have ever *done?*"

"Hah! Hardest thing *you've* ever done? I said yes, and I *never* thought *I'd* be doing that."

He chuckles and wags his finger at me. "Yeah, but *I* had to ask."

"Did Jackie help you?" I ask, half laughing, imagining Jackie with a huge binder dedicated to engagement ideas.

Ulysses snorts and shakes his head emphatically. "No. In fact, no one knows. I did this all on my own, thank you.

"Aww, I'm so proud of my man."

"I like the sound of that, Bellator."

We stay like that for a while. My head is on Ulysses' chest and his arms around me and I am perfectly content with that. Ulysses strokes my hair, and I draw circles on his chest. Even though I just woke up, I could fall asleep again.

Ulysses murmurs against my hair. "Everyone is probably waiting for us downstairs. We should get dressed."

"Do we have to?"

"Well, it would not be proper to present ourselves in night clothes, so yes."

Ulysses laughs as he gently nudges me toward the side of the bed. I grumble as I sit up, searching around for my suitcase. It is in the corner of the room with clothes falling out.

Classic me.

I plop down in front of the suitcase and flip open the lid. It isn't organized in the least bit. I can't tell my pants from my sweatshirts without holding up each item. I grab some jeans and an oversized sweatshirt that says, "I only like you for your dog."

As I tug it over my head, it dawns on me that it might be slightly weird considering who I hang out with these days.

Oh well, you only live once.

I glance down at my fuzzy socks with cactuses on them and accept that I'm a bum. Maybe it's that very nuttiness that makes me contemplate how slippery the hard wood floors might be, so I bolt out the door. I come to a sliding halt inches from the wall opposite my room. I have no idea where I am going.

If the heart leads you, you will follow.

I hear voices, so I follow them. I turn one corner and collide with a person. We both squeal as I fall on top of them.

"Get off me you, big ape. You're crushing my spine. *Spencer.*"

Spencer helps Ruby up, and I stay on the floor. Griffin lopes up to me, wagging his tail. I rub his head and try to stand.

"Thanks, I'm okay, too."

Someone takes my hand and yanks me up.

"Thanks, Paul."

"You're welcome, Luna."

"I've told you a million times, Paul. Don't call me that. I'm *not* Luna."

He raises an eyebrow. "As of tonight, you will be. Oh, and nice rock."

"Thanks. Hey, wait a minute, how did you…"

And he is gone. I twist my ring self-consciously.

Is he going to tell anyone?

The kids are at a table eating cereal. I snag a banana and a muffin from the buffet and sit next to David. They are all talking, or should I say *arguing*, so I elbow David.

"What are they arguing about?" I whisper.

He leans over to me. "Harry Styles or Tom Holland."

I snort and bite into my muffin, half-listening. The debate is over which one is 'hotter', has the 'bigger fan base' and blah blah blah. I chew my muffin in peace.

"So, what are you doing today?" David asks, poking at his oatmeal.

"I do not know. Jackie oversees all that stuff. What are the guys doing?"

"Aubrey suggested the guys just hang out at the house till we put our suits on. Not much guys need done, anyway. Although I could use a haircut, so could Patrick. He's looking like Shaggy."

"It's a cute little Shaggy, but you're probably correct. Okay, I'm going to make a break for it before Jackie notices me and drags me away."

He snickers, smiling, and I collect my trash. I sidle over to the trash can and throw my napkin and muffin wrapper in.

If I'm going to slip away before I have to do any preparing, I'll need to leave quietly and...

"Hi baby. Why did you run off on me?"

I shriek as Ulysses lifts me from behind, swinging me in the air. "Set me down, you big oaf."

He spins me around until I am two turns away from puking up my muffin.

"No can do, Bellator. I enjoy holding you."

"Well, do it later. I need Westries, so set her down." Jackie says, tapping her heels. The ground meets my feet again.

"Can I keep her for just a little longer? Please?" Ulysses pouts, still clinging onto my waist like a baby. Jackie grumbles and stalks to the door.

She faces us again. "No, she's coming with us. Down, boy, release the pretty girl."

Ulysses grunts and lets me go. "Fine, just bring her back to me in one piece, okay?"

"No promises."

I plead with Ulysses with my eyes, begging him to put an end to her nonsense and rescue me. He waves and dons an exaggerated frown as Jackie yanks me toward the door.

Aubrey, Daria, Hannah, Ruby, and two other girls wait by the door.

"Alright. Now that everyone is here, we really need to get ready. It's 11:07 right now, so we have a little over six hours till the coronation. Oh, I'm so excited!" Jackie leaps with joy.

Then Daria butts in. "Plus, it's all going to be aired on TV."

I stop dead in my tracks. *Aired on TV?*

No one told me about that part. "I'm sorry *what*? TV? Since when?"

They all stare at me like I am crazy.

"You didn't know?" The blonde girl I don't know asks.

"No…" I sigh under my breath.

"Oh, and I'm Karine, by the way."

"Westries."

I shake her hand.

"And I'm Anna."

"Hi."

I shake her hand, too. They both seem like they are in their late twenties.

"Great. Now that we are all acquainted, can we please hurry? We don't have much time. We've got a coronation to prepare for."

We follow Daria through a large oak door covered in ornate designs.

Inside is basically a giant bathroom, but fancier. There are blow dryer chairs and what, I think, are foot baths.

I am so out of my comfort zone.

Daria and Jackie charge personal beauticians to do our spa stuff: hair, makeup, nails, and whatever else royal women do. Can't be *that* much different from the lowly normal people. Jackie forces me to sit in a lounge chair and put my feet in heated water. A girl in a crisp, pale pink uniform sits in front of me and reaches for my feet. I jump.

I don't like people touching my ticklish feet… or anything on me, for that matter.

"Oh, sorry, my Queen. Did I hurt you?"

"Oh no, you didn't do anything. I'm just not used to this. In fact, I've never been to a spa before, so I don't know what I'm supposed to do."

She smiles up at me and gingerly reaches for my foot and massages it with a scented rock.

I try to relax and distract myself with conversation. "So, what's your name?"

"Meredith, my Queen."

"Please don't call me Queen. It's just Westries. So, tell me about yourself."

We proceed to talk about everything under the sun, including learning she's newly met her mate, and his name is Ben. I gaze around the room at all the other girls getting various services.

This is the strangest thing I've ever done.

Everyone is laughing and giggling while teen pop music blasts. Meredith dries off my legs after scrubbing them with salt stuff and shaving them. They feel smooth and fresh, and I will admit I like it, but that's *not* saying I would come here every day or something. She then shows me to a salon chair. I can't remember the last time a professional cut my hair. Kitchen scissors have worked fine till now.

"So, what should we do to this?"

Meredith fluffs and separates my hair, checking for split ends and what not.

No doubt admiring my fine work done in motel rooms.

"I don't know. Maybe layers, no highlights, and nothing too crazy?"

"I got you. Beta Female Jackie explained to me what she wanted me to style your hair like. So, no need to worry."

"Figures. She had that pre decided." I snort.

In fairness, it's not like *I* have any ideas about what to do. In the mirror, I can see Aubrey squealing with delight. Her beautician has just finished her haircut. She is beautiful, and I know someone who will agree with me.

"Hey, Ruby? What are you going to do?"

"Just a trim, I guess, and for the style I was thinking to have it down with big curls."

Meredith takes my head in her hands and turns it so I'm facing the mirror. She gives a terse smile, and it's clear she wants me to stop squirming around and stay put. I do as I'm told. For lack of anything else to do, I close my eyes. I haven't been this relaxed in a long while. Meredith is so good at her job; I actually start to fall asleep in the chair. She taps my shoulder, waking me. I look in the mirror to see my hair is ten times healthier. She whips the smock off me, and I stand and stretch my back.

"Hey, Westries, lunch break. It's almost 3 o'clock now." Aubrey called from the doorway before she disappeared again.

So, I guess it's "Linner" technically.

I face Meredith, who is sweeping up all our hair.

"Thanks, Meredith. Are you going to take a lunch break?"

"Yeah, just got to clean up a little here. You'll still have to come back so we can style you."

I nod and smile at the other women, who are also tidying the room. Following the sound of the girls leads me to a parlor with couches and a TV. They are watching a chick flick and eating pizza. I sit down next to Hannah and grab a slice.

I ask the question I've been dreading the answer to. "So, when are we changing into our dresses?"

"In, like…"

"Right now."

Anna and Katherine argue whether it is better to change into our dresses before or after our hair styling. Daria, sitting across from me, takes another doughnut hole and grins.

She leans in and whispers. "Ignore them. They're cousins. They'll be fine."

"Ah, okay, then. So, how many packs are in Romania?"

"Just one. Which means most of our subjects are human. It can be hard keeping the secret that the royal family and their court are werewolves, but we make do."

"And your son, Lucius? How did that work? If you don't mind me asking?"

Daria snorted and pulled her legs up on the couch.

"Oh yes, my little fire ball. Well, I met my mate *younger* and had Lucius. That was almost eight years ago. It isn't the most unheard-of thing here, for a teenager to marry and have kids young."

"What about this coronation? How is *airing* this going to work? Do you guys have like a secret channel or…"

Daria laughs. "Oh no, we don't have a secret channel. It's going to be on normal international TV. We are crowning you a 'Duchess of Avenge,' but to the werewolf world this is a Royal Queen's Coronation. The name was Patrick's and Corrine's idea. It's so perfect, though."

I guess that makes sense, sort of. But how have they gotten so much done in such a short time?

I can't be the only one who thinks it's crazy how fast this is all moving. Then again, Jackie *has* had in her possession multiple binders *filled* with plans, dresses, food, hairstyles, even the color scheme. And everyone knew they would have a queen someday.

I guess they just wanted to be ready.

"Alright everyone up. It's 3:47, you've had plenty of time to eat. We have a schedule to keep. Let's go, go, go."

Jackie shoos us up, which is fine, I don't think I could have eaten anymore if I wanted to. My nerves are setting in and I don't feel so good. Back in the spa room, seven dresses hang in plastic bags behind each chair where we will get our hair done. Jackie, Daria, and Anna are already sitting down and getting started. Ruby, Katherine, and Hannah are changing into their dresses. I stand still, clueless as ever.

"Would you like to change first or wait, Luna?" Meredith asks, holding a basket of curling irons, bobby pins, and ponytail holders.

"Umm, maybe dress later?" She curtsies and guides me back to my chair and starts pinning half my hair up to curl.

My thoughts are jumbled and switch from wondering where the guys, Aubrey, David, and the little ones are. Hopefully, they have their clothes together and are changing, too. A piping hot iron gets close to my skull, curling my hair. Everyone is talking loudly. Blow-dryers are droning.

Cue the panic attacks and nervous tremors.

I close my eyes and force my breathing to slow. Few things scare me. This one thing *terrifies* me. I haven't told Ulysses how extremely scared I am of what is going to happen in less than two hours.

I open my eyes again, and I have a full head of curls. I am losing my sense of time and awareness. I really need to get this under control before I walk into a room full of eyes and cameras on me.

Throw me to the wolves and I'll come back leading the pack.

That is what is happening, literally.

"Luna? *Luna?*"

"Huh, w-what?"

"You're nervous?"

"That obvious?"

Meredith pats my shoulder, then resumes pinning up my hair.

"Well, I would be, too, if I were you. Plus, I've been trying to get your attention for the past five minutes."

"Oh, sorry."

"No worries, you're almost done, anyway."

"Really? What time is it?"

Meredith checks her watch. "4:52. Curling hair usually takes a while if you want small curls. Pinning some up is pretty quick. And you're done. Should we change you now?"

"Aw, Wes. I don't think I've ever seen you with curls before."

Ruby is in the chair next to me and is also done. Her red hair is in wild, large curls with crystals pinned everywhere.

"Thanks and look at *you*. Now you really are like Merida."

She purses her lips and side eyes me while fluffing her hair as her assistant hairsprays her. Meredith also suffocates me in a cloud of hairspray. My hair can now withstand hurricane-force winds. She removes my smock and leads me to my forest green ballgown. Meredith unzips the plastic bag and delicately removes the dress. I carefully lift my sweater off, and she helps me maneuver the giant fabric trap over my head. I kick off my pants. The moment after she zips me up, I struggle to breathe. Not because it is too tight or anything, but because it is real.

"You are beautiful, my Queen."

I smile at Meredith and don't bother correcting her. I just need to accept it. I face the room. Everyone is done and wearing their dresses, too.

"Picture time, everyone get in," Hannah yells, getting out multiple phones and Polaroid's. We huddle close and smile as four of the spa girls snap various photos.

"Funny face."

We pose multiple times and dare I say, I am having fun.

Okay. Those pictures are going to be fun to look back on. When Hannah and Katherine declare we have enough pictures, we disperse. Jackie gives us specific instructions that we are not to see the guys and we cannot ruin our makeup, hair, dresses, blah blah blah, or else she will kill us. If I haven't said it before, I'll say it now. Jackie is intense.

Time to escape Drill Sergeant Jackie.

I wander through the castle until I hear voices. In the dining hall, the younger kids—all dressed and ready—mill around. Corrine and Aubrey are in cute pastel dresses with tulle. David, Patrick, and Lucius wear tuxedos with shiny black shoes. They all are so beautiful and handsome.

"Bear! Look at my tux. David, Lucius, and I match."

Patrick runs up to me with a big smile and a juice box. I put my hands up, ready to stop him from jumping or spilling juice on me.

"Patrick, you know I love ya, but Jackie will kill both you and I if this dress is ruined."

He screws his little face up, then shrugs. On the island are snacks, muffins, and juice boxes. Against my better judgement, I grab a juice box and lean against the counter.

"So, where are the guys?"

David sits on the cabinet eating a bag of chips and Aubrey, next to him, sprays Cool Whip into her mouth.

"In the coronation hall." Aubrey says around a full mouth. A blob runs down her chin and David wipes it away with a napkin, grinning. She giggles a thanks and cleans herself up.

"Right after we finished getting dressed, they all left."

"Why didn't you go with them?" I ask, taking the whipped cream can from Aubrey and spraying some into my mouth. He shrugs and jumps off the cabinet, throwing his trash away.

"I wanted to, but…" He mumbles. He can't hide it from me. I jab him in the chest.

"You sure?"

He scowls at me, and I roll my eyes. He has a mate crush, *hard*. He changes the subject. "Hey guys, it's 5:19. Do you know when Jackie wants us to go to the court?"

I throw my hands in the air. "Don't look at me. I'm clueless to how any of this works."

This whole thing will be on the international news. Lots of people, royals, Alphas and their mates, and whoever else is coming, too. And here we are, drinking juice boxes in ball gowns and tuxes.

Totally normal.

"Well, I'll tell you what I know, at least. The coronation will be in the grand old chapel attached to the castle. That's where you will be crowned. Then we will all go into the old throne room where the ball will be held. And of course, you can go outside to the courtyard where the food will be. Plus, you saw all the tables and chairs inside. That's where most of the action will be, but all the doors along the side wall will be opened. Okay?"

I gulp. It doesn't matter if I understand it or not, everything is still going to go down, with or without me.

Well, probably not without me since I'm literally half of the main attraction for the day.

David exclaims from the window. "Woah…"

My heart jumps. I immediately know what he is talking about. Aubrey beats me to the window and my heart rate picks up.

"Shit…"

"Shit? That's not *shit*. That's holy *fucking* shit."

I whisper yell so the other six ears can't hear me. Though they probably did. Cars fill the roads, parking lot, and roundabout. People are stepping out with magnificent gowns and tuxes, and uniformed staff take their keys and park the cars.

"That's a lot of people. Good luck trying not to fall in front of all of them." David laughs.

I glare at him, and Aubrey slaps him.

"Thanks, David. You're not helping me here."

"Oh, come on, I'm joking with ya."

I grunt at him and stand by the younger kids.

"And my mom said we could all sit in the front row." Lucius exclaims. The wild gleam in his eyes suggests a bit too much sugar intake.

"And we get to stay up all night with the grownups." Corrine says, clapping her hands.

"All night?" Patrick asks, leaning forward, clutching his poor juice box to death.

"Yeah. Are you excited, Westries?" Corrine asks. They all turn to me with smiling, glowing faces.

"Yeah, of course," I say with forced enthusiasm. "We're going to eat cake and hang out *all night*."

"Cake?" Patrick's eyes widen.

"Yeah, cake. What did you think we would have? Cookies?"

"But I really like cookies." Lucius whines.

"I'm sorry, Lucius. I didn't mean to use the word cookies in vain. How about broccoli?"

They all shake their heads in disgust.

"Can we all agree cake is better than broccoli?"

"What type of cake?"

I slam my head dramatically into my arms on the table.

"Lucius, you're killing me here."

Aubrey interrupts. "Jackie wants all of us to head toward the chapel hall."

They all rise, and I move to join them.

"Not you, Westries. No one can see you till the ceremony. You're coming with me. David, take these three to the hall. I'll meet up with you in a minute." Aubrey orders.

He herds the three toward the chapel hall. Aubrey takes my hand as if I might try to escape and leads me down the hall, but before we reach the grand front entrance, she takes me down to another door. She calls it the anteroom.

"The anti what now?"

"It's like a waiting room. You're just going to stay here until someone comes to get you. It will most likely be a guard or warrior. They will then escort you to the ceremony and you'll walk down the aisle, and the rest is pretty much self-explanatory. The pack pastor will tell you what to do once the service starts. Okay?"

My throat is dry, and I can't talk. Aubrey takes both my arms and rubs them. "Hey, you'll do fine, okay? This is nothing compared to everything else you've accomplished."

My head does something like a wobble-nod, and Aubrey leaves the room. I sit down at the vanity in the corner next to the giant stained-glass window and breathe in and out for what felt like a solid five minutes.

If I have to guess, I would say it was around 5:30. I play with my thumbs and mess with the loose hair on my forehead. I am bored, nervous, hungry, and now I feel the need to pee. I rest my head on my arms, careful not to mess up my make-up.

I'm in a black hole of existence. I can't go to sleep or leave the room. I can't figure out what time it is, or if anyone is ever going to come get me. I tap the wood with my nails and hum a tune. My nerves are not calming. Then, a faint knock raps against the door.

I jump up. "Um, come in?"

My heart thunders as the person opened the door slowly. When I see who it is, my heart bursts with relief.

"Corbin." I practically tackle the elderly man with the wrinkled face and cowboy hat in a hug.

"Slow down there, child. *You* can still stand on your own. I have a metal rod in my leg."

He chuckles as I unlatch myself from his neck.

"Sorry. What are you doing here? I didn't know you were coming."

"Well, I can't miss your special day, now, can I? Plus, Ulysses asked me if I would do the honor of walking you down the aisle today. Of course, only if that's okay with you?"

I nod and hug Corbin again. The threat of tears stings my eyes, but I won't cry. Not yet at least. I sniff a few times before Corbin pulls back and hands me a tissue. I mumble a thank you and he lifts his arm up for me to hold.

"Well, we mustn't keep the world waiting."

I take a deep breath and walk next to Corbin to the grand wooden double doors. There are ten guards standing at different locations all around the entrance before the doors.

"I will walk you down the aisle and then I'll hand you to Ulysses, okay?"

"O-okay." It comes out as a whisper.

Four guards open the doors. I gasp as dozens of eyes and video cameras come into view. The chapel is completely different with people in it. Corbin and I walk at a slow pace, and hundreds of eyes watch my every step. The clicks of cameras and whispers between people ripple through the great room. Part of my brain dimly registers there are news outlets I recognize taking video, pictures, and writing notes. Everyone here is a werewolf, except the reporters, I guess. Little do they know the "Duchess of Avenge" is being crowned queen.

Corbin squeezes my arm reassuringly. I'm guessing all these wolves can smell my nervousness. It isn't until I am at least halfway down the aisle that I realize I was looking everywhere except in front of me. I focus my gaze dead ahead and the first thing I see is Ulysses. His eyes are only on me. My cheeks heat. He is wearing a uniform that reminds me of a combination of Police and the Navy. It is navy blue, and he has a sword on his hip. He is very handsome, I'll admit. Corbin guides me all the way to the foot of the stairs and turns to me.

"This has been an honor, my Queen. This is a day I will never forget."

I lean in close and whisper. "I am not Queen yet. And you know I'd rather just be called Westries."

He smiles warmly at me and takes both my hands. "You will do great things. I can already see it."

Corbin then takes his light brown cowboy hat off his head and places it gently on me. My poor hairstylist, Meredith, is probably gasping in horror somewhere, but I tug it down a little, securing it. The old man grins, knowing full well the impropriety of the cowboy hat at the royal coronation.

And knowing just how me it is, too.

His smile and the warmth in his eyes say, *I'm proud of you.* And I don't think he'll ever know how much that means to me.

Corbin turns me to Ulysses, whose outstretched hand awaits. Corbin hands Ulysses my arm and the two of us, arms linked, walk up the small staircase.

At the top of the steps on the raised platform, Jackie, Ruby, and Hannah stand to the right. On the left are Coleman, Spencer, and Cade. In the center is the minister, who is dressed in white and gold robes, holding an ornate silver book. The minister begins, but I don't hear because Ulysses whispers in my ear.

"Nice hat, cowgirl."

"Thanks. Do ya think it will match my riding gear?" I whisper back.

"Definitely."

"Distinguished guests, members of the royal court, dear friends, and ladies and gentlemen, good evening. Once again, we are gathered here today to witness the coronation ceremony of the royal family Ronan. There are those who you will recognize and one person you will not."

Ulysses squeezes my hand as the pastor gestures to us.

"*Here* we have the fated of his majesty Ulysses Carter Ronan, Westries Clary Mikos. The subjects of Alpha's Dark Sun have long been awaiting this day, so let us begin."

Two small boys approach with a velvet rope and a golden chain of beads with a small dagger charm hanging off the end. The pastor takes one in each hand and motions to us. Ulysses kneels and I follow.

"This represents the bond that you both will share for eternity."

He places the rope around us loosely and tied the knot. He holds up the gold chain of beads with the small knife charm, takes our hands, and encircles it around our wrists.

"And this represents the trials and hardships that they will face together and…"

I snort.

I just freaking snorted in front of everyone. I hope no one heard that.

I instinctively glance over at Ulysses, who is holding back his own laughter. The minister peers at both of us, raises an eyebrow, and continues. I squeeze Ulysses' hand tightly, trying to force us back under control. He looks me in the eye and bites his lip.

"Stop it." I whisper.

His expression is of mock innocence. He whispers back. "Stop what?"

"*And now,* as tradition states, both parties will lay down their weapons that they will use to protect their people. Whether it be words, the power of the pen, or his sword."

Ulysses helps me off my knees, and we remove the ceremonial rope and chain. The pastor hands the items to the young boys, and they leave. Ulysses unhooks his sword, and I realize I need to remove my own weapons, not that anyone is expecting me to have any. I reach down to the bottom of my dress and raise it slightly. Several gasps erupted from the crowd. I smirk as I unlatch my revolver from my ankle. I hold it up to an also smirking Ulysses and set it on the table with his sword.

I lift my other leg and unlatch an extra magazine. I show the audience the black piece of machinery in my hand before I hand it to Ulysses, who is shaking his head but attempting to hide a smile. Next, I reach in-between my bra and pull out a black case. More gasps and murmurs ripple through the chapel, but I don't care about any of that.

I unsheathe the knife and pass it to the pastor, who carefully set it next to all the other weapons. The minister turns back to us, his expression pure disbelief, and I shrug. Coleman and Jackie step forward with a Bible and the golden tiara. Jackie places the Bible in Ulysses' hands, and he extends it, face up, out to me.

The minister says, "Now Westries, please raise your right hand and place your left on this Bible and repeat after me."

I do as he says and face Ulysses.

"I, 'State your name,'"

"I, Westries Clary Mikos,"

"Promise to protect and defend the values, people, and beliefs of the throne."

"Promise to protect and defend the values, people, and beliefs of the throne."

"To defend the defenseless, speak for the unheard,"

"To defend the defenseless, speak for the unheard,"

"And for my last dying breath, be for the one true Creator who has made me with a purpose."

"And for my last dying breath, be for the one true Creator who has made me with a purpose. Always."

The minister looks at Ulysses, who bows his head.

"Please kneel, your Majesty."

I remove my hand from the Bible and kneel before the minister, who has the crown held high above my head. Ulysses takes my hat off, handing it over to a page boy. I bow my head as his voice booms.

"And it is with great pleasure and my duty to crown you Westries Clary Mikos, Queen Westries Mikos Ronan. Rise."

Ulysses holds his hand out and helps me stand. It is like everything is moving in slow-motion. In my peripheral, I see everyone standing and clapping, but I can't hear anything. Warm lips press against mine. Ulysses pulls me close, and I wrap my arms around his neck.

Life is strange. I have finally found my forever home. I am no longer someone who lives in the shadows. Everyone knows me, or who I am.

Who I am now.

I have found my knight in shining armor, my partner in crime. Something I never dreamed existed for me. In his eyes, I see all possibilities. I am so glad I stopped running from this… from him.

veryone is shouting and cheering, but they seem a thousand miles away. My mate is officially mine, and now the universe knows it. *They also know that she is armed.*

That part makes Axel a little calmer, knowing that everyone saw her remove the weapons from her body. I pull away from her to see her beautiful eyes gazing back at me, and she is smiling.

"Shall we?"

"We shall."

Westries intertwines our hands and we head back down the aisle together. The Pastor is telling everyone they can move to the ballroom for the reception as we walk past the clicking cameras, guards, and giant wooden doors. We slow down in a corridor and Westries catches her breath.

"You know, we left our stuff back with that pastor dude, right?"

I grab her around her waist and pull her to me. "Yeah, Coleman and Cade will take care of it."

She rests her hands on my chest and straightens a patch.

"Don't we need to, I don't know, go to our own reception?"

"Maybe, but first…"

I kiss her. She links her arms around my neck and pulls me closer. Axel purrs and pushes himself to the surface, taking control.

"Ulysses is thrilled."

Westries laughs and traces our jaw with her thumb.

"Hi, Axel."

Axel full on hugs her like his life depends on it.

"I am very happy as well."

"Me too." She whispers into our shoulder.

I take control back from Axel and take Westries hand, leading her toward the grand hall where everyone will be by now. As we approach the double doors and guards, country pop music is playing on the other side. It isn't traditional, but it is Westries' favorite.

"You ready?"

Westries gazes up at me, absolutely glowing. "For anything."

I nod to the guards, and they open the doors. The room is filled with Alpha's and their Luna's from every corner of the planet. It is one giant melting pot. There are people in prom like dresses and suits, women in Chinese Hanfu and men in traditional robes, and women in African Kitenge and men in brightly colored shirts with indigo tassels. It is a breathtaking sight and Westries, clear by her open mouth and wide-eyed gaze, is equally impressed. Everyone claps as we step into the room. Westries squeezes my hand with a smile.

"Bear!"

Across the floor, Patrick bounds out of the crowd straight toward us. Westries prepares herself and catches Patrick as he jumps into her arms.

People *aww* as Westries hugs the boy and spins him around in her flowing green gown.

"Hey bud, what are you doing?"

"Did you know that there is a cake with six layers covered in chocolate strawberries?"

"Really? Did you show Corrine and Lucius yet?"

His eyes go comically wide, and he scrambles out of Westries arms and runs away, screaming for Corrine and Lucius. Westries turns back to me, and I take her hand.

"Come on, there are people who want to meet you."

She inhales and nods as I lead her toward a group of people. The music has started again, and people are dancing. I am searching around when I hear exactly who I am looking for.

"Ulysses. The man of the hour."

I face a large man who is an alpha from West India. "Raksha. How are you?"

He embraces me with a deep laugh and a tight hug. "I am well. But shouldn't I be asking you that question?"

I laugh, pulling Westries forward and presenting her to my old friend. "Raksha, this is my mate, Westries."

Westries reaches for his hand as Raksha bows. Westries retracts her hand and implores me for help.

"Sorry, I don't know what I am doing at all."

Raksha laughs. "It is fine, my dear. I know this can be quite confusing and new for you."

Raksha reaches his hand out and shakes Westries hand. Jackie then appeared out of nowhere, out of breath and ecstatic.

"Sorry, I am going to have to steal the Queen. We'll be right back."

And as quickly as she appears, she disappears, dragging a very confused Westries along with her. Raksha excuses himself as his mate calls him from the other side of the ballroom. I walk over to my father, who is mingling with the other pack Alphas.

"Congratulations, Alpha. I must ask, though, where is our Luna Queen?"

I smirk. "The Luna has been called by our Beta female for apparently pressing matters."

I emphasize *pressing* because it is of no true importance, really. Simply Jackie making Westries change into yet another dress that I am for sure going to hear about later.

"That is one thing I simply will never understand, mates," said one Alpha. "The other day Agnes asked me which color blinds I thought were best for the living room, but I couldn't tell a difference."

He laughs, throwing his arms up. His mate behind him slapped him with her clutch.

"You are just simply an old fart now. If your Beta can tell the difference, so should you. You've been married to me for how long?"

"Anything to make you happy, my dear."

He kisses her head, and she swats his stomach.

I hope Westries and I are like that one day. Still in love and getting on each other's nerves.

I wander around, meeting and talking with all sorts of people. There are people of all ages. From newborn babies, to teenagers, to old Alphas with their life mates. The music blares country and people dance along. I spot Paul, Cade, and Spencer, who were talking with a group of various people, and join them.

"Alpha. It's so good to see you. How have you been?"

"How could I be anything but perfect right now?"

"Oh yes, and where is this mate of yours? She couldn't have changed her mind so soon?"

Another woman chimes in, laughing.

"Oh no, she is presently..."

"Right here."

I whip around to find Westries standing in front of me in her black lace dress. The slit runs high on her leg, so her holster is clearly visible. Her tattoos are also perfectly outlined by the one sleeve and black swirl lace matches her tribal markings.

"You are beautiful, Bellator."

"Thank you, *your Majesty*."

I nudge her and face the group of people again. "*This* is Westries."

"Hi."

Westries acknowledges them with a simple head bow.

Not bothering with shaking anyone's hands again, I see.

"So, you're the infamous human Queen?"

"Yes, and no, I never thought I'd be here."

"I bet it was hard to adjust to. Knowing that werewolves exist now."

A young Norwegian Alpha says over his punch glass. Westries laughs and they give her a puzzled expression. She links her arm through mine. Axel purred in delight.

"Oh, no. I've known for a long time and I'm pretty sure some of you already know *me*."

Cade snorts, and Hannah shoves her arm into his gut. Westries is smirking.

God, I love this girl.

"What do you mean, my dear? We only heard Ulysses found you a week ago."

"You only heard about *Westries* a week ago, but before then I went by the Avenger."

A few people choke on their drinks, some just stare, and someone says, "That makes sense."

"Good God. How old are you?" An older woman exclaims.

"Nineteen. Well anyway, it was a pleasure meeting all of you, but I must go mingle now."

Westries waves and leaves them, jaws agape. I try to hold back my laughter as I catch up with my mate, grabbing her forearm.

"Hey. Wait a minute, cowgirl. You can't just say that and leave them hanging." I jerk my head in their direction. "Explain yourself a little."

Westries smirks with that mischievous glint in her eye.

"Why? It just makes everything so much more interesting this way. Plus, I will never reveal *all* my secrets at once. Now come on, dance with me."

Westries has a contagious laugh. She drags me to the dance floor. I groan. Dancing has never been my thing, and country is no exception.

"Oh, I love this song."

The song is about the "good ones." I assume the artist is talking about her boyfriend, because she kept saying, "He's one of the good ones and he's all mine." Westries sings along as we step on the floor. The song ends as we step out into the open and I am hoping Westries will spare me, but no. Another song begins and Westries spins around, absolutely in bliss. She has changed so much since we first met.

Axel growls at me to dance with our mate, and I give in. I lift her hand and spin her around to the upbeat country love song. She leans her head back and laughs. This song is about a bartender dancing in a club after a breakup. That's about all I take away from it. I recognize it from the time Westries controlled my car radio, though.

People's eyes are on us as we dance with no particular style, but my mate is happy, and that's all that matters. More people join us on the dance floor.

I motion to the gathering crowd. "I think we started a trend."

"See, isn't this fun?"

"Absolutely."

Her smile is adorable as I spin her away from me. She pokes her finger into my chest, singing along to the song, walking toward me.

She is sassy tonight, too.

We take frame again and sway around wildly. A tap on my lower back causes me to turn around. I am expecting to find a man. Instead, it's Patrick.

"May I dance with the lady?"

Westries looks at me, trying not to laugh.

"Of course."

Patrick starts dancing with Westries like a wild child would with his mother. Westries is laughing her head off as Patrick is 'flossing.'

"Lassie, dance with me."

Corrine jumps into my arms and I catch her.

"Yes, ma'am."

I twirl her around and she giggles. We sway with the music. It is another upbeat song about life and his perfect girl. Every time I glance over at Westries, it's to see she is singing every word with Patrick, Lucius, and a few other boys. Corrine jumps out of my arms and dashes back over to Patrick. I follow and pull my mate aside.

"Do you think we could pause on dancing so you could meet some more people?"

"Yeah."

She pouts, but then smiles, and I smile back. We stroll around and I introduce her to other people. She makes small talk and drops a few more bombs about her being the Avenger. The traditional speech I'm supposed to give never happens, which is right on par with the entire non-traditional… everything.

So, since this is the only plan anyone has, I go with it. A few people notice Westries ring, causing some raised eyebrows and curiosity. It isn't a tradition to propose to your mate. You find yours, mark them, and everyone knows they belong to you. It is simple.

Except Westries isn't like every other mate. She is human, and they have completely different customs. Customs I want to honor for her sake.

"And this is Alpha Samson Gage, his mate Lucky, and their son Colton."

"Oh, my goodness, it is such an honor to meet you, my dear."

Lucky embraces Westries in a bear hug, and Westries allows it. Yet another example of how much she's changed.

"Thank you, and I really have to say I like your name. It's very unique."

Lucky throws her head and back laughs. "Well, thank you, my dear. Apparently, I was a miracle, so thus the name. My parents thought I was a boy, so they didn't even have any girl's names picked out. The name was a last-minute emergency, courtesy of my father. Oh, my goodness, here I am yapping away about my name when there are others who would like to talk to you, too. This is my son. Now he is actually *my* little lucky charm."

Lucky runs her hand through her son's hair till he swats her hand off and fixes his spiked sections. Lucky and her mate are African American, and their son is Caucasian. It's clear they're unfazed by their differences and bonded by love.

"Hi, Luna Queen, I'm Colton and I'm eleven."

"Oh, well, hello to you too, I'm Westries."

"I like your name. It reminds me of my parents."

Westries blinks at the boy, her head tilting. I could be mistaken, but it seems that her face has paled.

His mother says, "Hey Colton, why don't you run along with the other kids?"

"But I don't know anyone, mom…"

"My friend Patrick can introduce you." Westries says, reaching out to touch his arm, then pulling her hand back.

Colton bobs his head eagerly. Westries is behaving oddly. To cover it, I call Patrick and Lucius and they bounce over.

"Boys, this is Colton. Do you think you could…"

The three boys are already gone. Where, who knows?

"Well, that's little boys for you."

Samson chuckles, sipping on his beer.

"Yes, I apologize for him. He doesn't really click well with the other boys too much because he's human. Like yourself, Luna."

Westries has this micro expression she gets when she is trying to piece something together. I watch her more intently, sensing she is struggling with something.

Her voice has a slight tremor when she asks, "Well, if you don't mind me asking. How did you adopt a human baby? Was that your intention?"

Samson laughs. "Oh no, it was completely accidental…"

"But the best kind of accident." Lucky chimes in.

"We can't have kids. We had been praying for such a long time that God would send us a sign, a direction, something, to show us what his plan was for us. He answered our prayers. One day we had a rogue make it past our border patrol. They chased it off as soon as we found out. We try only to kill when necessary, or if we know they did something worthy of death." Lucky says, shaking her head.

They've always had a very kind pack. I've admired and even been a bit confounded by their pack, as violence is something they try to avoid at all costs. For werewolves, it is uncommon.

"Later, after we doubled patrols, our guards found, in a *tree* of all things, a human boy. They brought him back to us and I just knew when I saw him, he was going to be a part of our family."

"She wouldn't let anyone go near him for at least a week after we found him."

Samson scoffs and Lucky elbows him.

"It was my maternal instincts, you brute. Well, anyway, the poor thing was scrawny, bloody, and would only say his name for the first day. After a bath, food and, of course, proper rest, he opened up to us. And long story short, he's our son now."

Samson kisses his mate's cheek as they both smile happily. I turn toward Westries, whose face is unreadable. She bites her lip, and I take her hand, giving it a squeeze.

"You good?"

"Huh? Oh yeah, sorry. I-it was really nice meeting both of you. I hope we'll get to talk again before you head back home."

Samson and Lucky give a polite bow, and Westries turns to leave, so I follow.

"Hey, Ulysses, I'm going to sneak away for a minute to use the bathroom."

"Alright. You sure you're okay?"

"Yeah, I just need to pee."

I drop Westries' hand as she weaves her way back through people toward the bathroom.

Something is wrong.

CHAPTER 36

WESTRIES

My heart pounds so hard it hurts. I don't even know *what* I'm thinking right now. My thoughts started to wander the moment the boy Colton was introduced, and everything is just… *strange.*

My body, disconnected from my brain, trudges along an empty corridor toward the courtyard outside. I never needed to pee. I just needed a second to gather myself and my thoughts. I am being paranoid and stupid.

Aren't I?

I slip out the back door and onto the stone floor where I can talk sense into myself. I pace across the patio. They decorated the deck in twinkling lights, and were I not so distressed, I'd admire the beauty.

I slap my cheeks, trying to push back the annoying thoughts plaguing my brain.

My family is dead. I saw the bodies; I read the newspapers; I know what happened, end of the story.

Then why am I doubting myself? They found five bodies at the campsite. Five. I was the only one missing. They even identified the bodies, or at least I thought they did. I will admit I have gone nowhere near there since that day. My gut wrenches for not visiting their graves, but I just can't. Especially if I am now not sure if one of my *brothers* is even there.

Because here I am, at my coronation ceremony, and there's a couple who adopted an eleven-year-old human boy named Colton…

That they rescued from rogues in Virginia.

Ok, reasons I am being paranoid: he doesn't recognize me, and I don't recognize him. Therefore, it's just a stupid coincidence. I pace until the click of the door stops me. I whip around to find Ulysses standing in the doorway with his arms crossed and a scowl on his face.

"Needed a bathroom break, huh?"

His stare makes me want to hide away and not answer.

"I-ah, well I was just…"

He strides toward me, but his gaze softens. He opens his arms out to me, and I step into his embrace. I bury my face in his chest and let out a deep breath.

"Are you going to tell me what's happening now?"

"You'll think I'm crazy…"

"We're past crazy, Bella."

I groan into Ulysses' chest. "I think Colton might be my brother…"

Ulysses laughs and pulls away from me so I can see him.

"Wes…"

"I'm serious, Ulysses. I think Colton might be my brother."

I scan Ulysses' face to see what he is thinking. By the look he is giving me, he thinks I am crazy.

I huff and try to break away from his embrace. "*See?* You think I'm crazy."

"Wait, wait. No, Wes. I don't think you're crazy. I just thought they were all…"

"Dead. They are supposed to be dead. My family *is* dead. But…" I shake my head hard to clear it. "Ulysses, please just tell me I am ridiculous."

I sigh as Ulysses strokes my back and sits me on a bench.

"You're not ridiculous, but can you explain how you came to this conclusion?"

"I don't know. It's just… he has the same name, age. He was even found because he was being chased by rogues. He looks like him and… I-I never saw my brother's bodies, s-so I just, when Lucky was talking, some old hope ignited…"

I trail off as Ulysses kneads my shoulders. Tears come to the surface, but if I cry, Jackie will kill me.

"Well, do you think he recognized you? Would he remember you?"

"I don't know. Ugh, I just don't *know.* I had this *moment,* and this idea that … What would I even do, say even? Hey, I know we don't know each other at all, but I think your adoptive son is my brother that I thought was dead."

I lay my head on Ulysses' shoulder. It isn't even 9 P.M. and I am exhausted.

"Well, why don't we go back inside to the party and figure this out? We've been gone awhile now."

I agree and follow Ulysses back inside. I am holding his hand, trailing behind him. My feelings are all over the freaking place. We enter the ballroom again from a side door. I sort of want to blend in with the crowd, but that isn't possible. I follow Ulysses around as he introduces me to even more people. I will not remember anyone's name in two hours. Sue me. After thirty minutes, I end up at a table with Ruby, Anna, and the three kiddos who are pigging out on cupcakes and cheese squares.

"Are you serious, Wes? Your brother is here?"

"*Ruby.* Could you say it any louder? I'm not sure that the old people across the dance floor heard you."

"Sorry, it's just I thought, well I thought you said they were dead…"

"They *are*." I whisper back to Ruby. "At least that's what I thought. This is just… this is my brain playing a cruel joke on me. That's all."

"But what if…"

"Please, Ruby, just drop it. I just thought I'd tell you."

"Well, I have one question. Are you ever going to tell him and his *parents*?"

I shrug. He seems so happy with his new parents. Why would I bring up terrible horrifying memories he may or may not even remember anymore? *I* still have nightmares. Why would I do that to him? He doesn't even know me.

"Well, did you hear Paul found his mate?"

"Hannah's brother Paul? Who?"

"An Alpha's daughter in Washington. He's going to be an Alpha. It's a pretty big deal."

"Woah, that's so great for him."

"Yeah, he hasn't left her side all night. It's pretty cute, Paul acting like a puppy."

Ruby laughs and devours her fourth piece of cake. Props to her because I haven't even finished my third. Spencer comes over to Ruby and tells her she cannot sit and eat cake all night, then drags her to the dance floor. Then it is just me and four little kids on a sugar high, left sitting at the table.

"Bear, why aren't you eating your cake? It's really good. Try it."

Patrick is extremely hyper. He is going to be impossible to put to bed.

"Did you know Lucius can fit an entire cupcake in his mouth?"

"Oh really? That's super cool, probably a choking hazard, but still cool."

"You wanna see?"

"Umm, let's not, okay?"

I stab a fork at my cupcake. Well, what is left, at least. I sort of mutilated it with repetitive stabs and smashes, turning it into a paste on my plate.

Where has Ulysses run off to?

I wish he would come back and keep me company. Everyone is dancing, laughing, and having a good time. Plus, Jackie said this party is going till 1am, so coffee is sounding pretty good. I sense eyes on me, and I glance around to find Colton staring at me from across the table. He has a contemplative expression on his face. I raised an eyebrow, hoping he will look away. He doesn't. The other three kids are still playing with their food and laughing their heads off.

"You look like my old friend."

"Oh, yeah? What was he like?"

"No, it was a *she*. It was back when I was little and me and my friends were in first grade."

I clench my jaw. If this kid is going to keep talking, I might cry. Old wounds are opening.

"What was she like?" I ask, my voice almost cracking.

"We did everything together. My other friends' names were Ian and Daya. My favorite memory before my parents adopted me was of us taking a trip to a water park. Do you have a best friend?"

"Yeah, I do." My voice betrays me, big time.

"What's his name?"

"Well, Ulysses is my mate, and Griffin is my dog, and I love them both." His eyes widen, and he half jumps onto the table.

"You have a dog named Griffin too?"

My heart pounds in my chest. I stand and walk around the table to Colton. I sit on my heels in front of his chair and stare him in the eye. He shifts and glances away, but I really needed to know.

"Colton, do you *know* me?"

He quirked his eyebrow, confused by my question.

"Yeah, you're the new Luna Queen."

"No Colton, do you *remember* me? At all?"

My voice breaks. Colton fidgets in his seat.

"Um, I don't know…"

"Colton, listen to me. Your friends, Daya and Ian, they weren't just your friends."

"Of course, they were my friends." He interjects.

My body betrays me, and tears roll down my face as I clench the chair Colton is sitting in.

"Colton, do you remember how the Gage's found you? The rogues? Camping? Griffin? Do you remember *any* of it?"

"Um…."

"*Please*, Colt, remember. Just try. Mom and dad, our siblings, the backyard with the tire swing that we made one summer, and adopting Griffin from the neighbors farm… anything…"

I'm dimly aware of the few surrounding people. Their awkward stares. Thankfully our table in corner is secluded enough. Colton blinks at me and I search his face. Does he not remember *anything*? Tears streak my face and I thank God and Meredith I have waterproof mascara on. Until now, I thought my entire family was dead. I thought they were gone. I am the last of my name.

If this really isn't Colton, I don't know how I can get over this again. I let go of his chair and wipe my face, not caring about smudging anything. My heart was shattered, and Ulysses helped glue the pieces back together again before. But *this*? This is a bull in a China shop.

"*W-Wes*?"

My head shoots up at the sound of the nickname my siblings always called me. I sniff as more tears stream down my cheeks.

"I-I remember… I remember Ian and Daya, but I thought they were dreams that…"

I cut him off by pulling him into my chest, hugging him like my life depends on it. I full on cry as I kneel on the ground hugging my *brother*. My actual flesh and blood brother is here with me, alive. He trembles and squeezes, and my shoulder grows wet from his tears. I squeeze back.

"I missed you so much, Colt. So, so much…"

"I thought I made it all up…" He cries into my shoulder. "I thought it was my imagination… I thought I made you all up because it was better than thinking no one wanted me…"

I pull back from Colton and take his face in my hands.

"No, no, no, don't ever think that. I would never abandon you. I thought you were dead. They told me… they said you were dead. Please forgive me, Colton. I would never have abandoned you if I knew…"

I hang my head in shame. How could I not have gone searching for them? Why did I ever listen to those bastards?

"I am so sorry…" I whisper. I failed him, big time. How could I?

"You are my sunshine, my only sunshine. You make me happy when skies are gray. You'll never know, dear, how much I love you. Please don't take my sunshine away."

Colton softy hums our special song that our mom used to sing us to sleep with, and my heart melts and anxiety washes away. It is one of the sweetest things anyone has ever done for me. I half smile as Colton flings his arms around my neck once again.

"I missed you, Wes."

"Me too, Colt."

But our reunion is interrupted.

"Colton?"

We turn to the small group that has formed around us. Lucky stares from Colton to me. She doesn't appear mad, just confused. As do most of the people watching, which thankfully isn't a lot, considering we are in the far corner of the ballroom, behind the food tables.

"Mom, this is my real sister, Westries. She really does exist; I didn't make her up."

Colton jumps up to hold his mom's hand, and I realize I am still on the floor. Not the most graceful position for the Queen, I suppose. I rise as Ulysses comes over to check on me. He has been watching the whole thing, I think. He gently places one hand around my back protectively and then tilts my face to look into his eye. My brain is firing a million a minute yet I feel relaxed for the first time. I stutter in a breath, trying to cope with what I just discovered.

"Are you okay, Bella?"

"Yeah. I found my *brother.* He *is* alive, Ulysses. I'm not the only one that survived."

I face him again, staring up into his beautiful eyes. I can't decide if I want to cry, scream, or praise God. Ulysses traces my jaw with his thumb.

"I know, baby, and I am so happy for you."

Lucky gasps to Colton. "I'm sorry, Colton, but *what* are you taking about?"

"All those dreams weren't nightmares. They were memories. They all really *existed.*"

Samson glances over at Ulysses and me, and I can't read his expression.

"Son, I need you to tell me the whole truth. How could you even *know* her majesty is your sister?"

"I recognize her. We recognize each other."

Colton smiles at me. Lucky and Samson appear anything but happy, and I feel the need to calm their nerves.

I place a hand on each of the distraught parent's arms. "Look, I don't want to take Colton from you. He has something very special with you, parents who love and care for him. I just want closure. I've spent the past five years thinking my entire family was dead and took out all my anger at doing terrible things. I'm not asking anything from you, just that I can maybe visit Colton from time to time. I understand though, if, if…"

"Oh goodness, no. We absolutely want him in your life, but for the sake of my conscience and my heart putting me into an early grave, could we run a DNA test?"

That doesn't surprise me, nor did it offend me. Some crazy human Luna Queen claims your kid is her long-lost brother. I would have doubts, too.

"Yes, of course, and thank you."

Lucky smiles at me and the small crowd disperses, for which I am thankful. Colton hugs my waist, grinning from ear to ear, then ran off with Patrick and some other kids like his world didn't just do a one eighty.

"Bellator?" I turn back to Ulysses, who has his hand extended to me. To the others, he says, "It looks like we'll have much to discuss. But for now…"

I place my still shaking hand in his large, calloused one. "What are you doing?"

"I'm dancing with my mate. What are *you* doing?"

Ulysses draws me to his chest, and we take frame.

To lighten the moment, I say, "I am being forced to dance with a really handsome old Alpha King, who has two left feet."

Ulysses fake gasps, and I snort laugh.

"I'm hurt, and also sort of flattered at the same time."

"You know what? I love you."

Ulysses spins me around and then pulls me against his chest again. A slow song plays, and I wrap my arms around Ulysses' neck, holding on tight. We sway together to an old country love song, and I rest my head on his chest as he inclines his head to meet mine.

He murmurs against my hair. "Could we just stay here?"

I hum a yes. My eyes drift close, then fly open as Ulysses dips me backward. Ulysses laughs as he brings me back up.

"If you keep that up, I'm going to puke."

"Now, how mad do you think Jackie would be if you did that?"

I groan, rethinking my next actions. "Fine, just be gentle. Motion sickness is a thing and I had a lot of cake…"

"Always, Bellator."

We dance and dance and *dance*. Ulysses twirls me around, tenderly, at my request. I am on cloud nine and Ulysses even surprises me with his waltzing skills. So, the werewolf King *can* dance. People are slowly leaving, and all the kids are gone, likely shuttled off by keepers and parents. It's way past their bedtime.

Mine too, now that I am thinking about it.

Ulysses and I stop dancing and bid farewell to the leaving dignitaries. Well, actually Ulysses sends people off, and I hold on to his hand, trying to look pleasant and not fall asleep standing up.

The last to go are Colton and the Gages. "Well, this has truly been an *unexpected* and eventful night, though one I am grateful for. Luna, I hope to see you soon. Although I don't think Colton would have it any other way."

"Mom says I can visit anytime, right, Mom?"

Lucky laughs and squeezes Colton's shoulders. "Not *any*time, you do have school, but as much as we can, okay?"

He nods and runs into my arms, almost knocking me over. He curls his arms around my neck and I hug him back just as strongly.

"Will you come visit our pack when you go home?"

"Yeah, if it's alright with your mom and dad."

"Of course, Luna, you are welcome anytime."

"Well, we better get going if we don't want to miss our flight. Say your goodbyes, Colton."

Colton hugs my neck again.

"Bye, Wes."

"Bye, Colt, I'll see you soon, okay?"

We watch them leave, then two guards close the large double doors as I let out a sigh of relief. That was intense, but now everyone is gone, and I can relax and bask in the glow of my complete happiness.

Oops, not everyone.

Daria says, "Well, I think that was a success. Don't you think, Stefan?"

"Yes, dear, I would say so. Though I will say that it's extremely late and I am exhausted. So, we are retiring for the evening, goodnight, everyone."

Stefan and Daria leave, making us officially and finally alone. I tug at my dress in a *get this demon thing off me* hysteria.

"Officially tired of being fancy?" Ulysses approaches, laughter in his eyes.

"You put this monstrosity on, walk in heels for like nine hours and then tell me how you feel after wearing it. Can we please go to bed now? I'm tired and it's way past my bedtime."

"Bedtime? Since when did you have that?" Ulysses crosses his arms, smirking at me.

"Since now and because you are copping an attitude, you will carry me. My feet have blisters, I'm not walking and you're strong, so…"

I raise my arms like little kids do when they want to be carried. Ulysses rolls his eyes and lifts me up, except he carries me like a baby.

"See? I'm light as a feather."

"More like heavy as a boulder." Ulysses grumbles. I slap his chest as he pushes open the door to our room. I am ready to collapse and fall asleep, but first I need out of this death trap of a dress.

C H A P T E R   3 7

Westries

Ulysses sits me on our bed and walks into the bathroom. I kick off my heels and fall backward onto the cushiony mattress. I wish I could just fall asleep right there, but I must at least change and wash off my makeup. I hear the sink faucet turn on and Ulysses hums. I undo the clasps from my pocket pistol—returned, as promised, by Cade—from their holsters and set them on the nightstand.

I struggle to unzip myself.

"So, how are we going to bring Justice back home?" I call out to Ulysses, who is still in the bathroom.

See, this is why I don't wear dresses, because it takes two people.

He calls back, "Well, we'll probably charter a freight plane. Boat would work too, but flying is faster."

I mutter *yes* when I finally unzip myself. "Isn't that, like, really expensive? I mean, it's okay if we have…"

"Babe, I'm a King who is a billionaire. I think I'll manage."

"Right. I *forgot* my mate is a rich *bachelor.* Does that make you my sugar daddy and I, a gold digger?" I joke as I tug on sweatpants and a shirt. Ulysses snorts.

"First, you're my mate, so I'm not a bachelor, thank you. And as for the gold digger part, you definitely aren't one, but that doesn't mean I won't spoil you rotten."

I laugh as I knock on the partially open bathroom door.

"Hilarious. Are you decent? I want to wash this makeup off."

Ulysses kicks the door open with his foot and I swear my face turns three shades redder. Ulysses' pajama pants sit low on his hips, and he is not wearing a shirt.

"You know, by law, we're married, so you don't need to ask to enter our room."

I feign nonchalance and give him an *'are you for real'* look as I turn on the sink and tie up my hair.

"Technically, our relationship is illegal in some places." I say, smirking as I splash warm water onto my made-up face.

Ulysses stands behind me and places his hands on either side of me on the counter, leaning in so his head is right next to mine.

"Really, because last I checked, you had a ring on your hand. So, what does that make us, then?"

I hold up my hand right in between our two faces, so we can both see the rustic ring on my left hand. It is gorgeous and I guess *technically* this makes us married.

"Married, I guess?" I say, smiling as I finish wiping the gross makeup off.

Thankfully, there isn't too much left to begin with. Ulysses wraps his arms around my waist and kisses my cheek tenderly.

"I like that."

"Me, too."

I fold my hand around Ulysses' larger one as he caresses my neck with his thumb.

"You tired, Bellator?"

"No, can we just talk for a while, please?"

"I thought you had a bedtime." He teases.

"Screw bedtimes."

Ulysses laughs and hugs me tighter. I lift my knees to my chest, and he carries me like this to our bed. He then dumps me on the comforter and climbs on, too. I lay in front of Ulysses with my hands supporting my face.

"So, what do you want to talk about, my *wife*?"

"Well, first nicknames, because 'wife' just ain't working for me. I'm too young to even be married." I say, scowling.

Ulysses twirls a strand of my hair and rolls his eyes at me.

"Okay, picky. How about you give *me* a nickname, then?"

"I did. Fluffy, remember?"

He groans at my nickname for Axel and throws himself backward onto the bed. I mean, it isn't 'manly' per se, but it's mine for him, so he just has to deal.

"Really?"

"Yes, and I'm not changing it."

"Then I'm calling you Wifey."

"Fine."

"*Fine.*"

Ulysses reaches over and pulls me beside him. I lay my head on his chest as I listen to the comforting sound of his heartbeat. I inhale a deep breath. He smells like clean pine air and charred red oak logs. It is a little particular, but it doesn't hurt to be specific.

"Ulysses?"

"Hmmm?"

"Does this mean we have our happily ever after?"

I expect him to say something sweet and memorable, but instead all I get is silence, which makes me nervous. I poke his chest to see if he is even paying attention to me, or maybe he is *dead*. Out of nowhere, he shoots up in bed. His eyes are changing color, so I know he is talking to Axel or someone in the pack. His jaw clenched and the veins in his neck and temples pop. He is terrifying, but I am not scared because I know he would never hurt me.

"Ulysses?"

I reach out to touch his shoulder, but before I can touch him, he jerks away and storms toward the bedroom door. He rips it open to reveal an out of breath pack warrior. I'm becoming more alarmed by the moment.

"Are you sure?" Ulysses booms in his Alpha voice.

"Y-yes Alpha. We only know of seven as of right now. Beta Coleman is in the office as we speak."

"Thank you."

Then he storms out the door with the warrior following behind. I am extremely confused about what just happened, so I do what's natural. I chase after them.

"*Hey*. Ulysses, what's happening?"

Screw my short little legs. Being five-foot-four has its advantages, but chasing after a six-foot Alpha king just isn't one of them. When I eventually catch up with the two, they are already in Stefan's office with almost everyone else.

"And you are sure this is an act against the crown?" Ulysses asks Cade. Cade nods solemnly.

"There is no other way it could be anything else. How do seven different Alphas and their families get run off the road? By chance?"

Now I am piecing together why Ulysses is acting this way.

"Can someone maybe fill me in on what's happening?" I ask no one in particular. I am completely ignored.

"Have we received any contact from the attackers?"

"No Alpha, the motives are still unknown. Those who survived…"

"Wait. Survived? Can someone please tell me what is happening?"

"I want a list of every single person who was at the coronation today, human and wolf alike. I want background checks redone on everyone. I want to see everything, even a speeding ticket from thirty years ago. I want to know about it."

"Yes, Alpha."

The warrior leaves the room in a hurry.

"Spencer, I want contact with every Alpha here. Where they are and where they are going. Do we know the casualties yet?"

"Someone *please* tell me what happened?"

"Yes, Alpha, here's the list so far."

Ulysses takes the list from Spencer and glances over it, then at me, then back to the list.

"Start informing the families and packs immediately. Stefan, could we use your pack house as a temporary base of operations for the time being?"

"Of course, Ulysses. And I would like to start media damage control if that's alright with you?"

"Ulysses…?"

I try getting his attention.

"Yes, please do."

"*Ulysses. Anyone.* Someone freaking tell me what is happening or so help me, I will strangle it out of someone." I scream, officially tired of being ignored.

I'm the damn Luna Queen. I should know what is happening at all times.

Everyone startles. Ulysses turns his gaze to me with an expression of grief and rage. It makes my heart ache to see him like this.

"There has been an accident…"

"*Accident*? You said act against the crown. This sounds like an attack! What is happening?"

Ulysses takes a deep breath and continues.

"Some Alpha's cars have been *shot* off the road and we believe it was an act of terrorism against the crown."

I gasp. They were shot off the road?

"You said you knew who was... killed? Who were they?" I asked, scared.

Ulysses doesn't answer. No one does. Everyone avoids my gaze, even Ruby, who won't look me in the eye.

"Ulysses, they are now my people, too, and I deserve to know who they were" I state.

I want to know. They are my subjects, the people I serve. I deserve to at least know their names, even if now I won't ever meet them. Ulysses stares at me with pain mixed with sadness.

"A pack warrior and the Alpha's sister from the Night Hawk pack. The Luna from Twilight pack. An Alpha's daughter from Pine Air pack. The Alpha of Mountain Valley pack. Two warriors of Racing Spirt pack. And an elder from Ocean Side pack."

Ulysses takes another deep breath as he sets down the brief.

"What about the seventh? You said seven families, so who was the seventh?"

Ulysses casts his eyes down.

"Ulysses, who was the seventh family?"

"Wes, maybe you should sit down..." Ruby takes my arm and tugs me to the couch.

I rip my arm away and narrow my eyes at Ulysses. My voice shakes and my body is cold. "Who was the seventh family?"

Ulysses comes around from the desk and takes my shoulders into his hand, looking straight into my eyes. "Bella, I'm sorry."

My body already knows, but my mind won't accept. "Why are you sorry? Just tell me who they were."

His eyes search mine. "Bellator, the seventh family was the Gage's."

Colton.

"A-all of them?"

"I'm so sorry Westries."

I cannot talk, move, or say anything. I stare into Ulysses' chest, willing him to take back those words, make them untrue.

How? How can this be happening?

Mere hours ago, I find out I wasn't the only one who survived that horrid night. I reunite with my baby brother. Now, not even a few hours later, he's *dead*?

No.

Ulysses pulls me against his chest and holds me tight. My arms are slack.

I found my brother and now he is gone?

"H-he's gone…"

Ulysses kisses the top of my head. I stare blankly. Tears are streaming down my face, but I don't make a sound. I don't think I could if I wanted to.

Ruby speaks. "Wait. Ulysses? This says the Alpha and Luna. It doesn't say anything about a boy. He might still be alive."

My heart soars when Ruby said those three words. He isn't gone. There is still hope.

I step out of Ulysses' embrace and address each of them in the room. "Then where is he? What happened?"

Spencer runs in, out of breath. "Ulysses, I have the list of survivors. Some were airlifted out, some by ambulance, but they were all taken to Saint Mary's hospital twenty minutes from here."

I beseech Ulysses, who knows what I am going to ask.

"I'm taking Westries to the hospital. Coleman, you take over for the time being. Anyone who wants to go better start moving people."

Stefan throws Ulysses a pair of car keys and we are out the door. Ruby, Cade, and David follow us to the car. I don't know if I should be relieved or nervous. All I know is he's in the hospital from a car crash that just killed both his adoptive parents. My heart races as Ulysses goes well above the speed limit. We turn onto the highway, and I feel like all the air is being sucked out of me. Ruby, knowing my distress, rests a hand on my shoulder.

Through the pitch black of night, the red lights of the ER stand out. Ulysses drives us straight to the doors and slams on the brakes.

"David, go with her."

I jump out of the car and run into the ER. David is trying to catch up with me as I slam into the reception desk, out of breath and disheveled. The poor receptionist nearly jumps out of her scrubs.

"Colton Gage." I say, brushing back the wild strand of hair from my face.

"I'm sorry ma'am but…"

"He was just in a car crash, and I was told he's here."

"I'm sorry I can't give you any information without his parents present and…"

"They're dead and he's my brother. Please just tell me if he's okay. I just need to know i-if he's okay…"

My voice cracks as I beg the woman behind the desk. I plead with her with my eyes, and she sighs. I grip the desk and lean over, trying not to strangle her for keeping me from my brother. She types something into her computer and glances back up at me.

"All I see is that he is coming out of surgery and is in the ICU. That's all I know, ma'am."

"Can I see him?"

"I…"

"Please…"

"I'll see what I can do. For now, please take a seat over there. I'll call you when I know something."

I nod as David leads me over to the scratchy green and orange chairs where I sit, waiting for news about Colton. David rubs my back as I bury my face in my hands. I refuse to cry, not again. I don't even think I have any more tears left, anyway.

"I'm going to go get you some coffee, okay?"

I nod.

"Ulysses is on his way with Ruby. They just parked the car."

David pats my back and walks off to get us some energy. Staring down at my feet, I notice I never put on any shoes during all the commotion. The side doors open and the heavy footsteps of my mate storming in follow. I pick my head up to see two strong arms circle around me, pulling me into his chest. I sniff a few times. I want to cry. I really do. I just can't.

He is alive. That is all I can ask for.

"He is in the ICU."

"He's going to be okay."

I nod and pull on the strings of Ulysses sweatshirt he must've just found. I don't know what to do, think, or say anymore.

"Family of Colton Gage?"

I jump, almost taking Ulysses' head off with me.

"Yes?"

"You can see him now. He is in a coma."

"A c-coma?"

We follow the nurse down the hall as she flips through her clipboard.

"Medically induced, but still a coma. His body needs time to heal from his injuries. It's a miracle he even survived. He must have had an entire armada of angels watching over him. This is his room."

The nurse opens the door to Colton's room, and the air is once again ripped from my lungs. Colton's' face is cut and bruised a sickly green. He has tubes and wires hooked up all over him and bandages cover the entire upper half of his body. I freeze in the doorway, the tears that I refused to cry now stream down my cheeks. Ulysses is behind me, nudging me inside the room. I step in, walking cautiously toward Colton's bedside. My hands shake as I reach out to hold his.

"Will he make it?" I whisper, not taking my eyes off Colton for a second.

"It is hard to say right now, but he'll be under twenty-four-hour watch for the time being. If anything were to happen, we will do everything we can. I'll leave you alone. Press the red button if you need anything."

I clench my fists as Colton's heart monitor beeps at a steady pace.

"Who did this?"

"Bell…"

"Ulysses, if you have even the slightest knowledge of who did this, you better tell me right fucking now."

Ruby excuses herself from the room.

"Wes, it's not that…"

"I will hunt them down and kill them in the most agonizing ways. I haven't added onto my *kill* tally in a while. Maybe I should start back up."

I am fuming. Screw crying and sobbing over this. I am going to do something about it. I am already planning how I will murder these sick son-of-bitches as I stand in front of Ulysses. All I see is red. Someone is going to die for what they just did. Not only for my brother, but for every other innocent life that was stolen tonight.

"I know you want to get them and so do I, but right now, we don't know *anything*. No one has claimed the assassinations yet and until then, we don't have much to go on. We are going to get them, I promise you."

"I'll tear their arms off one by one. Someone just signed their death warrant."

All the muscles in my face tighten as I turn away from Ulysses and back toward my unconscious brother. I sit down in the chair next to his bed and take his hand in mine, careful of the needle. My tone changes from violent and filled with murder, to sweet as I can muster.

"Hey there, Colt. Listen, I don't know if you can hear me right now, but I got to go do something, okay? I am not abandoning you. Not again, I just need to go on a little trip. They won't get away this time, I promise, bud. I'll visit every day. I just need to make sure you're safe. This won't ever happen again. I swear my life on it."

I kiss his forehead and cover Colton more with his hospital blanket. Ulysses mutters something into his cell phone.

As I approach, he says into the receiver, "Alright, thanks, bye."

"Any news on who my Barrett will meet?" I say through clenched teeth.

Ulysses types something into his phone and shows me.

"We just got this."

Ulysses clicks play on a video of a man with a hideous face in a dark room.

"Well, hello there. I am an advocate for the Black Death pack and today is a momentous occasion, I hear. Our Luna Queen has been *crowned*. Although I was a little disappointed when I didn't receive an invitation. Our Queen and I go way back, don't you know?"

The man menacingly chuckles, and an icy chill runs up my spine. Once he stops cackling like a loon, he continues.

"Now, if you ask me, a historic day like today deserves some more celebration than what I understand you are doing. I saw on the news some of our *precious* rulers were in some *very* tragic accidents. Not a very fun way to end such a happy day.

Westries, so naïve, so simple, so very *stupid*. Oh, did I forget to introduce myself? Silly me. Well, my name is Judas Nether, but you already knew that my sweet, or did you? I can never remember to introduce myself to all the women I've fucked."

Ulysses lets out a low monstrous growl. I can't find the power to care though because I am shaking. He is right. I know him. He was the man who killed my family and raped me when I was fourteen years old. The scars, the carving into my leg, that revolting beard that scraped my face. I remember every bit of that night in detail. Those and his vile face live in my nightmares. Judas cackles again on the tape, making Ulysses shake with fury. The worry that he might shift is enough to break through my thoughts. I rub his arm.

"Now, I can imagine the state that your precious *King* must be in right now. Knowing that another man took all your first pleasures away. Oh, I would give anything to watch him *reject* you for the *whore* you are. But sadly, I cannot, because I have many responsibilities to keep up with. Maintaining the rogue army and, of course, declaring *war* on the Royal family, of course. Did I forget to mention that?

Your sins are catching up with you, Westries. And there's only *so* much you can do to stop your impending demise. You've made some very interesting enemies over the past few years, my sweet. And I have made *very good* friends with them."

He grins like the Cheshire cat, and I gulp. Ulysses clenches the phone in a death grip that I am afraid it might pop.

"Well, my little video must end now. So many people to kill, *so* little time to do it. We're coming for you and everyone you ever loved. I'd watch my back if I were you, *Avenger.* Until we meet again. Tick, tock…"

He bows and tips an imaginary hat, then pulls out a gun, and aims it at the camera lens. The screen goes fuzzy, and I exhale a deep breath. I never wanted to see that *thing* ever again, yet here we are. And it's my fault.

"I'm going to fucking kill that bastard," Ulysses rages, finally crushing the poor phone in his fist.

"Yeah, well get in line, buddy."

Ulysses takes my face in his hands, kissing me hard. I wrap my arms around Ulysses' neck and return his kiss with equal passion. Ulysses pulls away for air and we rest our heads together.

"This means war." He growls.

Oh, I agree, my dear.

"I'm going to need one thing."

Ulysses waits.

"How fast can we raise an Army?" I say darkly, smirking.

Ulysses kisses my forehead forcefully. "How good of a shot are you, Bellator?"

"You already know the answer to that question, Ulysses." I purr.

He draws back and gazes into my eyes. If he's seeking confirmation of something, he sees it. "I mind linked Coleman to notify all the packs. We are ready."

"Alright then. Let's go hunting."

Sic semper tyrannis.